American Requiem

J. R. ORTIZ

ISBN: 0615796648
ISBN 13: 9780615796642
Library of Congress Control Number: 2013906951
AMERICAN AMARANTH LLC Miami, FL.

FOR ALINA

The angry storm arrived. The sky went from calm blue to hostile gray. Nature's living colors faded. Martial thunder rolled from the horizon in a deep ominous rumble, quaking the ground and dampening calls of warriors from across the valley.

I firmly pressed my bare feet into the soil of my beloved motherland, slowing the rotation of the earth. With steady hand and steely eye, I aimed the arrow high at the dark clouds.

Time stopped. The world went still. The furious din of impending battle was replaced by silence. Only echoes of duty sounded in my mind. All eyes, friend and foe, gazed upon me.

I prayed that honor and courage would guide my labors to victory. I could not be vanquished by the enemy and fail my mission. I would defend my country to the last. I halted breath and let faith fly.

A great force of freedom sailed into the tempest, carrying the hopes and dreams of righteous many. In this moment, in this perilous age of all ages, Lady Liberty would stand or fall forever.

We knights, we few and fortunate paladins of justice and virtue, we devoted legionnaires raised in 'American Amaranth', marched forward with sword and shield to seize the day.....

J. R. Ortiz

"The amaranth flower..... A symbol for all things we wish eternal..... A metaphor for eternal honor and courage, hope, justice, and freedom..... Most of all, an expression of everlasting love.....
The ancient Greeks tossed them onto the graves of their dead warriors to honor them in the after-life, and placed them on the heads of champions as crowns to praise their victories..... Poets and lov-ers have used the amaranth as a symbol of love throughout the centuries..... The amaranth flower never fades and never dies....."

J. R. Ortiz

Contents

Maps

Italy

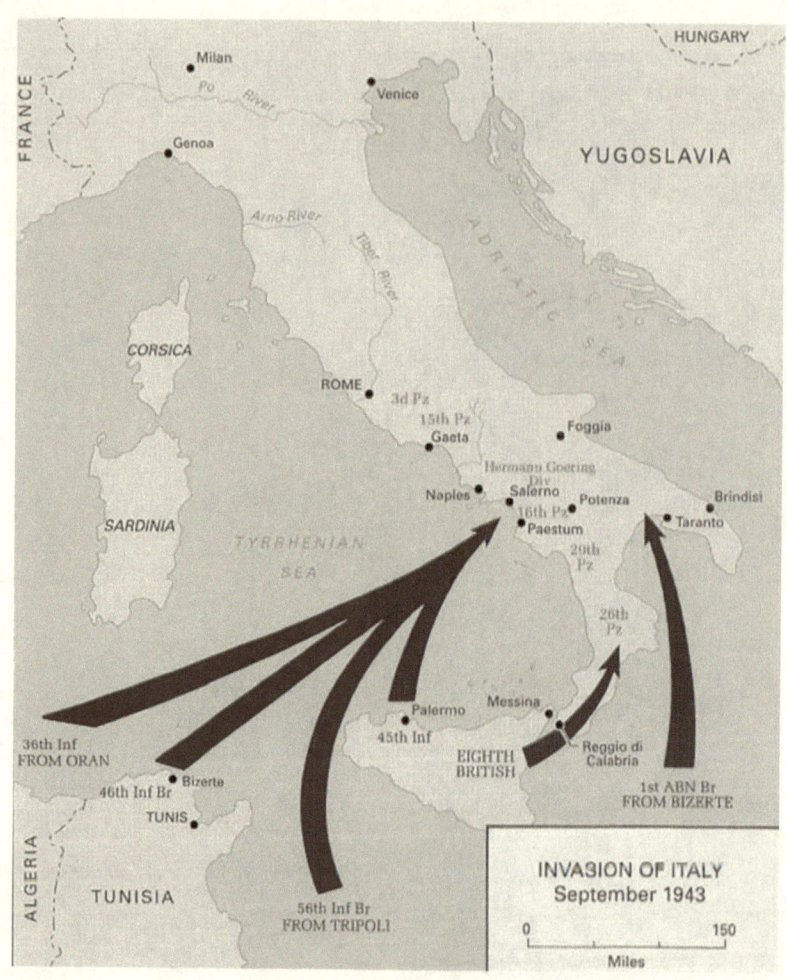

Allied Invasion of Italy 1943

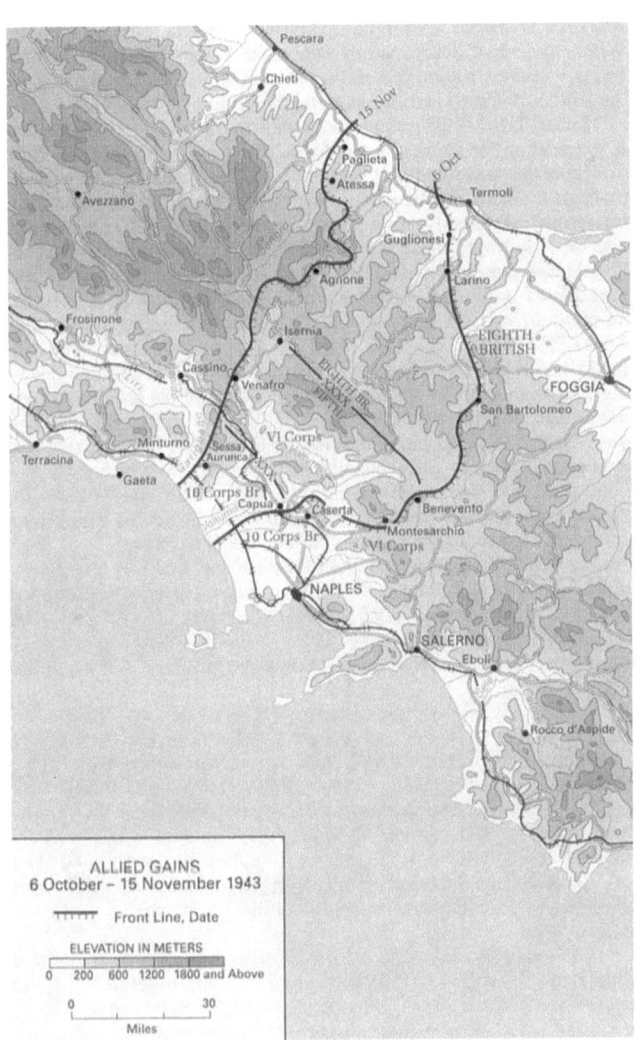

Allied Gains to Cassino 1943

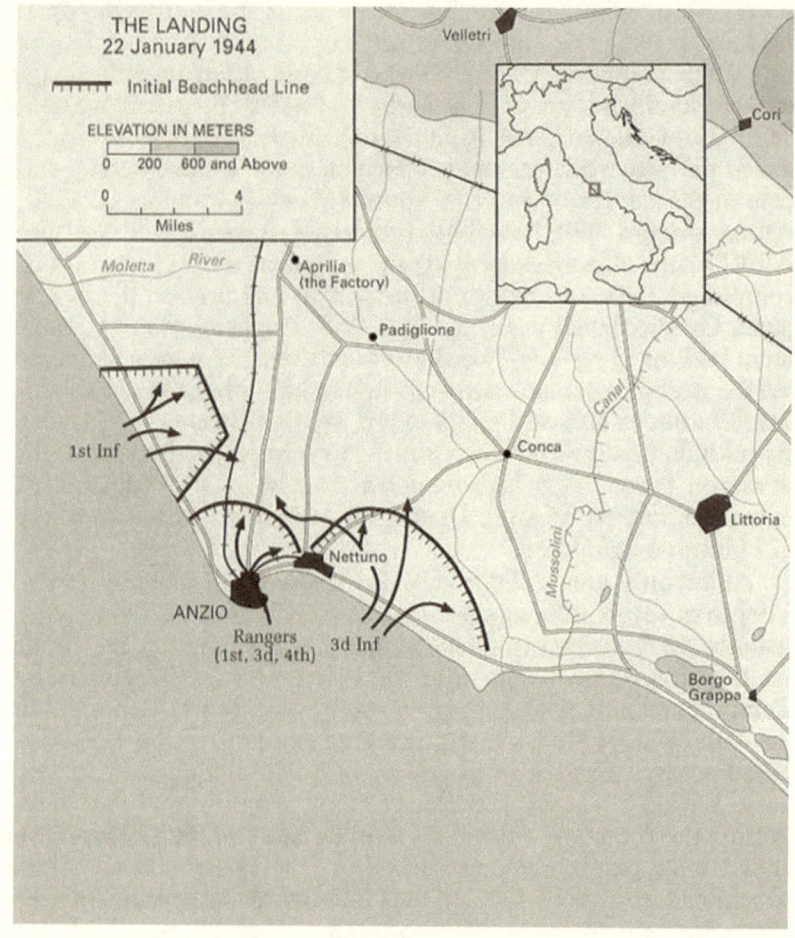

Allied Anzio Landings 1944

Acknowledgements

Creating the story of *American Amaranth* was not difficult. The three novels evolved in front of my eyes like a moving picture. I simply sat down, watched the movie, and wrote down what I saw. Characters were born from my imagination spontaneously without much mental labor. At times, characters and scenes were created on the run in the middle of a chapter. On other occasions, the features of the novels were developed over several days of thought. But always, all the ideas, locations, situations, and people flowed easily like a cascade. The creation has been a joyful experience and one that I will never forget.

The organization and structuring of the writing was not so pleasurable. I am a medical scientist at heart. Spelling, punctuation, grammar, and sentence structure are not my strengths. I had to work very hard at it. Although I did not have the luxury of one, professional editors are extremely important to the success of a novel. I was my own editor. I feel this was my weakness throughout the development of the three novels of the anthology.

I am certain a creative writing professor would be greatly disappointed in my treatment of the 'paragraph'. Throughout the books, I often approach the 'paragraph' as a personal encounter. I hope that I have maintained clarity in the story and not confused some readers. I must say that a more 'correct' form did evolve through the process of writing the three novels. I could have changed some of the 'errors', but I didn't. I rather enjoyed watching the evolution of my self-improvement. Like becoming a physician, the art of creative writing is a growth process. I feel it's a testament of how difficult it is to write according to accepted practice; and how different creative styles often evoke emotions similarly, without much confusion.

At its very core, writing is about the story. The story is what counts most. Passing a thought and emotion to the reader is the writer's objective. There are many ways to accomplish this. My way is not the conventional one, but I hope it is still effective in communicating my story.

The essence of the *American Amaranth* books are life's loves and losses, and how they shape us as human beings. Many times, it is a challenge to work through the losses. We must always maintain the fire to live a good life, and share our experiences with those we love and still have.

It is better to do good in this world than to fester in bad. Live your life passionately and always remember opportunities are fleeting. Grasp onto them and make them count. This is the key to happiness - sharing our love and growing into the best human beings we can be.

Preface

Our universe was born 13.8 billion years ago. From the infinitely hot and dense 'Singularity' of the 'Big Bang', a cosmic inflation and exponential growth of space occurred in trillionths of trillionths of a second. At one-millionth of a second after the 'Big Bang', sufficient cooling allowed energy to be converted into various subatomic particles. Thousands of years later, the first electrically neutral atoms - hydrogen, and then helium and lithium - were formed. Eventually, a billion years later, giant amorphic clouds of these elements coalesced through gravity to form star systems and galaxies. The heavier elements needed for life were formed within the stars and their explosive supernovae.

A 'Dark Energy' drives the progressively accelerating expansion of the universe. Composing seventy per-cent of space, this hypothetical force counteracts the effects of gravity and may eventually lead to 'heat death' and a 'Big Rip' dissolution of the universe. On the other hand, gravity may seize the day, combat 'Dark Energy', and cause the universe to contract in a 'Big Crunch'. This, in turn, may lead to another 'Big Bang' and further cyclic reformations of the universe in an eternal process.

Man only partially and simplistically understands the natures of the titanic physical forces at play in the universe. We don't know what came before the first 'Singularity', or what will come after a potential 'Big Rip'. Metaphysics, philosophy, and religion can never adequately explain the truths of the 'Big Picture'.

However, one thing is certain. Man occupies a tiny planet, orbiting a star in the Milky Way Galaxy. There are hundreds of billions of stars in our galaxy, and there are hundreds of billions of galaxies in the universe. There may be other intelligent life forms on many other planets in the universe. There may even be parallel universes in a multiversal space. Human beings appear to be insignificant particulate matter in the vastness of the cosmos. This fact is difficult for the human mind to accept. Our insignificance to cosmology is ego-dystonic. It is also spiritually disruptive to those with the mental inclination to consider it.

Mankind may be unimportant in the infinite scope of the cosmos, but we are not unimportant to ourselves or to each other. We need each other on this journey through 'Time and Space'. Human interaction, discourse, and peaceful coexistence are essential to the further cultural advancement of mankind. The evolution of our minds, necessary for future progress in science, medicine, technology, and governance, demands allowance for different religious and ideological beliefs. Race and creed should not be discriminated against. Freedom and justice for all peoples must be safeguarded.

Not all forms of government allow equally for the freedom of thought required in the advancement of humankind. Totalitarian and radical theocratic systems generally do not open a way for personal growth. Racism, bigotry, and religious intolerance and unacceptance do not stimulate creative and constructive thinking. The only result of oppression is fear and stagnation of thought. Limited interpersonal trust and interaction leads to dead societies which drown in their own self-perpetuating misery. Radical restrictive governance is not an acceptable template for the future of mankind.

At present, constitutional republican government with strong 'rule of law' and a deep system of 'checks and balances' is the only viable path for our planet. It is often imperfect and combative. Recently, many Western democracies have found it challenging and difficult. Nevertheless, it remains the best option we have.

The process of man's moral and spiritual growth is never-ending. It may take thousands of years for us to reach an acceptable state of equilibrium that encompasses the world. In the interim, we must not allow discord and belligerence between nations to spin out of control. 'Uncooperative' elements, dedicated to primitive theological thinking and restrictive 'de-civilization', must be slowed down enough to allow more progressive, educated factions in their midst to rise and overcome them. If they don't self-digest, they may require more persuasion from the leading nations of modern civilization. The culmination of efforts must be freedom and justice for all.

The road of human history is pockmarked. Justice and injustice, good and evil, have vied for control of man's destiny for thousands of years. The twenty-first century is no exception. However, our present circumstances are much more complicated and perilous than ever before.

Worldwide economic instability and aggressive posturing by major nations have unsettled relations between governments. China and Russia have pursued angrier anti-American positions, and evolved more supportive relationships with North Korea and Iran. Terror states are becoming major military powers. Cyber-warfare has grown immensely, jeopardizing prospects for peace and increasing chances of war.

Shortages of energy resources, food, and clean water have become existential threats to many countries around the world. All the major powers have battle plans made for the planet's resource-rich areas. China and Japan vie for the oil and gas of the East China Sea. Vietnam and the Philippines are preparing to contest China over the energy riches of the South China Sea. India and Pakistan plan for war over the water of a major river. Europe is energy-starved, and increasingly dependent on unstable sources from Russia and North Africa. The threat of Shia Iranian hegemony over the Persian Gulf throws her neighbors into a wild race for nuclear weapons and destabilizes oil commerce through the Strait of Hormuz. Africa is becoming a large proxy-war battlefield between the Western democracies and China. African sectarian divisions are fanned by the major powers. America and Europe support the Christians, China provides aid to the radical Islamists. Major oil, gas, and mineral fields in Africa are the prize of victory. China and Iran continue to make social inroads into Central and South America, and are gaining share of the region's rich mineral, agricultural, and energy stores. The United States and Russia fight for influence in Eastern Europe, and prepare for the scramble into the arctic and the conquest of its oil deposits. If the world economy doesn't improve dramatically, major war seems inevitable.

Ballistic nuclear technology has proliferated into the 'Terror' regions of the world. Pakistan and North Korea have significant nuclear stockpiles already. Iran seems unstoppable in her quest for nuclear independence. All these nations are shrouded with radical ideology and extreme anti-American sentiment. Atomic weapons have become miniaturized and deliverable by a single person carrying a backpack. The concept of suicide-bomber has suddenly become much more ominous to the nations of the 'Free-world'. In the future, will the truck-bomber be replaced by the nuke-packer? Millions of lives will be at the mercy of a single terrorist and his fanatical thoughts.

Before the horrors of World War Two, totalitarian despotic governments of the Axis nations ruled over approximately 200 million people. They saw America as being distant from their regional ambitions. The anti-American sentiments in the Axis countries did not reach the fever-pitch levels of our enemies today. Two of the three Axis nations were Christian. None had nuclear weapons or advanced ballistic technology which could target the American homeland. The American heartland did not know the concept of 'Terror'.

The 'Cold War' of the past century pitted the United States of America against the communist ideology of the Soviet Union. They had been allies in the prior world war. Although they were post-WWII enemies, they respected each other. Neither society was suicidal. Neither carried a fanatical religious banner. And both believed in the concept of 'mutually assured destruction'.

Today, our enemies on planet Earth number in the billions. They are radically despotic. They are totalitarian. Some are religiously fanatical, and even suicidal. They are not interested in a balance of power with the US. They seek hegemony and are actively working for it. They hope to project their power around the world. They do not allow for free speech in their countries, and extinguish it violently when confronted with it. Dissent groups within their borders are exterminated. If not outright elimination of our country, they wish at least for a severe weakening and diminution of America. Worst of all, they have nuclear weapons and means to deliver them on our homeland.

Whether the world realizes it or not, American principles of free and democratic government are essential to future global stability. The eventual 'civilization' of humankind rides on the wings of 'American Amaranth'. Man's tiny speck in the cosmos will soon disappear if freedom and justice do not reign on our planet. As Americans, we must not allow domestic struggles or the antipathy of enemies to extinguish our flame of freedom. It is truly the only hope for the world.

This anthology presents the concept of the 'noble American warrior'. The idea may be controversial to many persons around our planet, and unpalatable to some people even in our own country. Notwithstanding, I use the concept generally to represent all Americans, in all walks of life, who take honor in just doing the right thing. Americans who follow the law and do not steal from their neighbors. Those who take responsibility for their families and support the community in times of stress. Those Americans who work hard in their chosen fields and support fair government. Those who don't subsist from our government's largeness unnecessarily and don't abuse the charitable giving of our citizens. The Americans I hold in honor are those who do the most they can to make our country safe, ethically moral, and productive in all of her endeavors to remain a bastion of freedom and justice for the world. We can all be warriors in this struggle.

The *American Amaranth Anthology* is set in the near future, and follows a family through several generations of personal, national, and international struggle. The Stansfields are not perfect, but they attempt to be in their upholding of the values which have made our country the envy of the world in the past. It is intended to be dramatic and occasionally metaphorical in order to make specific points known. The anthology illustrates the grandness of our country, and reveals the hopes and aspirations of many of our equally responsible citizens. It uses our history as a people to light the path for the future.

Book One, *American Amaranth*, is seen through the eyes of an aged and sick warrior, Admiral Julian Stansfield, while he carries the weight of his country on his shoulders. Handicapped by personal grief and medical illness, he directs the United States through a major conventional world war. He worries for his three sons who are all scattered around the planet in their respective duties as American military men. Throughout the story, the admiral remembers his beloved late wife, Olivia, and retells all he learned from her about life and freedom.

Book Two, *Libertas Americana*, takes brothers Julius and Michael Stansfield on a heroic odyssey of high adventure through eastern and central Europe. Ordered to stop a developing terrorist attack on the United States, the brothers face great obstacles and dangers throughout their spy mission. Through their ordeal, they remember the glory of their youth and the greatness of the 'Amaranth'.

Book Three, *American Requiem*, is a complex tale involving four independent stories in one. A continuation of the saga from books one and two, it incorporates a long lost family diary from the Second World War in North Africa and southern Europe. The journal functions like a time portal into the past as it's read by eldest brother Julius Stansfield, while involved with his two brothers on a CIA mission to Italy in the near future. Julius learns emotional secrets about his paternal grandparents in the US Army Medical Corps during 1943-44. He also gets a privileged insight into the young life of his father, then Lieutenant Julian Stansfield, from the summer of 1975 as the lieutenant spends time caring for his dying mother, Ann Nelson Stansfield. Four parallel stories are carefully interwoven to better illustrate the love between different generations of Stansfields during separate critical times of their lives.

American Requiem highlights the reality that we are, as individuals, an amalgamation of all our life experiences. Like physical traits passed on in our genes, philosophies of life may also transcend generations in a family. Frequently, our ancestors contribute mightily to our 'Gestalt' of being. *American Requiem* reminds us of the fact that we are often times complex reflections of those who came before us. The struggles of the past help forge us in the present. Many times, we are what we were. Our 'garden of life' was planted before us. We simply tend it, and help it to grow and prosper further. We have a duty to remember loved ones who set the path to the garden, and insist those who come after us continue to nurture the flowers already planted. Common sacrifice leads to common goodness. We must make the world better.

Common to all the books of the anthology is a deep love between individuals caught in the trying times of war. All the heroes attempt to uphold the principles of freedom and justice, knowing they are the framework from which great cultures evolve and prosper. They all do the most they can to increase the small benevolent imprint that mankind makes in the vastness of the cosmos.

Love is the nucleus of the anthology. It sits at the core of the story. Without love, there is no reason for our existence in the cosmos. It simply would be too unbearable. Without love, there is no purpose for freedom. Being 'free' is pointless if you aren't free to love. Love is the oldest and most powerful energy source in our universe. It is our greatest and purest resource. It needs no refinement. Love defies gravity and 'Dark Energy'. In its truest form, it explodes more brightly than the splitting of atoms and outlasts the nuclear fusion powering the stars. It is all-consuming, conserving, and regenerative at the same time. No laws of nature can explain it. None can control it. No force can stop it. It is the ultimate 'Singularity'. It is from where all goodness comes. It is where we all seek to go. It will continue to be all these things into tomorrow. Young love is eternal. It is the driving force of the world. Its power existed before the 'Big Bang', and will radiate long into the future - unknown but to God.

CHAPTER 1

Ghosts of Annapolis

"Mother, I'm ready," spoke out Alexander Stansfield, walking into the study of their home near Cape Florida.

"It's still early, Alex," said Nasrin. "Sit with me for a while, I won't be seeing you for a good time."

"All right but don't baby me, Mom."

"I won't," smiled Nasrin, as Alex threw himself across the couch next to her.

The warm summer South Florida sun beamed into the room. Morning light shined on a large red-bordered flag, hanging vertically on the wall. Two upright five-pointed gold stars reflected the sunlight back into Nasrin's green eyes.

"You look just like your father," she said proudly, enjoying her son's company. "Tall, dark, and handsome were traits of his also. I'm sure you'll drive the girls in college wild."

"I'm looking forward to that," he laughed.

"I'm sure you are, lover boy.

"Sweeping girls off their feet must be a distinct trait inherited from your father. He certainly had an easy time with me," she smiled.

"Tell me the story again, Mother," said Alex, lying on his back and staring at the ceiling.

"You've heard it many times," she answered.

"I know, Mother.

"But it's a cool story. My parents fell in love as secret agents in Iran.

"It doesn't get any cooler than that," he shouted.

"I guess it doesn't," she agreed. "Love and danger seem to strengthen each other. It's a curious mix of escalating emotion. It certainly kept us on the edge of our seats twenty years ago."

"Was Iran as dangerous as they say?"

"It was, Alex, perhaps even more so. That war was horrific.

"But your father was very brave and gallant."

"So were you, Mother."

"Yes, so was I," she said softly.

"Was Iran more dangerous than Dad's last mission?"

"Your Father's last mission?" she asked in a hushed voice.

"It's okay if you don't want to talk about it," said Alex tenderly.

Nasrin stared at the service flag on the wall. The gold stars brought tears to her eyes. She remained silent for several minutes and regained composure.

"I'd like to show you something," she said, while walking to the desk at the center of the room.

Nasrin opened a locked drawer and returned with a large box. She handed it to her son.

"Open it, Alex."

Alexander sat up on the couch and carefully removed the box's lid. Inside, he found two old notebooks. The larger of the two was much older than the other. Each had an amaranth flower pressed into its cover. Both flowers were still a brilliant red.

"That box hasn't been opened in nearly twenty years," said Nasrin. "I was the last person to read those notebooks. I'd like you to look through them on our trip. They'll explain everything you need to know about your father's last mission. It's time for you to understand it all."

"I'm sorry Mrs. Stansfield," politely interrupted the man by the door to the hall, "but we must leave if we're to arrive on time."

"Thank you, John."

"Alex and I are ready," said the still beautiful middle-aged Persian princess.

Before leaving their home on Key Biscayne, Nasrin pulled a red globe amaranth from the bouquet in the hall and placed it into Alexander's jacket lapel. She kissed his cheek and caressed his face.

"I love you, Alex, and I'm very proud of you.

"We'll talk more on the plane about Dad and his last mission," she whispered to her son, thinking back many years on the love of her life. Her mind regressed nearly two decades to a time that permanently impacted her, the entire Stansfield family, and America..... The clock of time was turned back eighteen years....................

CIA Director Joseph Mitrano arrived early for his breakfast appointment at the US Naval Academy. He had been personally invited by his dear friend, Vice Admiral Walter

Zume - the Superintendent of Annapolis, for a meeting at Buchanan House later in the morning. Mitrano would first go to Memorial Hall before seeing his old classmate.

The director knew the grounds and deeply appreciated their glory. He had graduated from this hallowed campus in 1973. Although not a frequent visitor, Mitrano had attended Admiral Julian Stansfield' s memorial mass at the Academy Chapel a year prior. For Mitrano, Annapolis was a place of sacred memories. He had become a man here at the confluence of the Severn River and the Chesapeake Bay, only thirty-three miles from Washington D.C.

The coastal Maryland air was chilly and damp on this early September morning. Escorted by his usual security detail, and wearing a long dark trench coat, the CIA director slowly stepped across the heavily canopied Quadrangle. He passed along the familiar red-brick paved Stribling Walk, staring into a thick pre-dawn fog. The path toward Tecumseh Court and Bancroft Hall was still dark. Light from old lamp posts and a full moon lost itself into an ethereal cloud hanging above the ground.

Mitrano remembered jogging this path many times with his friend Julian as young plebes, before reveille at the Bancroft dormitory complex. Although long ago, the memory was seared into Mitrano's mind. They would awaken at 0430 hours on their own, run a ten mile route, and shower before the bugler played his morning call at 0630 hours. They had bonded closely on those runs. They had shared their dreams and aspirations. They had encouraged each other to work hard and be at their best to protect their beloved America.

Many years had now passed. Mitrano's rapid physical decline could not allow him to run this path again. Youth had been replaced by age. His friend had been taken from him. But the memories of his "Glory Jogs" were vividly relived in his mind.

Although his body was failing him, Mitrano still had important tasks to perform. The director needed every ounce of energy he could muster to keep his country safe in these dangerous times. He was still the leader of his secret army of patriots. An army always on alert and in the fight. Challenges to his America would continue to arise into the uncertain future. Mitrano would carry the torch as long as his capabilities allowed. He could not soften to the demands of the job. He would continue the struggle as his friend Julian had. His love for America demanded that he persevere with steadfast dedication until the final out of the game.

Tecumseh Court was drenched in moonlight haze as the CIA detail left the forest of the Quadrangle and approached the sublime, monumental entrance portico of Bancroft Hall. The fog rolled from the forest in waves across the plaza, further accenting the sacrosanct edifice for Mitrano. This had been the director's dormitory all fours years as a midshipman at Annapolis.

A heavily armed Naval Academy security team checked Mitrano's identification papers and allowed entrance onto the court. Midshipman First Class Harold Milsap waited in full dress blue uniform at the top of the steps. He stood at attention in front of the large impressive doors to the complex. The three-story facade of pale granite and medium gray marble glistened with morning dew. Tall fifty foot columns rose high above the fog, bracing the entrance. The doors were topped by a sculpted sailing ship and the trident of the United States Naval Academy crest.

Milsap and his detail of three midshipmen saluted the director and led the CIA security team into the Rotunda.

They passed under a large mural of the *USS South Dakota* in action at the Battle of Guadalcanal in October 1942. The cavernous Rotunda's carved limestone walls and moulded plaster vaulted ceiling rose three open stories to a skylight above. Dark and light green, pink, and cream colored marble covered the floor of the iconic 110 year-old vestibule.

"Good morning, Sir.

"The US Naval Academy is honored to have you and your team as guests," politely stated the tall and proud midshipman Milsap, while again saluting the CIA director.

"I have been ordered by Vice-Admiral Zume to escort you into Memorial Hall and be available throughout your stay with us this morning.

"I understand you have specific interests to see in the Hall. I was also informed of your attendance at Annapolis and your personal familiarity with this building."

Director Mitrano smiled at Milsap, nodded affirmatively and said, "Yes, we share this heritage. We are all family."

Young cadet Milsap led Mitrano up the broad marble stairway to the second deck and the entrance atrium of Memorial Hall. The midshipman-kept hall commemorated the nearly four thousand graduates of Annapolis killed in battles throughout the history of the United States. The core of cadets maintained it in order at all times. It was an integral aspect to their education as warriors. The memory of the fallen was eternally present here. The midshipmen slept with the souls of their brave comrades.

Milsap remained at the entrance. "The point of interest for you, Director, is to your left at the end of the hall, by the large bronze light sconce and double doors leading to the terrace. I leave you now, Sir, to your privacy and personal reflections." He slowly saluted Director Mitrano and stepped back.

Joseph Mitrano had not entered this sacred hall in almost forty-five years. He walked into the long rectangular room, passing battle helmets, cannons, swords, axes, arrows, and maces from ancient wars. Four heavy chandeliers hung from the high ceiling, each with thousands of Czechoslovakian crystals. The ceiling was vaulted and accented by a large central oculus skylight. Being 5 AM in the morning, only the moon's rays permeated through the glass above. The varying shades of oak parquet floor creaked under Mitrano's feet as he stepped past captured flags of America's enemies in prior wars. British royal standards, Mexican battle banners, German Iron Eagles, swastikas, Japanese Rising Sun battle flags, North Korean, North Vietnamese, and Chinese war pennants paraded before his eyes. An "Honor Roll" inscribed with the names of Annapolis' war dead, plaques, sculptures, busts, and portrait paintings filled the walls of the memorial. A large mural of the Battle of Lake Erie, and the defeat of the British Navy off the coast of Ohio in September 1813, covered a wall. Mitrano took a deep breath as he finally arrived at his destination.

At the end of the hall by the large bronze light sconce, isolated on its own, appeared what Mitrano had come to see: a magnificent life-sized oil portrait of Admiral Julian Stansfield, painted shortly after he was named Director of Naval Intelligence. A plaque beneath the painting commemorated Stansfield's contributions to the US Navy and the defense of the United States. Mentioned boldly were his years of Naval Intelligence, his significant involvement in developing offensive and defensive missile technology, and his central importance in the defeat of Iran, North Korea, and the People's Republic of China a year earlier. The admiral's leadership in planning for the Pacific War against China was highlighted, as was his participation in the Battle of Taiwan. Stated at the end were his injuries suffered in the last great war, leading to his death from cardiac failure six weeks later. The last sentence proclaimed him, "A hero for our times."

Another plaque to the right of the portrait enumerated Admiral Julian Stansfield's awards and decorations - including a Bronze Star for his intelligence mission to Vietnam in 1979, a Navy Cross for his intelligence actions in the Battle of Taiwan, a Purple Heart for his injured left eye in Vietnam, and another Purple Heart for the leg trauma off Taiwan which led to his rapid physical decline and sudden cardiac death. He had also been honored with a Navy Distinguished Achievement in Science Medal, a National Intelligence Distinguished Service Medal, and the rarely given National Intelligence Cross.

In the portrait, Julian stood elegantly wearing his dress white hat and blue jacket, with gold admiral's lacing on the sleeves topped by a gold star. Colorful battle ribbons blazed across his left chest. A soft board on each shoulder held a naval anchor and a grouping of four white stars. He wore a bright white shirt and a black tie with a tight knot. A black patch covered his unseen blind left eye. Julian's right eye was hazel-green. His face projected both proud determination and introspective contemplation. The artist had captured both the hard and soft edges of the man.

Over the admiral's left shoulder sat a portrait gallery depiction of his four children at young ages. Joseph Mitrano glanced over Julian's right shoulder into the background and a mirror painted on the wall. Fixed centrally in the mirror was a reflected clear image of Olivia, lovingly smiling at her husband. Julian's right eye, Mitrano noted, stared directly at his wife's beautiful face.

The painting depicted the entirety of this noble warrior, husband, and father. Mitrano couldn't believe his eyes. Seizing the enormous significance of the portrayal, the director thought of his friend and of the contributions to America made by the Stansfield family.

He had come early this morning to see the portrait by himself in private. Mitrano knew it would be an emotional moment for him. He needed to be alone with his thoughts. The painting would be presented to the rest of the US naval community later in the week with the unveiling of Admiral Stansfield's statue at the US Naval Academy Chapel.

The director remained in front of the portrait for another forty minutes, silently reminiscing of the passion and glory of his friend - the consummate American patriot.

A bugle call echoed into the hall. Morning reveille awoke America's midshipmen and women for another day of freedom. Dedicated young people would learn the conduct of war with honor. Mitrano pondered the greatness of courageous youth enamored with the idea of saving liberty. He understood their mission was difficult and full of risks. It was a lifetime calling that never ebbed away, persisting until their final days. Perhaps in the future, thought Mitrano solemnly, many of them would also be honored in this hall.

With reveille sounding in his ears, a tear flowed from the director's right eye to his chin. It finally fell, like a raindrop, onto his dark blue jacket.

"James," he whispered..... "James....."

Mitrano slowly returned the way he had come. As he passed with his cane, he glanced one more time at the "Honor Roll" and took a deep breath.

Officer cadet Milsap stood rigidly at attention by the entrance to Memorial Hall. He saluted Director Mitrano as he exited the sacred chamber.

"Did you see what you intended to, Sir?" asked the young Milsap.

"Yes, and so very much more," said the director.

"My deepest sympathies, Sir, for your personal losses."

"We've all had personal losses, young man. They were family to you as well. America has buried many sons and daughters."

Joseph Mitrano was led down the marble stairs to the lower deck.

Thousands of midshipmen and women in their summer working blues congregated into the square for roll call and the beginning of their day of education. Mitrano walked into them and shook their hands in thanks. He looked into the crowded plaza with deep inspiration. He knew Julian's dream of a great America would persist into the future. The proud young faces around the director were familiar. They displayed the same confidence he and Julian had shown so many years before. That was the beauty of America, he thought. The dream would never die. Freedom and justice would never fade away. The Stansfield creed of "American Amaranth" was alive and well in the eyes of the young cadets.

Mitrano thanked officer cadet Milsap for his dutiful attention and stepped through Tecumseh Court. He had met many future American heroes. Inside his heart, the director was content. The America of tomorrow was in good hands.

Mitrano made his way across "The Yard" to Buchanan House and his breakfast meeting with the superintendent. Vice-Admiral Walter Zume had studied at Annapolis with Joseph Mitrano and Julian Stansfield. He had worked with Julian at Naval Intelligence for many years. Shortly after Julian became DNI, Walter moved to the Academy and assumed the superintendent position. He had always been a good friend.

Buchanan House, home of the USNA superintendent since the early 20th century, sat next to the Academy Chapel. The residence had received more dignitaries over the years than any other government house in America, except the White House. Named for Admiral Franklin Buchanan, the Academy's first director in 1845, it was surrounded by vivid canopies of trees and colorful flower gardens.

Joseph Mitrano walked through a ground cover of blue and white periwinkles, and up to the front landing of Buchanan House. His security detail took up positions around the home. Walter Zume, in formal white Navy attire, greeted the CIA director at the door.

"Good morning, Joe. It's nice to see you back home at the Academy," said the tall and trim Zume. The men embraced warmly and passed together into a hall leading to an open porch at the rear of Buchanan House.

A long line of portrait photographs of young men hung on the corridor's walls. Mitrano noticed their significance immediately.

"These are USNA graduation photographs of Navy and Marine officers killed in action since the beginning of the Global War on Terrorism in 2001," stated Zume. "They are all awardees of the Medal of Honor, posthumously," murmured the vice-admiral.

The CIA director took his time and read the exploits of each hero, moving slowly down the line. Occasionally he'd look at the superintendent, nod his head in silence, and say he knew the boy's father or mother at the Pentagon.

Zume stopped halfway down the hall and added, pointing with his right hand, "From here down, the boys performed their final acts of selfless devotion in the Great War against Iran, North Korea, and China. There are twenty-three of them in this final grouping, all younger than thirty-five years of age. We have aviators, submariners, surface fleeters, and Marines. All our branches are represented."

Acts of bravery were captioned in bronze beneath the framed photographs. Mitrano seemed to slow down even more, giving each boy his due respect. Many young American lives had been lost on our most recent path to freedom, and these boys had led the way. They had given their blood, and everything else they had to give, devotedly fulfilling their responsibilities to America. Their full sacrifice demanded Mitrano's full attention.

The CIA director finally arrived at the last portrait. He bowed his head for several minutes and prayed. The handsome naval aviator from the USS Ronald Reagan had been the last man to receive the Medal of Honor during the Great War.

Mitrano gently stared up at Walter Zume, before returning his gaze to the caption beneath the final hero's photograph. With a strong sense of honor in his voice, the director read aloud, "After engaging in aerial dogfights with Chinese fighters at close range over the Taiwan Strait, and shooting down five of them, this US Navy Commander's F-18 was hit by rocket fire and disabled. Rather than eject and parachute into the waters of the strait, this hero directed his plane into a Chinese troop transport disembarking Chinese marines on the western beaches of Taiwan. While on fire, his act of projecting the F-18 onto the deck of the troop transport led to a disabling explosion of the enemy ship and its sinking a short time later, with the loss of most of its crew and human cargo. This act of valor, and others like it, allowed for America's victory in the Battle of Taiwan."

Joseph Mitrano closed his eyes and slowly passed his right index finger across the raised letters of the hero's name beneath the portrait. "Commander John 'Boomer' Zume," he said beneath his breath.

Vice-Admiral Zume also closed his eyes.

"These are only a few of our 'Ghosts of Annapolis', Joe. There are many more. Both you and I have had our personal losses.....

"I was deeply saddened by the loss of your son, Joe..... Very deeply saddened.....

"He was a great young man.

"As your old friend, I'm sorry.....

"My son was also a great young man. They all were. We'll miss them much. We would have wished to take their place. Unfortunately, fate and destiny are not negotiable. Our sons met their fate with valor. We must also.

"They can't be replaced in our hearts. Their absence leaves a lonely hole, which only becomes more profound with time. We both know it's an indescribable emptiness. Your insides feel evacuated.

"They were brave boys doing their duties for their country. All our 'Ghosts' were courageous warriors performing their duties. Their lives may have been physically lost, but their memories are kept for an eternity.

"Many families in America are missing their children as deeply as we are sensing our loss. It's a long 'trail of tears', Joe. It is a trail of love and memories.

"Let their souls rest in peace....."

Without saying a word, Joe Mitrano looked up at his friend's face and smiled kindly. Unspoken truth was shared in their eyes. He placed his right arm on the admiral's shoulder, and both men walked towards the veranda at the back of Buchanan House.

They sat at a breakfast table on the deck and remained quiet for a few minutes. The old warriors reflected through their pain. They were surrounded by a beautiful rose garden, and a tall sycamore tree shaded them from the morning sun. Vice-Admiral Zume's assistant brought the men coffee.

"Did you see Julian's oil portrait at Memorial Hall, Joe?" asked Walter Zume, changing the subject. "It's quite a creation, I think."

"I sure did, Zoomer," said Mitrano. "It's iconic. It captures the essence of the man. His depth and strength fill the canvas. Olivia and his children were included, just as he wished. It's a work of artistic genius. I'm certain Julian's children will be touched by its simplicity and emotional detail. It sure brought tears to my eyes."

"I had the same emotions last night when seeing it for the first time. It's perfection in style and color. It completely captures the love of the man. I was humbled. Julian is one of our ghosts also," softly stated Admiral Zume.

The Navy men ate breakfast on the chilly morning, and spoke of old times and America's challenges in the future. After finishing their meal, they returned inside to the home's library.

Joe Mitrano sat on a leather couch beneath a large panoramic painting of the Battle of Leyte Gulf. The contest for the liberation of the Philippine Islands from Japanese forces in late October 1944 was the largest naval battle of World War Two. The painting depicted a US destroyer under attack by organized kamikazes. The ship's anti-aircraft guns fired furiously into the air as a flaming Japanese plane fell into the Philippine Sea nearby.

"Zoomer, I'd like your opinion concerning a particularly delicate situation which has developed for me in the past few days," stated the director, with concern in his voice.

"Without getting into great detail, let me explain the context of the situation. A few months ago, the CIA and US Naval Intelligence were involved together in eliminating a serious threat to the American homeland from overseas. The combined mission was thought to be a complete success for us and our allies.

"Last month, one of our covert operation teams in the overseas area in question verified that a splinter terror group had escaped our attention and was preparing a follow-up plan with horrible implications for our country. Four days after this discovery, our four man team was ambushed and killed near the terrorist hide-out."

The CIA director paused for a moment, stood up from the couch, and walked over to the bay window overlooking the rose garden. Without blinking, he stared into the red flowers.

Walter Zume sat in a chair next to a bronze bust of Stephen Decatur, the American naval hero of the Barbary Wars and the War of 1812.

With his back to his friend, Mitrano added, "Aggravating the situation, the son-of-a-bitch Russians are kicking ass again in Georgia, and pressuring the Baltic and Polish borders. Our intel believes they're preparing to invade Estonia in the north, and Azerbaijan in the south. After a short calm, we have another shitstorm in Europe. Britain and France are mobilizing troops and equipment. For the time being, Germany is sitting still."

"We also have the Chinese murdering each other in a civil war," said Zume. "I'm told there were over a million deaths in the summer. Famine and disease are claiming more people than the fighting. It's absolute chaos."

"I don't know if I'll be able to keep the whole god damned thing together this time, Walter," murmured Joe Mitrano. "I think we've lost control of GD-93. The world has broken into a thousand pieces. Our nation is in grave danger. I'm feeling a fear unknown to me. The risk of nuclear war is the highest I've ever seen. We have loose nukes from Russia and China spreading across the globe. My men can't keep up with all the cases. If we get nuked, our forces will respond against everyone. We'll flame every bastard nation out there. It'll be the end of the Earth."

Zume remained silent. Minutes passed.

"What about the rebellion, Joe? Have you put down the neo-fascists in our country?"

"I believe so, and the communist fuckers as well..... That may be the only thing I'm certain of.....

"How did we lose control, Walter?" asked Mitrano, still staring at the roses. "It all happened so fast."

"Human nature, Joe. Poor and hungry people became angry. Risk of death became part of everyday life. The world turned suicidal."

"What do you think Julian would say about the situation, Walter?"

Zume smiled behind Mitrano's back..... "He'd stretch himself thin, covering all the bases. He'd give every ounce of energy to prevent a final calamity for America and the world. He'd chase down the terrorists with his teeth if he had to. He'd bring peace to the Chinese with political and economic assistance, and risk total war with the Russians. We have the defensive capabilities to prevent annihilation from Russia, they on the other hand do not. He would make them understand that reality. It's doable, Joe....."

"We have our asses to the wall," said the director. "I reckon I better get on my horse and re-direct GD-93 back on track.

"I may have just the man to help me do this. His unusual case is the real reason for my visit with you today, Walter.

"Captain Mark Stansfield, Medal of Honor winner and youngest son of our dear friend Julian, transferred to the Pentagon this past spring. In late July, he transferred to Naval Intelligence. Only two weeks later, he was responsible for discovering the secondary terror plan and directing our attention to the splinter group in question. He directed our CIA team to the terror safe house where our people verified the presence of the threat. Shortly afterward, the covert American crew was unfortunately ambushed and eliminated."

Director Mitrano returned to the couch. "The CIA has developed an operation to counter the terror group in question. Both Julius and Michael Stansfield, Julian's other sons and probably my best two agents in the field, have been assigned to the plan's covert team. Mark has requested assignment to this mission on the ground. He feels he knows the terror group, and perhaps sees himself partly responsible for the loss of the first covert team. He wishes to infiltrate the battle zone with his brothers and terminate the threat. I promised I would consider his request. The situation is delicate and emotional for me, Zoomer."

Walter Zume looked at his friend intensely and said, "I know these boys intimately. They have all performed courageously for the United States on repeated occasions. They are American heroes.

"Mark is in a wheelchair. A Congressional Medal of Honor hangs around his neck. What more can we ask of this boy? He has a loving wife and two young sons. He's a symbol for our country of sacrifice and honor. We can save him from becoming another 'Ghost of Annapolis'.

"On the other hand, he has a warrior heart and needs to feel more useful to his country. He wants to participate with his brothers on a dangerous mission to help preserve our republic.

"I believe you must accept his participation on the ground, Joe. Even in a wheelchair, his spirit is invincible. And it seems to me that America needs as many invincible spirits as possible."

Mitrano walked over to the sitting Vice-Admiral Zume. He extended his hand, thanked his friend for the advice, and stated with sad eyes, "I'm going over to the Chapel to confer with our 'Ghosts of Annapolis'."

Walter embraced his old friend. "Go and listen to their voices," he said, before escorting the CIA director to the front door.

Joe Mitrano walked the short distance to the Chapel. He entered the basement level and saluted the Marine Honor Guard standing at attention in front of the tomb of American hero, John Paul Jones - founding father of the United States Navy. Mitrano stood for over an hour in front of the nearly twenty ton sarcophagus, made of bronze and dark Grand Pyrenees marble. He read the names of Jones' ships inscribed in the marble deck around the crypt: Bonhomme

Richard, Alliance, Serapis, Ariel, Alfred, Providence, and Ranger. He bowed his head in contemplation.

The director stepped up to the Chapel and altar. The US Naval Academy Choir practiced nearby, singing the "Battle Hymn of the Republic". A large stained glass above the altar depicted Christ walking on water. Over the glass in stone were the words, "Eternal Father, Strong To Save".

Mitrano glanced over his right shoulder at another stained glass. It showed the Archangel Michael leading the way through the mine fields of Mobile Bay during the American Civil War naval battle.

He took a deep breath and nodded at the Marine Honor Guard standing in front of him, next to the silk sheet which covered Admiral Julian Stansfield's statue. The young Marine unveiled the rock for the CIA director. The "Battle Hymn" became louder.

Mitrano gasped as he viewed the large pale gray marble statue of his friend. In battle dress on the *USS Ocala*, Admiral Stansfield stood erect wearing a battle helmet. His binoculars hung low on his chest. With four stars on his helmet, and a dark gray patch over his left eye, Julian pointed with his right index finger towards the horizon. His left hand was to his side, open, as if waiting to receive a special something. While the Naval Choir finished the hymn, Joseph Mitrano touched the cold stone with his warm palms. He whispered to the colossus, "Welcome home, Julian."

CHAPTER 2

Father in Time

Julius Stansfield stepped out from the lake after a short swim. The Upper Rhine's water was warmer than usual in late summer. He laid his beach towel on the pebbly shore and sat for a while to enjoy Claudia's windsurfing. Through the dark shade of his sunglasses, Julius could see Claudia's magenta sail rising high into the air as she danced with the jet streams coming down from the Bavarian Alps. The weather was fine and so was Claudia, thought Stansfield, looking at the beauty surrounding him on the western shore of Lake Constance. The majestic mountainsides, covered with wildflowers of every hue, created a magical backdrop for the deep blue in front of him. He briefly removed his shades to appreciate the colors. This last day in August was the finest he had seen since returning to little Aborn, Switzerland.

Claudia's parents had stayed in Geneva for the summer, leaving the blue pastel home on the lake for the young couple to enjoy. More than two months had passed since their mission into Germany. Claudia and Julius had bonded and never left each other's sight. They were happy together, accepting the comfort each provided. She liked his composed demeanor. He was rational and stable-minded. He was responsible and devoted to his beliefs. Julius was a man that Claudia could believe in. A man who allowed her to express her natural freedoms.

The American had fallen into the temptress' spell. Her charms raptured his masculine spirit. She devoured love and passion. Julius understood her potent secret weapons. They were formidable and irrepressible. However, although quite a woman, Claudia was unharness-able. She was like a wild Mustang of the great North American West, free-roaming and untamed, thought Stansfield.

Julius stared out over the white-capped lake and took in the imagery of the athletic and graceful Claudia. The enchantress flew through the air but always landed on the water properly with her feet on the board. She was quick and coordinated like a mountain lion. Her muscular body was malleable and capable of any competitive challenge. He was mesmerized by her forms. It seemed she was always in control.

Stansfield glanced up at the warm mid-day sun directly above him. The solar rays burned his skin. He unfolded a mustard colored beach umbrella and secured it deep into the rocky sand. Laying on his towel, Julius opened a package sent to him from Washington by his younger brother, Mark.

He read the accompanying letter.

My dearest Julius:

I hope this letter finds you happy and in good health. We all miss you back home and hope to see you soon.

Sarah and I have visited your girls several times in the past month. They seem to be doing well, considering the new arrangements.

Rebecca has been playing across the United States this summer to full concert halls and is receiving good reviews as expected.

Michael is returning to London with Nasrin and Alexander next month. He'll be taking over European intelligence analysis at the CIA offices there. Let's see how long he lasts at a desk job. I don't think it'll be his cup of tea. It's not mine.

I was transferred to Naval Intelligence at the Pentagon in July. I hope to adapt to my limitations eventually. It's not easy, Big Brother. My mind is strong but my legs continue to fail me. I've become quite a driver of wheelchairs, both electric and manual. I'm impressed with the upper body strength I've developed over the past several months. It almost compensates for my body's atrophy below.

Sarah, the boys, and I have been living in Mother and Father's Georgetown home since arriving in Washington. It certainly has brought back many sentimental memories and emotions, as you can well imagine. They were good people. We are what we are because of them. Living here makes you realize how much they loved their family. The photographs displayed around the home capture special moments in all our lives. Snapshots in living, I would say. They have deep meaning beyond the first impressions. Layers of love wrapped tightly into a moment in time. We'll miss them dearly, and likely much more than we can appreciate at the present.

Recently, Sarah was cleaning out the closet in Dad's library study. She found an old cardboard box. Inside was a Silver Star and a letter of commendation to our grandfather, Dr. Robert Stansfield, for actions performed in Italy during World War Two. Dad never spoke much about his parents, Robert and Ann. They both died years before we were born. Nevertheless, I always found it strange how Father never mentioned his parents or his brother, and would subtly change the conversations if asked questions about his youth. I always sensed his pain in those thoughts. We never pressed and thus, we never learned.

Also in the box was a leather bound journal kept by Ann during her involvement as a surgical nurse in the 15th Combat Evacuation Hospital in Italy from 1943 to 1945. Interspersed throughout the long first person account of her experiences are loose-leaf hand-written notes from Dad on his thoughts and remembrances of his parents.

It appears our grandmother Ann died in a hospice on the shores of Lake Geneva, Wisconsin, in late July 1975. Father was given leave from the USS Tunny and travelled to Wisconsin to be with his mother in her last days. Some of Father's notes are dated from those days by Lake Geneva, caring for Ann and talking about her life, her beloved husband, Robert, and their two sons. The diary is a portal into another time, another place, and a life well lived. It is sad and dramatic. It is full of things unfamiliar to us, her grandchildren she never knew. I suspect much of the journal was unknown to Father at the time. I gather that much from his personal notes. But two things ring true throughout the emotional narrative - Ann's love for her husband

and children, and Father's love for his parents and brother, Bobby. Reading this album of memories allowed me to better understand our father, and know more deeply his love and devotion to our mother and to us. I now appreciate Father more completely.

So brother Julius, I urge you to read what I have sent you. Let it serve as a portal back in time into our family's heritage. I hope it inspires you as much as it did me. It is a portal into our own souls, a journey of self-discovery. It will make your heart ache and eyes tear, but it will be well worth it. The result will be an even greater appreciation of the life Father gave us.

I will soon see you and Claudia at Annapolis for the unveiling of Father's marble at Academy Chapel. I've been told Father's oil portrait at Memorial Hall, and statue near the altar of the Chapel, are magnificent. No matter how fine, they can't capture the true greatness of the man. Some things are difficult to define.

My love and deepest admiration always.....Mark.

Julius placed his brother's letter back into its envelope. He put on earphones and turned on his music player. He listened to the sounds of Tomaso Albinoni's "Adagio in G Minor" for violin, strings and organ.

The US Navy captain looked out over Lake Constance at Claudia's elegance on water. She seemed to move with the music. Power and grace were mixed to the extreme.

He opened the leather bound repository of memory. He sensed the portal into time and love was drawing him in. Julius allowed himself to fall into an alternate reality to help discover the essence of his father...................

CHAPTER 3

Paestum

My naked body seemed to glide through the water without effort. I felt weightless. The horrors of the past days left my mind for a moment. I had escaped hell, I thought. I couldn't see the horrible wounds and the blood, or hear the screams of young boys as they died in my arms. There were no bomb blasts or the rattle of machine guns around me. I was free.

I held my breath and kept my eyes closed as I swam underwater several meters. Closing my eyes and holding my breath was easy. I had done it so many times in the past few days. Darkness and silence were my friends today. They had come to rescue me. To save me when I needed it most. I was at peace for the first time in a long time.

The Tyrrhenian Sea felt warm on my skin. It bathed me, wiping away all the physical excrement of war. The dust, the grime, and most of all, the blood seemed to wash away into the sea. As I swam, I wished the sea could also claim from my mind the painful images I had seen. But that was asking too much. The memories, like scars, would have to stay.

I came toward the light, slowly letting the air out of my lungs in small bubbles which reached the surface before me. Nearing the interface of sea and sky, I opened my eyes and saw aliquots of air breaking up top. The sunshine above was diffracted into a multitude of randomly directed rays. Like sharp arrows, many of them pierced my heart. I had returned to my unkind reality.

I took a deep breath. The late September Campanian air along the Bay of Salerno still smelled of cordite, olfactory evidence of the battle that had taken place here. Treading water, I looked west into the open Mediterranean and saw only shades of blue - azure and cobalt, indigo and sapphire. Sea birds swept in peace low over the water, occasionally diving and scooping up a fish. There was beauty remaining to be found, I thought.

East towards land, the sun's beams of morning light peeked over distant green hills and reached the waters where I swam. I felt the warmth of the Italian sun on my face. More of God's beauty, I thought.

Alas, just beyond the beach and before the hills, billowing columns of black smoke rose to the sky from destroyed villages and towns. Many fires were still visible, signs of the struggle waged for the capture of this land. For several thousand meters north along the shore, destroyed Allied and German tanks, halftracks, trucks, and jeeps littered the beachfront. US Army morgue details walked the sands and accounted for the dead of battle. Rows of hundreds of American GIs in body bags lined the beachfront awaiting departure from sacred ground.

In a strange and surreal reality, close to the beach where I swam, rose the ancient temples of the Greco-Roman city of Paestum. The culture and civilization of the past mixed with the terrible truths of the present. A sick contrast in the evolution of history, I thought. We had become a mutated retardation of time. The scene exposed another developmental delay in the spiritual growth of mankind.

For days, we had fought and died near these shrines to Poseidon, Hera, and Athena. Their 2500 year-old altars were stained with a mixing of the blood of friend and foe. Many young American, British, and German boys had confronted each other with dagger and gun around the pillars of these temples, not always understanding the reasons why. Often, they had died together at the altars. Enemies lying close together in death, sometimes seeming to embrace each other. The pathetic and confusing horrors of war, I thought.

Still facing east, I again closed my eyes. I rubbed my naked skin with vigor to remove more mud, dust, and battle grime. I desperately tried to rid my body of the blood of boys I had tried to save. I was marked with my failures. Those that died outnumbered those I saved. I needed to start over, I thought. Perhaps, I could save more lives the next time. I hoped so, because so many had died this time. Had I done enough? I asked myself. Could I have been better? If only my soul could be so easily wiped clean.

A large bonfire on the sandy beach burned all of our soiled uniforms and boots. They were too encrusted with the smell of death to salvage. Better to burn it all. Changing old 'war-drobe' for new was part of the healing process.

Several hundred meters south of the bonfire, stood a palatial 16th century Italian villa where we would stay a few days before moving onto Naples. Rest and relaxation, they called it. Recovery was more like it. Like the ruins of ancient Paestum, the splendor and beauty of the villa's colonnaded and arched architecture seemed out of place. It made me more sad than happy. But on the other hand, it was more comfortable than sleeping only minutes at a time in a fox-hole next to a latrine. Lying in holes in the ground as shells burst over us, we never quite knew if they'd be burying us in the same hole. We all needed the rest and the recovery.

In the previous five months, I had crossed the desert of North Africa in an open truck, often under enemy fire. I had seen the destruction of war in Morocco, Algeria, and Tunisia. I had cared for both Allied and German soldiers alike. I had treated innocent civilians caught in the crossfire of battle. I had helped save lives in Sicily as our men fought to liberate it from the Germans.

I had walked the ruins of ancient Carthage, the Semitic Phoenician city-state on the Gulf of Tunis. I had strolled along ancient Greek and Roman temples in Sicily. And now, we had spilled blood on the Doric columns and travertine limestone of Paestum. It seemed odd that the ancient armies of Greeks, Romans, Byzantines, Turks, Venetians, and Napoleonic French, and now, the modern armies of American, British, and Germans, had all come and gone. Only the glorious ancient marbles remained. Ironically, the carved stones remained as silent symbols of what warriors thought they were fighting for - 'civilization'. This was my world in the fall of 1943.

I took another deep breath and dove underwater. I swam slowly towards the shore, where many of the girls were coming out of the water nude. *Without realizing, I had drifted out rather far. I had felt the need to be alone.*

After surfacing again for air, I heard the unmistakable rat-tat-tat. A Messerschmitt 109 German fighter flew low over the Bay of Salerno from the north. It swept down right over me. A British Supermarine Spitfire closely pursued it, firing its eight Browning machine guns. The 109 went into a steep climb over the bay, its engine humming in a low pitch. The Spitfire followed and fired. The high pitched whine of the Spitfire was musical. The dogfight continued for several minutes, with the Messerschmitt trying to maneuver and get the British fighter off its tail. Spinning away in a final desperate dive, the 109 was caught by a burst of bullets. An explosive puff of black smoke and red flame from its engine sent the 109 splashing uncontrollably into the waters of the bay, not far from where the girls stood exposed and naked - watching the action from the beach. Another life lost at Paestum. The Spitfire came back fast and low, close to shore. The pilot heroically flipped his wings in a victory lap, while the girls shouted and whistled.

Even now - with the Salerno beachhead secure, and our troops moving further inland and north toward Naples - our mornings were accented by death. The daily drama of loss of life had become routine. I could not become desensitized to the inhumanity. To me, it was cruel and unusual punishment. A young girl from Pleasant Lake, Minnesota could not accustom herself to this savagery.

I kept swimming to shore to begin my day at Paestum.....

Young Lieutenant Julian Stansfield sat across from his mother, Ann, reading the diary he found on the night table next to the hospital bed. He had travelled all night from Charleston, South Carolina, after receiving word on the USS Tunny that his mother was dying. Julian had served on the nuclear attack submarine for over a year; but in his mind, he had remained close to his mother throughout her illness.

Ann Nelson Stansfield had been in a major depression since the death of her husband in 1966. She had evolved multiple health problems after being hospitalized in a Wisconsin psychiatric institute in 1970. After a recent diagnosis of cancer, she refused treatment and was transferred to a hospice on the shores of Lake Geneva.

Julian stared at his mother, sleeping comfortably as the sun rose over Lake Geneva. A nurse entered the room, greeted the young lieutenant, and opened the large window looking out onto the water. She stepped over to a table nearby and placed a record on an old vintage RCA portable player. She smiled at Julian and said, "She has only one request for me. I'm to open the window at sunrise and play for her the soprano aria 'Vissi d'arte' by Maria Callas, from the Puccini opera TOSCA."

Julian nodded at the nurse. "It was a favorite of hers and my father."

Rays of sunlight illuminated the spartan white-walled room. Julian noticed the tall pink vase on his mother's night table. It held a single red rose. Next to the record player by the window, sat a photograph of his parents in military uniform on the Spanish Steps in Rome, Italy, dated June 1944. Another photograph showed Julian with his older brother Robert on their father's sailboat, cavorting on Lake Michigan in 1960. Maria Callas' voice seemed to invigorate and enliven everything in the room. The sound gave life to the pictures.

The beams of the sun rose slowly on Ann's face. Her son noted how sickly pale she looked. Although only in her mid-fifties, disease had ravaged her physical beauty. Long ago, she had attracted attention with her face and figure. Her long blonde hair, porcelain white skin, deep emerald green eyes, and tall athletic body had always made her the prettiest girl in the room, thought Julian. Time and life's circumstances had not been merciful to Ann Nelson Stansfield.

Ann opened her eyes and saw her son standing next to her, caressing her face with his right hand. Julian gently kissed her forehead.

"You look handsome in your white dress uniform, Julian. I'm happy to see you," she smiled.

"I came as quickly as I could, Mother. Your doctor cabled me in Charleston, saying you had taken a turn for the worse."

"I'm feeling more tired than usual. The doctor says my blood is thick with leukemic white cells, and my organs are failing. I don't have much body pain with the medicine they're giving me. I only hurt in my heart and soul. There's no medicine for that, I'm told. I always hoped not to leave you alone in this world, Julian," said Ann with tears welling in her eyes.

"I understand, Mother. Like with Robert and Father, we don't decide these things. They are what they are. I'm here now to help you with anything I can. I want you to be comfortable and not feel pain. Let me ease your mind," softly said Julian, holding his mother's hand.

"Well, I'm happy to see you strong and handsome, Julian.

"I hope the Navy can get along without you. The *Tunny* is a very important ship. I wouldn't want America to be short-changed," smiled Ann.

The nurse returned to take vital signs and give Ann her pain medications. The young woman, pretty and polite, looked at Julian as she performed her duties.

"Your mother speaks about you all day, Lieutenant. Ann is very proud of your accomplishments. The entire staff here is proud. We know all about you. And with all due respect, you are as handsome as she says."

She finished her tasks and walked out of the room.

"Mother, I took the liberty of reading your war diary. I found it on the table, next to the rose. I didn't know you had kept a personal running narrative of the war. You and Father never spoke much about those times."

"You haven't read the whole album, have you?" asked his mother. "I wouldn't call it a war diary. I think it's more of a long love letter to your father, the greatest man I've known. I would like you to finish it after I'm gone. You'll understand what I mean. One day, when you love a woman like I loved a man, you'll understand completely the emotions expressed in that journal. It's yours to keep for always, Julian," said Ann warmly.

"What do you remember of Paestum, Mother?" gently asked Julian. "Can you talk to me of those times? I'll understand if you wish not to."

"Paestum....."

"Paestum," repeated Ann Nelson Stansfield in a hushed voice as she closed her eyes.

"I remember the flowers..... So many flowers.....

"The white, pink and purple geraniums.

"The blue irises.

"Bright red and yellow poppies.

"Pink dahlias and tall yellow sunflowers.

"Creamy white magnolias and orange lilies.

"But most of all, I remember the roses.....

"Pink, yellow, and especially the red roses growing around our tent hospital at the Roman amphitheater of Paestum.....

"The beauty and grace of the roses, however, could not extinguish the pain we all felt there....."

Ann turned her head on the pillow towards the open window and the cool breeze from Lake Geneva.

"I was a young and innocent twenty-three year-old girl from a small town in Minnesota. I hadn't grown up much before the war. I had graduated from a three year nursing program in big city Minneapolis. I followed my friends and volunteered for the US Army Medical Corps. Next thing I knew, I was mending young boys torn by war in North Africa and Sicily. I don't think anybody can be ready for the things I saw over there. There is no preparation for hell.

"Before the war, I'd never seen even a fist fight between angry men. I wasn't exposed to violent trauma in nursing school, except for the occasional farming accident. In Africa and Europe, I saw every evil thing a human being could do to another. It shocked me to know that one could have such hatred inside.

"I landed near the Scoglitti beachhead on Sicily with the 15th Evacuation Hospital. On July 14, 1943, I waded ashore from an LST in shoulder deep water with my pack above my head. We spent the next month fighting and healing across central Sicily, from Gela to Caltanissetta and Nicosia. We were attached to the US Seventh Army under Lt. General George S. Patton, II Corps, 1st Infantry Division. I thought I would never see more death and dying than what I experienced the first week of August during the Battle of Troina against the German 15th Panzergrenadiers. That's to show you, Julian; in war, always expect the unexpected. It only got worse when we invaded the Italian mainland a month later."

Ann Nelson Stansfield took a sip of water and continued with her story. "In September, 700 Allied ships assembled in the Tyrrhenian Sea for the Salerno invasion of Italy. Ships came from Algeria, Tunisia, and Libya. I went over on an LST convoy from Palermo, Sicily. Troop carriers, ammunition ships, destroyers, cruisers, corvettes, and flak ships of all sizes filled the Mediterranean as far as you could see.

"We had a blackout that night. The only visible light on deck came from the volcanic eruptions on Mt. Stromboli in the Aeolian island chain off the northeast coast of Sicily. Balls of red fire shot high into the night sky, illuminating our ships in silhouette from miles away. We all hoped German U-boats wouldn't take advantage and attack.

"The same evening, we learned the Italian government had surrendered unconditionally to the Allies. When served steak, mashed potatoes, dessert, and fresh coffee for dinner, we didn't know if it was celebration for Italy's surrender or a last meal before the invasion. For many, it was the latter.

"In the pre-dawn morning of September 9, 1943, the first assault waves of Operation Avalanche and Lieutenant General Mark Clark's US Fifth Army began hitting the beaches at the Bay of Salerno. The British landed two attached divisions in the northern sector, closer to the Sorrento Peninsula. Our doctors landed in the first wave to the south at Paestum with the spearheading US 36th Texas Infantry Division. A few days earlier, Bernard Montgomery's British Eighth Army had landed further south at the toe and heel of Italy.

"The invasion of mainland Italy was proposed and heavily pushed by Winston Churchill. He hoped to draw German Army divisions away from the Soviet Eastern Front, and from the Normandy beaches of the planned Allied invasion of northern Europe. The Americans reluctantly agreed. It's not easy to fight up a long peninsula, crisscrossed by difficult terrain.

"Italy slowly became the 'Forgotten Front'. Many of our boys died there. Some of them in my hands. I've never forgotten any of them.

"The nurses on my LST - a large carrier of reserve troops, combat supplies, and medical equipment - were scheduled to disembark on September 12. Our boat sat in the southwestern sector of the bay, waiting to move closer towards the beach when ordered. German air raids had claimed several ships.

"Every evening, I would go to the top deck and watch red tracers shoot up into the sky from the fighting ships. Occasionally, a burst of red, white, and blue flame would pinpoint the loss of a German fighter-bomber. P-38s from airfields in Sicily would swoop in later and kill off injured German stragglers. Their splashes into the Mediterranean around our convoy would electrify the men and cause them to break into cheers.

"In the very early morning of September 12, as I slept with twenty other nurses in a small crowded bunkroom, a heavy barrage of anti-aircraft fire shook our ship. We awoke in panic. The bright glow from belching guns outside our porthole illuminated the room in fiery red light. We heard men on the fighting deck above us, yelling, 'Stukas, Stukas!' A German dive-bomber unloaded her deadly cargo right over us.

"I closed my eyes in bed and listened to the shrill of the Stuka, and then the tight whistle of her bomb coming for me. A great explosion knocked us out of our bunks. Smoke filled the room and the hallway outside. We all searched our way up the stairs blindly to the top deck and found a horrible spectacle of screaming, dying men everywhere. Fires raged at the stern while crews fought to limit its spread to an ammunition depot below the main deck. We helped those we could. Many men had been blown apart by the violent blast. Some bled to death in front of us.

"Moments later, another Stuka found us and delivered the final blow. The ship convulsed and began splitting apart. An 'abandon ship' order went out while deadly fires raged out of control. Lifeboats with the injured were lowered into the water first. The remaining nurses went next. Luckily, we all survived, but most of the young boys did not. The ship exploded in a massive ball of fire and sunk into the Tyrrhenian Sea. I watched the pitiful display from a lifeboat, caring for an injured seventeen year-old sailor from Louisiana.

"We were picked up by another LST and delivered to shore at dawn that morning. I waded in hip deep water to the beach, wearing olive drab woolen shirt and pants, combat helmet and boots. I carried essentials in a Musette Bag over my head. The shore was heavily mined, and engineers had set a safe path for us to get to the coastal road ahead. Destroyed and burnt out tanks, halftracks, and jeeps littered the beach. Swollen, bloated, blown-apart blackened bodies lay scattered like driftwood on the sand. Many of them were partially eaten by rats bigger than alley cats. As I approached the coastal road, most of the dead wore charcoal gray German uniforms of the 16th Panzer Division. They were as blackened and half-eaten as our boys.

"By the afternoon of September 13, the 15th Combat Evacuation Hospital was fully operational in an ancient Roman amphitheater at Paestum, 300 yards inland from the beach and only two miles from the fighting front. Two other hospitals set up in ruins nearby. We were surrounded by architectural relics of a civilization long dead. Tall fluted

Doric columns, Roman arches, and fallen marble stones, accented by yellow and pink hibiscus, oleander, and the finest roses I had ever seen. The magnificence and the horror of it all," sighed Ann, before falling asleep.

Julian pulled the bed cover over his mother's chest as a cool morning breeze off Lake Geneva swept into the room. He returned to his chair and opened Ann's diary....................

Over the past week, we've treated thousands of military casualties, both American and German. We cared also for Italian villagers - men, women, and children caught in the crossfire. We had ten operating tables running 24 hours a day in the surgical tent. We triaged cases from the battalion aid stations in the receiving tent. Aided by tech sergeants, we tried to stabilize the shock patients with intravenous saline and blood plasma before rushing them to surgery. We temporized with those more stable to wait. Initially, we had little oxygen, little whole blood, and no penicillin. We treated shell fragmentation trauma to heads, chests, abdomens, and extremities. Traumatic amputations were common, particularly from Schuh mines and 'Bouncing Betties' which blew away legs, buttocks, and genitalia. Many patients arrived at the receiving tent already dead, having bled out travelling the short distance from the battalion aid stations. It was completely disheartening.

We gave topical sulfadiazine powder and intramuscular morphine liberally to help prevent infection and alleviate pain. We had many gas gangrene cases from wounds not promptly treated on the battlefield. Anaerobic bacteria would invade necrotic, oxygen starved muscle in the extremities and spread quickly, killing the patient. Amputation was the only cure, if done early in the process. I was constantly checking wounds with a flashlight, looking for the tell-tale signs of purple mottled skin and cracking, hissing gas in the tissues. The putrid smell was unmistakable.

In the operating tent, surgeons steadied their hands against their patients' internal organs while US destroyers and cruisers a mile offshore lobbed shells into the hills east of us. German artillery sent shells back in the opposite direction. We sat in the middle, always worrying about 'shorts' from both sides.

Our 400 cots in the medical ward tents were always filled with recovering patients. Several hundred more patients filled litters between the cots. Along with the post-operative surgical cases, we had malaria, dysentery, venereal diseases, and combat-fatigue. As soon as patients were stable enough for travel, we sent them to hospitals in North Africa.

By September 15, Albert Kesselring's German 10th Army was on the defensive. Allied bombardments from ships at sea and fighter-bombers had broken their resistance. The Germans had inflicted heavy casualties on the American and British troops before pulling out north of Naples by October 1. Nearly 15,000 killed and wounded Allied soldiers had suffered at Salerno.

By the early morning of September 19, heavy fighting around Paestum ceased. Some of the girls gathered to go down to a secluded beach at dawn, just south of the landing zone. I had spent the night caring for a young soldier we had received four days before. The nineteen year-old boy from Houston, Texas, had stopped his studies in English Literature at Princeton University to volunteer for the army. He had been caught in an ambush south of the Sele River. Surgery to repair a ruptured liver and spleen had initially gone well. However, during the last 24 hours, he had developed sepsis with high fevers. The doctors had given up hopes for recovery.

In solemn dawn twilight, under the dark blue sky still filled with twinkling stars, the boy asked me to take him out to the ruins of Paestum so he could see the roses I always talked to him about. I had an aide help me wheel his stretcher in front of the temple of Poseidon. A low whispering wind from the sea was cool and warm at the same time. There was silence of voice, except for the calls and cries of the gods.

Next to a row of beautiful red rose bushes, I held the boy's hand as his breathing shallowed. The heavens above the hills became pink with early eastern light. The boy opened his eyes and asked me to bring a red rose to his nose. I passed the soft petals lightly across his cheeks and lips. He breathed in the aromatic scent and smiled.

'I love flowers... like I love 19th century romantic English poetry..... Roses and Keats go well together,' he said..... 'More so when in the company of a beautiful girl like you, Ann..... Do you enjoy romantic poetry, Ann?' he asked, before taking a deep breath and closing his eyes.

'I'm not familiar with it,' I answered..... 'It does seem romantic, though,' I added, crying quietly while I watched the young soldier struggle with his words, his breath, and his life.

'John Keats is my favorite,' said the boy. 'He died very young in Italy, not far from here..... I too will die young in Italy..... Legend says that in his last moments, Keats thought of flowers and their beauty, and felt them growing over him.'

The Texas boy from Princeton again asked for the rose. I caressed his face with the velvety petals. He slowly breathed in and smiled. The wind from the sea gently passed - bending the rose bushes near us towards the rising sun, and drying my tears. The stars in the sky seemed to brighten. The calls and cries of the gods became quiet. The sacred temples went back to sleep. The poet squeezed my hand with tenderness and whispered, 'I too feel the flowers growing over me.'

Julian Smith - the Ivy League boy from Texas who loved romantic poetry - took his last shallow breath and died among the ruins of Paestum, surrounded by red roses and the pink sky of an early morning Italian sunrise. He would never again recite beautiful words or enjoy the scent of a flower. Neither would he feel the warmth of the rising sun on his face or the touch of an ocean wind. Most of all, the boy would never again feel the love of a woman. He had joined all the other boys I had lost at Paestum. Their names, perhaps, would lose themselves into the blur of history. But I would never forget them. They would always remain in my heart. Especially Julian - the gentle poet soldier who loved Keats and a young innocent girl from Minnesota.

CHAPTER 4

Beyond the Call of Duty

lay shirtless and uncovered in bed, smoking a cigarette. A long thick scar ran down the middle of my abdomen, a remnant of a past but not forgotten battle. Above me, a ceiling fan's blades cut through the air, creating a monotonous repetitive sound. The noise reminded of my escape from the Hunza Valley sixteen months ago - helicopter rotor blades above the din of battle - cries of injured, both friend and foe - battle yells and commands in English and Chinese - automatic gunfire from all directions - fire and smoke of rockets and mortar - the look of death and selfless devotion in the eyes of my friend, Marcus Callanan - despair and sadness in the eyes of Marcus' sons, Martin and Gilbert. These nightmare images came to me in rapid succession. Shishkat Bridge had been a nightmare alright, I thought.

The actions had happened all so rapidly, and all so slowly. I could recollect each of my moves. Like slow-motion instant replay, I could rewind and replay at any speed I wished. Sometimes fast, sometimes slow - jump forward, slide back - any way you cut it, any speed you ran it, it was horror in the first degree.

I had used a light machine gun and an AK-47 rifle to cut down dozens of attacking Chinese infantry. I could see their faces as I ran through them like a hot knife through butter. Some were my age, others younger, but they all appeared bewildered and shocked at what I was doing. The Chinese infantrymen had expressions of disbelief. They seemed to ask themselves what they were doing there with me. Their faces expressed more surprise than fear. I had given them no time to react. Fractions of seconds had decided their fate. They were to die in the Hunza Valley, just like Marcus Callanan was to die a short time later. A hail of bullets and smoke, and a quick ebbing away of life. There had been much blood on stone and flower in the valley of Shangri La.

I had spent another sleepless night. Sure I slept, but only minutes at a time. Nightmares intervened as usual. One thing was coming home a "hero", another was the consequence. I was staring at a lifetime in a wheelchair, dependence and drag on those I loved. I had to accept an inability to satisfy my beautiful young wife sexually. I would never again play ball with my boys. These things didn't sit well with me. They were ego destructive, and not part of the image I had of myself.

September was unusually cool in Washington. Sarah had left the bedroom window slightly open all night. Morning sunshine hadn't yet warmed the room. The ceiling fan only made it colder. But I needed to hear the sounds of the blades. In a twisted way, I needed to live the experience again and again to fully recognize its consequences. I finally needed to accept its result.

Natural light from the sun fell on my mid-section. The purple scar, running from below my breastplate to the pubic bone, was smooth and shiny. The surgeons had split me down the linea alba to save my life. Perhaps they shouldn't have tried so hard.

I took another drag, before putting out the cigarette on the full ashtray next to my bed. Today was a big day for the Stansfield family. Later in the morning, the US Naval Academy was honoring my father - Admiral Julian Stansfield - with the unveiling of a life-sized oil portrait painting in Memorial Hall and a marble statue in the iconic Chapel. The formal affair was to be attended by many dignitaries, including the President of the United States, Secretaries of Defense and State, the British Prime-Minister, and hundreds of Father's friends and acquaintances from his years in the United States Navy. My brothers, sister, and I were guests of honor.

I pushed myself up in bed and looked across the room at the wall where Sarah had placed my Medal of Honor Flag. The sky-blue flannel had thirteen upward pointed white stars in chevrons centrally and was fringed in gold. The blue of the flag was the same color of the sky over the Hunza Valley. I remembered seeing the clear cloudless blue as I was carried to the waiting rescue helicopter with a bullet in my back. It was the last color I saw before losing consciousness on the copter. The blue had stayed in my mind. Without rational explanation, the color was imprinted and repeatedly flashed before my mind's eye in dreams. I couldn't interpret its significance. Perhaps, it reflected how close I came to dying that day in the Hunza. Maybe it was the blue of Heaven. The costs of freedom, I thought.

Today was also a big day in another respect. I would tell Sarah about my move to Special Operations at Naval Intelligence. It had taken two weeks to convince Admiral Culligan and CIA Director Mitrano of the transfer. I needed to do this. I had uncovered the secondary terrorist plot and knew the players. I had offered the specifics of the counter-terror plan, finally accepted by the Pentagon and the CIA. I desired to be on the ground and help implement the mission. A wheelchair was not going to prevent me from accomplishing the directives of the mission. I could do this.

While Sarah prepared breakfast and awoke the boys, I pulled my stubborn legs over the side of the bed and reached for the wheelchair, a short distance away. I'd usually wait for Sarah to help me, but today I tried alone. Grabbing the chair with my left hand, I slipped off the bed and fell to the floor. The stumble created quite a ruckus.

Sarah and the boys ran into the room as I crawled to the chair and pulled myself onto it with my arms. George and Robert, only eight and six years old, watched as Sarah held them back from helping. She allowed me to gather myself.

I smiled at her. Sarah smiled back, before quietly returning the boys to the kitchen to finish breakfast. I took a deep breath, and rolled to the bathroom to catheterize myself and wash-up.

"I can be more than this," I whispered to Sarah.

After bathing, I returned to the first floor bedroom of my parents' Georgetown home. The children had taken Father's room on the second floor. Sarah prepared my formal US Marine "Blue Dress" uniform on the bed. I closed the door behind me.

"I'm sorry, Baby, for embarrassing myself like that. I slipped. Couldn't catch myself."

Sarah turned and stared. Her kind loving blue eyes filled with tears. With a hushed voice she said, "Listen, Captain Mark Stansfield, you are a man through and through. You are brave and dedicated to your family and country. You have given everything for us. You are incapable of embarrassing yourself. It's inconsistent with the very fiber of your being. You fell, and you will fall again. You will continue to pick yourself up. It's the only way you know how to do things, Captain."

"The legs aren't coming back, Baby, neither is my ability to give you pleasure as before."

Sarah smiled again. "It all depends on how hard I work you, Captain."

She unbuttoned her blouse and removed her brassiere. She slipped off her dress and underwear. Sarah stood nude in front of me and began touching herself. Within minutes, she had prepared me for her body. We made love.

"You see darling, you're still my Captain. I can bring you back whenever I wish," said Sarah playfully. "You're the only man for me. The only man I've ever loved. The only man I'll ever love. You fulfill me and I fulfill you. It's very simple, Captain. Our love conquers all."

We laughed like children. Sarah had not disregarded our predicament. She simply refused to make it an issue in our love affair. She was a woman in love, and a wheelchair was not going to get in the way.

A while later, I sat in front of the mirror in the room. I wore a form-fitted long sleeved dark blue coat with high collar.

Shiny buttons displayed the Corps' eagle and anchor insignia. Underneath, I had a starched plain white shirt and sky blue trousers with blood red stripes down the outer seams of each leg. The red color was to honor the memories of fallen Corp comrades. I wore a midnight blue web belt with a gold M-buckle around my waist.

George placed a black sock and dress shoe on my right foot. Young Robert did the same on the other. George then carefully placed a white peaked officer's cap on my head. Robert placed Medal of Honor and Navy Cross battle ribbons on my left chest, as George set other battle ribbons on the right.

Finally, Sarah came from behind and secured the light blue, moiré pattern, silk Medal of Honor band around my neck, outside the shirt collar but under the coat. America's highest military decoration for bravery and valor had been given 894 times since the beginning of World War Two, most of them posthumous. Authorized by President Abraham Lincoln in December 1861, it was a distinction of honor and selfless devotion to comrade and country. It made me feel uncomfortable, reminding me further of the Hunza Valley.

Sarah lovingly positioned the five-pointed inverted bronze star over the base of my neck. Each point of the star was tipped with trefoils, and centered with a crown of laurel and oak. Within the crown, the Goddess of War and Wisdom, *Minerva*, stood holding a shield with America's coat of arms in her right hand. Her left hand rested on fasces, symbolizing "strength through unity". She repulsed a figure of "Discord" in front of her, representing America's enemies. The medal was suspended from flukes of an anchor, attached to a shield of blue ribbon with arrangements of thirteen white stars in three chevrons. The shield extended into the sky-blue silk neckband, 1 3/8 inches wide and 22 inches long.

I looked into the mirror and noticed Sarah's proud stare. The boys had tears in their eyes. I kindly smiled at George and Robert individually, and said simply, "Let's go honor your grandfather."

CHAPTER 5

Reflections

We arrived at Bancroft Hall as scheduled, an hour before everyone else. Vice-Admiral Walter Zume had asked Midshipman First Class Harold Milsap and his Honor Detail to provide guidance and comfort.

The Stansfield family van parked next to the "Marine One" wheelchair ramp, adjacent to the front steps of Bancroft Hall. Twenty cadets in full Academy Dress Blue Honor Guard Sword and Scabbard stood at attention in the morning sun waiting for our arrival. Harold Milsap opened the van's door, saluted me, and said in loud voice, "Welcome, Sir, to your Alma Mater."

George and Robert brought the wheelchair around. Sarah stood by as I maneuvered into it and allowed George to push me in procession in front of the Honor Guard. The cadets presented their swords, and looked in deference while I passed slowly by them.

The US Naval Academy Band played "Semper Fidelis". I held a rigid salute throughout the procession. Six year old Robert - wearing a huge smile - walked with his mother and Milsap behind us, also saluting the Honor cadets.

At the end of the line, Milsap requested to push me up the ramp to the ceremonial entrance of the Rotunda. We entered the marble enclosure as the last notes of the Sousa march played.

Cadet Milsap accompanied the family to the Memorial Hall entry vestibule and handed the wheelchair back to George. "Please forgive me, Captain Stansfield, for my personal show of respect, but I must say for all the troops at the Academy that we are honored greatly by your presence here today. May God bless you and your family, Sir." The midshipman looked directly at the Medal of Honor, hanging at the base of my neck, and saluted.

We passed slowly down the hallway of the memorial, until reaching the station of Father's portrait. George placed my chair directly in front of the silk curtain covering the painting. Sarah stepped behind me and asked the boys to gently roll the curtain away. She let out a soft gasp as the presence of Julian Stansfield appeared.

The boys rushed quietly to my side. Sarah stared at the portrait with a hand cupped over her mouth. The family remained in silent contemplation for several minutes.

Young Robert blurted, "Who is that lady in the mirror? She's smiling at us!"

George quickly enlightened him, "That's your grand-mother, stupid! And she's not looking at us. She's loving Granddad."

I placed my arms around the boys and brought them in front of me. I embraced George, and then Robert.

"That's my mother, your grandmother," I said. "She's the woman behind us all. You were only three years old, Robert, when my mother died. I regret you have no recollection of her. But if she was alive, she would be spoiling you rotten. I'm sure of that," I smiled.

I studied Father's image.

"Rear-Admiral John McLaren, the painter and old friend of the family, captured all of his character," I told Sarah. "The portrait reflects the man in detail. Like Shakespeare allowed his heart to guide the pen, John freed his heart to direct the brush. His love for my father shines through. What more can I say....."

Sarah sensed my feelings. She and the boys left me alone for a few moments.

The memory of Father's visit in the middle of the night to the intensive care unit of Bethesda Naval Hospital came to me in a rush of emotion. I remembered the expressions on his face. He had great worry and concern over my injuries and chances for recovery, after I arrived by air ambulance from Germany.

I quietly spoke to him.

"You see, Dad, I'm alive and in one piece. Not all the pieces work as well as before, but I'm here, still fighting. I have no intention of dropping my guard. I'm staying in the ring and coming back. Before the final bell sounds, I'll be victorious just like you."

I paused for a moment, searching for the right words.....

"You never mentioned you were leaving for Taiwan, Dad..... I would have likely urged you not to..... You wouldn't have listened and gone anyway, I suppose..... With Mom gone, and your deep responsibilities for our country, I guess it was the only decision you could make..... You never stopped fighting, Dad. I respect that. You lived the 'American Amaranth' credo. You fought through physical disability, deep personal sorrow and hardship, and ultimately performed your duties to America with honor and courage. Although you went through hell, you helped preserve our freedom. You were instrumental in winning the 'Great War' for the United States. Your family and country are deeply appreciative."

I paused again.....

"I've made a decision, Father, I suspect you would argue against..... I must get back in the fight according to my own personal rules and beliefs..... I don't perform well behind a desk, or parading around social events for the Navy. They have me showing off the Medal of Honor. I don't like doing that. It makes me uneasy and uncomfortable. I find it dishonorable, and not reflective of the way I've lived my life..... I understand I'm in a wheelchair without functional legs, but my heart and mind are strong. My will to fight is strong, as it is to live. I'm willing to pass through great hardship, like you, to fulfill the expectations I have of myself. I don't appreciate this easy life that they have created for me. Pain and suffering are fine with me, as long as I believe in my actions and sense of duty..... I'm willing to allow the 'Law of Natural Selection' to run its course. Survival of the fittest, I say..... I need to be on the ground and in the field. I want the ball in the last ten seconds of the game. Don't sit me out coach, I say..... In your reflection, Father, I'm willing to pass through hell to get to heaven."

I sat in solemn repose for several more minutes. I prayed for the souls of my parents. Finally, I looked up to my father one last time and whispered, "See you in Elysium, Dad."

We exited Bancroft Hall. The Marine Corp Band struck up Sousa's "The Thunderer", as I filed past them and the Honor Guard. Harold Milsap directed his midshipmen at attention and saluted. He made direct eye contact with me, and I returned the gesture with a nod of my head.

The Stansfields met for breakfast at Buchanan House. Vice-Admiral Zume and the President of the United States welcomed all of us - Julius, Michael, Rebecca, their families and close friends - for a simple meal. Also in attendance were Admiral Culligan from Naval Intelligence and CIA Director Joseph Mitrano. The president gave his personal thanks for Father's service to the United States.

A short time later, everyone crossed the street to Academy Chapel for the ceremonial unveiling of Admiral Julian Stansfield's marble image. The US Naval Academy Band played Samuel Barber's "Adagio" adapted for Brass. The somberly impressive music quieted the place where Father had given his well-remembered speeches on freedom to his beloved cadets. The entire First Class of midshipmen in Dress Blue uniforms lined the walls of the chapel. All of them stood at attention. We took our places in the first row with the president.

Michael stepped to the podium. He liked to give speeches, and we had chosen him to give the opening remarks.

"My family and I thank you for coming to show your respect and love for our father. Knowing him as I did, he would have been mortified with the ceremonial display. At the same time, he would have been honored to come back home to where he learned the ways of liberty and free-dom. To the place he worshipped until his last breaths. To the chapel where he taught his lessons of life to his beloved midshipmen. He would often tell us that the Chapel was his place of worship, to his God and to his Navy. He was a simple man with complex emotions. Throughout his life, he fought and loved furiously.

"Our mother was his companion in life, and now in death. She also taught him much about freedom. She was essential in my father's growth as a patriot. She gave her life freely and completely to him, and to our country. They always shared a deeply rewarding life together, exquisite in spiritual detail. They shared a single soul, I think. It was a gift, they'd say. For our family, our mother and father were an inseparable unit. Like our nation, they were indivisible in every respect. We feel this celebration is as much about her, as it is dedicated to him.

"Our mother and father would have hoped that the admiral's image here would inspire young students of freedom to fully realize the greatness of our country and appreciate the costs required to protect her for all time. They would have wished for this lasting effect. I believe it is a noble wish, reflecting the strong faith they had in the young people of America.

"Finally, speaking also on behalf of my brothers Julius and Mark, and sister Rebecca, we would like to impress upon all of you the certain reality that our father's legacy was and always will be of love. Love for our mother, our family, our Navy, and our country."

Michael walked off the altar and sat down. The US Naval Academy Choir sang "Eternal Father, Strong To Save". A Marine and Navy Honor Guard carefully removed the silk sheet covering the greater than life-sized sculpture of Admiral Julian Stansfield.

The gray stone was solid like the man. His iconic eye patch was part of the captured image. The four stars on his battle helmet, signifying his station, could just as easily reflected love and faith in his four children.

I immediately noticed Father's open left hand. It laid softly to his side, almost kindly inviting us to hold it. I thought it too was reflective of our father. He always had an open hand to help anyone who needed it. Mother and we could count on his support at all times and in all occasions.

After the ceremony ended, and everyone had filed out of the chapel, my brothers and I stayed sitting in front of the marble. Each of us took our turn holding Father's left hand.....

Joseph Mitrano secretly watched from the entrance, understanding the Stansfield men and their need to stay a while longer. He then witnessed something remarkable.

Julius and Michael helped Mark to his feet, and assisted him closer to the admiral's image. They hoisted him up on their shoulders as Mark removed his Medal of Honor from beneath his jacket and placed it around his father's neck.

Mitrano slowly walked away with his mind firmly decided. A unique situational challenge required unique people to solve it. Hard problems demanded hard people, people as hard as the stones at Annapolis.

CHAPTER 6

Cauldron of Fire

Julius Stansfield returned to Aborn on September 20. He had spent ten days with his girls in Washington after the ceremonies at Annapolis honoring his father.

Claudia impatiently waited for her man back in Switzerland. She had not accompanied Julius to the United States. She didn't want to upset the delicate balance that Julius maintained between his old life and his new. His daughters were young and impressionable. Appearing as a "new girlfriend" with their father was ill-timed.

Claudia generated an energy in Julius which he found unfamiliar. She alerted his basic instincts more than any woman he had known. Her intelligence and crude natural habits hypnotized him, and aroused his sensitivities. Often dark and unpredictable, she could also be soft and charming. For reasons he couldn't completely understand, Julius now felt free with her - physically and emotionally. A natural love had evolved, born from primitive lust. The sensory wonderland was fulfilling for both of them.

Julius and Claudia lay naked on a buckskin rug in front of the warm fireplace. The Austrian Alpine Red Stag hide was soft and porous. It had soaked up their sweat while they made love. The living room's large plate glass window faced out over Lake Constance. A low hanging crescent moon lit up the lake's black surface. The peaks of the dark Bavarian Alps also stood below the moon rays. The whole scene was both beautiful and wicked, just like Claudia Coffigny.

A nude Claudia sat up cross-legged on the red deerskin and placed her strong back to the fire. Her blonde hair fell on her shoulders. Facing her, Julius stayed laying with his head on a jewel-green colored satin pillow. Both lovers drank French cognac.

Claudia read from her book of sensual French poetry. "La sueur et la semence se sont mélanges. Mes jus femelles coulant comme un fleuve. Le pinacle d'orgasme accompli plusieurs fois. L'odeur d'amour dans l'air. Notre loins se bloquait dans la contraction, a plusieurs reprises. Rendez-moi lourd avec votre amour."

The femme fatale looked up from the book at Julius. She smiled and translated in English from memory. "Sweat and semen mixed. My female juices flowing like a river. Pinnacle of orgasm achieved many times. The smell of love in the air. Our loins locked in contraction, again and again. Make me heavy with your love."

Claudia closed her eyes and pressed her pelvis against the buckskin. She slowly licked her lips.

"Words are powerful, Julius. They evoke emotion. They make you feel all sorts of things. These words, like the hot fire burning behind me and the animal skin beneath me, are erotic. They flame me up. Imagine, a simple collection of letters strung together in French or in English prepare me to have more of you," she said, opening her eyes widely and biting her lower lip.

"Do me now!

"Make me heavy with your love!" demanded Claudia.....

The hours passed. The lovers - exhausted from drink and passion, and entwined like rapturous vines in summer – caressed each other's bodies. The fire crackled behind them.

"I remember shooting this stag with my father's bolt action Italian hunting rifle when I was fourteen years old," said Claudia, laying on her belly and softly passing her fingers through the fur.

"On a hill near Innsbruck, I got down open legged, just like this."

Claudia pressed her breasts to the buckskin, and opened her legs and ass wider to the fire behind her. Stansfield lay next to her, mesmerized by her sexual energy. Everything about this pussycat turned on his awareness. Her physical looks, her gestures, her body odor, all seemed to draw out his manhood at once. She was simply irresistible.

"I stabilized myself, and peered with my right eye through the telescopic sight. Out of the dark green forest and cool hazy morning fog, he appeared on a ridge only two hundred meters away. His fifteen points shined with morning dew. I thought of him having more points than I had years.

"God's creature seemed to look up directly at me, as I held my breath and fired a round into his head. He fell to the ground, convulsed and died."

Claudia sat back up again, whirled her thick blonde hair to one side, and took more cognac.

"I felt sad when walking with my father over the ridge to see my first kill. Father held my hand as I trembled. I had ended the life of a strong and proud animal, I thought. He had done no harm to me.

"Standing over him, the dead buck looked peaceful. A bullet had entered his head, right between the eyes. Perhaps a bullet elsewhere would have caused suffering, I thought. Better this way. A quick death without pain or knowledge of what just happened, I said in a low voice to myself."

Claudia finished her glass of cognac and quickly poured another.

"Tonight, you and I lie on his skin and make love. Life is full of disconnects, Julius. Contradictions and ironies. Complications and hardships. Disillusionments and disappointments. You simply have to run through it, expecting less than what you hopefully get. The reward in life is simply 'living'. I seek pleasure and avoid pain. I fill my soul with what I wish, when I wish. I like to pack light and move quickly when I can. I'm not held up by complication. I live one breath at a time."

Julius stared at Claudia's face. Her blonde hair, deep blue eyes, fine cheekbones and nose seemed created by a Renaissance sculptor. She was Venus at her birth. Michelangelo could not have created better. But she was elusive, thought Stansfield.

Paraphrasing Winston Churchill's characterization of Russian geopolitical maneuvering with the Nazis in 1939, he whispered to her, "You are a riddle, wrapped in a mystery, inside an enigma."

"What do you mean, Captain?"

"You're ultimate pleasure to the senses, that's all," he laughed. "You go 0 to 60 in a split second, forward and in reverse. Hot or cold, you tantalize before delivering every time. You rapture with both your mind and body.

"But also, you have a sharp edge I can't quite figure. Volatile and potent, it's a mixture of Tasmanian devil and black widow spider," grinned Julius.

"Oh, I can be much worse than that," she smiled.

In spite of these realities, however, Claudia was thrilling. She was fantasy and ultimate entertainment. She was an exciting roller-coaster ride from start to finish. Her way was so profound that she could give you poison, and you didn't care. You still scrambled to be with her.

Her French-tinged English was enchanting and endearing. She was a special attractive creature, thought Stansfield. She was intrinsically kind, loving and hopeful. But in an instant, she could also be murderously insane to the first degree. Claudia was bottled lightning. Bipolar dynamite embodied in flesh and bone. She could go from reciting love poems or dancing ballet to insanely rich sex, and return to soulfulness in perfect choreography. She could make it all seem part of the same dance. She could just as easily run a man through with a stiletto and cut out his heart, as she could make love to him and conquer it. And had probably done so in reverse sequence many times, thought Stansfield. A queen tigress in the jungle could not match her mating skills or killer instincts. Like liquid mercury, Claudia was dangerous and difficult to handle. She could be toxic. A man needed to be at his best when around her. If not, he would not be around much longer, figuratively and literally. Claudia sharpened all of Julius' senses. She made him a more skilled and powerful man and warrior. She made him want to survive in order to experience more of her.

Julius and Claudia talked and loved by the fireplace until early morning. He was happy to be back in Switzerland. Maybe there could be something to this relationship, thought Stansfield.

After Claudia went to sleep, the US Navy captain stayed by the fire reading Ann's war diary. The journal was like a time machine. It had been written with deliberation and sensitivity. It was keenly expressive in imagery. Julius again fell into its portal and drifted away....................

I climbed to the top of the hill. An old 15th century monastery sat at its summit. The Benedictine monks still faithfully operated the sanctuary. They guided me onto an elevated rock garden with terraces of recently planted tulip bulbs. From the promontory, I had a clear view of the green valley below. I saw our hospital with its big red cross, two miles to the south. Further south, the temples of Paestum rose up near the blue Mediterranean Sea. Several miles in front of me stood Mount Vesuvius, with a dark plume of black and gray smoke rising from its hot hole. The active volcano divided the Bays of Salerno and Naples. Both waters were filled with half-sunken wreckage of Allied and German ships. Many of them smoldered. My world, land and sea, was an angry world.

Ship horns and sirens blared across the bay and harbor of Naples. Looking north at a distance, a squadron of Stukas came into view. Escorted by Fw 190 fighters, they approached in fury. American and British warships hurriedly threw their metal into the sky. Puffs of black broke in the air between the German dive-bombers as they descended to drop their bombs over the targets. The wail of their dives chilled me to the bone. Although outdated and obsolete, the Stuka could still kill with ease.

One bomb hit an Allied destroyer, breaking her back in a mighty explosion which sent shock waves across the water. Two Stukas disintegrated in the air simultaneously, sending debris down on the ships below. A British grouping of Spitfires entered the fray and fought with the 190s. Swarms of planes flew into each other, firing their machine guns. Multiple individual battles formed in the sky. Every few moments, a plane came crashing down into the bay. From my position, the sounds of aerial war were muted but still clearly heard. The occasional explosion from a ship was louder and was felt on my skin. The dramatic terror of it all, right in front of my eyes. The killing went on for almost an hour.

I returned to the hospital in the afternoon. We had arrived in Naples on October 5 and occupied an old Italian medical clinic. The Germans, abandoning the city on October 1, had retreated strategically north of the Volturno River. They fortified the Volturno's banks and dug in for a fight.

We were expecting to stay in Naples for a while as the Allies tried to break through the new German lines of defense. Our four-story hospital had no electricity or running water. Gas generators provided minimal electric lighting. A water tank truck outside supplied clean water for drinking and medical purposes. The elevators didn't work, and materials and patients needed to be carried by litter between floors.

The basement cellar provided a bomb shelter from the nightly Luftwaffe raids. But most of us would stay with our patients on the second and third floors, who were usually too sick to be moved. The first floor was organized for receiving casualties and performing surgery. The fourth floor provided living quarters for the doctors and nurses, who would frequently mix at night. I never did.

The city of Naples had been destroyed by the retreating German Army. Water and power supply stations were blown up. Street signs were removed to confuse incoming Allied traffic. Booby traps, firebombs, and mines were placed everywhere to create chaos.

There was no local civilian government in Naples. There was no police. Meat, butter, sugar, coffee, tea, and cigarettes drove high prices in the black market.

To prevent typhus in the general population, the US Army sprayed the civilians with DDT. This also helped decrease the number of malaria cases. US Army personnel had been given the new typhus vaccine. We all took daily Atabrine to help prevent malaria.

We spent the days and nights repairing the usual shell shrapnel and bullet wounds from the Volturno front. Close hand to hand combat brought more knife and bayonet abdominal injuries. German snipers near the outskirts of Naples caused many Allied head and chest wounds. Booby traps and mines inside Naples continuously generated scores of casualties on a daily basis, both civilian and military.

Like at Paestum, the wards smelled of blood and burnt flesh. This unforgettable scent was mixed with the putrid smell of infected muscle tissue, and the oily emissions from suction machines keeping lungs expanded and stomachs empty. The guttural sounds of dying men were as common in the dimly lit wards in Naples as in the tents at Salerno and Paestum.

Unlike Paestum, however, we didn't wear our helmets in surgery. In Naples - we operated in a concrete block *hospital, not the soft canvas tents of before. We also didn't eat, bathe, brush our teeth, or do our laundry out of our steel helmets. We had sinks at Naples. In that respect, we lived in luxury. Surgery by candlelight was also less common.*

Young Lieutenant Julian Stansfield closed his mother's diary. As evening progressed, Ann had spiked a high fever. The doctor prescribed anti-pyretics and warned Julian that sepsis was setting in. Infection would overwhelm her final defenses.

Julian passed his hand across her face and gently wiped off the perspiration.

Ann softly opened her eyes and asked, "What time is it?"

"It's nearly midnight, Mother. You've been asleep the past six hours. You haven't eaten.

"Are you hungry?"

"No," she said. "I haven't been hungry in a long time, Julian. Being alone takes your appetite away."

Julian nodded. "I understand."

He set the journal down on the night table, next to a fresh rose.

"I was reading about you in Naples, Mother.....

"What do you remember most of those times?"

"Before or after meeting your father?" she asked.

Julian thought for a moment and answered, "Before, Mother."

Ann Nelson Stansfield closed her eyes and let out a quiet sigh.

"The cauldron..... The cauldron of fire."

Ann paused to regain strength.

"One night in mid-October, while we worked furiously in the operating rooms on the first floor, the air raid sirens began to scream. It had been a bruising day, with hundreds of grave casualties. We couldn't just stop surgery on our patients, so we ignored the warning and continued our duties.

"A heavy German bombing raid spread from the northern sector of the city into our area. The abdominal surgeon I assisted was finishing up a complicated multiple shrapnel injury to the belly with stomach and small intestinal perforations. The young boy soldier had bled out during the operation, requiring several transfusions. I had just hung another fresh unit of whole blood and stepped out of the OR for more from the lab, when a bomb blasted out the wall next to the operating table. The surgeon, scrub nurse, and boy were torn apart. Many others in the room were killed and injured. I spent the rest of the evening picking up their pieces.

"I went out for a smoke at dawn and sat atop a jeep looking at Mount Vesuvius. The angry mountain would throw her occasional ball of red fire into the early morning sky. Streams of red lava rushed down one of her sides.

"Holding my 'Chesterfield' in my mouth, I started the jeep and drove towards the volcano. I crossed the valley and rode a back trail up near the summit. I parked and went the rest of the way on foot.

"Trekking to the crater's rim, the ground around me trembled and hissed. Every few moments, molten debris would explode out of the crater and fly high into the sky.

"I reached the rim and stood for several minutes looking down into its cauldron of fire and gas. It was hell on earth, I thought, but not any worse than the man-made hell we were living every day.

"I felt an urge to jump into the cauldron. I could barely resist it. The heat singed my eyebrows while I balanced on the edge.

"It's hard to explain, Julian. Your mind, tired and beaten, plays with you. Decision-making suffers. You become numb to fear. Death becomes attractive.....

"Naples before meeting your father..... A cauldron of fire all around me, eating away at my abilities to think and react..... Fire from above, fire from below, an inferno for those still alive..... Those are my memories."

Ann drifted back to sleep. Julian held her hand until early morning.

Julius closed Ann's diary as the warm glow of the fire died away in the living room. Dawn broke over Lake Constance. A thick fog crept into the town, basking the view of the surrounding Alps.

The captain stood at the picture window and watched the white fog pass over the lake. He thought of lonely young Julian helplessly watching his mother, Ann, lose her life. Years later, the admiral lived through even greater loss with his beloved Olivia.

Julius had been present during his own mother's final days. He remembered the agony his father had gone through. Like the fog over Aborn, his father had been shrouded by the pain.

Julius drank the last of the cognac and tried putting his memories to sleep.

Climbing the stairs to bed on the second floor, Captain Stansfield heard a knock at the door. He grabbed his pistol and returned downstairs. He carefully opened the front door to the chalet and found his brother Mark in his wheelchair with CIA Director Joseph Mitrano.

Life was changing, again.

CHAPTER 7

Project X

Rather than lifting with sunrise, the fog over Aborn and Lake Constance densified. The lake and mountains became invisible from the chalet living room's window. A white, creamy cloud engulfed the region.

Mitrano and Mark's presence implied the seriousness of the situation. Something heavy and ominous was coming down, and everyone was involved. There was a foreboding sinister sense to the visit.

Without saying a word, Julius restarted the fire and sat on the couch next to his brother. Mark also remained silent in his wheelchair. Joseph Mitrano walked over to the window and stood with his back to the Stansfields, staring out at white emptiness. A moment passed without verbal exchange.

"You would never know where you were, looking out into that," said Mitrano.

"You could even be in Heaven, I suppose," mumbled the director.

"Or just as easily be crossing the Acheron, with no hope of returning," quietly sighed Mitrano.

"As you age you get less hopeful, Julius. Whether you realize it or not, you see an end to things. The idea of eternity begins to disappear from your mind. One becomes harder on the facts, I reckon. Statistical probability of terminal failure becomes more realistic. You realize there's an end to every-thing, including oneself. I would best describe it as a realiza-tion of risk and impotence. You want a winning record, but you doubt your chances of remaining undefeated."

The director stopped speaking for several minutes. He remained motionless at the large window, staring into the white fog.

> *"There was a time when meadow, grove, and stream,*
> *The earth, and every common sight,*
> *To me did seem*
> *Apparelled in celestial light,*
> *The glory and the freshness of a dream.*
> *It is not now as it hath been of yore; -*
> *Turn wheresoe'er I may,*
> *By night or day,*
> *The things which I have seen, I now can see no more.*

"Those are the words of English poet William Word-sworth from his *Ode*. They begin the centuries-old poem on intimations of immortality, as one looks into the abysm between the idealism of youth and the realism of age.

"In the last year of his life, your father often repeated them to me. They've stayed in my mind. I now also recite the words frequently to myself, as he did.....

"That's what I loved most about Julian. That clever SOB could fight off his own melancholy. He forced himself to see the bright side of things through the darkness. Even in this crazy, confused and angry world, he saw the good overcoming the bad. He saw more with his one eye than most see with two. Your father remained a romantic till the end. He believed in the righteousness of his cause. He never doubted the results of America's actions. Julian felt America's success was preordained. He always expected to be perfect. He never thought of failure because he felt he could prevent it.

"Julian was the smartest man I ever knew....."

Mitrano paused again. His body did not move as he stared into the fog.

"Your father was hopeful and optimistic about one's soul..... He believed in the immortality of the 'good' soul.

"After Olivia's death, he was convinced he'd be reunited with her. He felt in his heart he'd see her again. He looked forward to it, completely disregarding his own death.

"Julian remained young in his spiritual ideals. I loved and respected that about him.

"I wish I would have learned his secret. I suspect it was your mother's love.

"I can honestly say I envied both of them for what they had. They kept each other young and immortal," gently stated the director.

Still standing at the window with his back to the Stansfield brothers, Mitrano continued.....

"You boys may remember I had a son named James.

"He was a Marine first lieutenant.

"James would have turned thirty years old this month.

"To my great sadness, he died on Taiwan last year, trying to defend against the Chinese assault on the international airport outside the capital. His company was overrun near the beaches in a fog just like this.

"I was told visibility had degraded to six feet. They could only hear the yells of the oncoming Chinese horde as they approached the American foxhole positions. US artillery air burst and machine gun fire filled the remainder of the sound space.

"Along the interior beach, men fought hand to hand for hours. Their common blood pooled in the wet, sandy foxholes where they died. Short range pistol shot, knife, and bare hands were the weapons of choice. Some even eviscerated the enemy's eyes with their fingers, while struggling in the trenches to get an advantage.

"Imagine that.

"I suppose in close combat, your fingers and mouth can be as invaluable as your bayonet or pistol. You use what you can to kill the enemy before he kills you.

"Many hundreds of fine American boys died in the fog on that beach; as they have on many other beaches, In other places, in other times.

"It's regretful we must continue to suffer losses of our treasured children.

"James joined our long roll call of young and brave 'Immortals'. I don't think I'll ever get a handle on that."

Director Mitrano silently wiped a tear off his face.

"God, how I wish Julian would have taught me his secret..... An elixir for the pain..... Enough to get you through

the day..... Enough hope to allow thoughts of tomorrow.....
More sunshine and less fog.....

"I miss James very much. Much more than I could ever
express in words. The visceral hurt of losing a child is hard to
describe. It's depersonalizing. Quite literally, it takes you out
of yourself. Sometimes you're unsure of the reality. It gets
lost in a jumbled mind.

"At times, you ask yourself if it possibly could be a bad
dream? Could he still be alive? Am I alive? How awake am
I to the reality?

"Unfortunately, the depersonalization is never complete.
You stay aware just enough to continue sensing the reality
and the pain.

"What I feel is not unique. Millions of fathers have felt the
same pain. Many more will feel it into the future.

"War appears to be an intractable and incurable plague
of human evolution. It's a stain on the cloth of life. 'Survival
of the fittest on the field of battle,' Darwin would have said -
Tactical Combat Darwinism.....

"When you get right down to it, the battle for the airport
on Taiwan was representative of war in general. It reflected
combat's most extreme axiomatic principle: Use what
you can to kill the enemy before he kills you. Stay alive!"
lamented Joe Mitrano.

The director appeared aged and worn. His physical
health was visibly declining with his spirit. He was approaching the end of the road, and he knew it. His personal life,
and the intense demands of maintaining the national security of his country - perpetually at war - had finally taken their
toll. His demons were beginning to get the upper hand. He
was in war with himself, and valuable energy was being
expended.

Mitrano sat across from the Stansfields.

"Julius, let me explain my visit.

"As you are well aware, after 9/11 America entered a new era.

"We live with our enemies at the gates. Many of them remain invisible, gnawing at our bones. America's intelligence services are at the forefront of this never-ending war on terror.

"Regardless of our victory in the last world war, we are still in the midst of the most dangerous period in the history of the United States, both domestically and internationally. This is the reality that we must all live in. The survival of our country as a free constitutional republic hangs in the balance. Washington, Jefferson, and Lincoln are awake in their graves listening to our every move. They wait to see if our efforts will be enough to rescue our endangered nation. They all would have understood the consequences of our failure in this great task. This experiment in freedom, which we call America, has lasted over 240 years. Our jobs are to securitize it continues long into the future. We live in hard times, but we as people must be harder."

The director slowly gazed at Mark Stansfield, sitting in his wheelchair by the fireplace.

"A new Islamic terror movement has developed over the past three years. The *Kilij* is composed of radical Sunni fundamentalists from Libya, Egypt, Syria, Jordan, Turkey, Pakistan, and Saudi Arabia. Many of them belonged previously to other radical groups broken up by the United States in the 'Global War on Terrorism'. They are the survivors. Combat Darwinism has left us with the most dangerous, battle-hardened, and evil terrorists on the planet. Their sharpness is emblemized by their name. A Kilij was a light-weight curved cavalry sabre used by the 15th century Ottomans and the Mamluks of Egypt. It is, perhaps, the most destructive one handed sword in history.

"In a report from Bamberg three months ago, Pavlo Mitnick communicated to Langley that two North African Arab nationals on the *Katarina* had deported in Passau, Germany, two days earlier. Their presence on the ship had been kept secret. Each of the Arabs carried two large steel suitcases to a waiting car before speeding off. Mitnick sent digital photographs of the men to CIA headquarters. They were identified as agents of the *Kilij* movement, Aqeel Sultan - codenamed 'Gremlin', and Ameer Samara – codenamed 'Goblin'. Unknown to Mitnick at the time, American agents in Passau tracked the Arabs southwestwardly along the Inn River - a tributary of the Danube - to Innsbruck, Austria, and later to St. Moritz, Switzerland.

"Our surveillance in St. Moritz showed them at the home of another *Kilij* agent, Anwar Nejem - codenamed 'Condor'. This character owns a popular hang-gliding school in the area. Our people followed these guys for two weeks. Nejem's home in the Upper Engadin Valley is near Lake St. Moritz. The fortified villa is in a heavily wooded area. Over fifteen agents of the *Kilij* movement lived on the large compound.

"Throughout the surveillance period, the *Kilij* members would regularly take the cable railway from town to the Corviglia Summit of the Piz Nair. The Condor's paragliding center lies on the mountain at 8200 feet elevation, overseeing the Engadin Valley and St. Moritz. Two dozen *Kilij* agents were being instructed personally by Anwar Nejem and his assistant, Yousef El-Amin, on a daily basis. We have codenamed Yousef, 'Mole Rat'. All the players appeared to be competent hang-gliders.

"Why were these men training to be hang-gliders? And what was in the steel suitcases?

"A plot was evolving before our very eyes, and it seemed to be directed by Anwar Nejem.

"The Condor is no idiot. He comes from a prosperous Egyptian family and is heir to a vast fortune. He's a well-educated 40 year-old veteran of the civil wars in Libya, Syria, and Egypt. He was a highly respected ground commander in the Syrian Rebel Army and was instrumental in the great rebel offensive on the city of Aleppo. He has personally killed hundreds of men and ordered his soldiers to murder thousands more.

"Anwar is not a novice to the terror game. He is evil, pure and unadulterated. He was recruited out of Syria and into the *Kilij* international team three years ago. Since, he has been involved in multiple terror acts around the globe. The CIA has him as the main perpetrator in numerous assassinations and bombings in Indonesia, India, Pakistan, Lebanon, Israel, Europe, and the United States."

Mitrano walked back to the window over Lake Constance. The fog still obscured the view of the Alps. The director turned and faced the Stansfields.....

"Mark joined Naval Intelligence in early July. Working with CIA on the St. Moritz gang, he noted communications between Switzerland and the GPNR in Moscow. References to the 'boxes' were made repeatedly. Deeper analysis with Michael at the London offices tied the 'boxes' to four 'lost' battlefield tactical backpack nukes which the Russian GPNR smuggled into the Ukraine three years ago. They were sold to the *Kilij* and transferred to them on the *Katarina*.

"After the failure of the *Katarina* mission, the Russian GPNR cut away from their dealings with the *Kilij* and tried to buy back the nukes. Apparently, Anwar and his boys have no interest of returning the nukes to the Russians. The present Russian government, not involved in the GPNR dealings but aware of the nuke sale, is now panicked. They're worried the CIA will consider them part of the evolving *Kilij* plot. Strange enough, Moscow has not communicated any of this to our intelligence agencies. Certainly, they have not informed me of anything. They're still more concerned with eliminating all traces of connection to the *Kilij*.

"The GPNR, now disorganized and disbanded, is missing in action. They are unable to force the return of the nukes from Anwar. The Moscow federal government, still heavily infiltrated with fascist lunatics from other groups other than the GPNR, is caught in a bind. They didn't sell the nukes to the *Kilij*, but they will be held responsible if the nukes are used nefariously. The bottom line is that the Russian government is up to its knees in shit and doesn't know how to get out of it.

"I don't expect the Russians to inform me of the 'situation'. My people inside the Kremlin tell me the armed forces are planning to invade the Baltics and southern Caucasus after a 'major event' in the US. They will stop our flow of oil and gas from Central Asia to Europe, through Azerbaijan, Georgia, and Turkey. With confusion and chaos in America, the Russians hope to negotiate a settlement with the West, allowing their re-occupation of old empire lands in Eurasia. Poland, Romania, and Bulgaria are arming to the teeth. France and England are mobilizing troops. Germany is playing the middle.

"If a nuclear terrorist action succeeds in the United States, we will retaliate against fascist Russia and several Sunni nations. Our strategic nuclear commanders believe they can incinerate Russia and defend against a similar attack. I am not so confident of our abilities to prevent a global nuclear holocaust. We must find out the *Kilij* plans and targets.

"Mark picked up communications between the Condor in St. Moritz and his handlers in the Middle East. Although not completely deciphered, many messages referred to cities in the western United States. Seattle, Salt Lake City, Denver, Los Angeles, and Phoenix were repeatedly named.

"Mark and I have discussed the obvious implications of the data. The four suitcases from the *Katarina* in Passau were the backpack nukes previously 'lost' by the Russians in the Ukraine. They were placed by the GPNR onto the *Katarina* for delivery to the *Kilij* movement. *Kilij* members trained in St. Moritz to hang-glide over American cities and detonate their cargo over civilian populations.

"Each of these Russian tactical nuclear weapons consists of two tubes of Uranium, each five inches in diameter and twenty-four inches long. The fifty-five pound linear implosion device is finger-triggered and produces an explosion equivalent to 20 kilotons of TNT. This is stronger than the Hiroshima bomb. An air burst blast at 1900 feet above the ground would create a two mile circle of instant lethal destruction. Every physical structure and every living thing within that circle would be incinerated in the initial blast. Temperatures of 8000 degrees F would create a giant fireball within that circle. Lethal doses of direct radiation would seep beyond the edges of the circle and lead to acute radiation sickness in survivors of the blast and firestorm. These victims would succumb shortly afterward. Longer radiation effects in the surrounding populations would lead to increased incidences of cancer for two generations. In each of the mentioned cities, we could expect 100,000 dead in the initial blast, and another 250,000 dead within six months. Perhaps millions more would develop deadly cancers over the following years.

"On August 16, the goons packed the steel suitcases in a car and left St. Moritz. A CIA team followed them south on a highway out of the Engadin Valley. More CIA agents set up along their projected path. Shortly after crossing into Italy, our trailers were attacked and destroyed by a *Kilij* assault squad. An American support team which came to their assistance was also attacked. A total of six CIA agents were killed. Our failure allowed the *Kilij* agents and their contraband to escape capture. Other CIA teams in the area lost their trail until August 28. On that day, we tracked them to the town of Como in the Northern Lakes region of Italy. Anwar Nejem apparently owns another hang-gliding school on Monte Cornizzolo, a 4000 foot mountain near Lake Como."

Claudia came walking down the stairs in white under-wear and a loose-fitting sport t-shirt, interrupting Director Mitrano's discussion. She calmly sat on the couch next to Julius.

"This involves you also, Claudia," said the director.

"I've been listening from the top of the stairs for the past half-hour. I know the area of Como well. I've hang-glided the Northern Lakes region many times in the summer. I'm familiar with the school on Monte Cornizzolo," smiled Claudia.

Mitrano smiled back and said, "We know.....

"We're placing a team of eight specialist agents into Como to gather intelligence on the *Kilij*. They will be aided by many other agents already in the region. Our analysis in London and Langley supports the idea that the enemy will train in Como through October, and then move men and materials to the United States for action in the coming spring. Communications imply the *Kilij* will coordinate their attacks on at least five American cities in early June. We intend to acquire as much information as possible on their network in the US, before striking and killing all of them in Italy. We will not allow the nukes to passage from the Italian mainland."

The CIA director returned to his chair near the fireplace.

Mitrano looked at Claudia and Julius, "I want your participation in this mission. I have total confidence in both of your abilities."

Julius nodded. He stared at his brother and asked the director, "Who are the other members of the specialist team?"

"Michael will join you, as will two British Secret Intelligence Service (MI6) agents familiar with the Kilij and the Italian zone of operations. An Indian Intel agent, who has been tracking Anwar's activities across South Asia and the Middle East, will also participate."

The director paused for a moment in anticipation of further inquiry from Julius. The short silence spoke for itself.

"That's six of us," said the submarine captain. "Who are the other two?"

"Mark has requested participation on the ground with his brothers in this mission," slowly responded Mitrano. "He's gathered the intelligence and developed the final mission plan with the CIA. He deserves the opportunity.

"It took me two weeks to allow his transfer to Special Operations. It was not an easy decision at first; but after complete and thorough consideration of the full measure of the man, the final conclusion became obvious. Even in a wheelchair, his heart and mind are invincible. Courage, like loyalty and devotion, can't be created or bought. I'm willing to take our chances with Mark's wishes.

"Who could match up with America's 'Three Knights'?

"Besides, Mark would not have allowed me to exclude him.

"Lieutenant James Thomas, US Marine Raider, will accompany Mark. They were together on the Paraguana Raid in Venezuela, and the attack on Shishkat Bridge in Pakistan last year. They are close friends and have obviously worked well together in the past.

"The operation is codenamed *Project X*. You'll all be briefed on mission details over the next 48 hours and deploy to Como by September 23."

Joseph Mitrano rose slowly from his chair, thanked everyone for their patriotism, and wished the mission Godspeed. Little brother stayed by the fireplace while Julius walked the director to the front door of the chalet.

Returning to the living room, big brother looked at Mark and asked, "Why?"

CHAPTER 8

Invincible Bastard

Claudia rushed upstairs, leaving us alone. Julius threw wood into the fire and went to the kitchen. He returned with glasses of cold milk for both of us. He sat by the fireplace and quietly stared at me. A great silence was interrupted only by the crackle of the flames, and the mournful howls of a strong wind outside the chalet. Although daylight, the room was dark. The early sun, which typically rose over the Bavarian Alps to the east and illuminated the chalet with bright morning radiance, was drowned out by the thick fog. The lack of sunshine further depressed the mood.

"Drink your milk, little brother," said Julius.

"What's gotten into you, Mark?

"You're not thinking straight. Maybe you've forgotten your dependency on wheels. This is a rough game. Any disadvantage, whether mental or physical, is attacked by our enemies. You become a sitting duck in that chair. You'll be exposed to their worst machinations. Their deepest evil will be drawn out when they sense the disadvantage. These are not merciful people. They'd enjoy making you suffer.

"You've suffered enough, Mark. You've done your part for America."

I drank my glass of milk as advised. I played the part of good little brother, but only to initiate a productive dialogue with the big brother I loved and respected. I understood his concerns. I would feel the same if the roles were reversed. Each and every one of us, all Stansfields, had protective instincts for those we deemed unfortunate. I knew Julius could not withdraw from the responsibility he felt for me.

I had crossed the Atlantic to explain myself to Julius in person. My lack of fortune was not my lack of leg power; it was my inability to fulfill promise and duty. It was hard to convince others of the deep need I had to remain useful. I simply wished to be more than what I had become. I could not accept in my inner core that anyone, especially my brothers, consider me an unfortunate.

"Listen, Julius.....

"Look at my reality.....

"Open your mind's eye for a moment and pretend you're in a chair. You try with all your might to stand up and walk, and all that happens is a weak twitch of a muscle in one of your skinny thighs. Maybe, on a lucky day, a big toe moves a little. Your arms and chest are strong, but your lower body appears made of matchsticks. From the waist down, there's only skin and bones. Your mind and spirit don't match the atrophied physicality you see..... Now, remember your past – baseball glory, Annapolis, and wartime heroics.....

"America continues to face existential threats," I said somberly.

"First, China and North Korea teamed up with radical Shia Iran in an attempt to suffocate our country. We were initially able to convince the Russians of the dangers of collaborating with this evil axis. The risks of having an Islamic Caliphate in the Middle East near the Caucasus, and an all-powerful China on her southern borders, made Russia wake up. They realized these regimes had no intentions of stopping their expansions short of the Russian steppes and Siberia. They listened to us and cooperatively sat on the sidelines.

"Regrettably, the Russian government's willingness to work closely with their old arch enemy - the United States - coupled with deteriorating economic conditions in Eurasia, stimulated the ascendance of the GPNR. Right-wing extremist Neo-Nazis in Russia and Germany, in conjunction with the Turkish intelligence service, tried to infect the United States with a deadly plague virus. They attempted to weaken us, and force America out of Europe and the Middle East. They wanted time and space to conduct their evil design on the world. In essence, their plan was to subjugate lesser nations of Eurasia and profit from their enslavement. A fresh 'Fourth Reich', they called it.

"The brave people of America defeated both of these threats and survived to control their own destiny. A dominant America may not be to all people's liking, but it sure is a better option than the alternatives. Future world peace and the advancement of human civilization depend on our success. American leadership in science and technology, industry, agriculture, and energy production is essential to the future prosperity of mankind. Our principles of free democratic government must not perish from this earth. Freedom and justice in this world would become extinct without our presence. We are the main catalyst for advancement on this planet. No one can seriously argue these points. History is the evidence.

"Today, America faces a new existential menace. The recalcitrant remaining members of the GPNR in Russia, and the increasingly fascist central government in Moscow, are working with radical Sunni Islamists from North Africa and the Middle East to create a human catastrophe on our homeland. Again, the enemy tries to free themselves from our oversight to perpetrate their evil misdeeds around the world. Their fanatical ideologies directly imperil the foundations of our republic and the future freedoms of people everywhere. Their plan is ingenious, Islamists using hanggliders to detonate tactical nuclear bombs over multiple major US cities in air burst fashion and creating incalculable damage on our nation, followed by a Russian invasion of the free countries of Eastern Europe and the Caucasus.

"I will not sit this one out, big brother. I'm not a bench player. I need to be on the front line, seeing my enemy up close. I can't stay back at the Pentagon watching things evolve on a screen and hoping for the best. Particularly so when my brothers are in harm's way. Making plans and not carrying out the mission does not agree with my constitution.

"I'm not afraid of dying for my country, Julius. I'm sick with weakness, unable to defend her as I have done in the past. I'm not a computer-screen warrior."

I paused and stared into Julius. My eyes watered.

"Do you remember when Mother lay dying at our home in Georgetown?" I asked. "It's been almost three years. The last two months of her life, she could not get out of bed. Her pain was so severe she couldn't even reach for a glass of water. Father sat next to her day after day, reading her poetry, feeding and washing her. His love was incessant. He simply could not give up.

"We saw her shrivel away. Mother's physical decline was horrific to all of us. But Father never looked at her with pity; we did.

"Regardless of her pain and physical wasting, Mother always maintained a smile on her face. That was enough for Dad. That was the only fuel he needed to continue the fight.

"At the end, our pity allowed us to let her go. Not Dad. He never accepted her passing. He died the day she did.

"I sleep every night in Mother and Father's Georgetown home. I lay in the bed she died in, remembering her wasting away. How badly I felt for her. Her beauty and physical strength evaporating before our eyes. Becoming a heap of bones and skin. Physical decline and disintegration does not sil well with me.

"When I sit in my wheelchair in front of the large mirror in our bathroom at home, I feel the same pity I felt for Mother. I see the same wasting away, the same decline.

"I'm tired of having people open doors for me. I see the pity in their eyes too. It's pathetic. My mind and spirit are still strong. I will not allow my paralyzed legs to keep me from performing my duties to my country. My honor depends on it."

We sat silently staring at each other. We both understood the full gravity of the situation. Julius searched his mind for the right words.

"Your honor?

"For God's sake, you've done enough for your country!

"You've received both the Navy Cross and Medal of Honor for your brave actions.

"What more can you expect of yourself, Mark?"

"What more?" I questioned loudly in disbelief.

"I have lived by my principles all my life. My code of honor does not change just because I won a 'Most Valuable Player' award or because of my inability to walk, Julius.

"In my heart, I am the same man I was at Shishkat Bridge. I cannot settle for a lesser role because of my legs. Providing commentary in front of a computer screen at the Pentagon does not agree with me. I also can't convince myself to parade around in my wheelchair with the Medal of Honor draped around my neck and believe I've done enough. I don't know how to live in the past.

"Old glory dies, Julius, and I die with it!"

Julius sensed all of my raw emotions, but it was still difficult for him to restrain the instinctive need to protect me.

"How are you going to deal with your lack of mobility on the field of battle?" he asked.

"I'll compensate with a quicker, more agile mind. I'll get to where I need to be before the critical point. I'll think ahead and react pre-emptively. I'll be where my enemy doesn't expect me.

"My presence in a wheelchair is not alarming or threatening to the enemy. It's beyond his ability to conceive. I'll use that to my advantage. It's the perfect prop for a field agent.

"Who could ever imagine being challenged by a physically handicapped intelligence agent?

"My weakness in your eyes, Julius, may even be the deciding factor in the success of our mission. Besides, I can still shoot straight," I smiled.

"How about Sarah and the boys?" asked Julius. "What does she think about your decision?"

I bowed my head. Motionless, I couldn't speak. Several minutes passed.

"I love my wife and sons very much, Julius, and they love me. But I also see the pity in their eyes.

"I must set an example for my boys. I wish to show them that being in a wheelchair does not lessen you as a man. I can still meet my responsibilities. I can equal the challenge.

"The evening after the unveiling of Dad's statue at Annapolis, I sat with Sarah for hours expressing my decision. I explained the feelings and desires of my code of conduct. She understands my ways. She married the warrior, not the cripple. Naturally, she fears for my safety. But that was the case before as well. Nothing's changed. I told her my wheelchair was a secret weapon. I was stronger for being in it.

"Worse than dying for your country, I said, is impotence in defending her....."

Julius could not argue any longer. Inside his heart, he applauded my strength. He had never known anyone like me. I had been this way since childhood. I was stubborn and took challenges personally. Nothing had ever been too difficult or daunting. I always threw the first punch and the last.

My big brother nodded his head in agreement. I had made my case.

He smiled and looked directly into my eyes. "Let's get to work, you invincible bastard."

CHAPTER 9

The Meaning of Life

Julius finally got to bed in the late morning. Briefings for the operation would begin later in the day. Unable to sleep, he pondered Ann Nelson's World War Two journal and its significance. Mark had sent him the album as an introduction prelude to his own involvement in *Project X*. It was clear to Julius now. Mark had chosen to participate in the mission several weeks before. Somehow, Ann's diary had inspired the decision.

Julius accepted Mark's choice, but it worried him. He loved his brother and supported his independent spirit. But would his handicap hinder him on the mission? Would he be able to defend himself sufficiently to avoid suicidal risk? Indeed, Mark's physical limitations were potentially catastrophic.

The fog outside lifted. The winds died down. Julius pulled open the shades of the room, letting in a trace of sunshine. He pushed up the window slightly and breathed the cool mountain air. It was clean and refreshing. He gazed out at the distant Austrian Alps to the southeast; their majestic peaks pointed high to the sky like steeples. Nature's rocky spires reminded him of Totenkopf Castle, and his great turning from naval officer to CIA spy and hitman.

Claudia stayed comfortably asleep in bed beside him. She had shown no concern or apprehension over the new mission. Danger didn't seem to bother her much. She snored right through it. Claudia was complacent with espionage duties, unconcerned about killing or being killed. She had rare beauty, and even more unusual disposition.

Life for Julius the past months appeared jumbled. Like an old country road, winding up and down and all around, strewn with gravel and dirty, shifty and off the map – Julius had been everywhere - in the sea, on the ground, and in his mind.

He stretched across the night table and pulled out Ann's diary....................

By early October 1943, General Mark Clark had over 100,000 fighting men of his Fifth Army preparing to cross the Volturno River - twenty five miles north of Naples. The Volturno Line, the German Army's southernmost defensive positions north of Naples, stretched from Termoli on the Adriatic coast to the Tyrrhenian Sea in the west.

East of the Apennines, General Montgomery's Eighth Army fought the German 16th Panzer Division along the Adriatic on their way to the Barbara Line.

West of the Apennines, Clark planned a three-pronged attack along the Volturno River. British General Richard McCreery's X Corps, composed of the British 7th Armored Division and the 46th and 56th Infantry Divisions, would cross the coastal plain north of Naples to seize the strategic Mount Massico Ridge. The plain, 20 miles wide and stretching for 30 miles north, was a fertile region of vineyards, fruit and olive groves, and farm towns. A few miles further east, Major General Lucian Truscott would lead his US 3rd Infantry Division across the Volturno River to the critically important Mignano Gap. Even further east, Major General John Lucas' US VI Corps, composed of the US 34th and 45th Infantry Divisions, would protect Truscott's right flank from German counterattack.

The area east of the coastal plain was characterized by mountains and valleys, stretching to the eastern slopes of the Matese Range. Low hills, surrounded by olive orchards and terraced farm fields, slowly developed into barren rocky peaks more than a mile high. The steep slopes overlooked fertile green valleys, dotted by tiny crowded villages with centuries-old stone homes and contemporary pastel-colored farmhouses. Green of grass and gray of stone were mixed with blue and pink.

The US 3rd Division fought their way from Naples northwest to Avellino and Caserta, arriving on the Volturno River by October 7. The US 34th and 45th Divisions captured Benevento, and established a bridgehead across the Calore River by October 9.

The Volturno River posed a huge obstacle for Fifth Army. Three hundred feet wide, and swollen by the daily rain of Italian autumn, the river's swift currents prevented quick crossing by assault boats or wading infantry. All bridges had been blown by German engineers. The northern bank was ten feet high, and lined with bushes and trees. Interlocking bands of German fire blocked all the easier crossing points of shallower water. German dug-in gun pits, machine gun nests, concrete pill boxes, and mortar emplacements filled the entire stretch of river from mountains to seaside.

Field Marshall Albert Kesselring's German 10th Army - composed of the 3rd, 15th, and 26th Panzer Divisions, and the Herman Goering Division - had fought a delaying action across the naturally defensive terrain north of Naples. All bridges, water, gas, and electricity works, mills and industrial plants had been destroyed by demolition. German engineers had mined all access roads through the areas south and north of the Volturno River. Many houses and villages were booby-trapped. The lower Volturno Valley was cold and rainy, and under the expert gun sights of heavy German artillery and mortar fire. Snipers hid in hills and all the farm villages of the valley. There were few stonewalls, sunken roads, or dry stream beds to offer the Allies protection. The terrain was certainly favorable for defense, and the German Army engineers had taken full advantage of the topography.

On the late night of October 12, under dry skies and a full moon, Clark's 5th Army began a heavy artillery barrage on German positions north of the Volturno River. The eerie moon glow over the silent valley suddenly filled with the explosions and machine gun fire of men at war. The cries of thousands of men on both sides would accent the Italian countryside for the next twenty days. Many dead bodies floated down the Volturno out to the Tyrrhenian Sea, beaching themselves along the coast for weeks.

Young Julian stopped his reading and walked over to the hospital room's window overlooking Lake Geneva. He opened it and took a deep breath of fresh Wisconsin air. The dawn sky was still dark blue, lightening out to the east and the impending sunrise. An orange-pink glow previewed the sun's appearance. A mild cool summer breeze swept across the lake and into the room, causing a wind chime to sound music. Julian played Maria Callas on the record player.

The lieutenant sat at the edge of the bed and gently repositioned his mother's pillows. She had suffered a rough night. High fevers and sweats had required two bed sheet changes by the nurse. In her sleep, she had muttered unintelligibly.

Ann awoke and smiled at her son. "Don't worry Julian, I feel better now. I'll have some cereal."

Julian brought the small bowl of oatmeal close to his mother's mouth and fed her three small spoonfuls. She pulled her head away from the fourth.

"Do you remember the Royal Palace of Caserta, Mother?"

The Caserta Palace was an 18th century villa built for King Charles III of Naples. More lavish than Versailles, it had more than 1200 rooms, all with the finest luxuries. Its Baroque style frescoes were the envy of Europe. The palace apartments were richly decorated with gold, stucco, and marble, and furnished with the finest cloths.

"Yes, I remember the Caserta Palace, Julian..... I remember it well.....

"Our hospital was temporarily moved there in late October 1943, in preparation for operations into the Mignano Gap. We cared for many Volturno front casualties at the palace.

"It had beautiful gardens. Winding and picturesque, they were full of tall green cypresses and cedars. A small lake, with a statue of Venus about to bathe, was a favorite place to gather my thoughts. The gardens on hilly terrain were surrounded by fish ponds and cascading fountains. It was an oasis of beauty in a land of death.

"Yes, Julian, I remember it clearly."

Ann asked for water. She took only a sip and continued to recollect images from her past.

"It was there in the palace library that I finally had the courage to write a letter to the parents of the boy from Texas, the poet soldier from Paestum. He had asked me to kindly describe the details of his death to his mother and father. I was a young girl, unfamiliar with that sort of thing. It took me several weeks to develop the strength. But I did. I felt the boy poet and his parents deserved a description of a noble and rich life lived.

"One night, I asked the guard to allow me into the palace library. He owed me a favor. I walked into the giant hall, filled with oak wooden bookcases and ornate mahogany tables. Oil portraits of the Bourbon kings covered one wall. The room had a strong odor of old books, and the musty smell of neglected carpets and draperies. A large two story picture window faced an adjacent garden with statuary, and also the battlefront - not too many miles away. The black sky would light with the explosions and fire of artillery. Occasionally, the window and furniture would rumble and move with the shocks of shell and bomb.

"I sat down in silence and stared out the window at the silhouetted figure of *Aphrodite*. The lights of combat flickered on the white marble of the Greek goddess of love and beauty. She was naked and exposed to man's cruelties.

"I lit a candle on the table and began to write. I told Julian's parents of their brave son's love of romantic poetry and Tolstoy. Of how he would recite from memory the most beautiful words I had ever heard. I spoke of his gentle and kind nature, only strengthened by his casualty.

"I wrote of his liking Leo Tolstoy's 'The Death of Ivan Ilyich'. In the few days I had with him, he'd often quote from that novella. Living the 'good life', and what that might involve. He had said, 'The simpler a man lived, the better his life would be.'

"He had also quoted from the 'Tirukkural', the ancient classic of Tamil poetry by Thiruvelluvar. He would repeat, 'Defer not virtue to another day; receive her now, and at the dying hour she will be your undying friend.'

"I reminded the boy's parents how much their son had loved them, and of how nobly and peacefully he had died. That he had felt no pain and expressed conscious thoughts of beauty until the end. I described his last moments by the sea, surrounded by the roses and temples of Paestum, and that I had held his hand and caressed his face tenderly to comfort him.

"Finally - I took a poem the boy from Texas had written his last day, and gently placed the blood stained paper into the envelope with my letter.

"I still remember his words. They are fortressed in my heart. He had an old soul, of someone who had lived much in little time. They were the noble words of a noble boy warrior:

"The light of life has guided me,
sometimes strongly, other times less so.

The journey has been shorter than what I
had hoped, but it was full of virtue.

I have tried to walk the path of good,
avoiding the ignoble and unjust.

I have been fair in my wanderings,
and broken no hearts willfully.

I have performed my life's chores,
and never refrained from my duties.

I have seen life's beauty and glory,
and its pain and misery, equally.

I have felt fear but wished it on no one.
It is cruel on the mind and soul.

I have judged no one differently than I
wished to be judged myself.

Although young, I have known love.
It is unmistakable, and inescapable.

I will miss earthly love and all its attachments.
I would have wished for more."

Ann Nelson Stansfield gently fell asleep with her loving son Julian at her side, also wishing for more.

CHAPTER 10

Her Eyes

Michael Stansfield sprinted along the short rocky plateau on the western slope of Mount Cornizzolo, and leapt off the 4000 foot high mountain into the strong winds and ridge lifts of the piedmont Lombardy region of Italy. Lying prone in a harness suspended from a rigid aluminum alloy airframe, he shifted his body weight posteriorly and allowed the air currents to lift the flexible fabric wing of his hang-glider up into the blue cloudless sky. He banked over the old gray and white stone buildings of the 11th century "Abbey of San Pietro al Monte" in a small valley, and flew high above the chapel of "Our Lady of the Seven Sorrows" at the foot of the mountain.

A quick learner under the tutelage of the MI6, Stansfield had just finished a week-long instruction on hang-gliding in the highlands of Scotland. Compared to HALO freefalls into enemy territory in the dark night from 30,000 feet, sailing through the wind in a harness on a strong wing was simple. It certainly wasn't fear provoking or death defying. Besides, he wore an emergency parachute. In the event of an unexpected calamity, he would cut himself away from the harness and drop safely into a beautiful green valley. Michael Stansfield knew life could be tougher.

The CIA man looked out over the scenic landscape. As far as he could see - blue mountain lakes, green valleys, and hills covered in mountain flowers stretched out in front of him. The vistas were remarkable in all directions. The natural beauty was inspiring and provided a short respite from the stresses of his mission.

Michael watched for soaring birds. They were a tell-tale sign of thermal updrafts. The strong sun heated the ground below, creating rising warm air. He had been instructed to follow the birds to gain height whenever possible. With the updrafts of the Northern Lakes region of Lombardy, a glider could expect to soar for hours if necessary.

He headed west off the mountains. He rose high above the town of Erba, and along the northern edges of Lakes Pusiano and Alserio.

The verdant hills of the Alpine piedmont reminded him of Nasrin's eyes. The green color was rich and deep like emeralds, he thought. Michael reached down to his belt and turned on his music player. Peter Gabriel's "In Your Eyes" sounded inside his helmet. The spy banked slightly to his left and sailed above the blue lakes toward the town of Como, only eight miles away.

Nasrin's eyes transmitted love, thought Michael. Deeply melancholic at times, they would darken from a light hazel to a deep forest green. They were eyes of someone who had seen the world and desired to change it for the better. Nasrin's spirit flowed from them. They shined with peaceful virtues. Kindness, tolerance, acceptance, and affection were all projected out in photonic waves of beauty.

How could her gentle eyes contrast so much with his - trained to destroy, neutralize, eliminate, and kill? Contemplation of the irony befuddled him. Her soft eyes simply brought peace to his hard warrior heart. Her love galvanized his soul, reminding him always of the good natures of human beings - of what life could be. As long as Nasrin's eyes shined for him, there was hope, he reasoned.

With the music in his head, Michael reflected on why he had volunteered for yet another dangerous mission. Only a few weeks before, he had arrived at the CIA's London offices expecting analysis work. He'd be home every evening to enjoy his wife and child. There were no more covert operations to test his courage. He'd manage the desk and computer screen, not the jungle. He'd provide expert opinion, not marksmanship at close range with a deadly eye.

What was he doing 3500 feet above the ground, flying a flimsy contraption and testing his desire to live? The answer was simple, he thought - "America".

If this mission was important enough for Mark to participate on the ground in a wheelchair, it certainly called upon him to sail with the hawks and eagles above northern Italy.

Michael Stansfield leaned the glider along the eastern edge of Como. The sun-washed terracotta red tile roofs of the town's buildings and homes contrasted sharply with the beautiful blue of Lake Como and the green of the surrounding mountains. Early autumn had arrived but the hills were still full of life, painted with the colors of summer.

Stansfield leaned forward, and dove the glider down two hundred feet toward the lakefront promenade and Town Center. He watched young lovers parade along the shoreline, stopping to buy flowers and Italian gelato at kiosks by the lake. A conductor-led orchestra sounded from a gazebo, surrounded by a garden of red roses. Children played in a park.

How free the people seemed to Michael, happily passing their morning with friends and family. They were oblivious to Stansfield's world, and completely unknowing of the criminal terrorist plot organizing in their idyllic piece of paradise. They were joyful and not burdened with fear. The scene brought pleasure to Michael, reminding him of life's goodness.

The American banked to the right along the edge of a mountain. The bright sunshine reflected strongly off Lake Como as he caught a ridge lift of warm air deflecting off the hillside, and elevated his glider to a higher altitude. He flew along the eastern shore of Lake Como towards the town of Blevio, only a mile away to the northeast. Many lavish homes and palazzos sat like porcelain crowns by the blue water.

Going from dreams to reality - from peace to war - Michael turned off the music and activated his scrambled radio communicator inside his helmet. His attitude changed from lover to warrior.

"This is Angel One to Heaven's Gate..... Do you read me?..... Copy?" he said to his colleague on the ground.

"I hear you loud and clear, Angel One, and so do Langley and Como HQs," answered John Mullen, an MI6 agent on the ground near Blevio.

"I'm coming upon 'Target Zero' and will be transmitting visuals shortly," communicated Stansfield.

Michael caught another thermal draft and flew up over the lake to approach his target from the west. His helmet's visor transmitted digital visual information to Mullen's computer on the ground.

"We're seeing the target, Angel One..... Continue your approach as planned," said communications officer Mullen. "We're receiving good visual and audio..... Now show us where this bastard lives....."

Stansfield leaned forward and dove rapidly down towards *Villa Vento Forte*, the Palladian lakeside estate belonging to Anwar Nejem - the *Kilij* superspy. The house rose like a monolith from the lakeshore, exposing three stories of arched colonnaded porticoes and classic Roman temple architecture. The 17th century villa was splendorous. Four acres of manicured grounds surrounded the estate. A winding private road descended from the mountainside to the home. Terraced gardens edged to the shore and the floating swimming pool on Lake Como. A private harbor with two fast looking Italian speedboats aligned next to the pool.

Michael Stansfield glided past the pool and four naked Italian beauties. The sunbathing women on the deck wore only sunglasses and fashionable hats. He waved, and they all smiled and waved back.

"Stick to the target, Angel One," laughed Mullen. "Keep your eyes on the target."

"I'm just giving you single guys down there a little bit of entertainment!" shouted Michael. "This Como scenery never stops thrilling the senses. Like cinnamon in coffee, I guess Italian girls are always a fashionable and required spice. For you Langley boys, who never leave your computers, perhaps you should consider special ops in the future. Fresh mountain air and beautiful naked women are worth the risks!"

Stansfield turned his head toward the villa's grounds. He transmitted images of a dozen heavily armed *Kilij* agents around the house. The guards wore ballistic vests and carried submachine guns. He then faced the third floor terrace, where three men sat at a table sharing a meal.

"Here we go, John," announced Stansfield. "The one with the big beak is the Condor..... He's the ugly one with the giant nose..... Tell Mitrano he picked a fine name for the ugliest mother-fucker I've ever seen.....

"The other two are Gremlin and Goblin..... They're not much prettier.....

"It's a shame to waste such beautiful women on these snaky desert-dwellers.

"I'm close enough to yank the cigarettes out of their mouths..... Or at the very least grab a mimosa off the table..... If we didn't need information from these goons, I could easily pluck each of them right now with my 9mm.

"What do you think? Do I send them to paradise, Johnny?"

"No, Angel One..... Keep the halo on your head..... We'll wait for a better time and place," said Mullen..... "At least we've verified they're here in Como.

"Claudia will get closer and initiate contact..... After we get the information we need, and the contraband is off the street, we'll send them to paradise where they all wish to go.....

"Now get your ass down here and let's put our plan into action!" shouted Mullen into Stansfield's helmet.

The American turned his glider around and made another pass by the villa. He rushed by Anwar Nejem on the third floor terrace and waved with his middle finger. The Condor stood from his brunch table along the balcony, looking warily at Stansfield as he flew by.

The CIA man continued a half-mile up the shore and banked into an adjacent valley. He landed on a dirt road between two hills, running to a stop. A pickup truck pulled out from behind tall cypresses.

"You turned off communications at the end, Mikey," said John Mullen, "you crazy son of a bitch..... What did you do?"

"I showed him my prick was bigger than his!" laughed Stansfield.

"You Americans are out of your minds!" shouted the Englishman.

"It was the crazy Cuban in me, John, not the cool and collected American half. No decent red-blooded American would show his dick to that scum!"

"Whatever, Mikey..... You're a mixed-blood bastard if I've ever seen one..... You likely scared the shit out of the Arabs with that Latin serpent of yours," laughed Mullen.

"I wanted him to see what he was up against, his nuke against mine," grinned Stansfield.

The MI6 agent shook his head in disbelief as he packed Stansfield's red wing into the back of the truck.

"Let's go into Como for lunch and meet the rest of our team, Mike. Along with your brothers and Claudia, we have Jimmy Thomas - a fellow US Marine Raider, Thomas Whitmore - an MI6 nuclear terrorism expert, and Daivat Kakkar - an Indian External Intelligence agent.

"Daivat has worked RAW (Research & Analysis Wing) for the past seven years. He's familiar with the Pakistani element of the *Kilij*. The CIA now believes that the Pakistani ISI transferred two more portables nukes over to the *Kilij* in Cairo six months ago. There may be more to worry about than just those four steel suitcases being carried around by your friends at the lake. We need to find out their complete plans for these bombs, their targets, and their networks in Europe and the US. We need to get those nukes under our secure possession."

Michael Stansfield sat in the pick-up and murmured to himself, "How in God's name is all this lunacy occurring in little Como, Italy? The vacation retreat of the rich and famous, town of lakeside music gazebos and rose gardens, is also a cesspool of ugly murderous action and intention..... What a world."

CHAPTER 11

Letter at the Garibaldi

I had an hour to kill before meeting up with Jim Thomas. I sat alone, thinking, on the terrace of my room at the Garibaldi Hotel on the southwestern shore of Lake Como. I watched the sun rise over the hills while strong winds passed from the northeast across the lake. Whitecaps formed on the blue surface. A sudden gust blew the red baseball cap off my head, exposing my short blond hair to the sun. Behind amber shades, my blue eyes squinted at the rays of yellow brilliance falling on the garden terrace. They warmed my face on this cool September morning. The day in Como had begun picture perfect. I smiled and thought it was good to be alive.

Atop a garden table in front of me, a white vase held a single pink rose. I stared at the flower as if it was the most beautiful thing in the world. It was magnificent, I thought. Although it had been cut and taken from its nurturing roots, the rose's stem was still robust. The pink petals were vibrant. The rose would remain this way for a while. But soon, the beautiful flower would die; its petals drying and falling one by one from the stem. The artistic symbolism of beauty would wither away. The rose's health and life were not eternal.

I looked out from the third floor balcony onto the lake and Como's promenade. The lakefront was busy with tourists and locals enjoying the sunshine, music, visual arts, and flower gardens. Young couples paraded through the gardens, expressing their affections. People in boats, many of them beautifully-crafted antique wooden cruisers, anchored near the harbor to experience the activities from a short distance. Majestic green mountains rose from the shore, and multiplied to the north as far as the eye could see. All the beauty was graced under a clear blue sky. The scene was picture perfect.

The people of Como seemed oblivious to the chaos engulfing the world. They appeared untouched by the horrors of global economic catastrophe and world war. They were unaffected by Islamic terrorism, civil war, political disunion and strife, and social anarchy. It all seemed clean and sterile - but also free and glorious and idyllic. The natural loveliness of Como, and the enchantment of its people, was mesmerizing.

I finally looked down at the white sheet of paper, picked up my pen, and commenced to write.

My Dear Sarah:

My love, where do I begin? I'm sorry to have left you alone again, with Robert and George. As in the past, you have been left in a state of unknowing. I'm understanding of this fact.

You are a brave and wonderful woman. Your deep serenity impresses me. It's a virtue I wish I had. Perhaps one day, you can finally teach me how to acquire and nurture it - as you have for so many years. Your peaceful soul is a gift for you and for me. My love, you deserve all the goodness in this life. I pray for your happiness.

My heart and spirit remained at home with you, the only place they wish to be. I am at ease when with you. Even thinking of you brings me peace. Your quiet nature, and gentle acceptance of things beyond your control, have always amazed me. You are not afraid of the unknown. To me, it is a sign of great moral strength - a strength unattainable by most and envied by all. I've always wished for your power. Your belief in love and the universal softer side of human beings is refreshing. It is very dear to me.

Thoughts of you calmly settle my restless mind. Why I have been so restless all my life, I do not know. But you are a salve for all of my psychic shortcomings. You complete my soul. This is a certain truth which I hold deeply. I love you for this truth, and many other things.....

I wrestled with this decision more than any other before. You have suffered so much. I understand your hurt and concerns. They are the same as mine. But my choice was clear and duty-bound. My options were restricted to my conscience and my sense of honor. My decision was led by my knowledge and sensibility of the situation at hand, my physical handicap notwithstanding. Knowing your love, and your trust and support in the past, allowed me to move forward and address my need to participate again in the defense of our beloved country. Others may not understand, but I know you do. I thank you for that.

At present, as I write to you, I hold in my left hand the ancient obsidian spearhead given to me by Father years ago. His gift upon my graduation from Annapolis is more than 280,000 years old. The polished black volcanic glass from central Ethiopia's Rift Valley feels fresh on my skin, although it is the oldest known projectile of war. In a long ago epoch, the sharp black stone was fastened on a long wooden stick. It was the killer point of a javelin in the hands of Homo heidelbergensis, a primitive ancestor of Homo sapiens. A thrown spear allowed the user to defend himself from a distance, decreasing risk of casualty. The complex advancement was transferred to modern man, and aided in his migration out of Africa. In my career in the US military, I have carried this token everywhere. You well know the story behind it. Perhaps, I am still alive because of its lucky properties. I will continue to carry the strong stone over my heart. Hopefully, its special character of fortune will allow my safe return to you. I consider the obsidian spearhead a symbol for 'Survival of the Fittest'.

In the years of my life of which I am consciously aware, I have always run toward the sound of the bugle and the gun. It's been unpleasant for those who loved me, but it is my way. It is difficult to change now. Sitting in my wheelchair has not changed my spirit. If anything, it has made me more determined to do my duty. I now know better the consequences of failing in our mission to keep America safe.

I don't want my sons to suffer my lot. More than my life, I want my children and my wife to be free. I don't want your choices limited. I don't want you living under fear and oppression. We live in a savage world. I have seen the 'dark side', and it is ugly. I have felt the fear, and it is uglier.

America's history has always been complicated. We fought for our freedom from the British Empire more than two centuries ago. We defended that freedom again in 1812. We expanded west across the North American continent, fighting wars against the Mexicans and native indians. We suffered through the Civil War, losing more than 600,000 of our brothers in the process. We abolished the indignity of slavery. We worked our way through the Reconstruction and the Industrial Revolution of the late 19th century. Two world wars and the war against international Communism were fought in the 20th century. We lived through the Great Depression for the decade leading up to the Second World War, and Americans suffered economic and social instabilities after the Great Economic Collapse of 2008. For several decades we have raged against Islamic terrorism, intensifying after the attacks of 9/11. We fought a global war against Iran, North Korea, and China. Yes, our history has been complicated. It has been replete with the trials and tribulations of maintaining a democratic republic. But certainly, it has been worth our sacrifice. We are still free.

In the last several decades, the world's great powers have clashed for access to energy deposits. A cheap alternative to oil has not been found. Coal, liquid natural gas, solar, wind, and nuclear power have not supplanted oil for a variety of reasons. Availability of oil has become progressively more difficult over the past forty years. There is less oil easily available. Much of it is in unfriendly countries. Still not fully tapped sources like shale oil and oil sands are expensive to process. The end result has been high oil prices, and markedly increased costs of agriculture and food around the world. The planet's exponential population explosion, coupled with the dramatically decreasing availability of potable water, have only worsened the situation. Scarcity of fresh water for irrigation has also added to the costs of food production.

The many years of economic crisis in the early twenty-first century has led to excessive inflation around the world and catastrophic global sovereign debt collapse. Financial misery was added to energy and environmental upheaval. Social anarchy forced governments into regional resource wars for energy, food, and water. Global war resulted.

Unfortunately, America will be dealing with the consequences of the aforementioned for the next several decades. Crises and threats to our nation will continue, many of them will be existential. The future of our country is not as clear as I would wish.

So you see, dear Sarah, my duty as an American fighting man continues unabated. A wheelchair will not stop me from duty to my country. By protecting her, I am protecting the future of my family. Perhaps accomplishing difficult tasks now will save my sons from even more difficult challenges in the future. The love I feel for them directs me in my cause.

*Naturally you, Sarah, are a different matter altogether.....
I am fighting for a future, for you, which may well be without
me..... This is an inconsolable thought for both of us..... I have
tried many times to reason the reality of it, but to no avail.....
It deeply pains me to consider a life for you without me in
it..... My senses fog when I think of it..... The uneasiness of it
all strikes at the very core of my being..... My heart hurts with
the sorrow of this possibility..... You are my only weakness,
the soft underbelly of my 'American Amaranth'..... I have so
profoundly loved you, and will so forever..... As my mother
would say to me as a child, 'You are my purity of purpose'.....
If I am to leave you in physical form forever on this mission,
may you hear my song of 'American Requiem' for eternity -
dedicated to my endless love for you and my sons.....*

Your adoring husband, Mark

I placed the letter into an envelope. I would later drop it
off at a Como flower shop - a clandestine CIA safe house -
for transport back to the United States.

I looked out again at Lake Como as a hang-glider with a
blood red wing flew over the eastern edge of town, heading
north to Blevio. I smiled gently, knowing of my own brother
Michael's sacrifices on this mission.

I slowly wheeled out from the table and looked into the
room. I nodded at Jimmy Thomas, who was waiting for my
order.

"Are we 'Tip of the Spear', Mark?" asked my dear trusted
friend.

"Yes, Jimmy," I said, patting my left chest and my father's
gift. "We have been, and we will be..... Let's get moving,
we have a rendezvous with destiny."

CHAPTER 12

The Blue Madonna

Julius Stansfield walked to the Como lakefront after breakfast with Claudia at their hotel in town. He strolled past the music gazebo to a mossy stone bench under a majestic oak tree by the flower garden. The late September morning was beautiful. The air was clean and cool, with the perfume of rose. He faced the length of the glacial lake between green Alpine foothills. The bright round yellow sun edged over the hills, lighting the garden with its warming rays. The red roses danced in a brisk wind. A blanched crescent moon lost itself behind the western mountains, surrendering to the new day.

Julius watched a young girl paint a portrait of two lovers kissing across the way. The man and woman sat on a patch of green grass near the roses with their passion legs entwined, embracing in the sun. He held her head firmly, and she his waist, as both expressed their souls' content with gentle vigor.

A breeze rustled through the upper branches of the oak tree, moving her thousand still dark green leaves in choral sound. Nature's breath matched the beauty of the time and place.

The precocious artist used water colors to reflect the scene's spiritual tenderness. Shades of blue lake, and green mountain and grass, red rose and yellow sun, filled the canvas on the tripod wooden easel as the young girl transferred herself to the work. She'd glance at the lovers, discreetly examine their body positions, and return to her creation. Julius sat in contemplation, appreciating and enjoying the artist's capture of love.

An old man in a wrinkled brown suit approached Julius with his violin.

"Good morning, Sir..... Would you like me to play something for you?" he asked in broken English.

"How did you know I spoke English?" enquired Julius.

"You are alone in the land of love..... It was a lucky guess, I suppose," answered the old man.

"I would enjoy your playing," said Julius.

"What would be your preference from my violin?"

"Play what you play best," suggested Julius.

The old man nodded kindly by the base of the oak tree. He placed the instrument on his left shoulder and smiled.

"With the moon soon to be lost for another day, conquered by the life of the sun, let us honor her last waning light," he said. The violinist closed his eyes and played Debussy's "Clair de Lune".

Julius inspired deeply and absorbed the splendor around him. The sound of the wind through the leaves was replaced by the crying melody of the old man's violin. The girl painter continued to image the beautiful young lovers on the grass by the red roses. Blue Lake Como reflected the sky and sun above, as the crescent moon died behind the green mountains.

Julius pulled Ann Nelson's diary out of his briefcase....................

Evening came once again. Mother's doctor auscultated her chest as she slept. He softly palpated her abdomen, checking her enlarged liver and spleen. Her breathing had become more labored over the previous hours, and she continued to spike fevers. He examined the petechial hemorrhages on her skin.

The doctor stood upright by the bed and returned the stethoscope to his coat pocket. He looked over his reading glasses at me and nodded. He put his arm on my shoulder and walked me over to the corner of the room by the open window. The moon's glow reflected across Lake Geneva; and a warm wind fluttered the white linen drapes, pulled to the edges of the large window.

"Your mother is dying, Julian. She's developed pneumonia. It's causing her great difficulty to breathe. She's asked me to provide only mild pain relief. She wishes no antibiotics or other medical interventions. I don't think I can alleviate much of her discomfort, Julian. There's not much time left, maybe two or three days at most. Please feel free to call on me if you need anything."

The doctor shook my hand and left us alone.

I watched her awhile, lying silently asleep in bed. Occasionally, she would utter an unintelligible word or slightly gasp for air. But she remained asleep, slowly fading away

to a place where she seemingly wished to be. I sat down next to her and opened the journal.

The Germans had fallen back from the Volturno River to the southernmost fortifications of the Winter Line, a series of three parallel defenses = the Reinhard, Gustav, and Hitler Lines - each separated by eleven miles. Halfway between Naples and Rome, the Reinhard Line bulged south from Cassino, incorporating the mountains over the narrow Mignano Gap. Through the gap passed Route 6, a direct road through central Italy to Rome by way of Monte Cassino at the entrance of the fertile Liri Valley. Just south of Cassino - the fortifications of the Reinhard Line transected the town of San Pietro, blocking the Mignano Gap.

The 15th and 71st Panzer Grenadier Regiments of the 14th Panzer Corps occupied San Pietro in September 1943. Kesselring ordered all non-essential citizen occupants of the town evacuated to the surrounding hillsides. Old men, women, and children were scattered outside of town. All able-bodied Italian men were ordered to help build defenses in and around San Pietro. Near the town, Mounts Sambucaro and Lungo overlooked Route 6.

The US 5th Army attacked on November 5. Camino Hill at the entrance of the Mignano Gap was taken early in the fight. As the Allies moved onto Mount Sambucaro, east of the narrow valley, and Mount Lungo to the west, the battle became intense and costly for both sides. The gap soon was known as 'Death Valley'.

The US 36th Infantry and 82nd Airborne Divisions assaulted San Pietro on December 8. Over the next nine days, four successive Allied attacks were strongly countered by the 14th Panzer Corps. German mines and anti-tank fire killed hundreds of American troops on their approaches to the town. Inside San Pietro, hand to hand close combat claimed many more on both sides.

Our hospital south of 'Death Valley' received thousands of casualties, including many innocent Italian women and children caught in the crossfire around San Pietro. A large cemetery grew around our hospital while the fighting raged in the Mignano Gap.

The Germans finally abandoned the town on December 17, moving a few miles north to the Gustav Line. Six weeks of killing had produced over 16,000 US casualties.

Two days before Christmas, we transferred our hospital north through the gap to San Pietro. Route 6 was a killing ground. The once fertile green valley had been made barren by war. Few trees stood upright. The ones still there appeared petrified and blackened by the soot of battle. There was no grass, only mud. Giant artillery crater holes sat nearly filled with dark blood-tinged rainwater, indicating their containment of bodies. Hands, arms, legs, and torsos of dead German soldiers in rigor mortis laid scattered across the valley. Their attached and tattered gray uniforms betrayed them to the end.

Amongst the many body parts, blown away from their owners in the violent assault, there were also heads. Some heads missed ears and eyes and nose, others - their top or jaw, making them less identifiable from the large rocks strewn on the field of battle. When definable, the faces of the dead expressed the horrors of their last moments on earth. You could see the fear in their open eyes and mouths. They seemed to stare and scream into the abyss. It was chilling.

I also saw the bodies of American soldiers still not claimed by our morgue details. Their faces expressed the same shock as the dead Germans. We all died alike. In the end, we were all humans. We all felt the same fear. We all felt the same pain. We all had our loved ones in our last thoughts. None of us wanted to die. But so many of us had. What a travesty.

Dispersed on the field too were fragments of US GI uniforms. Empty olive drab sleeves and pant leggings, torn from their owners in battle. All were blood-stained. Bodies had disintegrated into tiny fragments of flesh and bone in a mist of red, and scattered far from their death points. Many young lives were lost in the valley of death. The horror of it all.

I sat silent in my jeep while it slowly rolled through the sacred wasteland, consecrated by so many. I thought of the battlefield as a giant cemetery, where all the dead had fallen from common cause. It was a site of mass murder. These were all unnatural deaths. None had been taken by disease. All had been taken by war. None had been meant to be. All had suffered violent ends to life. There had been much suffering here. One could see it. One could smell it.

How could a piece of land be so important? I asked myself. How could the soil of the earth demand so much blood, sweat, and tears? From where in these boys did the courage arise to accept passage into the maelstrom of 'Death Valley', and allow hot flying metal to obliterate their young lives into pulp and mulch? Would any of their families really ever understand the horror of this place? Could loved ones ever know and feel the disfigurement of mind, body, and soul that occurred here?

Great fear had gripped these men in their last moments, I reasoned. Brave men performed their duty for their country in a war distant from comfort and familiarity. They had died far from their loved ones. These men were all children of someone back home, I reflected. They had siblings and *sweethearts. They had loved and been loved. These men - these soldier boys - would be missed by many.*

I withdrew into my citadel, my tranquil bastion of loneliness. Since arriving in war, I had escaped many times in self-preservation. In soulful isolation, in my fortress of calm and peace, I'd gather myself and prepare my spirit for further action. Like in a wilderness of the mind, I would refresh and enlighten my senses. The great solitude had shown me the greatest clue to life – the Rosetta Stone of Living – that for happiness to exist, there were only two required essentials – Truth and Love..... And in war, one could not find either of them.....

Up ahead, I saw the still smoking ruins of San Pietro - an ancient noble town in rubble. No buildings were left standing. The smell of death was everywhere. Bloated bodies of soldiers were scattered and mixed with those of innocents. Many women and children lay where they fell in the grotesque of war. Wild dogs in packs ran through the town feeding off some of the corpses. Our troops took potshots at many of them if they approached in a dangerous frenzy. The animals were seemingly as crazy as the people had been. It was a sickening sight.

We drove slowly through the eastern edge of town, trying to avoid passing over the crumpled bodies. At times, it was impossible, and the sound of cracking bone from underneath the jeep made you cringe with sorrow.

The partial remains of an old basilica were recognizable. Three of its walls still stood. The roof was gone, allowing direct sunlight into the interior. As we passed, I glanced into its open end and saw two small children kneeling inside. I asked the driver to stop.

I walked into the church, past fallen broken stone wall and spire, and gently crept up behind the young girl and boy. Rays of sunshine fell over their shoulders and onto the wall in front of them. As I got closer, their young ages became apparent. The girl seemed no older than eight years, and the boy younger. I saw they kneeled in prayer, both holding rosary beads in their small hands. Barefoot, their faces and emaciated bodies were soiled to a dark charcoal color. I came closer and knelt next to them. Neither looked up while they prayed. Tears streaked down their baby faces. They kept their eyes closed and trembled as they recited their sacred sayings. I waited.

Moments later, both children opened their eyes and wiped the tears from their faces. They looked up at me. The girl showed me a photograph of a beautiful woman holding two babies on her lap.

The girl's green eyes seemed big, even in their sunken sockets. Dirt had mixed with the tears, creating a dark mud cake on her eyelids and face. She pointed to the lady in the picture, gently rubbing with her finger to clean the image of the dust of war, and said sadly, 'Mama morta.'

The beams of the sun lightly fell on the wall in front of us. An ancient fresco of a 'Blue Madonna' was lit in full color by the sunshine. The Madonna's eyes were closed in despair, feeling deeply the loss at hand. A blue veil covered her head in sadness. I sat next to the children, embraced them both, and cried for the unbearable pain of their loss.

Julius closed Ann's album. He thanked the old man for the kindness of his violin, and walked the short distance from the rose garden to the lakeshore. As he passed, Julius kindly complemented the girl-painter for the grace of her art. He handed her a red rose.

A deep melancholy filled him. He stood by Lake Como, looking out.

Glancing up to his right, high above Como, he watched his brother Michael fly the red wing towards Blevio. Julius tucked the briefcase under his arm, smiled softly in acceptance, and began moving to the rendezvous point.

CHAPTER 13

The Devil Over Villa Vento Forte

The Condor stepped up to the third floor terrace from the swimming pool after enjoying a morning swim with his women. Wearing a long white silk robe and fashionable turtle shell Italian sunglasses, he sat at a long buffet table by the balcony with his house guests, Aqeel Sultan and Ameer Samara.

"Get my comb, Yousef!" yelled Anwar Nejem to his Jordanian aide, while pouring cold fresh fruit juice into a tall glass.

"Yes, Great Leader," said the meek and obedient Yousef El-Amin, before running to fetch his master's comb from the house.

"It is good to have reliable slaves," grinned the Condor at his guests, pushing back his wet shoulder length black hair behind his ears. He scratched his short-cropped salt and pepper beard and moustache.

"I have many women slaves, but only one man. Women don't aspire to wield power; they simply like the taste and bounty of it. Men, on the other hand, can't be trusted. They all eventually wish to give the orders. Yousef is more woman than man. I have his testicles in my pocket. He is my eunuch," laughed the Condor.

"Here, Great Leader!" gasped the Mole Rat, short of breath. "Your comb, sir!"

Anwar Nejem nodded and combed back his hair. He took off his sunglasses so his guests could see his eyes. A tall man of medium build, the forty year-old Anwar had dark eyes with unusually long eyelashes. A long nose hooked slightly downward at the end. Prominent bony cheekbones and chin angulated his face. Strong hands and a deep baritone voice added to his imposing physical presence.

Born in Paris to a rich Egyptian industrialist father and Italian mother, he was heir to a vast real estate and construction empire. Anwar considered himself Egyptian. He had been schooled at the finest academies of France. He had a degree in electrical engineering from the university in Berlin. He was polished in his manner, and highly informed in the areas of geopolitics, history, and world cultures. Anwar was as comfortable in the presence of kings and queens as he was with beggars in Cairo's bazaar district. He was also the *Kilij* movement's top superspy. He had killed many men in many places and boasted frequently of his talents to kill without remorse for the infidels.

Ruthless in his loyalties and allegiance to the idea of creating an Islamic caliphate from the Iberian Peninsula to Indonesia, the Condor had fought for the *Kilij* in the Libyan and Syrian civil wars. Although vehemently anti-Shiite, he had also conducted secret military operations for the Iranians against the English, French, and Israelis in Lebanon during the Great War. The Americans, Israelis, and Western Europeans were not Muslim. To Anwar, all non-Muslims were more infidel than the Shia Persians.

The Condor was experienced in all aspects of espionage and understood his Western adversaries. Surviving several assassination attempts by the CIA and MI6, he defiantly believed in his own indestructibility. As far as he was concerned, God would not remove him from this earth as long as he continued to kill infidels. His sense of invincibility on the field of battle made the *Kilij* superspy extremely dangerous. However, his delusional arrogant sense of self opened him to unnecessary risk-taking in his operations. The CIA would use this against him, and hopefully force a mistake from which he couldn't recover.

Anwar's grandfather had started the *Kilij* in Egypt after World War Two, in an attempt to rid North Africa and the Middle East of English and French influence. Initially a peaceful political movement, the *Kilij* slowly evolved over the decades into a Jihadist paramilitary organization fighting for the manifest destiny of a Sunni Islamic Empire. They fought for freedom from foreign imperialism. In the eyes of the *Kilij* leaders, the global movement wanted social justice, the elimination of the poverty and corruption of secular Arabism, and political freedom to the extent allowed by Islamic law. With mainly Egyptian, Libyan, Palestinian, and Turkish origins, the *Kilij* had re-organized into a much larger and better financed organization after the global war. They added loose elements of al-Qaeda, Hamas in Gaza, and former intelligence agents and Jihadi fighters from Jordan, Syria, Iraq, Yemen, Morocco, Algeria, Tunisia, Sudan, Somalia, Saudi Arabia, Pakistan, Afghanistan, and Uzbekistan. The common thread of these men was a deep rooted hatred for Israel and her main supporter, America.

The Condor leaned back in his chair and put his bare feet on the table in front of him. He rested his head against a yellow satin pillow and closed his eyes. The Egyptian opened his silk robe, exposing his nudity to the sun.

"Bring me American cigarettes, Yousef, and the maps!" shouted Anwar. "I need to show my friends how the United States will burn in the near future, while we smoke North Carolina tobacco. We will alter the whore's landscape considerably," laughed the Egyptian.

"The sunshine today is strong for late September," murmured the Condor, looking up at the sky and adjusting his penis to not get sunburn. "I must protect my large assets. My women enjoy its power as much as I," he grinned.

"The weather is good to keep training to fly like birds of prey. There are many things to learn before you can become a martyr. We have many men who want to die killing Americans. I hope to give them all much business!" yelled Anwar. "As far as I am concerned, no American deserves to live on this planet. They are all a scourge on the Islamic people. Their vices and immoralities are like toxins to the world. Like poisonous vipers, we must decapitate these creatures of evil and feed their bodies to the vultures."

Yousef returned quickly and placed a lit cigarette in Anwar's mouth. He offered the same to the guests. The Mole Rat opened a large map on the table in front of the Condor.

"Look, martyrs!

"See the cities which will disappear from the North American continent.

"Many will die instantly without pain, but many more will suffer for months before dying like rats. This fact brings me great pleasure. The vermin deserve to feel the pain my people have suffered for more than a century. Let them all go to hell," screamed Anwar with his face to the sun.

The Egyptian turned and looked at Yousef, "Take these maps away and get Tatiana from the pool. The tall one with the large juicy breasts knows how to feed an Arab. I want her to serve breakfast nude. She is fit and capable to exercise me later. Let her tantalize my stomach before she spirits my snake. She will also give me a pedicure while I sit and talk with my guests," laughed Anwar. "These fine Italian women are respectful of an Arab's needs. I will continue to add to my collection, Yousef."

The Condor finished his first cigarette and immediately asked for another. "I still relish the first American I ever killed. He was a young US Special Forces officer assigned to our group of rebel fighters in the desert east of Tripoli. One night, after a successful attack on a Libyan government convoy, I sat with 'Tony' on the side of the road smoking a cigarette - just like I am now. We had fought together for two weeks, and he thought he knew me. It was a cool night under the stars. He asked where I was from, and why I wanted to eliminate Gaddafi. After telling him I hated Gaddafi, and that I believed the dog was under imperial control, 'Tony' laughed and said, 'You stupid Arabs can't get your shit together.' The American then got up and went to urinate a short distance away. I took my long knife, crept up behind him, and slit his throat completely through. I then castrated him and placed his testicles in his mouth. The American's blood on my hands was warm, unlike his viper heart. The other rebels watched and laughed as I performed my good deed. You cannot trust these American pigs. They are worse than the Jews. I wish to kill many more while I still breathe."

The Egyptian paused for a moment, stood up, and removed his robe completely. He smiled and told his guests, "I want Tatiana to enjoy all of me as she clips my nails. It will prepare her for the afternoon exercises."

The Condor sat and pressed forward in his chair. He stared into the eyes of his guests and said, "Over the past several decades, America has created havoc in our countries. Your nation of Libya, Aqeel, was systematically divided and conquered by the imperialists to take your oil. Tunisia, Ameer, was also dominated in the process. Egypt, Syria, Iraq, Iran, Saudi Arabia, and all the others were coerced to follow the new plans for the Middle East. The new map, the Americans call it. We are all expected to follow their orders and fall in line. We have been exsanguinated by civil war and war against the imperialists. The oil riches of our lands have been taken away to North America and Europe. Our people have been starved into submission. Our old allies - Russia and China - were bought out with money and promises of a better future, or defeated outright in battle. China now suffers the same effects of American imperialism as we do in our lands. Israel still stands strong in the heart of the Middle East. They have been given rich natural gas resources in the eastern Mediterranean Sea which actually belong to our brothers in Turkey, Gaza, and Egypt. Israel is now a 'Superpower'. It makes me sick. We have failed in our duties to free our people. We have failed in our hopes for an Islamic empire. Like wheat in drought, we are withering away with no chance of harvest." Anwar broke bread and passed his offering to his guests.

"We have plans to change all this. Our friends in Germany, the FNNP, have been subdued. The GPNR still survives in Russia, although greatly weakened. As you both know, they have supplied us with the materials to humble America. In addition, I was able to purchase some added benefits from the Pakistani intelligence service. In Cairo this past spring, I personally received two additional tactical nuke weapons to use on our enemy.

"My Saudi connections have also provided added insurance, by way of China. Chinese hatred is almost as deep as ours. They want revenge implemented on our mutual enemy.

"So gentlemen -- we have the plan, the weapons, and the martyrs to be successful. There will be no more excuses for failure. We will not be subdued this time. It is God's will.

"Both of you are aware of the operation to send our falcons over populated cities in the western United States. I expect to obliterate several shining examples of American urban life. But that is not enough. I have bigger plans than that. These additional desires are secret for now, known only to me and a few people above me in the *Kilij*. My Turkish banker friend in Berlin has financed all my wishes. He is a true fighter for Islam. If we achieve our goals, America will be weakened beyond repair. Millions will die, and the social fabric of their country will be changed forever. They will die a devil's death. It is God's will."

Anwar poured more juice for himself, and stepped over to the balcony overlooking the swimming pool behind the villa. He took a long drag on his cigarette and waved at the beautiful Italian girls getting sun.

"Bring me Tatiana, Yousef! And bring her blonde friend as well. I have a strong appetite today!" shouted the Egyptian, before returning to the table.

"I have chosen both of you to join my cadre of fliers over America. You will be carefully trained here at Mount Cornizzolo, by Yousef and myself. My falcons will learn to be free in the air. You will understand the science and mechanics of control in strong winds, and become proficient in recognizing city landmarks near the planned detonation points. I have chosen ten of you to train for martyrdom in our cause. Only six will be picked at the end for *OPERATION STRONG WIND* over the western United States. Those not picked may be added to our still secret mission plan for three cities in eastern and midwestern America. We need many martyrs for many American deaths. This will change our future. No more servitude. We will rise to where we should be in the hierarchy of the new world order. We will disrupt America's new map of the Middle East. It is long overdue."

Out of the blue from the west, a hang-glider with a blood-red wing sailed in with a powerful wind. He flew at the Palladian villa and dove down over Lake Como. The rider of the red wing waved at the beautiful girls lying topless by the pool. They laughed and excitedly waved back. The glider swung around again, and sailed from south to north over the colonnaded portico and terrace.

The naked Condor, with a cigarette hanging from his mouth, sped back to the balcony.

"Who is this red devil?" he shouted at his armed men on the premises. "Is he one of ours?"

All of Anwar's men shrugged their shoulders, not recognizing the 'devil'.

Yousef said, "He cannot be a *Kilij* commando, Master..... Who among us would muster the courage to invade your space, Great Leader?"

Michael Stansfield flew low over the villa and waved at Anwar, giving him a middle finger. With his other hand, he saluted the Condor with his pecker.

Still standing by the balcony, Anwar screamed, "Who is this bastard?"

CHAPTER 14

Cowboys in Como

Michael Stansfield rode past the 14th century Gothic facade of the Como Cathedral and entered nearby Piazza Cavour. He slowly circled the lakefront plaza twice on his black Italian motorbike, before coming to a stop in front of the CIA's flower shop safe house. Wearing dark sunglasses, a western style flannel shirt, American blue jeans, and a white cowboy hat, Stansfield stayed atop his motorcycle for a few moments reconnoitering the scene. The waterfront square, just off the promenade, had a fine view of Lake Como. Ferries came and went from its small harbor. Tourists and locals shopped at stores facing the water. Outdoor cafes served early lunch. A large contemporary style hotel stood next to the inconspicuous flower shop. Everything seemed usual to Stansfield's eyes.

Across the way by the water, Julius walked up to Mark without making eye contact. Jimmy Thomas fed the ducks close by.

"I guess this is the point of no return, little brother."

"We passed that point a long time ago, Julius....."

"I reckon we did," said the big brother, buttoning his blue blazer. "It's damned cold out here."

"You're just scared for me."

"Yes, I am."

"Don't be, Julius..... I'm a bigger son of a bitch than you are."

"That you are," laughed Julius. "That you are....."

"Have you read the journal?" asked Mark, looking away from his brother.

"I'm into it right now. I'm half-way through. It's been revealing."

"It certainly is," said Mark, now gazing at his brother.....

"It seems to me that Father was a great facilitator. He eased his mother to her end," whispered Julius.

"He did much more than that..... He led her to a final glory. She died with a smile on her face and an open heart," whispered back Mark.

"He did the same for our mother," said Julius.

"Yes indeed, big brother..... He was a facilitator on many occasions."

"I love you Mark," said Julius in a low voice, before moving on to the flower shop.

Jimmy Thomas threw his last bread crumbs and also walked towards their rendezvous site. Mark followed after a few minutes.

One by one, Michael saw his colleagues arrive and enter the safe house. He took one last look around before entering himself. He passed the pretty Swiss receptionist, Diana, and tipped his hat.

"Hello, cowboy," winked the young woman, as Michael returned a smile and walked to the back of the store. Diana, a covert CIA operative in Europe for years, had worked previously with Stansfield.

An American male agent allowed Stansfield through a secret passageway and directed him two stories down to an operations center, equipped with the most advanced communication systems available to the United States. Another young female led Michael through a cavernous area, filled with analysts and signal officers hard at work, to a sealed assembly hall behind the main room. There he found the rest of his team sitting at a large round table.

Stansfield pulled a chair between his brothers on one side, and Claudia and Jimmy Thomas on the other. Jim, an African-American from Buffalo, New York, had been a star running back for Colgate University before joining the military. A US Marine lieutenant, and close friend of Mark Stansfield for many years, Jimmy had fought with the younger brother on both the Paraguana Raid in Venezuela and the attack on Shishkat Bridge in the Hunza Valley of northern Pakistan. He had personally witnessed Mark's medal winning courageous actions. The friends had been transferred together to US Naval Intelligence at the Pentagon only months before.

Sitting opposite from the Stansfields were John Mullen, Thomas Whitmore, and Daivat Kakkar. Mullen, a middle-aged British MI6 communications expert, had worked previously with Michael Stansfield on several projects in the

Middle East. He was well acquainted with Michael's tactics and methods, and had an excellent working knowledge of the *Kilij* movement. Whitmore, an MI6 nuclear terror specialist, had tracked down clandestine nukes all over Europe, Asia, the Middle East, and Latin America. He still had not failed once in stopping a nuclear terror attack, although coming close to catastrophe in London during the Olympic games of 2012. Kakkar, an Indian Intelligence agent assigned to research and analysis of the Pakistani ISI, knew the *Kilij* movement in Central Asia intimately. He had worked tirelessly to prevent the transfer of nuke material from the Pakistani intelligence services to Anwar and the *Kilij*. Unfortunately he had failed, the exchange taking place in Cairo six months earlier.

Timothy Ryan, the CIA's Chief of Covert Operations and Mitrano's deputy director, entered the room and sat beneath a large wall map of the world. "Good afternoon to all.....

"This is the first and last time any of you will enter this operations center. Regardless of risks, you are not to compromise our secrecy here by ever returning. Other safe houses will be provided for you as the case warrants.

"From here forward, you are a 'lone wolf' team. You will all coordinate your functions with each other only. None of you will communicate to the outside for anything. Vital mission information will be transmitted directly to you at our discretion only. You must all be self-sufficient in *Project X*. Extreme secrecy is the order of the day.

"The CIA will continuously monitor the situation and provide assistance only when absolutely necessary. We will have people on the ground in surveillance roles observing your moves. Two additional CIA assault teams will provide cover around you at all times. We will deflect any large scale attempts by the *Kilij*, Russian GPNR, and China to eliminate your presence.

"Your only objective is to find where the *Kilij* has hidden the contraband nuclear material. Secret phantom operation is the only way your team will find the deadly nukes.

"Avoid killing the targets, particularly the Condor, before safeguarding the contraband. These freaks are our only hope for finding the nukes, and uncovering the *Kilij* network of spies in Europe and the United States. Only Anwar and the upper leadership of the *Kilij* know the final plans for attacking America.

"Presently, the CIA has ongoing operations against *Kilij* leadership centers in Istanbul and Cairo. Our people in Russia and China tell us that the GPNR and Chinese Intelligence have facilitated the *Kilij* plans, but are not privy to particular details. This shows the desperation with which the Russian GPNR and Chinese are working. They are blindly providing assistance for the *Kilij* to destroy American infrastructure, killing millions of Americans in the process. Their hope is to break down American society, generate anarchy, and possibly instigate revolution on our home turf.

"Let's review the facts.

"The *Kilij* is an ultra-militant Sunni Islamist organization intent on establishing a world-wide Sunni Caliphate, controlling the energy riches of the Middle East and Central Asia. They have increased tremendously in relative strength since the demise of the Shia power centers in Iran, Iraq, and Syria in the last great war. Directed from their clandestine leadership centers in Cairo and Istanbul, the *Kilij* has been successful in establishing a world-wide terror network to further their aims. The Egyptian and Turkish governments are infiltrated with their people from top to bottom. The levers of these governments are now in their hands. Strong presence has been established in Syria, Jordan, Saudi Arabia, Qatar, Kuwait, Pakistan, and the North African Maghreb.

"The *Kilij* has sufficient financial backing from several sources to execute their plans. They have established a friendly alliance with elements of the Russian GPNR and the Chinese Revolutionary Council (CRC). Both the GPNR and CRC are trying to gain power in their respective countries. China is embroiled in a civil war, and fascist Russia threatens Eastern Europe and the southern Caucasus. Our failure in this mission would cause the United States to become entangled in a dangerous military confrontation with both Russia and China. In my estimation, we would be forced to use secret nuclear weapons, unknown to our enemies. Although our homeland would suffer, their cultures would be erased from the surface of the earth. Let's triumph in our challenge with the *Kilij* and avoid a world catastrophe. Our goal here is to force peace on our enemies. I don't believe in Pyrrhic victory or martial insanity.

"The *Kilij*, with help from Russia and China, has supplanted the more moderate US-backed Muslim Brotherhood movement in the Sunni nations of North Africa and the Middle East. They wish to destroy Israel and eliminate America's presence in their area of the world. Radical nationalistic elements in Russia and China want the same things, at risk of allowing the evolution of an Islamic world empire. In simple terms, they all wish to weaken America as they share the spoils of controlling the oil and natural gas reserves of the Middle East, Central Asia, the western Pacific, and the South China Sea regions. By controlling the major energy reserves of our planet, they will dictate future terms to the free democracies of North America and Europe.

"Similar philosophies led to a limited conventional global war last year. Apparently, this problem will confront America and the free democracies into the future. There appears to be no end in sight. Short of total destructive world war, and the complete annihilation of our enemies and their cultures, the CIA and other intelligence services of freedom-loving nations will continue to be called upon to save freedom for our people.

"We know the Kilij and Anwar Nejem have acquired four tactical nukes from Russia through the courtesy of the GPNR. Each of these bombs is the equivalent of 20 kilo-tons of TNT - stronger than the Hiroshima bomb. Kilij fliers will hang-glide these bombs over four western American cities and detonate them at 1900 feet above urban centers. Each will create a 2 mile circle of total devastation and lethal destruction. Over 1.4 million Americans will die within six months of the attacks. This is more than all our losses in previous wars combined. Several millions more will die of radiation induced cancers over the next two decades.

"Additionally, this past March in Cairo, the Pakistani ISI hand delivered two more tactical backpack nuclear bombs to Anwar. We believe these will target US cities in the east and midwest. Boston, Atlanta, and Chicago have been mentioned several times on secret Kilij communications picked up by the National Security Agency. The CIA feels certain the aforementioned bombs are all under the Condor's supervision in Como. Other Kilij operatives in Como may also know the whereabouts of the nukes. But none in Como, other than Anwar, know the final plans for those bombs. Thus the importance of taking Anwar alive if we can't find the locations of the contraband on our own. Only he can tell us where they are, and where they were destined to go. This is particularly important if we can't isolate all the bombs, and some slip out of Italy to the United States. The Condor would be our only hope for stopping those bombs before reaching final targets.

"We have also learned of a recent transfer of an unspecified 'dangerous material' from the Chinese People's Liberation Army (PLA) to Taiwanese businessman, Sheng Hong, living in Como, Italy. A tele-communications magnate, and rare art and book dealer, Mr. Sheng has a lakeside villa near Anwar's home in Blevio. He owns a fine art gallery and rare book shop in Como. Sheng is a secret member of the Chinese Revolutionary Council (CRC), which is trying to re-unify the Chinese nation during their present civil war. He is a Maoist Communist in the fake skin of a Taiwanese capitalist. The CIA believes Sheng is brokering a deal with Anwar to pass this 'dangerous material' into the United States in a terrorist attack. We don't know if this 'material' is biologic or nuclear, but we suspect it is extremely lethal and game-changing for the CRC to take these risks. We must find this material before it passes to Anwar for distribution to America. *Project X* must get to Sheng Hong.

"In the next several weeks, Turkish banker Bahadur Burakgazi will meet with Anwar and Sheng in Como. Burakgazi, code-named 'Babar', is a banker in Berlin for the *Kilij*. Monies from anti-American groups around the world are funneled through Burakgazi's bank in Berlin, laundered, and passed to the Condor in Italy. It has helped establish a vast *Kilij* terror network throughout Italy, the rest of Europe, and the United States. Anwar has major operations in Milan, Florence, Genoa, Bologna, Rome, and Naples. All funding comes from 'Babar'. The Turk is planning to pay Sheng for the transfer of the 'material' at this meeting in Como. We want to infiltrate both Sheng and Anwar before the meeting with 'Babar'.

"The CIA has loosely subdivided the *Project X* team into three groups. Michael Stansfield, Mullen, Whitmore, and Dakkar will be responsible for surveying Villa Vento Forte and Anwar's activities. You will make any contacts necessary to enter those premises, and any others, in search of the nukes. You will observe the Condor and his cronies for leads which may enlighten the discovery of the contraband elsewhere if indicated. You are not limited in your reach to Como and its surroundings. Go wherever you need to go to find the clues necessary to stop this plot.

"Julius Stansfield and Claudia Coffigny will locate *Kilij* safe houses in the Northern Lakes region of Italy. We need to know how many *Kilij* agents are involved regionally in this plot, and if the nukes are in any of these safe houses.

"Michael and Claudia, who both have experience in hang-gliding, will combine their flying and espionage talents to infiltrate the Condor's Mount Cornizzolo school. Yousef El-Amin, the Mole Rat and head instructor at the school, is a weak link. He may be capable of spilling information. We want Claudia to use all her powers to get close to Yousef. Turn him around as soon as you can, Claudia. He knows where the nukes are being stored. He also may have information on Sheng Hong's Chinese contraband.

"If these *Project X* squads cannot acquire the information necessary to locate the contraband nuclear material, they will kidnap important Kilij agents to further their aims. Severe interrogation techniques will be utilized to hasten the delivery of the needed information. The CIA will not restrict you for the methods used. The gravity of the matter forces us to use whatever means necessary to extract the details. The future of our country depends on your effectivity.

"Finally - Mark Stansfield and James Thomas will infiltrate into Sheng Hong's world, and find the 'dangerous material' before it's transferred to Anwar and the *Kilij*. You will get to the Chinese revolutionary through his love of rare art and books."

Timothy Ryan got up and excused himself from the room. He returned with two more individuals.

"Let me introduce two of our finest intelligence agents, Rafael Alvarez and Simon Westcott. These are their aliases.

"Rafael is an expert in special covert tactics on the battlefield. He is a highly decorated CIA veteran of the Global War on Terrorism. Rafael is also one of the world's foremost experts on 19th and 20th century paintings, particularly Picasso and Matisse. Sheng has several Picasso and Matisse pieces in his Como gallery.

"Simon is a twenty-year veteran of CIA covert operations around the world. He speaks and reads in five languages, and happens to be the leading expert in rare manuscripts of America's founding fathers. Sheng Hong has the world's largest private collection of American manuscripts of the 18th and 19th centuries in his Como rare book shop.

"Both Rafael and Simon, functioning as brokers, have gotten an interested American buyer - Mr. Mark Harrity (aka Mark Stansfield) - into discussions with Sheng Hong for the potential purchase of very expensive artifacts in his Como collections. Harrity and his assistant, James Jones (aka Jimmy Thomas), have a meeting with Sheng scheduled for tomorrow morning. By then, Mark, you will understand more about rare American manuscripts, and Picasso and Matisse art, than anyone you've ever known. I assure you. Both Rafael and Simon are excellent teachers of their trade.

"You will get close to Sheng. Hopefully, he'll invite you to a dinner next month in honor of his famous international financier friend - Mr. Bahadur Burakgazi. We expect the 'dangerous material' transaction to occur at this party on Sheng's yacht. If you must, 'physically' coax Sheng to surrender the material before it's passed to Babar. The CIA needs to eliminate it from the battlefield. However, before we can move against Sheng, the other *Project X* squads must secure the nukes under Anwar's control. The mission requires timely coordination for its ultimate success."

Timothy Ryan stood again and slowly circled the table, clasping hands behind his back. He stared down at the floor in contemplation as he walked.

"The urgency of this mission is obvious. However, what truly makes it immediate is that the *Kilij* has plans to move out of Italy in force by late October. That is only four weeks, people. They will have their killer contraband out of Italy and on its way to America in less than a month.

"They're planning their attacks for springtime next year. That would give them six months to hide the materials in the vastness of the North American continent.

"The CIA must stop the *Kilij*. The nuclear materials and the dangerous Chinese contraband must be removed from the battlefield before their departure from Italy. The Condor's final operational plans must be deciphered and destroyed. Enemy agents in Italy, and their networks in Europe and America, must be eliminated. Burakgazi's financial empire in Turkey and Germany must be torn down and confiscated. This money cannot get into other terrorist hands. Sheng Hong and his Chinese Revolutionary Council comrades, who want to harm and disable America, must be killed. *Kilij* leadership centers in Cairo and Istanbul must be dismantled.

"Those are all tremendous responsibilities for the CIA and our *Project X* team," said Ryan, returning to his chair.

The Chief of Covert Operations looked at his people around the table. He kindly smiled at each and every one of them.

"This operation is another important one in our agency's long history. We have often coordinated our efforts with the intelligence services of other freedom-loving nations. Duty to liberty on earth is the essence of the CIA. The foundations for freedom around the world rest on our shoulders and our attempts to uphold those foundations right here, in this place, in this time. Perhaps long from now, people will say all over the world, 'Freedom rings, freedom rings, because of the efforts of so few for so many.' I hope and pray that will be the case.

"Director Mitrano and I wish you all success on your sacred mission..... Godspeed to all."

CHAPTER 15

God Bless America

I was asleep and awake at the same time. Since my wounds, I had developed a tendency for this. It's mysterious how the mind drifts when the body is trapped. The mental journeys run back into the past much more than look into the future. The wheelchair may be a ball and chain for the physical, but it gave wings to my mind and thoughts.

I remembered, from years ago, my summer trip with Sarah to the western North Carolina mountains. We hadn't known each other for more than a few weeks, but we were in love.

We hiked the Blue Ridge Mountains and surrounding forests for days. We rock climbed and bird watched. We'd stop and rest whenever we wanted, swimming in lakes and rivers, eating wild blueberries, picking wildflowers, and sleeping in lush valleys under the stars. We lit campfires at night and read poetry. We also made love many times and in many places, always buck-naked in nature. We became untamed, like the deer and bears in the woods.

One day, Sarah and I found a 'Garden of Eden' near Upper Creek Falls. The forest around the fifty-foot waterfall was full of orange lilies, yellow daffodils, and Firepinks. The rushing waters fell in cascades into a series of large pools. Giant boulders sat to the sides; their smooth brown surfaces were comfortable for sunbathing.

I walked along a narrow and slippery rock corridor beneath the steep cliff. The power of the cataract was on me. The energy of the falling water shook my insides. I brought my head out from under the torrent. The cascade's jet spray massaged my back and neck. I stepped carefully to the edge of the ridge and dove down twenty feet into the largest pool. I touched the bottom with my hand and rose to the surface. It was cold but beautiful.

Squinting under the noon sun, I stared at the finest woman I'd ever seen. Sarah lay on a massive boulder in front of me. She was naked on her back, with her knees bent and feet flat on the stone. The sun shined strongly on her, tanning her shapely legs and thighs and chest. Her lips, all of them, were pink in flow. A warm wind played with her blonde hair. Like a wolf, the scent of her body brought me out of the swimming hole.

I lay beside her on the warm sun-drenched stone and kissed her mouth. I firmed my body close to her pleasure centers; and with my palms and fingers, I felt the curves and crevices of her hips and rear, the fullness and firmness of her breasts, and softness of her face. She passed her hands over me. We made love at high noon by the rushing waters of Upper Creek Falls.

Afterward, Sarah looked into my eyes and said, "To love, and to be loved..... What more can one ask of life?"

"Will you marry me?" I asked.

"I married you, Mark, the day I was born," she whispered into my ear, before kissing me.....

There was a knock on my door at the Garibaldi. My mind returned from its trip. It was time to go.....

Wearing Italian suits and ties for our meeting with Sheng Hong, James Thomas and I entered the fine and rare book shop off the promenade in the Como town center. Busy early morning pedestrian traffic had already developed along the lakefront.

An immaculately dressed middle-aged Chinese woman greeted us in the vestibule of the shop and locked the front door. She posted a 'closed' sign in the window and pulled the shades.

We were escorted through an oak wood paneled hall to a collection room with a large display of European and American Enlightenment manuscripts from the 18th century.

"Feel at ease to browse through Mr. Sheng's collection, gentlemen.

"Mr. Sheng's assistant, Mr. Hsu, is available to select manuscripts for your entertainment interest," said the receptionist, as she left the room with the tall Mr. Hsu standing by the door.

"Good morning, gentlemen," welcomed the young and fit Mr. Hsu in formal black attire and white gloves. "Mr. Sheng will present himself shortly. Please feel free to look through our library. I am here to answer any questions you may have concerning our classic manuscripts."

I sat in my wheelchair in front of a table display of rare books and personal writings of famous European and American scholars, political theorists, philosophers, scientists, mathematicians, and musical composers of the "Age of Reason". Original signed copies of Adam Smith's *The Wealth of Nations*, Thomas Paine's *Common Sense*, Edward Gibbon's *Decline and Fall of the Roman Empire*, and Alexander Hamilton's *Federalist Papers*, sat in glass enclosed display cases on the table. My attention was most captured by the German philosopher Thomas Abbt's treatise on patriotism, *On Dying for One's Nation*. Jimmy Thomas sat next to me, waiting for the arrival of our target, Sheng Hong.

Hsu was notified through his earpiece of Sheng's arrival. The bodyguard opened the door to the collection room and stood at attention. The casually dressed, short and fat 52 year-old Chinese billionaire was accompanied by Rafael Alvarez and Simon Westcott.

I noticed a small yellow-fire breathing red dragon tattoo behind Hsu's left ear. The insignia for Chinese PLA Special Operations Forces was familiar to me. I had seen it more than once in the Hunza Valley.

"Good morning, Mr. Harrity," smiled the fatman. "I've read much about you in the American newspapers as of late. Your passion for art inspires me greatly. Your recent purchases of the Impressionists in London and Paris shocked me favorably. I never realized the agriculture business in America could be so prosperous."

"It is inherited wealth," I said, shaking Sheng's hand.

"I am what I am financially because of my deceased father's labors to establish an agricultural empire. Perhaps, you could say, I have been fortunate in my commercial dealings since taking over the business eight years ago.

Harrity Food Enterprises is now larger and more diversi-
fied. Our company is a leading genetic modifier of crop
plants. Harrity Inc.'s drought-resistant wheat and corn are
exported all over the world. Whatever of the world is left
with the capacity to pay," I grinned.

"But nevertheless, I'm still in the shadow of my wise and
industrious father. He began the business and left it to me to
prosper from it."

"Don't be so modest, Mr. Harrity. I understand your
genetic engineering background is responsible for many of
the company's lucrative patents. It also seems to me, from
all I have read, that you are a young business genius. You
should be proud of your great achievements. There is no
reason to be so humble in your thoughts. Your father may
have been a great man, but you too are a great man - certainly worthy of your fine reputation and fantastic wealth.

"Professional success has allowed you to become a
connoisseur of the world's great visual arts and literary masterpieces. I am honored to entertain your interests in my collection of fine manuscripts and art.

"Mr. Alvarez and Mr. Westcott have communicated with
me for over a month. They have stated your particular fond-
ness for some of my collection pieces," said Sheng, motion-
ing to Hsu.

"I have taken the liberty of transferring here for your con-
venience the two paintings of interest from my art gallery
across the street. We also have the manuscript you have
been searching for the past three years. I hope they are
well received.

"Both these paintings have been lost for many decades.
They were forgotten. In fact, most people thought they
had never existed in the first place. They were only recently

re-discovered. I acquired the art from secret private collections, and re-introduced the works into the marketplace so sophisticated worshipers like you may enjoy them once again. It is a gift for the world. An expensive gift, I believe is well worth the investment," smiled Sheng.

The PLA soldier returned to the room holding an elegantly framed oil on canvas painting. He gently placed the 42" by 32" Pablo Picasso masterpiece on a steel tripod under perfect lighting. Sheng Hong stared at me for reaction and grinned like a fox.

"Be my guest and approach the beauty of Picasso," stated the Chinese fatman.

Jimmy stood behind my wheelchair.

"Let me introduce to you my longtime friend and personal aide, Mr. James Jones," I said. "At times, he's also the best substitute I can find for my legs."

"Any loyal close friend of yours, Mr. Harrity, is a friend of mine," said Sheng. "I respect friendship between men of strength. It is rarer and more priceless than my finest works of art."

Thomas slowly wheeled me in front of the painting. I appeared awe-struck.

"Absolutely splendorous..... Magnificent," I whispered. "Young Pablo painted this in 1905, when he was only 24 years old. It is an important early work of his 'Rose Period'. *The Virgin Queen* once belonged to Pablo's principal patron, Gertrude Stein. It was her favorite, after the somber tones of Picasso's earlier 'Blue Period'.

"She is so erotic and sensuous," I added in a state of exultation. "The woman is an aphrodisiac for the eyes....."

The painting was of a Renaissance era European queen, standing nude and full bodied - facing the viewer. Her beautiful face was carefully outlined. Her eyes closed in passion. A golden crown sat on her head, tipped with dark blood-red rubies. Blonde hair flowed freely onto her shoulders. Round and perfectly formed breasts pulled your eyes centrally. The queen's pink skin was accented by a green emerald pendant hanging from her neck. On her right wrist, she had a bracelet of large red rubies and small green emeralds. Her right hand rested on her hip, her left hand temptedly close to her upper, inner left thigh.

"She is so beautiful," I repeated.

"If you look closely, Mr. Harrity, her vaginal lips drool," snickered the fatman.

I glared at my host.

"She reminds me of my wife," I said in a slow harsh tone.

"I am sorry for my ugly comment," said the Chinaman in a low and embarrassed voice.

"I lost my queen years ago in the car accident that put me into this chair," I said, breaking hard eye contact with the fatman and returning my gaze to Picasso's painting.

"Yes, I know of your unfortunate loss, Mr. Harrity," said Sheng, looking at Hsu. "Those we love are never forgotten. The void can never be filled, not even with the brilliance of Picasso."

"Be more careful with your words, Sheng. Let Picasso speak for himself. Allow the client to conjure up his own notions about the art. Each masterpiece may signify different things to different people. Some things may be sensitive....."

"You are quite correct, Mr. Harrity. I did not mean any disrespect. Please forgive my statement of obvious manly observation. I didn't realize the painting's significance for you," said Sheng with slight sarcasm.

"In this business, one must consider all avenues of significance. It is usually wise for the host to keep his mouth shut, and permit the guest to appreciate his own mental images and private ruminations. A slip of the tongue could ruin a potential transaction," I retorted with composed anger.

Playing Shakespeare, Jimmy patted me on the back in an attempt to calm my temper. Sheng looked at Hsu in disbelief.

"I've searched five years for this painting..... It has been out of view for a very long time," I said.

"How did you come to it, Mr. Sheng?"

"I bought the masterpiece two years ago in Moscow from a rich Russian imbecile with no taste for art. Hurt by American economic sanctions during the 'Ukraine Crisis', the owner needed capital to keep his many women happy. He was a caveman in full respect of the word. He looked, spoke, ate, and acted pre-historic. He was not worthy of this beauty. I saved *The Virgin Queen*. I am now ready to sell her to you, if you wish," stated the fatman.

Sheng nodded at Hsu. The tall assistant removed the Picasso from its stand and walked out of the room.

"You may have her for $160 million in gold, Mr. Harrity. You can return to America with your virgin queen if you so desire."

I neither commented nor made eye contact with Sheng.

Hsu returned promptly with a second painting. He placed the larger work on the same tripod display.

"Here you have your Matisse, Mr. Harrity..... Enjoy!" said the Chinese spy.

I carefully looked at the 1907 masterpiece for several minutes. I analyzed the wild and dissonant colors of Matisse Fauvism, a forerunner of Expressionism. *Women Cavorting*

Among the Flowers had been one of the 20th century's best. Nude beauties danced in a field of white tulips.

"Sensuality in evolution," I whispered while observing the painting, loud enough for Sheng to hear.

I turned and looked at Jimmy Thomas. He pushed me back to the long display table.

"I am ready for the manuscript," I declared.

Sheng snapped his fingers, and Hsu removed the Matisse from the room.

"Are you appreciative of the Matisse, Mr. Harrity?"

I nodded my head slightly.

"It can be yours for $50 million in gold, Mr. Harrity, if your heart desires," smiled Sheng.

Hsu returned with a large, flat, black leather box. He placed it on the table in front of me and delicately revealed the antique parchment document inside.

"Do fighting men interest you, Mr. Harrity? Why your appetite for this particular piece?" questioned the fatman.

"We are all fighting men, Sheng..... You and I are fighting men..... No matter how old or rich, educated, sophisticated, and polished in the ways of the world one may be, we will always be fighting men..... Scratch a little below the surface and you will find the makings of violence and aggression. There are ruthless killer warriors inside us. They're restrained for reasons of civility. But they are still there, waiting to be unleashed in a moment's notice. There is burning fury inside you and I. Bloodthirsty, bellicose, and primal we are..... Don't forget, Mr. Sheng, humans are the most vicious animals on the planet. We will continue to be till our extinction....."

I grinned at the yellow fatman and returned my eyes to the document. "This man was the ultimate warrior. He's the reason why I'm here....."

Sheng said nervously, "This is the first Dunlap print of the *Declaration of Independence*. It was printed the night of July 4, 1776, by order of the US Continental Congress. It was specifically made by John Dunlap in his printing shop on the corner of 2nd and Market streets in Philadelphia, Pennsylvania, just blocks from Independence Hall. Two hundred prints were made. Only twenty still exist. However, this one is special. It was the first print, and it was given to George Washington. The general signed it and wrote in his hand, 'God bless our country for the struggle to come'. It is a unique document of American history, Mr. Harrity, and it can be yours for only $20 million in gold."

"Priceless..... Priceless," I repeated.

"No, Mr. Harrity..... It has a price..... A good one, I believe," said the Chinese businessman spy.

"No..... You don't understand, Sheng.

"General Washington saw the struggle to come. He realized it would not end after the American Revolution. He knew it would continue forever..... Perpetual war, Sheng..... A never-ending struggle for freedom.....

"His vision was frightening, but it didn't deter him from his duties. Washington was a champion of the cause for freedom and the rights of men everywhere.

"The man and his thoughts are priceless, not the document, Sheng..... The man and his thoughts," I repeated.

CHAPTER 16

Horns of Satan

The ancient white stone mountain lodge stood in a green grassy clearing, a thousand feet above the town of Valbrona. The retreat's hundred foot tall tower had provided Alpine hunters a commanding view of the surrounding hills and valley for centuries. From here, men with their guns could survey the dense green woods. Animal life was everywhere. No creature could hide from the naked eye for a mile radius from the top of the watchtower.

Creeks meandered through the forest. The sounds of rushing waters from every direction could be heard from the top of the watchtower. The pasture surrounding the lodge was filled with wild mountain flowers. Hues of red, yellow, blue, and purple dotted the lush green landscape. Verdant ivy grew up the tower and curled itself into the large open window at the top. The ivy sprouted a small white flower which easily fell away with the wind.

Wearing a dark green windbreaker and black beret, Julius Stansfield looked out from the watchtower through his US Navy binoculars towards the town of Como - twelve miles to the southwest. He scanned slowly to his left along the ridgeline of Mount Cornizzolo to the Corni di Canzo. The mountain's two steep rocky peaks rose like devil's horns nearly four thousand feet above him. The white stone of the piedmont contrasted sharply with the vivid colors of the valley. Four cows and a calf grazed in the fertile grassy plain below his watchtower; their bells clinked in the early morning chill. The submarine commander turned CIA spy finally concentrated his focus on the summit of Mount Cornizzolo and waited for Claudia to make her move.

One hundred steps beneath the navy captain, Michael Stansfield and Daivat Kakkar sat on a stone floor at opposite ends of an open air breezeway. They cleaned their pistols while occasionally glancing at a juvenile Golden Eagle perched on a tree outside the window. The dark brown predator bird stripped clean a white hare, betrayed by his color against the greens of the forest.

"That unlucky son of a bitch rabbit," said Michael, holstering his two 9mm weapons and walking over to the window. "His little brown friends are still alive. He should've stayed brown a little bit longer. He jumped into his winter color too early. Three months from now, his whiteness may have saved his ass. Bad DNA leads to poor timing and demise of the unfit, Daivat. Espionage mirrors the game of Natural Selection. Jump too early or too late, one can lose his head."

"It's not as simple as that, Stansfield. Fate plays into it also. You may be in the right place at the right time, or in the wrong place at the wrong time. Good and bad luck are significant factors in what we do," murmured the Indian, still on the floor.

"Don't give me that ancient Indian Hindu fatalism crap, where lives and events are predetermined. We can control our fate most of the time," said Michael, turning his back to the hare's bones.

"Yes, most of the time, Michael, but not all of the time," emphasized Kakkar. "You Americans feel you're always in control of events. Frequently, you blind yourselves to reality. Geopolitics is not watchmaking. It's easier and more certain to engineer the perfect Swiss timepiece than it is to build a perfect world. Shit happens, and often you can't do anything to prevent it."

Michael Stansfield smiled in sensible agreement.

"Don't take it personally, Indian. I'm just riling you up for an afternoon of fun in the Alps. I like to keep my international colleagues on the edge of their seats. An excited brain, firing across all synapses, is a prepared brain," laughed the American agent.

"All of you Americans are such bastards," grinned Kakkar. "You're like that fucking Golden Eagle outside, ripping the flesh of the poor rabbit. Everything is prey to you. You'll even eat the bones if given the chance."

"No, Daivat..... We'll save the bones..... They'll make good soup for a rainy day."

"Keep me out of the stew, alright," smiled Kakkar.

"Don't worry; the cowboys and indians are on the same side this time," assured the American.

The men laughed, and threw their troubles and doubts out the window.

"What the hell is an Indian doing in the Italian Alps, Daivat?" asked Michael, placing a clip of ammunition into his M4 carbine. "One would think Indian intelligence would have enough on their hands with the instability of a broken Pakistan, and a China in civil war, crossing over your porous borders. Instability has infiltrated into your homeland and is wreaking havoc. I read a few days ago that over 650 of your people were dying weekly in bombings across India. Islamists from Pakistan and Bangladesh, and Communists from Burma and China, are getting payback. I would think your presence in India would be essential at this time," opined Michael as he checked the rest of his gear.

"You would think so," said Daivat Kakkar quietly, before he loaded a short-nosed .38 revolver and placed it into his ankle holster.

The Indian looked up at Stansfield and began filling a pistol magazine with .45 rounds.

"One certainly wouldn't expect me to be here in the Italian Lakes region, I suppose.

"But naturally, you don't know the whole story..... Do you, Michael?" stated Kakkar with mild annoyance, answering the question before asking.

"My country, like yours, has been in perpetual war since her creation. If not the Muslims from the east and west, it was the Communists from the north and south. No one likes or trusts a free democrat, Michael," grinned Kakkar.

"Besides, I have important things to do here.....

"If America is rocked with a calamity, and is subsequently thrown into chaos, does India stand a chance of surviving the savage hordes?

"I don't believe so," said the Indian. "My country's survival, as well as all other free nations, depends on America's survival. I'm here to help you maintain your country free," winked the tall slender Hindu.

"Since our independence from the United Kingdom in 1947, my homeland has struggled to keep democracy intact. It hasn't been easy. China, Pakistan, and Bangladesh have been at our throats the whole time. We have had separatist movements in our remote northwest and northeast provinces for decades. At present, over three hundred groups are actively fighting for independence from India. The majority are in the northeast frontier lands of Arunachal Pradesh bordering China - and Assam, Nagaland, and Manipur further south, bordering Bangladesh and Burma. Several dozen Islamist groups are creating chaos in our northwestern frontier along the border with Pakistan. Like you, Michael, my country and I have perpetual war," said the handsome Indian.

"It all basically comes down to borders and boundaries, American. The world is composed of multiple closed communities, each eternally defending its limits. Man's boundaries are self-imposed, and dependent on race and creed, religion, and tribal identity. Lines drawn haphazardly on maps, along rivers and mountain ranges, create paranoia and a constant foreboding sense of threat from others on the opposite side of the lines. Wars are fought over differences in national ideology and identification, and needs for natural resources. The tribes have to maintain themselves at the expense of other 'different' tribes. Whether you're Hindu like me, or Jew, Muslim, or Christian, your group won't assimilate with the others. They all feel 'different', each group believing they were 'chosen' by God to be 'special' and 'better' than the others. Because of their 'specialness', they feel they deserve more. More food, water, energy, land, and power dictate the course of world history. Wars of conquest are fought to keep the tribe 'special', and to lower the standard of living for the other 'less deserving' tribes. Keeping our rigid sense of nationality will only generate perpetual war for both you and I, American," said Kakkar.

The Indian intelligence officer slid a fully loaded magazine into his .45 pistol, charged and holstered it at his waist.

"Both you and I, Michael, have 30,000 genes in our genomes. That is a scientific fact. I may be Hindu, and you a Christian, but we are the same where it counts. We are both human beings. Our insides are the same. We can suffer from the same afflictions and causes of death. We both have a heart which pumps red blood to our vital organs. We both have the same neuronal tissue in our brains, with the same synapses and chemical neurotransmitters. We have minds that feel the same emotions and needs for love and spiritual fulfillment. We are the same, and not any 'different' from a Muslim or Jew. Until the rest of the world understands and believes in that reality, you and I, and people like us into the future, will be sent to far off lands to protect the 'special' interests of our 'special' tribes."

Stansfield turned and watched the Golden Eagle fly away, satiated with the flesh and bone of a Darwinian loser. The strong had overcome the meek once again. Power was essential for victory on nature's field of battle, as it was on man's.....

"Listen, Daivat, I can appreciate your reasoning. I have thought about these issues many times in my past, particularly when in harm's way. One's impending death seems to stir these questions from time to time. But the reality is that man has evolved these 'boundaries' over thousands of years; and it will likely take thousands of more years to arrive at a settled and peaceful solution to our problems. These are truths, whether we like them or not. You and I are just soldier ants protecting our colonies from the enemy. It's rather simplistic, really. Our functions are to follow orders to the best of our abilities, and allow time to model our cultures' sensitivities and sensibilities. The world will eventually reach a rightful place, and our species will evolve to a rational equilibrium. It will take time. Hopefully, people like you and I will continue to prevent gross human calamities. Perhaps, the course of human history will be pacified. Let's give time for evolution to replace revolution," said Michael with a sparkle in his eye.

"Your perspective is that of the eagle, Michael. You are strong and agile, and able to bring all your advantages to the combat. You are a powerful victor; and thus, you are comfortable with the allowance of time - eons of time – to pass before a peaceful equilibrium. You can wait for evolution to grind the earth into powder without losing patience. Time and space are your allies..... But what if you were the hare?

"The weak cannot afford to wait for evolution's graces, because the weak receive no graces. They cannot allow for time to bring solution to the disequilibrium, because none will come for the extinct. Their only hope to prevent the rip and tear of the eagle's sharp beak and talons is to avoid the attack in the first place. The fear and terror of revolution are their only means to do this.

"Unless the stout and sturdy share the bounty of the earth with the feeble and fragile, humans will continue to feel the wrath of revolution until it ends in our blackness."

Stansfield stared at the Indian before charging his M4 rifle.

"I get the feel that you have a bigger crusade to fight than what perhaps others may have," said the American. "There's a rumor you have personal stakes in this particular battle, Daivat. I've had enough time in this game to tell. I see it in your eyes, Indian. The fight in you is not only for God and country. There's more to the story, I'm certain."

"Listen, Stansfield, the bastards we're trying to take down are planning to kill millions of your countrymen. They want to incinerate innocent women and children. That alone is enough for me to give my best to prevent it.

"If the *Kilij* is successful, the Russians will invade and occupy Eastern Europe and the Caucasus. Another world war will proceed to kill millions more.

"My country will be pulled into the conflict. India's old enemies in China and Central Asia will mass against us. Our freedom would suffer with yours.

"Just because I understand and feel for the hare, doesn't mean I'd choose not to be the eagle. Sympathy for the weak doesn't overcome desire for the strong. My instincts to survive, like yours, are engrained into me by Darwin himself. We are programmed to survive at any cost. Every human being is a survivalist. There lies the crux of the problem - survival for you, and perhaps me, through evolution - and survival for the *Kilij* through revolution."

"Cut the bullshit, Indian..... What is your personal connection to this operation?"

The tall Hindu freedom fighter slung an AK rifle over his shoulder. He slowly walked over to the edge of the breezeway and remained motionless under an ancient Roman stone arch. He faced the small creek flowing along the side of the hunting lodge. Only the sedate sound of flowing water over river rock broke the silence. The strengthening morning sun rose over the mountains in the east and lit the Indian's hazel eyes in a fire burst. He turned his head toward Michael, sitting in the corner cold shade of the breezeway.

"I've worked research and analysis in our northeast frontier states for over seven years. Hundreds of our agents have died in this region. It's a mostly unknown war to America and the CIA. If it doesn't affect Westerners, it doesn't make your news, Michael. But believe me, my region reflects the chaos going on elsewhere in the world. China provides arms and training to communist terrorist separatist groups operating out of Bangladesh and Burma. The Pakistani ISI backs the Islamist groups coming out of Bangladesh. These groups enter our frontier lands and terrorize all who oppose them.

"China and Pakistan have not been morally interested in truly 'freeing' these lands from the Indian state. They simply are interested in creating as much anarchy as possible for our national government. Their goal is to eventually destabilize and overthrow the democratic Republic of India.

"Almost two years ago, during the fierce direct hostilities between my country and Pakistan and China, I was assigned to the Imphal Valley of Manipur. Fighting had intensified that summer in the jungles surrounding the capital. Chinese commandoes and Islamists from Pakistan had reinforced the rebel groups as they made a push for Imphal. Indian forces were in heavy combat around Imphal until the end of last year. Things began to settle down a bit.

"However, this past February, I picked up information that the Chinese PLA and CRC were planning to sell the Bangladeshi *Kilij* two portable nuke devices. 'Babar' would make the payment to the CRC from Berlin. The Pakistani ISI was to assist the transfer of the material from Bangladesh to Pakistan. From there, the ISI would escort and protect the Pakistani *Kilij* to Cairo - where they would hand deliver the nuclear material to Anwar Nejem and the European *Kilij*.

"I was ordered to follow the trail as far as possible, and find the ultimate target for the materials. In Cairo, my contacts informed me of the Condor's terror network. We suspected a target in Western Europe. We and MI6 attempted to stop the transfer to Anwar. A city street shootout in Cairo led to the death of four MI6 and three Indian Intel agents. We were unsuccessful. Anwar returned to Europe with the nukes and went into hiding. The contraband trail went dry, and the nukes were lost.

"Months later, British contacts in Italy informed us that the target was America. This was soon complicated by the unloading of the steel suitcases from the *Katarina* in Passau, Germany. The CIA now had six nukes loose in Europe with a likely American homeland target in the near future. The trails led us to St. Moritz and Como.

"So you see, Michael, how events in tiny Manipur, India, affect the mighty United States of America. Threats to freedom anywhere eventually come home to America, Michael. I am here with you today to provide my services in the defense of your country against savage terrorism from a common enemy. My interest is for America to stay free, in order for my homeland to remain free. It is simple logic. Common mutual survival comes from common mutual patriotism and the love of liberty."

Kakkar nodded at Stansfield and charged his AK-47.

The American kept staring at the Indian.

"There's more to the story, Daivat. The look in your eyes is deep. It seems bottomless. I've seen that look before. Your eyes are full of both love and hate. There's always more to the story when love and hate are involved. These emotions are felt passionately, and also differently. One softens the heart, the other hardens and emboldens it for revenge. The presence of both emotions at once creates an unpredictable animal, particularly when the vengeance is contained for a lengthy period of time. The beholder of the tender and ferocious is dangerous to all around him..... This mission is personal to you..... Isn't it?"

Daivat Kakkar grimaced, trying mightily to hold back rage. He turned away from Stansfield and again looked out over the valley.

"Yes..... There's much love and hate in my heart. I'm unable to hide it, it seems.

"There is a personal side to the story. It is not all 'God and Country' as you say it.....

"Love and hate..... One gives life, the other takes it away.....

"How can both exist at the same time, in the same person?

"But they do..... Believe me, they do....."

Daivat pulled a golden heart-shaped locket from his pocket. He gently opened it and looked at its contents for a while. He showed Michael the photograph contained inside.

"This is my wife, Neha, and my two young sons."

Michael held the pendant, open in his hand. Neha was a beautiful young wife, and Daivat's sons were handsome like the father. He slowly returned the precious keepsake.

The Indian carefully closed the pendant and gently put it back in his pocket.

"Shortly after my discovery of the nuclear plot, the CRC and ISI assassinated my family in Mumbai. One morning, like every other school day morning, Neha prepared to drive the boys to school. She started the car, and it exploded with all of them inside.

"The explosion disintegrated and burned their bodies beyond any recognition. This pendant hung around her neck. It was the only thing the investigators discovered at the scene.

"My life changed that day..... I am no longer the me of yesterday.....

"Love and hate..... That is a very good description, Michael Stansfield..... I am full of love and hate....."

Inside the coffee hut on top of Mount Cornizzolo, Claudia sat with her flight instructor, Yousef El-Amin, studying the details of tandem hang-gliding. While Yousef described the difficulties of maneuvering through a sudden change in wind patterns, Claudia finished her cup of hot espresso. She pulled her blonde hair back into a ponytail and secured it with a pink rubber band. Seemingly uninterested in the Mole Rat's prolonged discourse, Claudia put on red lipstick and stared with her blue eyes at the bearded Jordanian. She lowered the front zipper on her bright yellow Italian ski-suit, exposing her delicious cleavage. She smiled intensely as Yousef stuttered his words.

"Your speech is on flying, and your mind's on fucking. That's why your words are shaky," laughed the Swiss seductress. "Tell me the truth, you want to plunge into me like an Arabian stallion. Here's your chance, Yousef. Fly me into the woods and juice me up."

"Clau...Cla.. Claudia, you're a se... sex.. sexy woman. Wh... Wha.. What I would dddo to taste your fruit."

With only them in the hut, other than the bartender who couldn't keep his eyes off Claudia, the killer temptress pulled down her top. She pinched both of her hardened nipples.

"You can start up here and milk me down to my papaya. You'll never want to eat any other fruit," she smiled, before licking her lips.

"You'll give yourself to meeee?"

"It works both ways, Arab. You'll be giving me some power also. I'll make sure of that.

"Your attractive primitive look thrills me. There's no clean sophistication in your primal appearance. It gives me an interesting feeling just where I like it. It takes me back a million years. I become a jungle woman in your presence.

"I'm wetting through my pants.

"Are you caveman enough to fill me?" challenged Claudia.

"Go for the pussy, Yousef!" yelled the bartender. "If you don't, I will!"

"I'm not selling my pussy, Fuckwad!" shouted Claudia at the coffee server. "You stick to your mocaccinos!"

"Ye... Yea.. Yeah!" Screamed Yousef..... "I'm not sharing herrrr!"

The Mole Rat accidentally knocked over a cup of coffee onto his lap. He cringed and nervously laughed it off.

"If your balls weren't on fire before, they are now! They must be burning up!" grinned Claudia.

"You are a fine looooooooking woowoowooman..... Perhaps, the most beautiful woowoowooooman I've ever seen," stuttered the Jordanian.

"Since we both like each other, I think we should not waste time and consummate our friendship," smiled the Swiss bombshell. "Let's fly into one of these fertile valleys and explore. Show me all your animal spirits, caveman.

"Get me some German Schnapps before we go split the turf, handsome Yousef. It gets my hot papaya sweeter and juicier," winked Claudia.

Yousef stumbled out of his chair and retrieved the alcohol from the bar. Claudia took a big swig from the bottle and said, "I'll save the rest for the jungle."

The Arab prepared a purple hang-glider and sheepishly gave final instructions to his student. Claudia played Led Zeppelin's "Whole Lotta Love" on her music-box. The sexy CIA agent put on French sunglasses, gripped the handle-bar in her tight-fitting ski jumpsuit, and ran off the side of the mountain into the cool morning air with Yousef.

Julius Stansfield peered through his binoculars and saw the purple wing come off Mount Cornizzolo. The target flew into the valley and moved north towards Canzo and Valbrona, only two miles away.

The captain looked again at the Corni di Canzo's rocky horns and murmured to himself, "The Mole Rat doesn't stand a chance against that crazy bitch."

He yelled down to Michael and Daivat on the first floor, "Lot's roll!"

In a lakeside villa, halfway between Como and Blevio, John Mullen and Thomas Whitmore sat with communications equipment eavesdropping on a conversation. The Turkish banker Bahadur Barakgazi in Berlin, and Anwar Nejem, just a quarter-mile north in his Blevio mansion along Lake Como, were setting plans for an important meeting.

"I'll arrive in Como tomorrow night," said Babar. "I have the gold arriving in two days..... I want to discuss the final terms with Sheng Hong personally. You are not, for any cir-cumstances, to meet with the Chinese brother outside my presence. Remember my strict guidelines, Anwar. I negoti-ate all transactions..... If the CRC has the material we want, and I can lower the price, the deal will be made. If these criteria are not met to my liking, the *Kilij* will proceed with the plans already implemented..... I don't trust Sheng Hong and the Chinese infidels. They treat us like they do the Afri-cans. They're using us against the Americans because they don't have the courage themselves. I hate these pan faces almost as much as I do the wicked Westerners. I'd prefer to destroy both their cultures..... Today America, Anwar - tomorrow, the stinking Asiatics."

The glider came down the valley. Claudia listened to Led Zeppelin and pointed to a clearing at the base of the Corni di Canzo. Yousef leaned on the purple wing and descended across the treetops of the green forest, scatter-ing mountain goats along the hillside. The wind died as the glider coasted onto the grassy plain.

The Mole Rat and his lady unstrapped from the flying machine. They ran hand-in-hand into a thicket of cypresses next to a small lake. Two young deer scattered away in front of them. The couple stripped bare by the blue water. Yousef grabbed a blanket from Claudia's backpack.

"This is beautiful!" gleefully shouted the Arab without a stutter.

He lay on the cool grass and covered himself with the blan-ket. He closed his eyes and patted the ground next to him.

"Come to me, pretty lady. Let me feel your beautiful body next to mine."

After a few moments without a response from Claudia, the Arab opened his eyes. Michael Stansfield stood in front of him, aiming a pistol at his head.

"Lombardy is beautiful this time of year!" laughed Michael

"Don't you think so, pretty lady?" the superspy asked sarcastically.

A naked Claudia sat next to Yousef with a large stiletto pointed at his crotch. She carefully lifted one of his testicles off the grass with the blade.

"What's colder, the steel or my heart?" asked the sexpot.

"The ssssssttttttteeel?"

"You don't sound convinced Yousef..... Try again."

"Your heartttt?"

"Yes..... My icy cold heart....."

"I wouldn't think twice about leaving your balls by the lake for the red squirrels."

"Please don't, I neeneeneed them."

"We need them also," smiled Michael Stansfield, still pointing the pistol at the Arab's head.

"I agree..... This forest is wonderful!" Claudia grinned at Michael. "We should start a campfire and have a weenie-roast! I love weenies, even Arab ones!"

Stansfield couldn't contain his laughter. He bit his lower lip and dryly said, "I think I'll pass on the weenies. But nevertheless, Yousef, we're happy you've come down with your woman to enjoy the forest scenery with us. This land is bucolic beauty. Everyone should have the opportunity to enjoy this place at least once in their life."

The superagent looked across the green field of grass and waved over his brother.

"Let's talk business, Yousef..... A friend of mine is very interested in meeting you. He'd like to ask you some questions. I suggest you answer them carefully. Your life and the welfare of your family depend on it. Do you understand, Arab?" asked Michael.

Yousef nervously nodded – yes.

Daivat Kakkar stood nearby, providing cover with his AK-47. Julius Stansfield walked up to Yousef and asked him to stand.

"Let me explain..... We know of the *Kilij* plans to attack America. We are aware of the dealings between the CRC and the *Kilij*. We are aware of the Turk banker and Anwar Nejem. We know of the nukes. We are following Sheng Hong, and know of his impending materials transfer to the *Kilij* and Anwar. We know of the hang-gliding plot over American cities and the desire to kill millions of our people.

"My team and I are here to stop all this before it gets to our homeland. We are prepared to kill each and every one of you in the process."

Julius smiled at Yousef like a fox planning his next move.

"We have taken the liberty of bringing your wife and young daughter from Jordan to sunny Italy. They are safe under our care. Don't worry, Yousef," said Julius Stansfield as he grinned at the naked Arab trembling in the cold. "If you cooperate with us on this mission, you will see your family again. We'll provide protection for you. On the other hand - If you don't help us, Yousef - we'll kill you; and you'll never know what happens to your family."

Captain Julius Stansfield pulled his pistol and placed it up to Yousef's left temple. The Jordanian crapped down the back of his thighs and onto the green grass.

"We need to know several things.....

"Where are the nukes? And what are the final plans for them?

"Who works with the Turkish banker in Germany, Egypt, and Turkey?

"How large is the banking empire behind the *Kilij*?

"What is Sheng Hong transferring to the *Kilij*? And where is it being stored?

"What are the *Kilij* networks in America and Europe?

"Where are the *Kilij* safe houses in Italy?

"These are simple questions, Yousef. You can help answer all of them."

Julius looked up and down at Claudia. She stood nude next to the Arab, still holding her knife near his tight scrotum.

"You should invite this sexy woman to Anwar's house by the lake in Blevio. We know he has a weakness for pretty things. And things don't come any prettier than this.

"Naturally, always keep in mind that your wife and child are in our custody; and only we will decide whether you ever see them again. Your cooperation will decide your fate.

"This fit and attractive lady – with fine golden hair - without a blemish or fault of skin, muscle, or bone - with sensuous eyes, lips, and mouth - with every curve and bump in perfect proportion and position – exuding sexuality from every pore – will track you night and day. She seems made by God for making love; but take it from me, she is more carnivorous than a hungry tigress in heat. She can make you a martyr in less time than it takes her to put on red lipstick. Believe me, I know. She is more malevolent than Satan. Give her an opportunity, and she will show you how sharp her horns are."

CHAPTER 17

Patriotism

I had known Sarah for only a few days, but it felt much longer. Her ways were familiar to me, as if attached to my being somehow. Her spirit and mine seemed to be old friends. Her manner of speech, with inflections on certain words with her voice and eyes, and the delicate but strong movements of her hands, were remembered in my mind. In some extraordinary mystical way, she had been part of my life all along - this or some past one. Somewhere in the recesses of our souls, we had been tied.

I had first seen her only a week before, at a formal dance in Washington. My attention was caught initially by her physical beauty. Her strawberry blonde hair, the almond shape of her blue eyes, her face with perfect lips, and her fine figure, all captured my eyes at the beginning. Yet, I was drawn to her by something else.

She had a magnetic power of being that conquered me. It pulled me in to her without any objectivity on my part. I didn't calculate or reason my approach, or consider different designs for meeting her. I simply went to her side as if she was expecting me. And the funny thing about the experience was she seemed to be waiting for the special encounter.

For me, Sarah was a unique and bewitching creature. She was glamorous and sensuous, and alluring in every detail. She spun a magical web of love around us in a puff of smoke. I couldn't get away from her spell. I was caught in it, like a small helpless boat at sea in the eye of a hurricane.

Our first date was unusual. She picked me up at Annapolis, and we drove towards Ocean City for the weekend. A young and electrifying exotic beauty behind the sporty wooden wheel of an old red Alfa Romeo Spider – Sarah was a sight to behold.

My classmates looked in awe as she drove up to Bancroft Hall in the convertible, and sat waiting for me. Every pair of free eyes stared down on her from every window, astonished at her sexy look. Her wind-tossed golden hair, and long strong legs in short shorts by the stick-shitt, gaped open many mouths. She'd look up and laugh at them, only entrancing my friends even more. It was good to be young and able-bodied in the presence of such magnificence.

On the way to the Maryland seashore, we stopped for ice cream. She held the dark wooden steering wheel with her left hand, and the cherry vanilla cone in her right. She'd occasionally pass the cone to her left while changing gears, leaving the wheel unattended on the highway. She would do this elegantly, like a professional Grand Prix car racer on a weekend jaunt into the European countryside. I ate my chocolate cone, staring at her sun-tanned legs. She'd look over occasionally and catch my focused stare. Sarah would smile and lick her cherry vanilla.

"Are you in school?" I asked.

"Georgetown," she said.

"What do you study?"

"Words," she laughed.

"Words?"

"Literature..... I'm an English Literature major..... I study the power of words to describe emotions."

"That's interesting."

"Words can carry a punch, Mark, perhaps a stronger punch than your battleships," she smiled, exposing perfect white teeth behind the sensuous pink lips.

She looked over at me, her eyes shaded by amber glass, and shifted gears. The red Alfa sped down the highway to the sea.

"The great tales of Shakespeare and the beauty of English romantic poetry..... There are no written words more beautiful than those," beamed Sarah. "They let you see light through the darkness of night. You hear the song of life in the words. They quicken your pulse and enliven your blood. They can make you cry in sadness and in joy. Love and ruin are explained with letters of the alphabet. One's mind can see the pictures. The power of words, Mark....."

The red Spider sped even faster. I thought the red paint on the old 75' Alfa would peel away with the wind. I saw she hadn't buckled her seat-belt, and I slowly unfastened mine.

We arrived at her family cottage by the sea in the early evening. We changed into our bathing suits and walked out to the beach. There was an early summer warm breeze and a quiet ocean at sunset. The sands were empty of people.

"Take off your shorts," she demanded, while stripping bare. She ran and dove into the surf under the moonlight. I joined her.

We relished in our bodies for hours. After making love many times on the beach under the stars, we fell asleep – curled in each other's arms.

I awoke at dawn with the sound of waves breaking on the shore. A warm wind settled on our naked skins. Sarah sat observing the horizon.

"Have you been awake long?" I asked.

"Not long.....

"I never miss a sunrise, Mark. The beginning of a new day is special for me. It's holy."

I sat up also and placed a towel around her cold shoulders. She instantly removed the drape.

"I need to feel the warmth of the sun on my skin," she said, smiling and looking into my eyes.

I smiled back.

"It's here that one can truly appreciate the power of words, Mark."

"What do you mean?" I asked.

"I'm closing my eyes," she said. "Look at the horizon and express to me in words what you see. Force my mind to sense the beauty of a new day."

I gathered myself, pulling away from Sarah's energy. I needed to, in order to perform my task. I realized how important this exercise was for her.

"The interface between sky and sea is defined. The dark sapphire ocean is marked from the heavens by a pumpkin orange band of dull light. Above the band, the azure and oyster shell white of sky spreads over us like a shroud. A lonely star, here and there, can still be seen bright in the darker shades of blue. A melon of a sun rises half-way above the special line of God's nature, beaming its radiance in narrow geometry towards us. Rays of diffuse light shoot into the celestium, silhouetting the lower hanging clouds. The brilliance of the sun squints my eyes..... There is glory in what I see."

"There is glory in what I sense also," said Sarah, opening her eyes.

My lady kissed me, using her tongue to soothe mine.

"So you see, Mark..... There is a Shakespeare in all of us..... The power of the word can describe the glory of the universe. It only requires an open mind and heart. From here to eternity - you will think of me, and I of you – with each sunrise. Let our lips meet with every new day. Let my love fall on you with the warm wind and hopeful sunshine of morning..... I love you, Mark....."

"I love you, Sarah....."

The power of a beautiful woman, graceful in every way, had opened the world to me. Her words and thoughts illuminated the earth and sky in a new way. I was alive with love and its energy. The power of the word was mine.....

I drifted back to my reality, away from Sarah and her love. I returned to my duty of saving the United States of America. My mind focused on the ugliness of human beings, leaving behind the sacred goodness of my girl.....

Accompanied by James Thomas, I wheeled myself into the Chez Voltaire on the lakefront promenade. Sheng Hong had invited us to dinner at Como's most popular French restaurant to further discuss our pending deal. The headwaiter led us through open French doors to a private dining area on the outside terrace by the moonlit lake. A large table was set up for a sumptuous dinner under the stars. Three tall white scented candles provided additional lighting. Two young attractive Chinese women, immaculately dressed in white, stood next to Sheng Hong. The Chinese tycoon spy sat at the center of the table, patiently waiting for me.

"Good evening, Mr. Harrity and Mr. Jones. Welcome to the finest spot for the finest food in northern Italy. The ambiance could not be better. It was special-ordered just for you, Mr. Harrity. Clear skies, cool breezes off the lake, and the moon and stars have accommodated us for a splendid dinner together. I hope you and Mr. Jones have an appetite for rich French food tonight."

Sheng snapped his fingers, and the women in short tight dresses poured Perrier-Jouet into large crystal champagne glasses.

"Let us toast to a successful arrangement, Mr. Harrity.....

"As the famous Prussian king, Frederick the Great, once said, 'The greatest and noblest pleasure which men can have in this world is to discover new truths; and the next is to shake off old prejudices.'

"Cheers, gentlemen....."

Sheng drank the whole of his glass. More was poured for him.

"French champagne is the classic spirit!" shouted the fatman, after smacking his lips. "It is cool and sharp on the tongue, and its effervescence is felt down to the soul. Like a beautiful woman's kiss, it is a drug for the senses. It brightens the mood and sets the pace for an interesting evening.

Particularly so when it is served by such enchanting, sensuous ladies."

The rich communist grinned and passed his hand under the back of one of his assistants' dress. He massaged the standing young woman's ass for several minutes with one hand, while drinking champagne with the other. Her face remained expressionless, and her tall body tightened into an erect, rigid posture. The woman's eyes fluttered, but that was all.

"Have you had time at the Garibaldi over the past few days to consider our deal any further, Mr. Harrity? Or have the seductive powers of Como enthralled you into altered consciousness?" asked Sheng in a tart manner.

I stared at the Chinese girl's pretty face while the fat tycoon aggressively groped her from the rear. Unconsciously, the girl's eyes finally closed as she bit down on her left lower lip. The communist pig extracted his hand and wiped it with his dinner napkin.

"My consciousness, Mr. Sheng, never strays from the deal at hand," I assured, now directing my steely stare at the fatman. "A mind asleep is a deal lost, my father would often say. I believe in quick decisiveness. Much like you - Mr. Sheng - if I find a way in, I go in all the way."

I drank champagne and watched the girl elegantly step off from the table.

"$230 million in gold is an expensive proposal for the works in your possession, Mr. Sheng. My advisors, Alvarez and Westcott, believe I'm being overpriced. My intuitions tell me the same. Perhaps, you have miscalculated your proposal, Mr. Sheng," I stated forcefully.

"There is much inflation in the world, Mr. Harrity," retorted the CRC delegate. "Most of it produced intentionally by America and her corrupt bankers.

"I do not set the values on priceless items. The market dictates to me the worth of these masterpieces. I have recently been offered $27 million for the George Washington Declaration of Independence," said Sheng, before snapping his fingers and pointing to his empty champagne glass.

"Freedom is becoming a very expensive commodity, Mr. Harrity. I suspect the less there is of it in the world, the more people search for it in material goods. They want to own a piece of the 'American Dream'. Washington's handwritten anecdote on the manuscript only entices the dreamers that much more, Mr. Harrity.

"They are dreaming, aren't they - Mr. Harrity?"

I looked quizzically at the short stubby communist. His fat belly and disgraceful behavior betrayed him. Here was a man interested only in himself - unable to dream of anything substantial, other than monetary wealth and power. I was disgusted by his presence.

"What do you mean exactly, Sheng? Are you implying to my senses that the 'American Dream' doesn't exist? Or that it has never existed? Do you mean to say freedom, cultural liberty, and the pursuit of happiness are all imaginary ideals of the American mind?

"I need to understand your implication clearly, Sheng. Or perhaps, I may begin to think your mind is as soft as your belly. I wouldn't want to believe this of someone with whom I am negotiating the purchase of rare pieces of human creativity. It may put you at a distinct disadvantage."

"I did not intend to insult you or your country, Mr. Harrity. Please do not misinterpret my comment. I am not a miscreant. I was simply stating an unbiased, objective opinion. The facts, I believe, speak for themselves. Naturally, an American would be the last one to see the truths.

"The reality is the 'American Dream' is only a figment of the American public's imagination. Is it not?

"A country maintained by tremendous military power - but also saddled with endless amounts of social, political, and economic chaos. A sick nation torn by racial disharmony, religious persecution, and uneven and unfair economic stratification. A culture in perpetual war - overextended materially, exhausted morally, and corrupt politically.....

"Can you describe America any better than I, Mr. Harrity?"

"Your description may be accurate from your obtuse Chinese eyes, Mr. Sheng. But it is not accurate through American eyes.

"Unlike China, we are still a unified nation. Long ago, our founding fathers saw to it that disharmony was to be accepted as part of the political process. Our civil war and national reconstruction only cemented the fact further in the American mind.

"We have had social, political, and economic issues over the past fifteen years, but so has the rest of the world - in multiples of ours. Racial and religious disagreements are to be expected in a free society where free speech is allowed. Americans may argue, but we are still united in cause and effect.

"It is easy to see our faults, Sheng, when viewed from a far off coast. But believe me, the spirit of the American people is as strong as ever. Unlike most of the world, we have hope for a better tomorrow. Our faith in the American Constitution, and in our people, is limitless. Like my mother would say, 'American Amaranth' is timeless. It is eternal. It is everlasting."

Sheng Hong was taken aback. He was not accustomed to dealing with a mind so set and determined. I was in a wheelchair physically, but my senses were lofty, quick, agile, and piercing. The communist devil collected himself and carefully measured his thoughts.

"What is 'American Amaranth', Mr. Harrity?" Sheng asked politely.

"The power of the word," I answered, thinking of Sarah and my mother.

"American Amaranth is my family creed, Sheng. It is my method of life. It is the strict compass by which I navigate. American independence is founded on love and hope, honor and courage, liberty and justice. These virtues form the common base of our lives. It is the source of our freedom and power. Without these virtues, America falls.

"As Americans, we wish this creed upon all..... It is an invention for the world, Mr. Sheng."

"What if the world rejects this American creed of yours?" asked the red spy. "Why should any country desire the procedural plans of another? Perhaps the rest of the world wishes to follow a different course from that of America's. Are they not entitled to choose for themselves how they wish to be governed?

"It seems the United States, since the times of Teddy Roosevelt, wants our planet to function according to her rules and dictates. America appears to order, coerce, and corner other countries into ultimatum conundrums. Forced choices may not be in the best interests of the people. There is much rejection of your creed around the world, Mr. Harrity. I don't think you can argue the fact. I believe the Chinese model of state capitalism was perhaps a better one for the world."

"I find it interesting and intriguing that a rich capitalist tycoon from Taiwan entrusts so much in a socialist form of tyrannical government control. Especially one that has spent the past seventy years trying to topple your island home's system of rule," I said with a bewildered look.

"I won't argue countries 'must' follow America's example. But I will say it may behoove them to at least try.

"Chinese mainland culture is ancient, but it is closed. Politically, socially, and economically, it is a robotic society.

"Was there more spread of wealth among the populace in the People's Republic or in the USA? How well accepted were immigrants into PRC culture? How accepted were Christians and Jews in mainland China? Were they as accepted as Chinese Taoists or Buddhists in America? Were Africans freely admitted into the People's Republic?

"Chinese culture on the mainland was not plural from a religious, racial, or ideological perspective.

"Could people debate and discuss political choice in China? Could they vote freely? Was there free press or freedom of speech? Did the right to bear arms exist in the People's Republic?

"I don't believe any of these questions were debatable in the past. However, they are debating these questions now in China. The present civil struggle will decide the future course of their country.

"I hope for peace on the Chinese mainland. But it will come with a cost. True freedom always does. If freedom does not exist entirely, then it does not exist at all. 'Selective Freedom' is not the best model for government. Only 'Total Freedom', with a strong system of justice to regulate it, can be a model for the evolution of a productive and creative world. That is my opinion," I declared strongly.

Dinner and wine were brought to the table. The space went silent, except for the occasional clink of a glass. One of Sheng's girls went to the edge of the terrace, overlooking Lake Como, and sang old romantic Chinese folk melodies. Sheng Hong became more self-aware. He softened with the wine and song.

The tycoon looked across the table at me and nodded.

"I was born Taiwanese in the sixties. My family originated from Qingdao on the mainland - a coastal city in northeast China on the Yellow Sea - across from the southern Korean Peninsula. My father was an industrial laborer, my mother was a homemaker. My upbringing on Taiwan was poor but not deficient of love," quietly said Sheng.

"After becoming a wealthy businessman, I took my first trip to the mainland in 2001. I returned to my family's Qingdao, now a bustling metropolis of several millions. It was quite an experience.

"My father and mother were born in Qingdao in the late 1930s, during the Japanese occupation. Imperialism has been formative in the history of Qingdao. The city was occupied by Germany from 1898 to 1914. They considered it a strategically important port, and based the German Navy's 'Far Eastern Squadron' there. With breakout of World War One, the German Navy abandoned all Pacific ports and returned to the European theater of operations. Opportunistic Japan occupied Qingdao and other German possessions in the Far East. Qingdao was finally returned to Chinese control in 1922.

"Unfortunately, the Japanese returned to China in 1931. With their plans for territorial expansion along China's east coast, the Japanese re-occupied Qingdao in 1938. During the years of Japanese occupation, more than 35 million

Chinese were killed or wounded. It was our greatest national calamity.

"After World War Two, the US Navy's Western Pacific Fleet Headquarters was based in Qingdao. My father's father worked on the US base as a day laborer until the Red Army entered Qingdao in the late spring of 1949. My family was not communist. They fled to Taiwan.

"Qingdao became the headquarters of the PLA Navy's Northern Fleet. It was heavily damaged by US missile and air attacks during the last war.

"My paternal grandfather fought with the Chinese resistance against the occupying Japanese forces. Much of his fighting was concentrated in the hills and mountains surrounding his home of Qingdao. On my trip to mainland China in 2001, I explored the old mountain bunkers and tunnel networks where he spent much of his time during those years. Pillboxes and sentry houses were connected by tunnels and natural caverns to ammunition depots and mess halls. The networks were all reinforced with steel and concrete, and heavily fortified against intruders. Occasionally, a tunnel would lead out to a machine gun nest built out of solid rock on the mountainside facing the Yellow Sea. It was eerie to walk the same tunnels my grandfather walked and bled in. I carried a kerosene lamp to light my way, just as my grandfather had done so many years ago. At the time, the experience made me yearn for a unified China - a China at peace with herself and in charge of her destiny. That is our dream, Mr. Harrity. It appears impossible at present. As you well understand, civil war is a messy proposition.

"So you see, Mr. Harrity, Americans aren't the only ones who wish for unified national independence and freedom. We all do in our own way. We may have different opinions regarding liberty, and its many forms of expression, but you and I are in agreement regarding the desirability of its totality.

"In the fervor of our individual national patriotism - we often forget about world peace, and our own individual country's repercussions on that peace. There lies the danger of patriotism and nationalism.

"At certain times in history, nations' struggles for freedom may become anarchic. Political disorder may spread, and lead to the epidemic social convulsions and geopolitical earthquakes we've seen around the world the past several years. Freedom is a difficult commodity to control; and thus, some governments choose to allow it only selectively - refraining from its totality to prevent chaos. This does not signify we would not wish for its totality in the future."

"I understand the dream of attaining 'American Amaranth' is not monopolized by my people, Mr. Sheng. Our spin on freedom is not the only spin. Yet, I recognize the ideological desirability it may have for the planet. Practically speaking, I also understand its difficult task. Much of the present world may be ill-equipped to handle it. Each culture must try to find its own form of just government to rule its people. They must search for their own particular 'spin' on freedom and constantly work to improve it with time.

"However, with all that said, I still believe 'Total Freedom' with a strong rule of law - if achievable - is the best form of government. Limiting liberty in its totality, or allowing it without a strong rule of law, only increases the risks of tyranny in the future. In my country, the spiritual concept of 'American Amaranth' stabilizes the nation and prevents it from falling into tyrannical chaos. Its purity of purpose sustains us ideologically.

"You must also recognize the importance of the US Constitution and Declaration of Independence for the American people. They have provided us a legal roadmap for freedom. They have kept my nation balanced in times of trouble. We remain free and whole after more than two centuries. That reality is the 'American Dream', Mr. Sheng. It's a testament to the enlightened men who devised these articles of liberty, and to the thoughtful people who followed the power of the word.

"As the famous French philosopher, Voltaire, once said, 'Man is free at the moment he wishes to be'."

CHAPTER 18

The Firecrest's Song

Young Julian Stansfield looked into his mother's eyes as he held her head slightly off the pillow with one hand and placed a glass of room temperature water up to her mouth with the other.

"Drink, Mother..... You must take water. You're perspiring out your fever," he said.

The lieutenant saw his mother's bloodshot blue eyes deeply sunken into hollow orbits. Her beautiful face was ravaged by a merciless disease. Ann's facial bones screamed out her fate; they were sickly prominent like an unearthed skull.

This was an enemy Julian couldn't fight. A blood cancer was eating Ann away, and her son couldn't do anything about it. His mother's short blonde hair was matted on her head, wet from the night sweats. A once elegant white skin was mottled with a purpuric rash, and tiny petechiae covered her body. The red spots were indicative signs of poor coagulation from leukemia. Physically, there was only sick skin, atrophied muscle, and weak bone left of her.

But above all, it was his mother's eyes that told the story. The orbs were filled with melancholy. Great sadness and regret channeled out of them like beams. As water flowing down a mountain stream, Ann's life rushed from her. Dreams, hopes, and aspirations had died long ago. Now her body followed her soul. Julian wished to ease her from this world and into the next, where his father and brother waited.

"Mother..... You spoke Bobby's name while you slept," whispered Julian, as he repositioned Ann's head back on the pillow. "You didn't say very much I could understand, but you repeated his name many times."

"I was dreaming of you and your brother," replied Ann with a tender weak voice. "My boys.... We were on the boat with your father. It was a handsome day on Lake Michigan. I sat with Bobby, watching you and your father man the sails. Bobby laughed while I played with his golden hair..... But I mustn't speak of that..... Too painful, Julian," gently uttered Ann, as she closed her eyes.

"Yes Mother, I understand," softly said Julian.

Only pain filled his mother's life now, he thought..... He pulled the bed sheets around her and returned to the chair by the bed. Julian rested his head back and took a deep breath.

A quiet breeze passed from Lake Geneva, sounding the wind chimes by the window. He closed his eyes and listened to the music. It was a tranquil melody, probably similar to those his father had loved. Peace and hope effused from the song.

Julian opened his mother's journal and fell into her hidden world. It was a lost secret kingdom. It was a stirring story of a metamorphosis, a tale of a girl's change from innocence to hard reality. It was an account of a life lived long ago, but never again revealed or discussed. They were the private recollections and thoughtful impressions of a young woman struggling to stay sane in a crazy world.

The book was also a history of a young beautiful girl hurtling at the speed of light towards the love of her life. Like a crash of a meteor on earth, the chance eventual meeting of two wonderful people would come in a land of destruction, chaos, and suffering. As if strapped into a time machine flight to another era, the sounds, sights, and smells of that hidden world surrounded Julian.

"I felt like I was with her, looking up at the rock and thinking how men could survive all that trauma. Like army ants at war, men came out of their holes and battled each other for control of a stone mountain, desolate of life except for those still fighting. The battle for Monte Cassino and the Liri Valley was emblematic of man's cruelty to man," wrote Julian on the margin of a page in the diary....................

We had fought several weeks to get through the Mignano Gap. I personally cared for hundreds of casualties. Many good American boys died in my embrace. We all hoped for a reprieve, but it was not to be. There were no delays of punishment in the world I lived.

On a cold early February morning, shortly after sunrise, I sat on a mountain ridge facing Monte Cassino. The sun's glorious orange glow radiated gently down at an angle from the east onto the white Benedictine abbey atop the rock. Still pristine, the Allies had avoided dropping bombs on the sacred monastery. We all knew that German spotters used the heights of the abbey to help pinpoint their artillery barrages on key sectors of our lines. But the relic remained untouched by the fire and flying metal of war surrounding her.

I smoked a Chesterfield, while I rested my head back on a smooth stone and thought of the killing that had taken place around this mountain. For two weeks - twenty-four hours a day - the Germans, Americans, British, French, and Moroccans had fought hand to hand for control of Monte Cassino. Some days, hundreds would die for a patch of territory, only to give it back the next day. The dead were piled on top of each other in heaps across the battlegrounds. Unrecognizable mounds of charcoal gray and olive green intermixed. Vultures circled above the piles of dead men, not differentiating friend or foe in their scavenging. I could see all this from a short distance – only two miles away. The sanctity of Monte Cassino and its abbey had grown.

The historic hilltop abbey on the mount, founded in the early 6th century AD by Benedict of Nursia, dominated the town of Cassino and the Rapido and Liri valleys at its base. Cassino was the linchpin of the German Gustav Line defenses preventing travel up Highway 6 through the Liri Valley to Rome, only eighty miles distant.

The heavy and fast flowing Rapido River rose in the central Apennine Mountains, flowed west through Cassino and across the entrance to the Liri Valley, finally joining the Liri

River to form the Garigliano River out to the Tyrrhenian Sea. The Germans held the Rapido, Liri, and Garigliano valleys surrounding these rivers, peaks, and ridges. The fortified defenses of the region had to be overcome in order to liberate Rome before the scheduled invasion of northern France in June 1944. It would take four bloody Allied assaults on the Gustav defenses - between January 17 and May 18, 1944 - to expulse Kesselring's army.

For miles around Cassino and adjacent hilltops, German defenses had been prepared for a long fight. German generals would not be lured by the Anzio beach landings to the northwest in late January. Kesselring would reinforce the Alban Hills east of Anzio and remain steady at Cassino without retreat. The Allies had fallen into a meat grinder, for which they were initially ill-prepared.

I smoked my cigarette and watched the sunrise over the Rapido Valley. It was cold. I wore a dark green woolen head cap, mittens, and a heavy olive drab coat. My hair and ears were tucked beneath the warm covering. My boots, draped in mud and stained with the blood of my patients from the long night before, exhibited the difficult conditions of the war in Italy. The misty air and wet wind on the mountain ridge froze my bones, as I sat looking down on the German defenses.

Barbed wire, concrete pillboxes, bunkers, and blockhouses filled the valley and the face of Monte Cassino. The ridges and gullies between the surrounding peaks were scattered with booby traps, mines, and snipers. Interlocking lines of machine gun fire, flamethrowers, and mortars created an unprecedented killing zone. Up to three hundred meters below the abbey, German defenders sat steadfast in their holes defending the entrance to the Liri Valley.

West of the Apennines, there were only two routes from Naples to Rome. Highway 7, the ancient Roman Appian Way, ran up the west coast into the flooded Pontine Marshes. It was impassable to the Allied army. Highway 6 ran through the maelstrom of the Liri Valley, and the fortifications of the German Gustav Line. The US 5th Army would break their back trying to penetrate the mountain defenses and difficult river crossings.

We had reached the staging area south of Cassino by January 15, 1944. On January 17, the British X Corps forced a crossing of the Garigliano River near the coast. General von Senger's XIV Panzer Corps stiffened the Allied advance, causing 4000 British casualties.

In the evening of January 20, Major General Fred Walker's US 36th Infantry Division assaulted centrally across the Rapido River. Facing the 15th Panzer Grenadiers, only three US battalions successfully forded the river. No armor came to their support, and they were destroyed by the evening of January 22. Over 2100 Americans were killed or wounded.

On January 24, in the mountains northeast of Cassino, the US 34th Infantry Division under Major General Charles Ryder attacked across the flooded Rapido River Valley and into the mountains behind Cassino. Upstream of Cassino, they fought for eight bloody days with the German 44th Infantry Division. Further to the right - French and Moroccan troops fought the German 5th Mountain Division, taking the nearby Mount Cifalco by January 31.

By early February, a US battalion of the 34th Division had reached a point 370 meters from the abbey. German paratroopers and Americans fought hand to hand over bare rock for the advantage. After more than 2200 casualties, the Americans withdrew. The first Battle of Cassino had been won by Kesselring.

I finished my smoke on this particularly cold and clear February morning. Except for the occasional burst of automatic gunfire from afar, the valley below me was quiet and still. Strangely so, the area was peaceful. I closed my eyes and rested on the flat stone awhile.

I thought of my home in Minnesota, and of Mother and Father. I remembered the summers of childhood by the lake, and growing up free of worries. I remembered running barefoot through the farm fields with my friends, laughing and smelling the early harvest in the air. No one was trying to kill me, and no one was dying in my arms. Sweet times for a sweet girl, I thought. Reminders of how life should be, not of how it had become. I rested for several minutes in my alternate universe.

Still with my eyes closed, I listened to the wonderful sounds of a songbird. They were happy sounds, full of energy and hope. There was no tristesse in the call, only love.

I opened my eyes and found a small Firecrest perched on a ledge near me. He had bright olive-green upper parts and whitish underparts, washed with brownish-gray on the breast and flanks. With pride - he displayed a bright orange crest on his head as he sung his heart out, trying his best to attract a lover. I thought it unusual for a Firecrest to be so high up on the ridgeline. They mostly stayed down in the forests. But then again, I realized he had been displaced like everything else around Cassino. He was out of his environment, as I was.

I stayed quiet and enjoyed the Firecrest's love song. I thought of how courageous he was to be so high up, near the hawks which flew from the ridgelines over the valley. He seemed less afraid to die than I was. He sang through his fear. A brave creature he was. I again closed my eyes and continued listening to my bird friend's melody.

In slow development, a low-pitched rumble formed and interrupted the songbird's call. Little by little, the threatening sound intensified, and the small bird was drowned out. Scared, I opened my eyes and looked out over the valley.

A large squadron of low flying B-24 Liberator heavy bombers flew from the south over the valley. Each dropped its payload over Cassino and surrounding hillsides. Nearly one million pounds of bombs crashed down on villages and concentrations of German troops. The roar of the plane engines and exploding munitions hurt my ears in the cold air. My insides trembled with every explosion. German anti-aircraft flak filled the sky as the American planes kept coming. Many times - I saw a burst of red fire in the blue, followed by the sound of a shattered aircraft. Pieces of planes rained down on the valley. With each fragmented B-24, eleven men lost their lives. Our warriors were too low for parachutes or crash landings. No one survived a low altitude hit.

The horror of war in color passed before my tired eyes. It was apocalyptic. My short respite of morning peace had disappeared. Mass death had returned to me, and there were no words to express the sadness of it all.

I gazed at the rocky ledge near me, searching for the brave little bird. He had gone. My friend had flown away to a better place, I hoped. If I could only do the same, I wondered.

As the last wave of B-24s passed on, US howitzers began an artillery barrage on the German emplacements. The eruptions of hundreds of long guns deafened me. Soon, another assault on Monte Cassino would begin. Many more hundreds of American boys would come to our hospital in the cellars of the church below the ridgeline.

Our medical camp smelled of death, urine, and feces. The macabre image of decomposed bodies of American GIs outside the cellars will stay with me forever. Insects and rats crawled over the sacred dead. We wore bandages, soaked in cologne, over our mouth and nostrils as we passed by. It was a horrible sight to behold.

Inside the cellars, we had twelve operation tables working around the clock. There were no breaks during offensive operations. The crowded underground rooms smelled like a slaughterhouse. We were all scared kids - soldiers, nurses, and doctors alike. When we would run out of blood for transfusion, the artillery boys nearby would donate, as would the hospital staff. It was a scene out of Dante's Inferno. It's amazing what the human spirit can endure and tolerate.

I walked down the mountain to our base camp. I continued to search for my tiny singing lovebird friend as I descended. He was nowhere to be found. Perhaps, he had found a refuge from the turmoil of the day. Maybe he would live to find his mate. His song resonated inside of me, a short melody of beauty and hopeful aspiration in an ugly upset world. The natural graces of life were in short supply where I lived.

The Firecrest and his song would become an eternal memory for me. His melody of love would remind me to always search for the beauty and glory in life. It could be found anywhere, and at any time, even in life's saddest moments.

Today, the cellar would be manned by a new unit. Our evac hospital was returning to Naples for redeployment.

They needed us elsewhere. Where could the US Army need us more? It was frightful to think there may be some other place needing our services more deservingly. Was there some place worse than Dante's Inferno? I wondered.

We drove off heading south for rail transfer to Naples. I sat in the back of an open truck, remembering my two weeks at Cassino. The cruelty of man against man was truly unimaginable. I had seen it personally elsewhere in North Africa, Sicily, and at Salerno - but never with the appalling intensity of Cassino. There had been too much blood and death for a girl from the serene American prairie.

We passed through a small village in the valley. Dotted with small gray stone buildings, and beautiful pink and light blue farmhouses, the town seemed untouched by war. Italian villagers walked between homes carrying burlap sacks of food given to them by the Americans. I stared at a young mother, openly breastfeeding her baby as our truck went by. I smiled at her, and she smiled back.

Amongst all the death, there was still life. Hope still existed. Life would go on, I thought..... I closed my eyes, remembered my songbird, and cried.

Julian closed the diary and went to sleep in his chair. He hoped to learn more about his mother while he could.

Julius Stansfield read Ann's album until late in the evening. He got out of bed and stepped to the bar. He took a shot of Scotch whiskey and walked onto the terrace overlooking Lake Como. The Alpine autumn air was refreshing. Como was quiet. The night sky was filled with bright stars which seemed close enough to touch.

Julius remembered his father's trip to Subic Bay in the Philippines before the Battle of Taiwan. The old man had wanted to see him before combat operations with the

Chinese intensified. The admiral urged his son to live by his intuitions in the naval battle to come. He desperately wanted his son to survive and come home. "A father's love", thought Julius.

The captain returned to bed. He turned off the lights and thanked his father.

CHAPTER 19

White Knight

W hen fortunate on this earth, you may live to see thirty thousand days; but in each and every one of them, you'll fight for your life. The contest between body and Time is never-ending. In hours awake or asleep, it goes on. Time vanquishes the physical, pummels it into submission, and entombs the residual. The battle is waged inside each of us every day. No one escapes its wrath.

In the war against Time, Nature can be ally or foe. Our minds decide whether to use the natural world's graces for benevolent creation, or its power for destruction. As we tussle with many combatants, trying to overcome the various hindrances placed before us, we choose our way.

Time's victory over our physical body is inevitable - - we are all fighting at Thermopylae. Yet, regardless of defeat of flesh and bone, the mind and soul can remain invincible. The only essential fuel for the human spirit to triumph, and to drive for goodness, is Love. If there's no appetite or struggle for Love – your body, mind, and soul simply cease to be.....

In my dream.....

There was a wide expanse of green field under a bluish white sky. Fully fledged trees cast their shadows in the warm Carolina afternoon sun. A smell of rain was in the air, downwind from an approaching summer storm. Rumbling thunder from afar was heard. A slow moving stream ran by my side; clear mountain water slid past colored rocks. Thousands of pink and lavender blossoms carpeted the valley, sprinkled with thick clusters of vibrant yellow sunflowers and purple thistles. All things glowed to my eyes in the fading light.

Sarah walked ahead of me, passing her outstretched hands through the tall stands of wildflowers. Separated petals of every living color danced up in windswept circles around her.

She sat by the dandelions; the yellows of sunlight, hair, and flower mixing together into a golden sheen. On her upturned palm landed a butterfly, the bluest of blues. Its fluttering wings slowed to a stop. Sarah smiled and released her gentle creature back into the wild.

The winds increased, and the sky darkened. The thunder became louder, accompanied by streaks of dangerous electric current. The colors of the valley, field and stream, were washed away. The world changed.

Sarah said to me, "Beware the Great Turning."

Her blue eyes moistened as I held her hand. I closed my eyes and kissed her lips. Our embrace was strong, before my sight went black.....

I heard only my racing heart and breath. All other noise was drowned out. I was aware of blood rushing through my brain, and the deep rhythmic inspirations and expirations of air from my lungs. Thick dark gun smoke from mortars and attack helicopter rocketry occluded my vision. What laid in front of me was invisible. I couldn't see the enemy confronting me, but I didn't care. My instincts were to move forward and engage them with all my might. All fear had been lost at the initiation of my actions. I was possessed by something greater than myself. My mind was not of the order to try to understand the power overtaking me. It was supernatural and beyond my abilities to comprehend.

The gray smoke was heavy and still, like a pregnant summer rain cloud about to empty its contents on a dry grassland below. There was no thunder or lightning, just bleak blackness and deafening silence. This was my ominous landscape.

After running several hundred feet through blind darkness, the smoke thinned. Light from the sun became visible. I heard the dangle of my dog-tags on my heaving chest. The bipod at the end of my light machine gun rattled as I raised the M249 in anticipation of the action to come. My feet in combat boots pounded the uneven ground beneath me, pushing forward towards the fury. My arms and legs ached in my sprint.

The familiar sound of Chinese automatic gunfire surrounded me, as I left the false safety of my cloud and entered my inferno in heaven. A high wickedness animated my space. The forces of good and evil directed the scene unfolding before me. Thunder and lightning appeared in my world. Everything went into slow motion, and life stopped in the Hunza Valley.

I held my gun at the hip and spat fire at the enemy. Dressed in mountain camouflage, the PLA troops fell like toy soldiers - one after the other. I ran through them like a skate on wet ice. They all had similar expressions of disbelief on their faces - as if questioning why I was there, and why they were there. Too late. A rush of metal into their mid-sections ended their amazement and bewilderment forever. Their hopes and dreams faded with the smoke. They were no longer for this world.

A Chinese infantry captain, with a whistle in his mouth, raised his pistol at me as I ran towards him. He fired multiple rounds at me, missing with every one. His eyes grew big with my approach. Emptying his gun, the PLA officer lowered his weapon and waited to die with a tranquil smile on his face. He accepted his lost duel fearlessly. He envisioned the 'other side'. He honored me and himself with his expression of chivalry. He too fell dead to the ground, joining his comrades. A devil out of the black cloud had taken all of them in surprise. They were conquered in a frenetic moment of martial valor.

I ran out of men to kill, as I ran out of bullets. I stopped my sprint and stood alone - facing emptiness. In a surreal reality, I had hollowed the battlefield of all life. In just a few seconds, I had removed several dozen enemy combatants from play. I touched my body and felt no pain. I had no blood on me. In disbelief, I turned slowly and sprinted back in the direction from where I'd come. Back into the dark cloud, I faded. The fog of war cloaked my escape. My men and I would all be out of here soon, I thought.

The sounds of copter blades cut through the thin mountain air. The further I ran, the louder they became.

'They are waiting for me,' I said under my breath, running as fast as I could. 'Just a little bit more to go,' I murmured.

I left the black cloud and approached the American positions.

As I reached Callanan and Thomas near the landing zone, I felt a sharp ripping pain in my back. I lost all my breath, falling to the ground next to Callanan.

With the left side of my face flat on the rocky soil, I opened my eyes and saw Marcus. He lay motionless on his back next to me. His eyes looked up to the sky. Blood flowed copiously from his right chest, forming a red pool between us. My right hand was in the crimson, and I felt its warmth. He slowly turned his head towards me, winked his left eye, and grinned.

'Give me that fucking gun,' he said, pulling it from my hands. He sat up and loaded a fresh barrel magazine into it.

The Hunzakut-American coughed up a torrent of frothy blood onto his lap. He removed the pakol hat from his head and placed it on mine. He stared into me with a sure face and shouted above the gunfire and yells of battle, 'It's time to take my sons back home, Captain! It's where they belong, now!'

His expression was of a loving father, not a warrior under attack. His serenity amazed me. Callanan knew he'd die on this day; but also, he'd save his sons with his actions. That realization brought him the peace he needed. It was a worthy sacrifice. He'd stay in the Hunza Valley with his beloved

Amara for eternity. His children would return to America safely. They would be free, and he and Amara would be free. Marcus accepted this fate with ease.

Callanan shot the machine gun into the horde of Chinese infantry approaching our position. I saw enemy fire crashing into the ground around him, throwing the dust of the earth into the air. Still with my face flat on the ground, I watched him with envy. His courage and sense of honor was sublime. I felt lucky to be in his presence on this day. There was no fear in him, only determination. He would not allow the Chinese to kill his sons. They had killed his wife, Amara, and ended his idyllic life with her in Shangri-La. They would kill him also. But he would never allow them to take his boys. I looked at him, in all his fury, and admired his selflessness. He was devoted to keep his children alive and free. He'd now bear the costs of that freedom. I watched sweat pour from him, as did his blood. This was the end he had always expected. After the hail of bullets, he'd return to his beloved Amara. He was composed, accepting the fact with love in his eyes. He had hoped for this end. It was in the Hunza Valley where he would take his last breath. He'd never leave this land. He knew it; and now, I knew it.

Callanan yelled at Jimmy Thomas and two US soldiers who had come from the helicopter to help, 'Get Captain Stansfield out of here! I'm staying to greet my little yellow friends! Besides, I can't survive my wounds..... Now, get outta here!'

I was carried to the helicopter, where Callanan's two sons pulled me on board. As we lifted up from the Hunza Valley, Marcus fired the M249 into the fast coming enemy. We all watched helplessly while the PLA overran his position, killing him with bayonets.

Marcus Callanan found his glory in the Hunza Valley. Martin and Gilbert saw their father die in front of their eyes, unable to help him.

'For freedom and country!' they shouted, before dropping to the floor and sobbing.

I slipped down next to them, cried, and passed from consciousness into my own personal fog of war.....

There was no sound or color. Everything was in black and white. Our ship sailed on a kind sea. A light warm breeze slowly pushed us toward the sunrise in the horizon. Cape Florida's limestone lighthouse stood tall, visible at a distance next to the sun. Serenity was all around me. A peaceful full moon still sat high in the sky, its glow dampened by the rising sun. Venus was in view. Seabirds fluttered in the wind, crying their songs for me. I was sailing home.

I was very young, no older than five or six years. I watched my father work the sails. I marveled at his strength and good health. He had no eye patch. His hair was full and blond. His skin darkened by the sun. Powerful, confident, and courageous, my father was the man I remembered. He turned and gently smiled at me.

At the wheel, my mother sat in full splendor. Her poised elegance radiated kindness, like a halo on a saint. Her fine white skin and jet-black hair complemented her beautiful face and graceful body. My mother was the woman I remembered. She turned and gently smiled at me.

I sat between them.

'My White Knight,' whispered my mother. 'My brave White Knight,' she repeated.

Father took my hand and kindly stroked it with more love than I had ever felt. He looked at me with great sadness and said, 'To all greatness, there is an end. The only thing

*eternal is love. Noble love never dies. It only grows for eter-
nity.'* He held my head in his hands and softly kissed my
forehead.

'Never fear a storm, Mark,' said Father. 'It's only a test of
your moral strength. Be true to your convictions. There will
be many attempts to break your code of honor. At times,
you may weaken and falter; but don't fall. Believe in yourself and defend the things you cherish. Stay true to your
virtues, regardless of the risks and challenges. We are only
what we make ourselves to be. Expect the most from yourself and you will get it. Your instincts and intuitions will be
true to you, and will lead the way home.'

The moon faded from the sky. The light of Venus disappeared from view, as the sunlight blanched the day. The
wind grew stronger and warmer.

Mother held me in her arms and caressed my face. She
pushed her fingers through my hair and looked into my eyes.
Her soul enveloped me like a fire. Her love covered me like
the warm ocean wind.

I placed my ear gently to her chest and heard her beating heart. It sang her praise for me.

She whispered again, 'My brave White Knight, I miss you
so.....'

She kissed my cheek and slowly disappeared from sight.

With tears in his eyes, Father placed his arm around me
and said softly, 'Let's go home, Mark.'

I smiled and tenderly held his hand.....

"Sarah!" I yelled, awaking in my Garibaldi Hotel room.

My heart heaved. I turned in bed and looked out at
Lake Como. The morning sun was peaking over the eastern

mountains. I had slept with the terrace doors open and felt the warmth of the sun on my face in the cool autumn air. For a moment, I couldn't differentiate dream from reality.

My eyes welled with tears, and I whispered to myself, "Sarah, please forgive my American Amaranth."

CHAPTER 20

Manifest Destiny

J im Thomas found me sitting on the terrace. The day was bright and clear. A strong sun overhead warmed us both. Lake Como was a deep blue, contrasting sharply with the green mountains all around it. An occasional gust of cool wind from the Alps reminded you of where you were.

Jimmy could sense my solitude. He had known me for a very long time. He could tell when I was caught in thought. Jim pulled a chair and sat down next to me under the Italian morning sun.

A rustic, finely hand-painted planter, filled with red, pink, and white roses, lined the base of the balcony facing Lake Como. I had picked a red flower and placed it in the left jacket lapel of my dark blue suit.

"Good morning, Jim," I greeted, without making eye contact with him.

I twirled the obsidian spearhead in my left hand and stared at the detailed martial scenes on the flower container. A heavy infantry formation of ancient Roman warriors marched against a well-encamped enemy. Carrying shields, spears, and short swords, the foot soldiers appeared greatly outnumbered.

"What is it about man that he always turns to war?" I asked. "Why has war become such a permanent part of human culture?

"No matter the centuries, nor the scientific and technological advancements of human civilization, we find ourselves perpetually at war. We're not any better off now than those poor devils were two thousand years ago," I said, pointing to the roses with my sharp black volcanic glass.

"It's always America against the world, Jimmy..... Not much different from Rome, I guess..... My father was right..... We can't quite escape war or its consequences.....

"Can we, Jimmy?"

My friend remained quiet. He had seen as much killing as I had.

"The roses are misplaced with scenes of war," I said..... "They remind me of the ones we saw growing wild in the Hunza Valley last spring..... They were everywhere you looked - by streams and lakes, and scattered in mountain passes and fruit orchards..... The colors were spectacular..... What a place that was....."

"They too were contained in a land filled with war," said my friend..... "But yeah, the Hunza was a unique place..... It's hard to explain its idyllic beauty."

"Just as difficult as to describe the horrors of the Hunza," I murmured..... "What contrasts..... Paradise and Perdition..... Heaven and Hell..... Elysium and Inferno..... Violent rage and murder under a blue sky, and on fields of flower.

"The roses don't capture the unimaginable horrors..... Do they, Jimmy?"

"I suppose they can't, Mark - except for us."

"Blood and roses.... They don't seem like a natural pairing – neither in the Hunza Valley, nor here..... Yet, they sure are pretty to look at," I said in a soft tone.

"Tip of the spear, Mark."

"Yeah, tip of the spear," I whispered, tightly holding my obsidian lucky charm.

"You've carried that African rock on all our missions, Mark, but you've never told me the story behind it."

"I would never give up its secret," I grinned. "I'll only say it's an inherited relic of fortune."

Jim Thomas smiled and said, "You are one rich and fortunate bastard, Mr. Harrity."

I looked down at my frozen legs and burst out laughing. The irony of holding my lucky charm in a wheelchair seemed ridiculous for a moment. Jimmy and I appreciated the lightness.

Turning serious, my friend said, "We did have fortune in the Hunza, Mark..... Your bravery saved our lives..... You're alive, and got to see Sarah and the boys again..... I don't know if it was your special Ethiopian glass, or something else, but I've never seen or heard of courage like what I saw in Pakistan..... You amazed me.....

"Do you remember what you did there, Mark?"

"Do I remember what I did there?" I slowly repeated in a low voice.

Jim Thomas could not see my eyes. They were hidden behind dark tinted sunglasses. A long silent pause interrupted our conversation. It seemed to last forever. My blue eyes filled with tears, and my upper lip trembled. I tried to open my frozen heart.

"I reckon dreams remind me often of what happened there, even if consciousness doesn't," I answered. "Like a movie, rewound and played over and over again, I learn a little bit more every time I see it. Most of what I see, though, I don't like. I see many men died in that valley in the Hunza. Some were boys. Most were brave. And many had no time to think of their loved ones before they passed from this world.

"Yeah, life is sacred; but it became even more sacred to me after the Hunza. I have sanctified that valley in my mind. It is a holy place. The more I remember, the holier it gets."

I put the obsidian lucky charm in my left breast pocket. I gripped the sides of the wheelchair. My knuckles blanched noticeably.

"I remember the courage of Marcus Callanan. He commanded me to take his sons home. He was going to die in that valley so we could get home to our families. His children were going to live on, he was not. He left them a legacy of love and honor. What more could you expect from your father?

"While awake, the whole thing is sometimes a blur. But in my dreams, the moments are captured and recaptured again and again. With every dream, a few more details become apparent. It's as if my mind wants me to know the truth, but only a little at a time - protecting me along the journey.

"The dreams are now more complete, coming alive as if I was still there - the faces of those Chinese infantry boys, and the brave PLA captain who stood his ground and didn't cower from my attack. He firmed up and stood at attention, smiling as I approached. He had lost his duel, and acknowledged it. What things we do when placed in harm's way, and see our own end in sight.

"I remember the crimson pool of Marcus' blood, and my right hand falling into it. It was still warm with his life. I stared at my fingers in the blood and couldn't retract them. I needed to maintain the connection with this man.

"In all the dust and din of battle, Marcus winked his eye at death. He knew he'd save his sons....."

Like a brother, Jim Thomas took hold of my hand. "I was there and saw the movie played out in front of my eyes, Mark. I have never seen an act of conscious courage like what I saw you do in that valley near Shishkat Bridge. Your selfless actions saved the mission team and the crews of two helicopters from certain death. Your courage allowed the opportunity for Marcus to save his boys. If I hadn't seen it with my two eyes, Mark, I suspect I wouldn't believe the accounts. But I was there watching the whole thing go down. You were possessed, I think, by a power much greater than all of us. It's inconceivable you survived the action; but you did. I'm alive today because of your bravery in that valley, Mark. All of us who were there will honor you for as long as we live."

"Conscious courage?" I doubted. "How insensible that sounds. I didn't think much before I acted. It was more an unconscious reaction for survival. The moment took me away."

"You're wrong, Mark..... All courage is conscious," said Thomas. "The realization of the danger and risks is part of its very definition. You understood your own mortality, but still proceeded with the action. That's the basis of your Medal of Honor. You did what you did, irrelevant of the consequences to life. You accepted your own death. You threw your life to the wind. You measured the risks and took your chances in an attempt to save your men. It all stems from the love you have for them and for your country. That's what makes it so honorable, so unique – Mark..... I love you for that..... You will be my brother for as long as I live."

Jim Thomas embraced me in my wheelchair. He then walked over to the white roses and picked one for his lapel.

"White goes well with black," he laughed, raising my spirits. "Now, Mr. Harrity, let's go to our lunch appointment with our friend - Mr. Sheng."

An hour later, Jimmy and I were seated in a large hall at Sheng Hong's lakeside Italian villa. The 16th century estate sat on the southeastern shore of Lake Como - a short distance across the lake from the Garibaldi Hotel, and two homes south of the Egyptian Anwar Nejem's palace.

The hall took up most of the third floor in the four-story villa. Many glass doors opened out onto a terrace by the lake. High ceilings, white Carrera marble floors, and giant painted frescoes on the walls gave the room an 'Old World' European charm. The wall paintings depicted Dante's journey through the nine circles of Hell, from the 14th century epic poem - *Divine Comedy*. A music system played the aria, "Ebben? Ne Andro Lontana", from the Alfredo Catalani opera - *La Wally*.

I stared at an antique Chinese carved red sandalwood panel which ran for more than forty feet along the bottom half of a wall. It was carefully painted with military scenes, and encrusted with thousands of pieces of silver, gold, precious jade, yellow amber, and differing shades of red and green tourmaline stones. The panel contrasted with the European features of the hall.

The double entrance doors opened, and Sheng Hong passed into the large room. He was followed by Mr. Hsu, and his two young attractive Chinese female aides carrying silver service plates with decanters and crystal glasses. Sheng wore bright pink Bermuda shorts, an open dark blue silk shirt, and gold-rimmed sunglasses. He had pulled his long, greased black hair into a short pony-tail. He wore red Italian leather loafers without socks.

"Welcome, gentlemen, to my home away from home!" declared Sheng, before ordering the women to the bar at the far side of the hall.

He sat at a chair across from me and snapped his fingers twice. Hsu offered us hors d'oeuvres from a large serving platter.

"Those are my favorite - egg toast with white truffle shavings and a thin slice of manchego cheese - all topped with a sprinkle of white truffle oil. White truffles are in season now," smiled Sheng.

"Do you appreciate expensive Scotch whiskey, Mr. Harrity?" asked the Chinese tycoon.

I nodded, yes.

"Our meeting today is informal, but this whiskey is as formal as any spirit can get. It's an extremely rare aged blend which I purchased at auction in London last year. It's been stored in Spanish sherry casks for over seventy years. It cost me nearly half a million inflated US dollars. It's too expensive for the English," laughed Sheng.

The two Chinese exotics - dressed in tight white miniskirts, silk white shirts, and black high heels - carefully poured the liquid gold, a mixture of three separate batches from the 1940s. They gave each of us a whiskey glass with three ounces of spirit. Sheng grinned, and patted one of the girls on the ass as she returned to the bar.

"This whiskey may be finer than my women, but it's close," laughed Sheng.

"Salute to Mr. Harrity and his interest in my works of art!" declared the Chinese spy.

"How do you like the whiskey, Mr. Harrity?"

"It has a smokey smoothness with a hint of peat," I answered the prickhead. "This would have been too good even for Churchill."

Sheng drank merrily.

"Being Irish-American, Mr. Harrity, I know you can appreciate quality. You are welcome to drink as you like, and enjoy later the company of my beautiful girls as well..... All of mine is yours..... Please feel free to indulge yourself in all of my finest things.....

"My women are very educated in their tastes and pleasures. They are well trained in the sexual arts. Each is carefully selected by me, after a rigorous personal program of evaluation. You could say they are world-class athletes in the oldest contact sport," smiled the greaseball. "Both of these girls together is quite a pleasure indeed. Let them perform their ballet for you, Mr. Harrity. They will give you an unforgettable experience, perhaps more valuable than my other works of art."

I remained silent and continued to stare at the wood panel. I focused particularly on a scene showing a horseman's decapitation of his enemy with a sharp sword.

"Are you interested in my Chinese art, Mr. Harrity?"

I nodded again.

"That is rare tropical Zitan wood from India. The red sandalwood was greatly prized by the Qing emperors. In fact, all the furniture in this room is made of zitan and belonged to Emperor Qianlong – ruler of China for most of the 18th century. The antique panel was one of his most prized works of art. It depicts his 'Frontier Wars', and the Qing Dynasty's westward expansion into Mongolia, Tibet, and Xinjiang. His military campaigns doubled the size of the Manchu Chinese Empire. Earlier Manchu emperors had defeated the western Mongols and gained control of modern-day Mongolia by the late 17th century. By 1717, the Manchus had a protectorate over Tibet. And by 1759 - the Zunghar Mongols had been defeated, and their state annexed by the Qing Dynasty. The Manchu rulers created the China we knew until recently. Until, of course, the civil war induced by the Americans. The Manchu were astute diplomats, shrewd businessmen, and ambitious warriors. I suspect they sought their 'Manifest Destiny', just as you Americans did in the nineteenth century - Mr. Harrity."

"Many millions of people were killed in those campaigns for 'Manifest Destiny'..... Were they not, Mr. Sheng?" I asked with a wary eye.

"Yes, I believe many were," laughed the fatman..... "Many Zunghars were killed by my ancestors..... Just like in the American Indian Wars, where many native-American Indians were killed by your ancestors, Mr. Harrity..... In continental expansions, there are casualties of war. With the economic and military gains of expansion, there are winners and losers. It is always better to be among the winners and not expire with the losers. Conquests are like unsolicited business takeovers, Mr. Harrity.

"Both you and I are familiar with takeover tactics..... Are we not?

"It's never stealing when there's a contract, Mr. Harrity. Lawyer statesmen write up the papers, and all the dignitaries sign on the dotted lines. Lands are transferred legally to their rightful owners – owners who can increase the productivity of the land for the benefit of the greater masses. With the produce of the land, the fitter races can improve the future for mankind. The less fit can die away and make room for the more fit. It's all done for the welfare of the earth."

I sat back in my chair and grinned at Sheng. "Like the South China Sea was a business deal for the People's Republic of China..... The PLA considered the Vietnamese and Filipinos unfit to manage their rightful regions of the sea, and that the higher intellect and finer breeding of the great Chinese people made them a truer and more efficient developer of the region's bounty. So the communist statesmen of China drew up 'papers' defining true ownership of the South China Sea's energy reserves. Naturally, the People's Republic was performing a duty for the welfare of the earth. The PLA's control of the sea was for the betterment of mankind.....

"It's a complicated game - isn't it, Mr. Sheng? How empires form, grow, and fall..... A vicious cycle of eternal war to expand, capitalize, and defend your gains from competitors who want your head..... An endless struggle between nations, cultures, religions, and races to be the champion..... There are few rules in the game, and the few there are seldom followed. Everyone gets a shot at the top. No one stays there for long, though..... Like my father used to say, 'Eternal power, like eternal life, is a myth.'

"I don't like the idea of 'killing for your country's gain' being equated to a business deal, Mr. Sheng. I don't appreciate the minimizing of human life. I believe life is more valuable than whatever economic gains are won in a business trade. Your manner of thinking is much to blame for the casualties of the 'Great Game'. Unless these ideas are eliminated, our future world will only get progressively more dangerous."

"Are you telling me, Mr. Harrity, that America has not participated in this 'Great Game'? That they have not run the table, sort of speak?

"That is a forked tongue speaking, Mr. Harrity..... Your native Indian-American dead would agree with me, I think..... It is an incredulous statement to make, particularly so among an educated audience."

Sheng stared with big eyes at one of the exotics and snapped his fingers annoyingly. She quickly refilled the greasehead's whiskey glass with expensive golden amber and sat on his lap. Sheng reached into her shirt and fondled her breasts, while she played with his ponytail.

"You shouldn't distress me in that fashion, Mr. Harrity. It's not good for business."

"Please, Sheng, don't insult my intelligence. We both know you love my money more than I love your art. You are likely capable of tolerating anything from me as long as you sense the deal is still open. Your main objective is to empty my pockets, regardless of what distress I may cause you.....

"But I will be fair..... My country has made its share of mistakes," I said. "The Indian Wars and slavery were the two biggest. We have made amends. Everyone living in America today is free to live their life as they wish within the law. We are a nation of laws. We do not massacre our people because of a difference in political opinion. We also do not conquer foreign lands and enslave their people. We advise the people of the world to seek justice and liberty, but we do not enforce it upon them. They are free to choose their own rite of passage."

"Do you not believe in your country's 'Manifest Destiny', Mr. Harrity? Do you not want your nation to be powerful and free of enemy encroachment? Are you not a patriot, Mr. Harrity?" asked Sheng, pushing the girl off his lap and zipping up his pants.

"Do you see me in this chair, Mr. Sheng?" I asked sternly.

"I lost my wife in an automobile accident only a few years ago. I was left a cripple with no hopes of ever walking again. I have evolved several serious medical issues which affect my daily living. My life has taken on a somewhat pathetic character. I'm not much interested in war, or great national economic expansions, or even fine expensive Scotch whiskies for that matter. My only 'Manifest Destiny' is to hopefully awaken tomorrow alive, so that I may try a little longer to make this world a better and safer place for my children to live."

CHAPTER 21

Children of American Amaranth

The dark mountain loomed large over the grounds of the lakeside villa in Blevio. Early autumn night came swiftly in the northern lands of Lombardy. The quiet pitch blackness of the evening was uneasy. Only the occasional mysterious hoot of an owl in the woods interrupted the silence.

The lakefront was also strangely quiet. An old man on a small fishing boat drifted on Lake Como, a short distance from the Condor's *Kilij* compound. There were no other boats. The water's surface was glasslike in the calm darkness, reflecting the crescent moon's subdued shine. The sound of the old fisherman's spinning reel in action was the only man-made noise in the natural stillness of the night.

Men in motion descended from the mountain towards their target. They slowly crept down to the mountain's base and took up their positions across from Anwar Nejem's palace.

John Mullen, in full black camouflage, stopped behind an evergreen oleander tree. Between two thick branches, he looked at the villa through his infrared binoculars. A ten foot high cement wall surrounded the fortified citadel's three acres. There was only a single common entrance and exit gate leading from the house to the street at the base of the mountain. From his elevated angle, he observed four men walking the grounds behind the wall. All were armed with machine guns. Mullen knew there would be more *Kilij* inside the house.

The CIA had sabotaged the electrical grid a quarter mile up the road, creating a blackout in the area. Except for minimal moonlight, Mullen's men were cloaked in complete darkness. Two auxiliary CIA assault teams of six men each, dressed as electrical power company workers, had blocked the road in both directions for a mile under the guise of dangerous conditions.

"Attack Team Alpha in position..... Is support ready?" asked Mullen over the scramble phone.

A quick response came from the auxiliary teams down the road, "We're in lockdown..... The road is blocked..... No traffic will get through for an hour..... Get your asses in and out as quickly as you can..... Support will be provided as needed."

Mullen raised his body from a crouched stance and stared into the woods to the north. He signaled his squad with two short flashes from his red flashlight, and Attack

Team Alpha continued their trek down the mountain to the edge of the street. All of them carried M4 commando rifles, stun grenades, and automatic pistols with silencers.

Daivat Kakkar dashed across the road, pulled himself over the southern end of the wall, and disappeared from view. Thomas Whitmore and Rafael Alvarez did the same on the northern end. Mullen slid along the estate's wall to the entrance gate.

Kakkar slit the throat of a *Kilij* agent with his combat knife. Whitmore strangled one more and knifed another. Mullen and Alvarez confronted the final guard by the gate. The actions were conducted swiftly to avoid detection on the compound's security cameras.

The men, in teams of two, pried open separate side entrances of the dark house. From the poolside, Kakkar and Whitmore confronted an enemy agent in the living room and subdued him with strangle wire. Alvarez and Mullen shot two more with their silenced pistols on the opposite side of the villa. Within seven minutes, seven *Kilij* agents were dead - all in silence.

Mullen used his scramble phone to alert the auxiliary CIA teams down the road. "All deckhands are down..... We're proceeding to search for the pirate treasure..... Send in the clean-up team."

Mullen found the security room, and destroyed the cameras and their back-up generator. His men manually opened the front gate for the clean-up crew. They'd remove the bodies from the premises and leave no traces of the clandestine search inside the house.

"Whitmore, find the mother lode!" yelled Mullen. "Claudia picked up a nuclear signal downstairs at last night's party..... Start there.

"Alvarez, find the safe and clean it out! This scumbag will keep his money and gold where he sleeps. They all do....."

Simon Westcott drove through the entrance in a large electrical power company truck. He ordered three men with him to begin the clean-up. Westcott stayed at the gate and provided vigilant support protection with a light machine gun.

Using a dimpled hand-held detector, the size of a deck of cards, Whitmore walked down a flight of steps to the wine cellar. The detector emitted a repetitive alarm sound as it followed traces of high velocity spin off neutron particles from enriched nuclear material. The increasing cadence led him to a wall behind expensive collector wine bottles. He pulled out a heavy wooden panel, laden with French Bordeaux reds, and found a large lead door with a combination lock.

"Johnny, it's here!" shouted Whitmore.

Mullen rushed down the stairs. He pulled a device from his pocket which automatically turned the combination wheel in three alternating directions: left 28, right 72, left 13. The lock made an electronic click sound, and the door opened.

"That stupid Egyptian bastard!" yelled Mullen. "He brought Claudia down here to show ott his classy taste for French wine..... Wine he's been slowly poisoning with his fucking nukes!"

Two floors above, Alvarez and Kakkar entered the Condor's bedroom. Their attention was immediately drawn to a colossal painting on the wall by a lavish four-poster bed. The portrait depicted an Ottoman Turkish warrior beheading a Byzantine knight in the fall of Constantinople 1453.

"There is no better place to hide a good Muslim warrior's gold," said Alvarez, "than behind the lost head of an infidel Christian knight..... The Condor would keep his gold by his bed, behind the sword."

They tore down the painting and found the safe. Using a device similar to Mullen's, it was easily opened. Inside, there were over $250 million dollars' worth of European gold coins, Russian and Chinese marked gold ingots, and many Swiss gold bricks.

Mullen made another call, "Julius, we have an urgent problem..... I'm with Whitmore in Anwar's cellar..... We count thirteen portable nukes in the mother lode, many more than expected..... And they're all Chinese PLA..... There aren't any Russian marks..... The GPNR nukes aren't here. We're in deep shit..... The plot is thicker than what we know..... These mother-fuckers are planning a wipe-out..... Notify Mark immediately and tell him to move on the China-man..... Claudia needs to hook this son of a bitch, Anwar, now! If he has thirteen here, he likely has many more else-where. The fucker is collecting these things..... We can't wait to move on Sheng and Anwar until we've located the rest of the nukes. Take these sons of bitches alive now and get the information we need to shut this operation down..... Cut out their eyes if we need to, but get the details and the missing nukes! Get moving!" shouted Mullen.

A second clean-up crew arrived at the rear of the villa. The gold and portable nukes were carefully placed into separate compartments of the truck and carted off. Mean-while, Mullen and his men congregated around a table in the kitchen to discuss the situation.

"The night will be long, gentlemen," stated Mullen. "It seems the Chinese are even more involved in this sick caper than we thought. By the looks of things, the PLA has planned a nuclear meltdown of the West.

"The Stansfields will make their moves on the Condor and the weasel Sheng. The Egyptian will eventually figure out he's been stung, and he'll fight back ferociously. His actions will lead us to the rest of the lode. I predict Claudia's distraction will be his downfall.

"I want every airport within a hundred mile radius in lockdown. I want CIA teams on every highway route out of this area. Notify our people in Florence, Bologna, Genoa, Rome, and Naples to be on high alert for *Kilij* actions to get out of Italy. Tell them, 'Shoot to kill.' The missing nukes will not get off this peninsula."

A few miles south in Como, Julius and Michael Stansfield were parked in a black sedan on a chic street in the night-club district. Michael, behind the wheel, looked through a small spyglass at the entrance of a fashionable retro 60s club "No Way Out" - popular among the rich locals and tourists. They had worked the spot for several nights. Anwar and his boys would visit the club every evening - accompanied by the Condor's harem of women - to enjoy the fun, food, and music.

Claudia, who briefly met Anwar at a house party in Blevio nights before, would post herself with the richest and most handsome high rollers in the club. She made sure Anwar could see all her sexy moves.

Last night - after dinner at Anwar's villa, and after accompanying him to the disco - she had dumped the Condor for the most handsome of the revelers - Michael Stansfield. After refusing Anwar's advances the night before, she enraged him even more by her exit with Michael. The Condor had become obsessed with the spy extraordinaire.

Earlier this evening, Claudia told Julius, "I'm sinking the hook deep tonight. He may thrash and fight, but he will not get away. He's mine....."

"Is Mark ready, Julius?" asked Michael, while spying through his glass. "He should be on Sheng's yacht on the lakefront by now. The fatman may try to pull both deals tonight - Mark and the Turk Burakgazi. Our little brother is an invincible bastard - just like you said, Julius."

"A bastard with a giant lion's heart," answered Julius. "To put himself in this position is pure balls. He's been like that since he was a boy. Nothing's changed, except for the wheelchair. He was always so damned impetuous. Father worried his passion and drive would eventually claim him. Dad always worried about that," sighed Julius.

"Do you remember the night in Virginia years ago, when Dad had to go down to the D.C. Jail to bail Mark out?" asked Julius.

"You and I, Mikey, were home for Christmas..... I'll never forget that night..... I had never seen Dad any madder.

"Mark had gone with a girlfriend to a high-school party at a restaurant club in downtown Washington. Apparently, a group of young men at the restaurant started making some inappropriate comments around Mark's girl. 'Little Brother' took offense and went to war with his fists. Within a few minutes, he had left four guys unconscious on the floor - one with a broken jaw, and another with a fractured orbit.

"Dad was forced to pay for the damages at the club and the dudes' medical bills. The attorney's fees to get the charges dropped were even bigger. If I remember correctly, the Secretary of the Navy had to make a few phone calls to settle the situation.

"During his admission interview at Annapolis the next year, they asked Mark about the event. The news had circulated around the Pentagon, I suppose. Mark simply answered that everyone had gotten what they deserved; the pricks had their balls kicked in, and he had gotten out of jail.

"How clear he saw it all - bad guys and good guys..... They lost, and he won..... Pure and simple," laughed Julius.

"You gotta love the kid," smiled Michael.

"Knowing Mark, I think the Turk and the Chinese rat should be the ones worried on that yacht," grinned Michael, looking through the spyglass. "They're the bad guys, and Mark's the good guy. Little brother's mind and spirit don't break. After all he's gone through, he's the toughest badass I've ever known. He's incessant in his mission goals. One-mindedness rules his actions. The boy can't be stopped. He's a hurricane force of nature..... Those scumbags will meet their maker."

"Whatever it is the Chinese Revolutionary Council and Sheng are passing to 'Babar' and the *Kilij*, it won't get off the ship unless it's in Mark's hands," added Julius. "I understand his motivation.' American Amaranth' flows in his veins. It has since he was a kid. It's all personal to him. He is duty-bound to all of us, his country, and most of all - his wife and children.

"Sarah and the boys are his eternal flame. He sets his pace to the flame's light, and everyone follows. Imagine those freaks he wiped out in Washington over a girl whose name he can't even remember. Now put yourself as a fly on the wall, inside the fat rat's yacht on Lake Como. Can you imagine going up against Mark and his 'Eternal Flame'?

"My money is on the good guy. The slimy Turk and communist rat are finished."

Julius, in the front passenger seat, rested his head back and closed his eyes. His mind briefly drifted off to the night his mother died in their Georgetown home, nearly three years before...................

Late in the evening, Father retreated to his private study to be alone. It had been a long day of suffering for all of us. Rebecca cried to sleep in Mother's bed. And earlier, Father had agonized openly in front of us over the loss of his Olivia.

While my brothers and I sat quietly reflecting in a dark living room, we heard Father call for us. We softly entered the study and found Father behind his desk, staring at an old photograph on the wall. The large color picture, taken many years before in Greece, showed a young Olivia and Julian sitting in a field of red amaranth flowers near the base of Mount Olympus. Ancient Greek ruins of a columned temple stood nearby. The tall Corinthian columns provided them with some shade from the sun. It was a beautiful image of two handsome people deeply in love. The love was visible in their faces and their smiles.

Father asked us to sit down with him, and we did. My brothers and I did not speak. We just listened.

'Your mother was a wonderful woman - beautiful, elegant, and graceful to the fullest measure - kind, compassionate, and thoughtful to an extreme..... She was the love of my life..... I can hardly think of getting along without her..... She was my reason for being..... We will all miss her dearly.'

Father continued to stare at the photograph, never once leaving its sight.

'This picture was taken many years ago in Greece..... Your mother had just graduated from Dartmouth..... I was with the *Tunny* on a Mediterranean cruise..... She flew over while I had a few days leave. They were the best days of my life to that time. We drank much wine, made much love, and realized we couldn't live without each other..... It was rather simple, really..... How could I ever be without such a woman..... A woman who could make me feel the things she made me feel..... She was truly a remarkable lady..... Her kiss was like a drug. It numbed you into excitement. It could stop your heart..... Her beauty in every sense was life-changing..... She was what every man wished for. What love is all about..... I could have lived alone with her on this planet forever. I wouldn't have needed anything or anyone else..... She was unique and astonishing in all her ways..... She was my love.....'

Father wiped tears from his face with the palms of his hands and continued to stare at my mother in the picture.

'The sky was blue. The prettiest blue I had ever seen. The field of amaranth seemed to go on forever. The shades of red changing as the flowers swayed with the change of wind. An ancient Greek temple laid in ruins to one side. We walked down the mountain and into this beauty. It was like walking into heaven. We sat down near the columns in the field of the gods and laughed. Olivia placed a single red amaranth in my hand, embraced me, and kissed my lips.

'A young shepherd boy walked nearby with his two baby goats. I ran to him and showed him how to shoot my camera. I sat next to your mother as she smiled. She lifted her face to the sky and shouted, 'I love you.'

'She looks up at the sun in the photograph. The light falls gently on her face and captures all the details of her beauty - her thick black hair, porcelain white skin, and perfect smile. Her lips are puckered. Her handsome dark eyes are open.

'How could she not have made me the happiest man on earth?

'Her magnificence was so much more classical than the ancient Greek columns standing next to her. What a woman she was. What a soul she had..... And she was all mine.....

'We both fell in love quickly. All of you are the product of that love. We have cherished you..... We did the best we could to raise you to be great men - strong men - able to stand for what is right..... People of principle and coura-geous character - children of 'American Amaranth'..... Your mother and I are very proud of you all.....

'But your mother was also very concerned. She saw the world getting progressively more unstable and dangerous. She understood your duties in this world. She saw you all going into harm's way. She had much fear about this. You were all her babies.

'I want you boys to understand a large war is coming our way..... It is inevitable..... You will all be in the middle of it soon and so will I..... Be smart in your plans and depend on your intuitions. Sharpen them while we still have time. I have great faith in your abilities..... But you are my sons. I will worry about you..... I will have to accept the fear of send-ing you off towards the danger..... Take the time we have left to consider your futures. Place your minds in situations of critical decision-making and make your call. Think out the process before you are actually in physical harm's way. It will prepare you psychologically for what is to come..... Save your lives and those of your men. They are sacred..... Always believe in yourself and make decisions accordingly. Trust your intuitions. They will usually be right..... And always remember your mother's faith in you.

'I love you all to the core of my being.'

Father took his stare from his Olivia and looked at each of us individually. A tear swept down his face from his right eye and onto his shirt, darkening his blue collar.

Mark stood and walked around the desk to Father. He embraced him and kissed his cheek. He looked at his face and said, 'Do not worry, Father; we know what stuff is inside our souls. Its essence is strong and noble, like you and Mother. Its light will guide us through rough seas and dark terrain. Its wisdom will provide us clarity, when confusion reigns. Its spirit will nourish us, when we need hope. Its kindness will remind us of love, when none can be found around us. Its promise will bring us back home.'

Father nodded his head gently and smiled....................

A block down the street, two black luxury limousines arrived at the club. Michael Stansfield watched several of the *Kilij* henchmen get out of the first car and line up on the sidewalk in front of the entrance.

"We got Yousef, Aqeel, and Ameer," counted Stansfield.

From the second car, several women exited first - followed by the Condor.

"All our targets are here," said Michael on his phone. "Let's move."

The brothers shook hands..... Michael left the car first, walked around the corner, and was joined by Claudia from the opposite direction.

"How's my girl Swiss banker from Chicago – Jill Lamont?" smiled Michael.

"Ready to roll and kick some ass, like these fuckwads deserve," stated the best female CIA agent in the world.

Claudia and Michael entered the nightclub, arm in arm. Julius Stansfield followed them in, a short time later.

Anwar Nejem, not knowing of the attack on the Villa Vento Forte, had come to the club after dinner at a local posh restaurant. He came with the sole intention of hooking up with the sexiest woman he had ever seen – Claudia - introduced to him previously by Yousef as Jill Lamont, a Swiss banking executive from Chicago with a French accent. The Condor could not accept that she had rejected his advances the night before, and chosen Michael Stansfield for fun and games. He refused to be denied again, and Claudia knew it.

The exciting nightclub played retro 1960s music. Topless "go-go girls" danced in steel cages suspended from the ceiling. The main hall was lit in purple light, hiding much of the drug passing and sexual activity occurring at private tables and small side rooms. A run of music by "The Doors" had just begun when Michael and Claudia entered the main hall.

"Riders On The Storm" played loudly as Claudia attracted all the eyes in the club. Dressed in small, loose fitting white shorts, a colorful open blouse, and black Italian leather pumps, she stepped down onto the dance floor with Michael and set the stage for the rest of the evening.

Claudia's unique physical beauty attracted both men and women. Her long muscular legs in shorts and high heels, and her beautiful sensuous face and blonde hair, made people stop in their tracks all around her. Anwar sat at his table, surrounded by his harem of sexy Italian ladies, but stared at the only woman he wanted.

The Condor stared down Yousef, sitting across the table, and signaled him to go get the sexy bank executive from Chicago. The Mole Rat timidly walked up to Michael Stansfield on the dance floor.

"Annnnwar haassss.... fffffffallen," stuttered the Jorda-nian aide. "He ddddddemands your woman come to hiisss.... table for the evening. The rest is uupppp.... to you."

Michael stared at the Arab informant and winked. He grabbed Claudia's hand and stepped up to Anwar's table.

"Thank ya for invitin us for drinks. You are a true gentle-man," Michael Stansfield said in Texan drawl to the Egyptian.

The Arab stood and nodded silently. He forced the girl next to him to vacate her chair for Claudia and asked Stans-field to sit two seats away.

"Don't worry, baby, cum sit on my lap here with me," Michael told Claudia before she sat. "I don't reckon this raghead intends to split us apart. He simply wants to buy us some drinks and look like a bigshot with his harem of women. So cum over here with me and plant that beautiful ass of yours on my lap."

Anwar yelled in anger as 'Hello, I Love You' began to play. "No! You don't understand! I invited the lady to sit next to me! This is my table, and I set the rules!"

"I don't know where you're from, Arabman, and I don't particularly care; but from where I'm from, Texas, I make the rules with the woman I cum with!" shouted back Stansfield in southern Texan twang.

Anwar signaled two of his men to physically remove Stansfield from the area. In less than five seconds - Stansfield had side-kicked one of them in the chest, knocking him unconscious across the table; and fist punched the other in the face, breaking his nose and knocking out two front teeth. Michael stared the Egyptian back down into his seat.

"Listen, sand jockey! I could elbow bust your ugly face in pieces, use your beard to wipe the floor, and walk away from here with all your women; or, you could back off and run home to Creepistan! I'll let you decide my next move, Arab."

As club bouncers approached, Anwar called them off with a frustrated wave of his hand. He slowly and deliberately picked his henchman's two teeth off the table, and angrily threw them across the dance floor. He then collected himself, looked at Stansfield, and grinned.

"Why don't we ask the lady where she wants to sit, Texan?" the Egyptian calmly propositioned.

With The Doors' famous hit "The End" playing, Claudia sat next to the Condor. The Arab laughed and shouted at Stansfield, "Go home to America, Texan! You are not liked here! You Americans are not liked anywhere!"

Michael walked defiantly from the table. With his back to the Egyptian, he smiled and claimed total victory. He murmured to himself, "That stupid mother-fucker just bought himself a one-way ticket to martyrdom on the wings of a she-devil."

Julius joined his brother out the door.

CHAPTER 22

The Rubicon

I n January 49 BC, Julius Caesar trudged with his 13th Legion to the northern bank of the Rubicon River in northeast Italy. More legions marched behind him. Reddish sediment gave the river a blood color as it swept from the Apennine Mountains to the Adriatic Sea, fifty miles to the east. The Roman general had fought the barbarian tribes in Gaul for years, losing thousands of his soldiers and much of his patience. The Roman Senate had disintegrated into a corrupt and inept body of philanderers and spineless opportunists. The old ways of Roman government had been lost. Their complex constitution had broken down. The Roman system of 'checks and balances' had failed. Social chaos gripped

244 | *American Requiem*

the citizenry, and the republic was dissolving away. Caesar could not allow his men to die in Gaul for principles not lived in Rome. He had marched south with the intent of making history, and to create a new future for the Roman Republic.

Caesar had been ordered to return home and stand trial for activities inconsistent with the wishes of the Roman Senate. Tales of his unauthorized adventurous incursions into Germanic lands, and his great victories in Gaul, had made him a hero to the Roman people. An envious and paranoid Senate did not appreciate the grandness of his being. In their eyes, he had become a renegade threat to the 'stability' of the republic.

The legendary general knelt on one knee by the edge of the river and peered into its deep flowing waters. The redness of the Rubicon reminded him of the blood lost for the glory of Rome. It flowed like the red blood from the veins of his men. His army was dying, and so was his country.

Many soldiers had been sacrificed over the centuries to tame the continent and the Mediterranean. The ancient world had advanced to organized civilization under the republic. Roman law, supported by military strength, had been the source of their power. Anarchy could not be allowed to destroy what had taken five hundred years to create. Caesar refused to accept the demise of his beloved country.

He thought of the consequences of crossing the Rubicon with his standing army. The northern boundary of the Roman Republic was sacred to the Senate. If a general crossed with his complement of troops, without first disbanding his legions, he incurred a charge of high treason against the republic. Trial would certainly lead to death or banishment from Rome.

In deep contemplation, Julius Caesar considered the effects of his decision on his family, historical legacy, and life. He thought of the repercussions to his loyal legionnaires and the people of Rome.

If he crossed the Rubicon with his troops, their fates were entwined. If he died, they died.

He pondered the consequences to the future of his homeland. If he crossed the Rubicon with his army and was defeated - history would see him as a traitor, and Rome would likely disintegrate over time. All would be lost. If he marched on Rome and Pompey's legions - winning a civil war - he could be seen as a power-hungry dictator who wished for himself the glory of Rome.

There were no easy decisions. Caesar agonized for hours by the Rubicon. The fate of the Roman Republic was in his hands.

Finally, Julius Caesar assembled his warriors. He stood before them for a long moment, pausing to find the right words. He explained the possible outcomes on the far side of the Rubicon. To pass with him, only victory could save their lives. To be killed in battle, they would fall at the hands of fellow Romans. To be victorious, they would take the lives of many brothers. Down all roads, there was a price to pay for the saving of Rome.

Julius Caesar described the decrepit conditions of their beloved city. He expressed his devotion to the country he had once known. He spoke his sentiments and shouted his desire to create a better homeland. The honor and future fortunes of Rome would be decided by them.

Caesar gazed into the eyes of the soldiers, and saw the love they had for him and their country. He paused again, and realizing their allegiance, uttered his famous words, "The die has now been cast....."

I sat alone in my Garibaldi Hotel room, viewing a wall painting of Julius Caesar in battle armor by the Rubicon. On his knees, and with his head bowed, the general searched his mind for solutions. The red flow of the river near him was full and strong. A wind turned trees and loose leaves in the direction of Rome.

I could hear a grandfather clock in the room ticking off seconds, not keeping pace with my heart. Time had not stopped for Caesar, and it would not halt for me. As the world turned, one needed to turn with it.

I stared at the great leader's sword, stabbed deeply into the earth next to him. At Caesar's feet, the Rubicon bled, as soon would Rome. The gladius stood like a crucible of fate at the center of the large painting. Caesar's destiny would be ruled by blood and iron, as one's destiny often is.

The Roman general's predicament and final decision had altered history for the next five hundred years. The republic was not preserved. Imperial rule took hold, and Rome was changed forever. In the end, Caesar had not saved his country; and he had paid for it with his life.

The course of human history was pockmarked by many "Rubicons". Times and places dictated by a few brave souls who risked all for ideals of the mind. Some were successful in their challenges, and others not.

I knew mankind's story. I preferred victory to defeat. My country's fate had been entrusted to me. I could not fail. The future of America was in my hands. Again, destiny would be ruled by blood and iron.

I mentally prepared for battle. I was facing my own Rubicon. If I didn't cross because of physical handicap, I could return to my wife and sons immediately. Life would go on. People would say I had already done enough for my country; that no more could be expected of me, and that my honor and dignity were intact. Yet, I would know better. I couldn't live in the shadow of the past. Eventually, I would die a broken man.

If I crossed, I'd likely die in action. My mind had accepted this probability. But more importantly, I would help save my country from future chaos. My children would remain free. I had chosen to make the crossing. Blood and iron would decide my fate.

I waited for Jim Thomas. I loaded a magazine into my 9mm pistol and holstered it behind my back. I removed a red rose from a vase on the table and gently placed it into the lapel of my suit jacket.

I looked out across the terrace at the dark lake. Night had settled over Como. I rested my head back and closed my eyes. In my mind and spirit, I heard Rachmaninoff's Cello Sonata Op. 19-3. I thought of an earlier time, a more peaceful time, and listened....................

As a young midshipman at the academy, I had gone to a formal dance in Washington. The event commemorated 230 years of the US Navy, and was attended by many dignitaries and their families.

Dressed in my formal white uniform - I saw the most beautiful girl in the world, standing alone across the hall. She had stylish blonde hair and an incredible figure. Even from a distance, her blue eyes and delicate engaging smile lit up the room. Captured by her natures, I made my move.

"Champagne for a princess in need," I smiled, gently offering her a glass.

She looked into me with her piercing dark blues and smiled.

"I thought no one would ever offer," she said, accepting me.

"A girl like you doesn't come to a dance unescorted," I inquired, hoping to hear it so.

"My date is right there," pointed the girl from heaven with her eyes.

I stared in the direction shown, and saw my father speaking to a tall and heavy gentleman.

"My father?" I asked in astonishment.

"No my dear!" she laughed..... "My father, silly!"

Aphrodite clinked my glass and drank her champagne. I felt like the biggest idiot on earth. But she was gracious, and found the incident funny.

"My father is the American ambassador to France," she smiled.

"Mine is an admiral," I stated, still embarrassed.

"Father was one also, before he retired to become a diplomat. I'm sure our fathers are good old friends."

"They are certain to be," I added.

"Stop fretting, Navy boy. Finish your drink and take me out to dance..... By the way, I'm Sarah Jones."

"I'm Mark Stansfield."

"Lead the way, Mr. Mark Stansfield," smiled Sarah.

It was as if the entire dance hall had been emptied of people, leaving only Sarah and I alone. She moved gracefully with her own body language. Her face expressed emotion easily and without inhibition. She was gorgeous and magnetic. I could not keep my eyes off her. We seemed to melt into each other.

Without much effort, it just happened. Like a giant tidal wave, it swept us away. It quickly evolved into total mastery of the heart. It was peculiar, but wonderful.

Our world stopped. A transformation took place. Two souls somehow became one, like helium from hydrogen. Like stellar nucleosynthesis, a new energy had been created in the universe. Stardust had been converted into young love, the energy that rules the world. Nature had spun its magic once again. Love came in a 'Big Bang'. And it was a passionate collision and explosion.....

Later, we sat outside under the stars. We had ice cream, listening to a small chamber orchestra play Rachmaninoff.

"Cello Sonata Op. 19-3," said Sarah.

"How would you know?" I asked with interest.

"How would I not?" she smiled.....

At evening's end, before bidding farewell, I politely asked to see her again. Sarah grabbed my hand and pulled me closer. She took a red rose from a vase on our table and placed it into the lapel of my dress uniform.

She kissed my lips and tenderly whispered, "Goodbyes are not for us to say, for we will test eternity."

She placed her hand over my beating heart and added, "This will never stop for me..... I sense it in my soul."

In few words, Sarah reflected what I had felt for her from the moment our eyes met. It was inexplicable, but all true...................

The music in my mind stopped. I returned to my hotel room in Como. I had enjoyed my trip with Sarah.

Survival instincts took over. I quickly reviewed my plans for the evening. Actions tonight were critical to the success of *Project X*. The secret material in Sheng's possession had to be uncovered and kept away from the *Kilij*. I considered the mission a combat operation. It was the only approach I knew, and the one I understood best.

Would my physical matter respond accordingly? I knew the mind was sharp..... But was the body?

I hoped to compensate for the limitations. Spirit would rule the day, and the body would rise to meet the demands required of my "American Amaranth".

Jimmy Thomas entered the room. "Are you ready, brother?" he asked.

"Tip of the spear," I said, patting my chest.

"Noble warriors in a noble fight..... I'm with you tonight, Mark..... You can rely on me. I've got your back..... Now, let's go and kick some ass....."

We arrived at Como's dockside and were taken aboard Sheng Hong's luxury yacht, *Dealbreaker*. I had been invited to a party in honor of Sheng's good friend, Turkish banker Bahadur Burakgazi.

Hsu escorted us to the ship's parlor where two young Chinese women played lutes, and another sang a popular solo frottola from the Italian Renaissance period. We were mixed into a crowd of elegant guests. Waiters, dressed in white, offered small bites and aperitifs before dinner.

"This is Mr. Sheng's Raphael Room. It's his favorite place to be on the yacht," said Hsu, below the music. "On the main wall hang three priceless works by the famous painter. All are of Margherita Luti, Raphael's model and mistress. As one can tell, the artist was fond of her form.

"Would you like a refreshment from the bar, Mr. Harrity?" asked Hsu, ignoring Jim Thomas.

"Two dry martinis please, for my associate and I."

The PLA trooper snapped his heels, bowed at both of us, and went off.

"This tall bastard is a real racist fuck," murmured Jimmy. "He hasn't made eye contact with me yet. It's as if I don't exist."

"He senses something," I said. "He's a Red Dragon. Doubt and paranoia are trained into them. None of those sons of bitches like anybody; but I get the feeling that Hsu doesn't trust us any more than we do him."

"That's fine with me," laughed Jimmy.

"Just be aware and awake, ebony warrior," I added.....

The singer and girl musicians wore sleeveless white see-through silk shirts to the mid-thighs with no undergarments. Their legs and feet were bare. Adorned with large thick golden loop ear-rings, each had similar but smaller rings through the belly-button and nipples of both breasts. Their bodies, including their heads, were completely shaven of hair. They wore no make-up, except for bright pink lipstick. All three women were tall with strong figures.

The Raphael paintings of Luti showed the naked woman in different positions of self-arousal. The artist's sexual and psychic infatuation with his model was plainly apparent.

Hsu returned with the drinks. "They are the finest martinis, Mr. Harrity."

"I wouldn't expect anything less from such a gracious host."

I watched the PLA man listen intently to his ear piece. He walked away without excusing himself. I knew he'd be back soon.

I drank the martini in two gulps, somewhat both aroused and relaxed by the femininity around me. I was in an estrogenic pool, and it felt good. I thought of Sarah, calmed my nerves, and sharpened my killer instincts.

The moment drew near. Like a fast approaching freight train at night, the weight of the evening had finally closed on me. I focused on the task at hand.

The Red Dragon Hsu returned as expected. "Mr. Sheng would like your company in the library."

"I hope it's as stimulating as the Raphael Room," I snickered.

"You're asking for the impossible, Mr. Harrity."

"Getting the impossible is my job, Mr. Hsu," I grinned, before following him out of the parlor.

Jimmy Thomas remained behind, breathing the estrogens and mentally preparing for what was to come.....

"Hello, Mr. Harrity!" welcomed Sheng, as he stood from his chair at the long mahogany table and shook my hand. "Let me introduce to you a dear friend of mine, Mr. Bahadur Burakgazi.

"Bahadur is a famous international banker with a taste for expensive art, books, drink, and women; just like you, Mr. Harrity. You are both my kind of men," laughed Sheng.

Burakgazi also stood to shake my hand. "I'm sure you enjoyed the Raphael Room, Mr. Harrity. We have had many interesting evenings in that parlor. It's the finest foreplay room on the planet, when properly attended. Between the music girls and Raphael's woman, even a dead man would spring to life. Don't you agree?"

"Most certainly so!" I agreed with the Turk.

"The women and paintings of the Raphael Room are unique in my collections, Mr. Harrity," declared Sheng. "They are the only possessions I own which are not for sale at any price," he laughed.

"I find that hard to believe," I grinned. "You being unwilling to part with anything for the right price?"

"Perhaps you're correct in your assessment, Mr. Harrity," smiled the fat Chinese tycoon spy. "I suppose even my sexiest girls and paintings are for sale in a moment of need..... But then again, I have never been or plan to be in such a moment," he smiled wider.

"I've been told you are an American," said the Turk, an olive-skinned man even fatter than the yellow communist. "An Irish-American who believes in American imperialism!" blurted 'Babar'.

"That is quite unusual..... Isn't it, Mr. Harrity? An Irishman who believes in imperialism?" disbelieved Burakgazi, scratching his grizzled beard.

"Is it frequent that you speak without knowledge?" I sternly asked Babar, ripping his heart out with my clenched teeth..... "I'm not an Irishman..... I'm a pure red-blooded American..... And it's not because I was born in America, but rather the standards by which I live..... Americanism is an ideology, Mr. Burakgazi, not a birthright..... Secondly, American imperialism - as you call it, is not true imperialism. It is simply America defending herself against all the sons of bitches around the world wanting her destruction.

"Don't you think so, Mr. Burakgazi? Quite simply, is it not our reaction to other countries' actions?"

I smiled rigidly and extended a stiff hand to the Turk. "Regardless of your improper pre-conceptions, Mr. Burakgazi, as an American I'm open to dialogue and friendship. I wouldn't allow our differences in opinion to disrupt a potentially great relationship. I am friends with the world, if the world reciprocates."

The *Kilij* financier sat with an incredulous look on his face. He bit down on a big cigar and lit it. He stared once at Sheng and returned to me.

"Would you like a Cuban smoke, Mr. Harrity?" asked the Turkish meatball.

"No thank you, I'd prefer not."

"Are you certain? These are the finest in the world..... They are from Castro's private stock, given to me as a gift after a mutually profitable trade deal. The Commandante was a great and shrewd businessman, and also a keen judge of character."

"What is your area of finance?" I asked the Turk. "What do you specialize in?"

"Oh, Mr. Harrity..... I am a global financier..... I will buy and sell anything people need, anywhere in the world. I lend and take money on every continent of the planet. I trade with every religion and race. I can insert myself into any level of the food chain for a profit. I will move practically anything, from American hot dogs to Russian bullets. I specialize in making money," laughed Babar.

"All of us here specialize in making money," said Sheng, trying to defuse tension.

"You may believe what you're saying, Mr. Harrity, but I don't agree with your assessment," argued Babar. "America's instigation of a civil war in China, which has caused hundreds of thousands of deaths, and her occupation of the Middle East in support of Israel are not 'reactions', Mr. Harrity; nor is the instability in Russia, induced by the multiple coup attempts of radical nationalists. The American CIA is behind much of the chaos around the world, I think. I believe America's concept of 'Manifest Destiny' has gotten to her head," grinned the short and fat Burakgazi.

"All the cases you've mentioned, and the rise of Sunni Islamic terrorism, are not a product of American imperialism. They are the causes, I believe, of American actions around the world," I said. "China, the Middle East, and Russia must be re-ordered if we all wish for peace on this planet. For many decades, these nations have tried to destroy my country. Americans are not in the habit of watching renegade nations usurp the power of the United States. They will not sit idly by and allow it to happen. Americans will be merciful, but they will also use all the powers at their disposal to fend off the threats. Economic, social, psychological, and military means will be maximized against the enemies of our country. America will slowly bend her enemies' systems to suit a more favorable, peaceful world for the future.

"Besides, gentlemen, world peace is good for our businesses. Feeding, financing, and intercommunicating our planet should be in all of our interests.

"Naturally, these are my thoughts on the matter..... I am an American first, and a businessman second."

"You seem to have a good grasp of world geopolitics, Mr. Harrity," said Burakgazi, smiling at Sheng. "You are passionate about America's position in the world..... Quite passionate, indeed," repeated the Turk as he smoked his cigar.

"Well, I would hope so," I answered. "I sell agricultural products around the globe. I need to keep up to date with the workings of governments which may benefit or impede my commerce. I sell wherever they are friendly, and avoid areas I'm not welcome. One of my country's main intentions is to turn the unfriendly into the friendly, and stimulate American commerce everywhere. Eventually, the world will come around. Fair and free market capitalism is the only road forward. All other avenues of conducting business eventually lead to revolt and destabilization of government. We wish to lift the world out of poverty. We want all nations to prosper and advance their cultures peacefully."

"Mr. Sheng had mentioned to me earlier how interesting a man you were, Mr. Harrity," stated Burakgazi. "If anything, you are even more interesting than what I expected. Imagine, a businessman who is more patriotic than he is greedy..... And an American businessman at that," grinned the Turk.

"Sheng and I don't suffer from your affliction, Mr. Harrity..... Patriotism doesn't play into our crafty schemes. We would rather have our bellies and banks full than our hearts. This world is only for the rich, and those who place their pocketbooks before their 'Motherland'. The only true passion Mr. Sheng and I have is a passion to make money - lots of it, and as fast as we can," laughed Babar.

"I don't understand world geopolitics any better than you, Mr. Burakgazi..... Certainly not any more intensely than you," I retorted..... "Nor do I believe your personal emotions regarding the concept of 'Motherland' don't impact your deal making. A good chess player knows human nature and human emotion. Patriotism always bleeds onto the paper. It is a fact we all adjust to, Mr. Burakgazi..... We're just different sides of the same coin.

"As international businessmen, we both need to understand the world's condition. We can't make money walking around blind and insensitive. But always, even in denial, 'Mother Country' tugs on the heart and makes the deal making more interesting.

"Besides, it wouldn't be any fun if everyone agreed all the time," I smiled.

The *Dealbreaker* left the dock and slowly cruised north along the lakefront. I sat by a large window facing the bow of the ship. I could see several of Burakgazi's henchman bodyguards standing outside the entrance to the library. Jimmy Thomas leaned on the ship's railing, smoking a cigarette. Hsu stood a few feet to my right, next to the door. I quickly analyzed distance and angles of fire while we talked.

"Come on, gentlemen," said Sheng politely. "Let's look at our similarities, not our differences..... We are all very rich. We love the good things in life and spend money to acquire them. And we all love to make a deal.

"Both of you are here tonight because I have things you want. You are willing to spend big money on buying these articles of mine..... I'm a collector. I collect things that other people want..... It's a great world we live in," laughed Sheng.

The red spy looked at the Turk and said, "Mr. Harrity is a patriot. We must respect that. He loves his country, just like most do. Now, let's enjoy the evening of good music, food, and women."

"I see," said the *Kilij* banker as he slowly puffed Cuba's finest. "It's interesting both of us are on this ship here tonight..... Maybe it's a coincidence. Maybe not..... Perhaps your intentions are not as commerce-related as they seem..... You appear too American for my taste. It's a little unsettling on my nerves..... I don't trust your intentions, Mr. Harrity. I don't believe you are only an art collector-farmer from the United States, wanting to make a deal with my Chinese friend. Maybe you want more than pretty art and manuscripts."

The fat Turk motioned with his hand through the window at his bodyguards. Jim Thomas pulled a compact submachine gun out of his coat and fired several bursts at the enemy. I grabbed my pistol, shot Hsu by the door, and placed a bullet into the middle of Burakgazi's forehead.

I then pointed the pistol at Sheng and calmly said, "It's time to really talk the deal."

Eight men lay dead on the ship as Sheng raised his arms high in the air. Two CIA helicopters descended on the *Dealbreaker*. Guests stood silently while American agents slid down ropes to the deck.

"Now tell me, Sheng, what did you intend to sell the fatman?

"The United States of America is interested in the Chinese Revolutionary Council. We have a full appreciation of your participation in the plot to damage my country. I don't take kindly to this fact. It makes my trigger finger tremble with anger. I'm just as likely to put a bullet in your head as I was with the fatman. So give me the material you intended to sell the Turk. If you don't, I have orders to kill you right here where we speak. If you are gracious, and agree to cooperate with America, we promise to give you a cell overlooking the Potomac and three square American meals a day. No caviar or champagne, but it beats the fish in Lake Como eating you. So come clean and give me the material."

I fired one round into the Red's right hand, shooting off two of his fingers. He screamed like a hysterical woman. I took aim at his head.

"I've already shot one fatman in the head today; it's not any harder to say I've shot two..... Give me what I want."

Sheng cried in pain as several CIA agents ran into the library.

"Alright, I'll give you what you want!" yelled the communist devil.

With his hand bleeding onto the red sandalwood floor, Sheng walked over to a Picasso painting on the wall and pulled it away with his good hand. He turned the combination of the wall safe and opened it. He took out a shoebox sized container and turned it over to me.

"American imperialist pig!

"You may have taken us down today, but we will get you soon. China has survived seven thousand years. We have had many civil wars, and we are still here. America will not outlast us."

I read the Russian inscriptions on the front of the metal box - **Airborne Zaire Ebola Virus-handle with extreme caution......**

Across the lake in Blevio, Anwar arrived at his estate with Claudia and his entourage. Mullen, Whitmore, Kakkar, and the rest of the CIA assault team waited in the woods near Villa Vento Forte. Anwar found the entrance gate open and ordered his driver to speed through.

The *Kilij* agents rushed into the house with Claudia. Anwar ran to the wine cellar and found the lead safe open.

Claudia listened to Anwar yell in Arabic, "The American bastards have taken the bombs! Yousef, call Florence and tell them that if attacked, they must get out with the other bombs! Say I will kill them all if they don't follow my orders precisely! They must save those bombs! Get me a helicopter to Florence right now!"

Claudia stepped into the shadows by the pool and text-messaged Julius on her encrypted phone. Julius and Michael sat in a fastboat on the lake, less than a mile away.

Julius read the message to his brother, "Other nukes - safe house – Florence... Soon on helo to find exactly where... Anwar blind to me... Follow GPS coordinates - rendezvous Florence."

Julius radioed Mullen and gave new instructions, "Discontinue attack... Allow Anwar safe passage from villa... New target in Florence... Will coordinate after meeting with Mitrano."

CHAPTER 23

Noble Prince

We had been moved by rail to Naples without knowing our next assignment. It was all a big secret. Everyone hoped that, perhaps, the military hospital outside of Naples would be home for a while. Others even believed we were going home after our distinguished service at Salerno, the Volturno River and Mignano Gap campaigns, and Cassino..... But it wasn't to be.

We were soon loaded on two LSTs and put out to sea. Never losing sight of the coast, we sailed north. Sailing north was not good. It was German-occupied and dangerous. The American sailors on board talked constantly of all the recent Allied ship losses in the area due to aggressive U-boat activity. It scared me.

I didn't want to drown in a cold sea, or burn alive in a raging ship fire. If I was to die, I preferred to go with a large artillery shell explosion on land. I had imagined dying many times before, particularly when exhausted without sleep. My mind would play with this dark fantasy. I imagined hearing the high-pitched shrill of the approaching shell, and then ceasing to exist with a puff of smoke. I preferred this exit to being sunk at sea by a German torpedo. But it wasn't for me to choose. We placed our trust in the destroyer escort and left the rest to God.

We knew of the Allied landings at Anzio on January 22. General Mark Clark had sent elements of the 5th Army to land along beaches thirty-five miles south of Rome in a maneuver to outflank German forces on the Gustav Line further south. Allied Command hoped it would trap the German 10th Army at Cassino and enable an attack on Rome from the coast. Or perhaps, Clark thought the 10th Army would draw back from Cassino to reinforce the Anzio beachhead, allowing the Allies at Cassino to break out into the Liri Valley and onto Rome. It seemed like an intelligent plan to Clark and his generals either way.

The British 1st Infantry Division had landed six miles north of Anzio. Several US Ranger battalions had attacked the port of Anzio directly, and the US 3rd Infantry Division had landed six miles east of Anzio with support from the US 504th Parachute Infantry Regiment. In total - over 40,000 Allied troops were engaged with three German divisions of the 14th Army, led by General Eberhard von Mackensen.

However - rather than pulling 10th Army troops from Cassino and retreating towards Rome, or the 14th Army abandoning the Anzio beachhead to the Allies - Kesselring reinforced both fronts. No Allied breakout from the beachhead had been achieved, and the Cassino battlefield had become a bloodbath. Allied losses were heavy at both fronts.

We had also become aware of the catastrophic losses of the 95th Evacuation Hospital at Anzio. On February 7 - a German fighter-bomber had scored a direct hit on the hospital, maiming and killing dozens of enlisted men, nurses, and doctors. The 95th was withdrawn and ordered to Naples for rest, regrouping, and further assignment. Sailing north along the Lazio coast, we all began to realize we were destined for Anzio.

The further north we went, the more we envisioned in our minds a visit to another beachhead. Talk among the girls switched from going home to our parents and sweethearts, to ugly memories of Salerno. We had seen a lot of killing on the beaches south of Naples. Unlike our childhood memories, going to the beach had taken on a whole new meaning for us.

None of us could forget the look of blood in sand. The fresh rich crimson red under the noonday sun, mixing and baking with the tan of silica and gray of ash, congealing into a sick rusty curd with time. It would foam under the salt of the sea, creating swirls of frothy brown in the blue. Hardening into tarry tack, it would line our boots with the lives of our men..... I will never forget the look of blood in sand.....

As morning rose on February 10, our ship entered 'Bomb Bay' of Anzio. During normal peaceful times, the twin towns of Nettuno and Anzio would have been quaint and quiet seaside villages - summer resorts for powerful Romans since before the reign of Caesar. Nero, Caligula, Coriolanus,

Cicero, and Trajan had all feasted in villas here, enjoying the turquoise waters of the Tyrrhenian Sea. Ruins of these villas were still visible up and down the coastline..... But these were not times of peace..... War had intruded on another pearl of Europe.

Crippled American, British, and Canadian ships laid half-sunken in shallow waters, marooned near shore by their surviving crews to salvage their contents. Many more ships had sunk into the bay after Nazi air assaults and U-boat torpedo attacks. Black smoke billowed from the beachhead in several locations.

From the Alban Hills in the north, German artillery spewed their fire onto Allied fighting positions inland from the beach. Their locations were easily spotted by their red and golden yellow belches. Some shells landed near the Anzio docks, creating panic among the medical personnel evacuating injured troops from the battlefield.

I waded ashore, and passed a large salvage dump stacked to the sky with helmets, belts, canteens, boots, battle fatigues, socks, and other military odds and ends - all taken from the bodies of dead American and British soldiers. Graves had filled an adjacent cemetery. Rows of covered bodies waited in line to be deposited into the sandy Italian soil, so far, far away from home.

Regardless of my many months spent on battlefronts, I could not desensitize myself to the terrible realities of war. The indignity of it all was crushing. The pathetic sadness of boys being buried into foreign soil, so distant and removed from their loved ones. The unfortunates were far from their mother and father, siblings, and sweethearts. The horror of it all was like a total and final eclipse of the sun.

From where had all this hate come?

Where was the underworld origin of the abomination?
Could we ever know the birthplace of the devil?

It was easy to see the inconsolable results of war, to feel the loss of promise and hope, and to dread the coming of another day..... Much more difficult was to figure how we could make it all go away.....

I climbed onto a supply truck as air raid sirens began to blare. Fighting ships in the bay sounded 'general quarters' alarms and turned their gun turrets toward the northwest. People around me ran in different directions.

I rushed underneath the docks and sat next to a pile of cement bags. I buried my hands into cold sand and dug like a dog with a bone.

An American soldier nearby shouted to me, 'Not under the docks, girl! You dumb fool! That's what they want to destroy! Get the hell outta there!'

But it was too late..... The fear of bombs falling on me from above stopped me into inaction. I froze like a scared kitten and hunkered down the best I could. A spectator in fetal position, I watched the grotesque display evolve in front of me.

The guns of more than two dozen Allied ships fired their salvos into the gray winter sky. Small puffs of black smoke appeared high in the horizon, followed by distant crackling retorts of sound. I stared at the explosive black cotton balls mixed with red fire, realizing the wall of angry metal in each of them. Thousands of killer fragments waited to kill the enemy.

I defined a small wave of planes descending towards the bay. The fire from below became more intense as four Messerschmitt Bf-110 fighter-bombers swooped down on our destroyers, cruisers, and supply ships. Five more Heinkel

He-111 medium bombers approached at a higher altitude from the west, escorted by seven Focke-Wolfe Fw-190s.

A Bf-110 was hit by flak and crashed in a thousand pieces into the sea. Another luckier one scored a hit on a US destroyer, setting it ablaze. Munitions on the American ship exploded into a thunderous black mushroom cloud over the bay. The power of the destructive detonation knocked me back several feet.

Allied ground artillery fired shells into the advancing wave of Heinkels and Fw-190s. A German medium bomber, hit and quickly losing altitude, flew low over the beachhead and crashed in a ball of fire into the Pontine Marshes to the east.

The Fw fighters were engaged by spanking new P-51 Mustangs. I was deafened by the roar of the Rolls Royce Merlin engines as they raced across the sky in chase of the enemy. Acrobatic spirals and turns by flyers in combat, right above me, took my breath away. The spectacle slowly brought me out of my fetal position. The rattle of machine guns over my head was shocking and thrilling at the same time. I needed to see this. I edged myself from under the dock and sat alone on the beach. I couldn't close my eyes.

A P-51 rumbled at low altitude over my position on the beach. It pursued an Fw-190 as the German fired rockets at the Allied oil depot. Another massive explosion threw me on my back.

Lying on the sand, I opened my eyes and saw the undercarriage of another P-51 pass over me. I caught a glimpse of the big white American Army Air Corp stars in blue on its wings, as the American pilot emptied his .50 caliber machine guns at a German fighter.

I was shell shocked by the blasts and lost my hearing for several minutes. I remained stunned on the sand and deaf to the sounds of battle.

With my eyes open and looking to the sky, I could feel on my skin the fires on the beach around me. The heat scorched my blonde hair.

I had gone from a maddening fear to simple acceptance of my own death. I imagined my body in the cold earth of wintry Italy, devoid of rose and sunflower, without the gentle beauty of summer light and sky, with no salt of the warm sea on my tongue or the sweet taste of honey, with no arias to hear or boys to love, surrounded by endless silent rows of worthier and braver heroes. I too would die in the land of opera and romance, unlucky like so many.

The extreme experience had numbed even my fear of dying..... Alas, I didn't succumb.

God had saved me one more time. There would be more duty in my future. Even if to save only one more life, I suppose he needed me.

I rose from the ground and dusted myself off. The battle still raged, but I was required elsewhere.

What was this hell I was in? Had everyone gone mad?

I returned to the truck, accompanied by many courageous nurses. The driver tore up the beach, racing inland a short distance to the hospital. We arrived minutes later, as another huge explosion occurred nearby. I jumped off the medical wagon and ran to a slit trench by the road. We all buried our heads in the dirt and prayed for everything to stop.

The ugly noise of plane engines became distant, and the sounds of war became muffled. For a split second, a sacred silence replaced the screams of bombs. It didn't last long.....

Cries of dying men all around me began filling the air. I raised my head from the hole where I lay, and peered over the edge of the road. From under the brim of my helmet, my eyes could not believe what I saw. I closed and opened them again, testing the apparition in front of me.

Time stopped in a holy moment. Predestination, some would call it. Ironic fate, others would say. I would call it - glory.

I can't explain why I felt what I felt. But it filled me with warmth and hope. In all the misery, there was goodness.....

The entrance to the hospital tent had been blown wide open. Little remained of it. The large red cross on the canvas siding, shredded into strips of red and white cloth, waved in the wind. A battle worn and tattered American flag, atop a tall flagpole in front of the hospital, stretched out its stars and stripes. A ripped open roof allowed columns of sunlight to beam down into the tent, isolating the scene before me like an altar from heaven.

Here was the glory of man for all to see..... Intrepid, determined, dedicated, unrelenting, and courageous..... This was the sight I saw..... In all the terror, there was still faith - a belief in what was just - a trust in man's higher calling - a moral ground rarely seen in the indiscriminate anger and self-preservation of battle.....

A young surgeon in bloodied surgical apron operated on his patient – alone..... A nurse assistant lay dead at his feet..... His patient still lived, and the surgeon fought with all his might to keep it that way..... Small sprays of bright red blood landed on his white gown, as he cut and tied his way to life..... Like a stage actor in a tragic Shakespearean play, the beams of light from above shrouded him in a peaceful glory all of his own..... The surgeon dominated the space.....

All his energies were focused on saving his patient..... He was acting by himself and not retreating from the challenge..... Fear had not enveloped him..... He was not giving up..... At this moment in time, in this place, regardless of condition or hardship, he had been anointed by a higher power to save a life - not take one..... He had been called to rise above the reality of the conditions.....

The scene transcended everything I had ever experienced in my life..... Here was the hope of the world, right in front of me..... Here was my 'Noble Prince'.....

I rose from the earth and slowly walked into the remains of the operating tent. The American flag above me cracked in the wind. Like in a place of worship, I removed my helmet and quietly placed it down on the ground. I stepped to the operating table and humbly offered myself for his use.

The surgeon's eyes looked into me; his mind searched the universe to make sense of it all. I could feel the aura of his mighty soul, struggling hard to save a life someone else had attempted so intently to take. He wasn't giving up, and I wasn't either.

He gently nodded and invited me into his sacred space. He allowed me to participate in his moment in time. I smiled at him and could sense his smile back from behind the mask.....

Julius softly closed Ann's diary and went to sleep.

CHAPTER 24

The Biology of Man

L ate the night before, Joseph Mitrano had given out orders to his men at war with the *Kilij*. Mullen, Whitmore, and Kakkar would go to Florence - and with the assistance of two CIA special operation assault teams - attack the *Kilij* safe house where the Condor protected his remaining cache of portable nukes. The orders were to extract Claudia from Anwar Nejem's clench and capture the bombs intact. At the same time, CIA raiders and US Navy Seals would assault the *Kilij* headquarters in Istanbul and Cairo. The director expected heavy losses on both sides. Mitrano, without specifying further instructions for the

Stansfield brothers, requested a meeting with them in Como for the next morning.

At dawn on the last day in October, the Stansfields arrived separately at the Como lakefront gardens and waited for Mitrano. Nearby, an attractive young couple quietly fed the swans on the lake. A middle-aged man on a sporty motorcycle watched the sun rise over the eastern mountains. Two female joggers stopped and sat by the red roses for a rest. The gardens were full of CIA agents.

At a few minutes past seven, Director Mitrano strolled by with a young woman. Both were dressed in formal attire from a seemingly long evening out on the town. The lady stayed alone by a statue of the town's founder in the first century BC, Julius Caesar. Mitrano loosened his black-tie and sat at a bench between Julius and Michael. Mark was in his wheelchair across from them.

"Well boys, we're finally in position to end this thing, once and for all," said the chief. "The last piece of the mystery is in a farmhouse on a hill outside of Florence. Men and women of the CIA will attack that site late tonight. My raiders will also assault *Kilij* sites in Istanbul and Cairo. The show will be over, I hope, by this time tomorrow morning."

The CIA director paused in silence for a moment. He leaned back on the bench and closed his eyes.

"This road for America is long," he said with his eyes shut. "George Washington was insightful in his view of the future for our country. It's been a long and hard struggle to keep us free. It requires constant analysis, re-assessment, and re-calibration of our efforts on a minute to minute basis. There is never time to rest, and only little time to reflect. It's a daunting challenge we all have."

Mitrano took a deep breath and murmured, "The eyes of Picasso."

The puzzled Stansfield brothers looked at each other, not understanding the comment.

"You mean the famous artist?" asked Julius.

"Is there any other Picasso?"

The brothers didn't answer.

"Have any of you ever paid attention to old photographs of the greatest painter of the twentieth century?" asked the chief..... "He had the most intense stare. His look could burn a hole through you. It was likely impossible to know what he was thinking at any given time; but his eyes told you he was thinking big.....

"Your father in youth had those eyes.....

"Julian had unrelenting intensity. His eyes were like lasers, focused on the objectives. He thought big all the time.

"The Biochemistry I class at Annapolis was a damned hard course. Our final exam consisted of 100 questions. After studying for days, I got 74%; your father got 99 out of a 100 correct.

"Instead of celebrating, Julian ruminated for three days about the one question he missed.....

"The next term, we took Biochemistry II. We were given ninety minutes to answer 100 problems on the final. Many of them required mathematical analysis. It was the most difficult examination I endured at the academy.

"Coming out of the exam, Julian's eyes beamed an incredible intensity. I swore they could see through walls. They were cold and hard eyes.

"When he was like that, so focused and determined, he didn't speak. We'd just move out of his way.

"One of our friends joked out loud as your father passed by, 'The eyes of Picasso.' Everyone laughed but me. I said, 'No..... The eyes of Julian Stansfield.'

"I received a 76%, the second highest grade in the class. Your father aced out a 100%."

Joe Mitrano opened his eyes and laughed out loud. He took a moment to compose himself.

"Your father was always right about everything. His intensity propelled him to be.....

"He was most certainly correct about the concept of power. He'd often say, when discussing politics and history, 'Eternal power, like eternal life, is a myth.'

"He sensed power and freedom, like life itself, were fleeting. Yet, he hoped and strived for that eternal power and its just use. He fought for America more furiously than anybody else, as if only eternal power could keep America free and safe. It was a driving force in his life....."

The director lit a cigarette with his gold lighter. He looked at the initials inscribed on the keepsake, 'JM' on one side, and 'JS' on the other.

"Julian got me smoking these things at the academy. I never forgave the 'son of a bitch'.....

"He gave me this lighter a few years ago at the 40th anniversary of our graduation from Annapolis. He was sincere and proper with his gifts. All of them had the intention of making you think.

"I had been with the CIA only a year..... On a note, he wrote, 'Light the flames to protect America.' He had a way with words, that old bastard.

"He seemed to easily understand and accept the realities of our country..... He'd often mention man's innate tendency to be cruel; but contrasted that with man's innate abilities to be great, compassionate, and creative. He believed Darwin's Natural Selection perpetually sharpened both man's darker and lighter sides. Like alter-egos, both natures of man were being finely tuned biologically for 'Survival of the Fittest'.

"Julian wanted America to catalyze more constructive creativity and hinder dark cruelty. He looked at geopolitics as an experiment in Natural Selection. The cultures which evolved better traits for quality survival would last into the future. The losers would fade into oblivion. His self-appointed mission since the academy was to ensure America didn't drown in the Acheron. He only saw America in the green fields of Elysium."

Mitrano finished his cigarette.....

He slowly passed his eyes by each of the Stansfield boys and smiled..... "I suppose the old man planted his seeds in each of his children..... The seeds germinated as he had hoped..... I see his eyes and flame in all of you....."

The director stretched out his tired legs.

"Now, let's get down to business," said the chief. "Our analysts in London confirmed Anwar has at least six nukes with him in Florence. Four of the nukes are of Russian GPNR origin, the other two are Chinese PLA/CRC. The same analysts picked up information on a rendezvous – November 3 - on the island of Capri between Anwar and a *Kilij* yacht. The ship will transport Anwar and his nukes to Malta, where they will transfer to a Turkish freighter bound for the port of Wilmington, North Carolina. From Carolina, the nukes will be distributed to their destination sites of Seattle, Los Angeles, Salt Lake City, Phoenix, Chicago, and Atlanta - six nukes, six cities. The bombs will be delivered over western targets by hang-glider. Chicago and Atlanta will be attacked by motorcyclists with backpacks. If successful, our analysts now estimate the US will sustain over 750,000 killed instantaneously with the blasts, and an additional 3,500,000 deaths over the next two years from traumatic injury sequelae and cancer spikes.

"Mark will lead his team of Jim Thomas, Rafael Alvarez, and Simon Westcott in Naples. Julius and Michael will be stationed on Capri. All of you are supported by dozens more in those locations.

"There is a high probability the Condor and his nukes will escape capture in Florence. The *Kilij* organization is deeply organized in Tuscany, hindering our efforts there. We hope Claudia's presence inside the terrorist lair improves our chances.

"The enemy is not stupid. They are well prepared for any contingency, and Anwar can likely counter most of our potential actions in Florence. The CIA must plan accordingly and presume the nukes will arrive at the port of Naples for ferry transfer to Capri.

"Julius and Michael on Capri form our last line of defense before Anwar goes to sea. We could sink the yacht into the Mediterranean; but I'd rather rub the nukes in the Chinese and Russian noses, and later use them for evidence blackmail. The game of espionage depends on payback, and the captured bombs could pay a powerful dividend in the future. We want the nukes alive, and the terrorists dead.

"Do you all understand?"

The Stansfields nodded.

"Director, you don't sound confident of Mullen's chances in Florence," said Michael.

"We're going strong against the farmhouse on the hill," said Joe Mitrano. "But it's heavily fortified and positioned for defense. We can't even assure the Condor and nukes will still be present when we attack. I don't imagine Anwar getting cornered on that hill. We need Claudia to slow him down awhile. If he gets out of Florence, his network is strong enough to get him safely to Naples and Capri. That's where you guys come in."

"What about Claudia?" asked Julius.

"We know she's still alive and secretly messaging. That's all we know," answered Mitrano. "But she's a tough nut to crack, and a match for Anwar. Claudia's the bigger dog and I'd bet on her..... She's my best agent in Europe..... The *Kilij* shouldn't miss any of their prayer sessions. They'll need all the help they can get against that gal."

Michael looked hard at the chief and asked, "How far can Mark go with action duties, Director?"

Mitrano returned the stare and said, "As far as his lion's heart allows him."

Michael and Julius appeared concerned.

"If the bastards get by Mark's men in Naples, your team on Capri will be the final obstacle," stated the director firmly. "In case of your failure, F-16 Fighting Falcons from the airbase in Naples will stop the ship in the Tyrrhenian Sea.

"Let me remind you all that attacks with heavy firepower against the farmhouse in Florence, or the *Kilij* ship at sea, risks a nuclear detonation. There would be catastrophic consequences to the Italian mainland. We do not like these options.

"The attack in Florence will be conducted by specially trained assault teams with small arms. No heavy fire will be utilized on the farmhouse or against vehicles. It must be a clean operation. The Florence mission's success depends on the element of surprise. The *Kilij* must be taken off-guard.

We do not want to induce a nuclear explosion by our accident or their design. This must be avoided at all costs.

"If an attack on the ship becomes necessary, our planes will knock out her propulsion systems and leave her dead in the water. US Navy Seals would conduct a combat boarding of the ship. Stopping the nukes on the high seas is the highest risk option available to us. Many American casualties would ensue. We could also lose the nukes into the sea. We must also avoid this option if possible.

"Let me stress again that we wish to seize the nukes if we can. We neither want them detonated, nor lost into the Tyrrhenian Sea. Detonation would be a catastrophe for all; and losing them into the sea would initiate a testy underwater race between us and the Russians. I must have the bombs' bargaining power for the United States. Their negotiation value may save thousands of American lives in the future.

"The Condor would have to escape our efforts in Florence, Naples, and Capri, before buying his fate at sea. Somewhere, he will go down. He will not escape our efforts. I would not consider his odds of success against the CIA a safe bet."

Michael understood Mark's unrestrainable nature. He was worried for him.

"Listen, little brother! You just make sure the SOB and his toys get on the ferry to Capri. Let me take care of the rest.

"You're already a hero, Mark; let me get in on the action. Stay back and live another day for me. You've done enough.

"Just buy the Arab a ticket for the ferry..... You understand, little brother?"

Mark Stansfield nodded.

The morning sun warmed the cold air. Shops and cafes had opened on the square.

Mitrano rose from the bench, removed his black-tie, and shouldered his jacket. He took a deep breath and said, "I think I'll get some coffee and toast."

He walked over to the statue of Caesar and put an arm around his escort. They strolled across the street to a restaurant. The young couple feeding the swans on the lake followed, as did the two joggers. The world was a crazy place, and beautiful Como was no exception.

The old park violinist came by the Stansfields. He winked his eye at Julius and played John Philip Sousa's "The Stars and Stripes Forever".

The brothers stared and listened.

CHAPTER 25

Tuscan Fall

The rolling hills passed into the horizon without end. The green turned to a blue haze and melded into the distant sky. Brown, yellow, orange, and red were sprinkled into the natural canvas like lovely specks of colored paint from an artist's passionate brush. Leaves were changing from the verdant of summer to the varied shades of cooler autumn. Fields of golden grain, black olive, and dark blue grape spread out in all directions. Standing groves of chestnut and fruit trees intermixed; the peaceful earthy hues of the nut tree integrated with the yellow leaves of gingko, the red pomegranates and cherries, and the orange of persimmon. Tall cypresses in thickets of oak, rosemary and sage, calmly awaited the first rains of November. Forgotten grayish-brown hay bales sat alone, gathering moisture. Yellow and orange chrysanthemums, symbolic of mourning on "All Souls's Day", seemed more abundant in the fields than in years past. Perhaps, it was an omen of things to come in this Tuscan fall.

The serene yellow tones of early light beamed across the Arno River Valley and the Chianti hills. A dawn fog, still present from the evening prior, crept along the valley. The smoky mist clung to the ground and hesitated to leave with the coming of a new day. The blue and white of sky became defined as the sun rose on Tuscany.

John Mullen looked out with his binoculars across the valley to an opposite hilltop. His position on a second story of a 15th century Florentine villa, situated 1500 meters above sea level, provided him with an excellent view of the enemy on a lower hill. Three miles separated the hilltops. He scanned down along the asphalt road, across a small stream in the valley, and up the enemy hill. He followed a long caravan of SUVs as they wound their way up to the farmhouse.

The *Kilij* had congregated in a fortified 13th century farmhouse. There were heavy machine gun emplacements in several windows of the Tuscan limestone building. The black guns were easily seen against the sun-aged, hand-chiseled, large rectangular blocks of pale Tuscan stone. The enemy complex spread across the entire hilltop. Without a perimeter security wall, the compound was defended by several hidden bunker gun positions in the hill's rock. More than a hundred men were positioned for defense of the safe house.

Along with companions - Whitmore and Kakkar - Mullen was supported by two complete CIA Special Ops assault teams and one MI6 squad. His orders were to attack the *Kilij* stronghold, rescue Claudia Coffigny, capture Anwar

Nejem, and seize the nuclear bombs. The sixty-seven men were trained to assault well defended positions and handle dangerous materials. They had learned their trade under fire, forged in the recent wars of Asia and the Middle East. Nevertheless, overtaking the enemy hill would be a daunting task. There would be many casualties.

"Thank God for the high ground," said Mullen to Thomas Whitmore, who sat behind him at a table cleaning his rifle. "I can see every single one of them.....

"There's no hiding, boys!

"By this time tomorrow, all of those bastards are in eternal sleep.....

"Food for the crows, if they'll have them!"

Mullen slumped slowly down the wall to the floor beneath his view. He removed the Cuban cigar from the corner of his mouth and looked at Whitmore with concern.

"This is worse than bloody Hill 2309 in Afghanistan, Tommy. We can't knock out the buildings with airpower this time. Exploded nukes and radiation fallout would poison Tuscany for a hundred years.

"Imagine..... Florence under a nuclear cloud.

"I don't think the gods would forgive us for that one..... Highly unpleasant, I'd say.

"We can hit the gun bunkers with heavy fire, but the main buildings have to be taken with small arms."

Mullen sat up and raised his head above the windowsill. He returned to his binoculars and chomped on his cigar.

"These Cuban smokes from Michael Stansfield are a delight. The Americans got them from the dead Turk. It's hand rolled, genetically-engineered tobacco from Fidel's fields. No wonder the Commandante lasted so long. He didn't want to let go of this shit.

"It's a crying shame!

"It's good..... Very good!

"Goddam it, not even Sir Winston had royal leaf like this!"

Taliban Hill 2309, in eastern Afghanistan along the Pakistani border, had been taken by a large NATO force in 2007. Mullen and Whitmore provided intelligence for the successful secret mission, which had cost thirteen US and British lives. Many more would have died if not for the US air strikes on the Taliban positions before the uphill raid. The MI6 intel provided the coordinates for the air attacks on the heavy gun emplacements. Both Mullen and Whitmore had won medals of valor for their actions at Hill 2309.

Daivat Kakkar came up the steps and entered the room. "Johnny, everyone's here and ready."

Mullen turned and said, "Sit down, Daivat..... Relax!"

The Brit group leader pointed out the window and grinned, "We have several hours to kill here, before we go kill over there..... So, sit down..... Put up your feet and take a nap..... Think about home and go to sleep."

Kakkar pulled a chair and sat at the table.

"Where's home, Indian?" asked Whitmore. The rough-edged Englander didn't make eye contact as he cleaned his AK-47.

"I have no home, Tom," responded Daivat, while removing his combat vest and gun belt.

Whitmore looked up at the Hindu with more interest. "Everyone has a home, boy..... Where's yours? Do you have a woman in India?"

"My wife and children were taken last year. They were killed in my hometown of Mumbai by *Kilij* agents. I haven't been back to India ever since.

"I've tracked these dogs since that day. I'll persist until I've killed all of them, or they have killed me.

"There's no going home for me, because I have no home. Without my family, there will never be a home again," sighed Kakkar, slowly opening his heart-shaped locket.

The Brits stared at each other in quiet. Mullen returned to his binocular field glasses and peered at the enemy across the valley. Whitmore loaded his weapon.

The fog had faded, and the sun lit up the Tuscan countryside - only miles from Florence.

After a short pause, Mullen muttered, "Don't worry, Indian..... We'll get these bastards.....

"Tommy, go downstairs and tell the men to get some rest..... The night is ours."

Daivat Kakkar walked into the corner of an adjacent room. He removed his boots and laid a red prayer rug on the floor. He sat bare-footed on it.

The Hindu opened his knapsack and carefully set up a small shrine. He placed a large photograph of his wife Neha and two boys on the altar. Next to the image of his family, he burned incense.

Daivat closed his eyes and crossed his legs. He held Tulasi wood mala prayer beads in his right hand, and chanted mantras for the souls of his beloved wife and sons. With each repetition, he turned his thumb clockwise around another bead in sequence.

The ritual brought him peace. On this earth, this was the closest he could get to their memories. It did not take away the pain, however. It didn't even alleviate it. It simply brought his soul closer to them.

On the *Kilij* farm, Claudia sat by the window of an upper story bedroom. She looked out at the armed men collecting by the house's entrance. She counted at least six dozen fighters with automatic rifles near the building and adjacent fields. Some carried heavy machine guns and RPGs. All spoke Arabic.

"We're leaving for the coast in the morning!" shouted a terrorist. "But it's not Naples. Anwar has changed plans. No matter, soon we'll be in America to kill the infidels where they sleep."

The Condor stepped out among his men. "Shut your mouths!" he yelled angrily. "Speak of nothing or I'll cut out your tongues myself."

He gave orders on the defense of the grounds. The men dispersed, and Anwar re-entered the building.

Claudia sent an encrypted message to Julius and Mitrano, "leaving for coast-am..... not naples-elsewhere..... don't know....."

With her thumbs still on the text, Anwar stormed the room with two henchmen. He slapped Claudia's face and shouted, "Give me the phone, you pestilent female dog!"

The Condor screamed at his men, questioning how Claudia could still have her cellular phone.

"You idiots! No one can follow orders! I must do everything myself!

"Who are you calling, stinking bitch?" screamed Anwar.

The Egyptian threw Claudia to the stone floor and kicked her in the head. He looked at the unintelligible message.

"What is this shit?" he yelled.

"Tie her hands and feet to the bedposts..... Spread her wide open like a dog in heat! I'll find out myself what scum she is!"

Anwar tossed the phone out the window and ordered his men to strip Claudia bare. He stood over her naked body on the bed and pulled out a knife. He passed the sharp blade across her exposed breasts. He raised the knife up against her neck, and then went to her face. He passed the point along the edges of her pink lips.

"So beautiful you are to be such a dog," he whispered with clenched teeth. "What a waste it is to kill you. I could have enjoyed you for a while. It's a pity to waste such natural female beauty."

The Arab psychopath placed the knife tip close to Claudia's left eye. He then pulled it down to her left nipple.

"I don't know whether to stick it in your eye, or remove a nipple. Both would be painful," he laughed, looking at his imbecile guards. "Certainly an eye is worth more than a nipple. But your breasts are so full, they entice me to be generous."

Anwar softly circled each nipple with his blade.

"They are hard and erect, you whore dog!" he shouted. "Does the steel excite you?"

"I like rough play," said Claudia, grinning like a she-devil.

The Arab placed the knife on her vagina, lightly spreading the lips.

"How rough do you like to play?" he asked, entering her with the tip of the six-inch blade.

"As rough as you like, as long as I live," she answered.

The Condor entered further, watching her face for reaction. Claudia did not flinch.

"You are a sick bitch!" he screamed, throwing the knife out the window.

Anwar punched Claudia in the face. She bled from her nose and mouth.

"Now tell me..... Who were you calling? Were you calling Mama? Why Can't I understand the script, fucking woman?

You were calling your Texan handler, weren't you? You are an infidel working with the American pigs, aren't you?" yelled the Egyptian.

Claudia responded, "You Arab fool, I have done nothing! I don't know of what you speak. I went with you for some fun. Now, I see men walking around with guns and angry voices. You have me locked up like a whore in a castle keep. I didn't ask for this. I simply wanted to play with a rich Arab."

She cried and pleaded, "Let me go! I'll return to Chicago and keep my mouth shut! I've seen nothing! You can believe me! I will not talk! Just please let me go home!"

Her Machiavellian acting was worthy of praise.

"Keep her tied-up until morning," ordered the Egyptian.

He edged his face up to Claudia's and murmured, "I won't kill you right now..... Your beauty is too much for me to destroy, just now..... You can perhaps give me pleasure, and make me forget what I saw. Sex could buy you time..... Relieve me of stress. Give me more time to consider your fate."

Anwar grinned like a hyena and ordered his men out of the room. He removed his clothes and stood over Claudia.....

Night came to Tuscany. It became cold and windy. A light rain fell. A black moonless sky provided cover for Mullen and his men while they moved across the valley. All dressed in dark camouflage with anti-thermal coating, and wearing night-vision aids, the CIA and MI6 teams raced to take positions below the *Kilij* hilltop farmhouse. By midnight, the men had collected at the base of the mountain.

On radio, Mullen gave orders to quietly ascend the 800 foot hill. Approaching the first bunkers near the top, Mullen signaled his men to stop and lay low. It was 3 AM.

"Excalibur One calling Crusader..... Please copy," said John Mullen into his radio. "We are in position and awaiting word."

Seconds later, a return, "This is Crusader..... We copy..... Five miles out, and coming silent and fast..... We'll provide 'fire and brimstone' on your order, Excalibur One..... Do you acknowledge?"

Mullen smiled in the dark and ordered, "Fire at will, Crusader..... Fire at will..... Pump as much fire and brimstone as possible into target mark..... Empty your guns!"

Four US Army Longbow Apache attack helicopters flew from the southwest over Mullen's position in an instant. The Brit commander felt the wind on the back of his neck as they passed. Methodically, they shot Hydra 70 rockets into the enemy *Kilij* emplacements outside the farmhouse. Bunkers exploded with massive effect. Helicopter chain guns fired hundreds of 30mm rounds into groups of men in open ground. Red tracers filled the sky in both directions. All hell had broken loose.

Mullen looked at his watch. It was fifteen minutes past three in the morning. He radioed his men along the line, "For God and country, attack! Attack! Attack!"

Dozens of CIA and MI6 agents went over the last two hundred feet of rocky ground, and assaulted the *Kilij* positions. Grenades were lobbed by both sides, while men met in the middle and killed each other with bayonets and small arms fire. *Kilij* mortars landed around Mullen as he raced towards the farmhouse. Enemy machine guns blasted from every window. Two CIA heavy machine guns shot into the farmhouse gun emplacements from the hill's ridgeline. Many men fell on both sides.

Inside the house, Anwar quickly untied Claudia from the bed. He bound her hands together at the wrists and gagged her mouth. He dragged her down the stairs to the backdoor on the first floor. Two men behind him, along with Aqeel Sultan and Ameer Samara, carried the steel nuke suitcases.

Anwar threw open the backdoor and immediately confronted two US agents who approached their position. Two quick bursts from his AK into the dark cut down the Americans. Claudia pounded the back of the Egyptian's head with her tied fists. The Condor fist punched her in the face, knocking her unconscious. Aqeel tossed Claudia over his back and handed his case to the Egyptian. They ran toward an SUV parked nearby, as machine gun rounds landed around them. An Apache aborted its attack after seeing the steel cases. The *Kilij* men drove off into the heavy forest of cypress and oak, with Claudia and their deadly cargo.

Thomas Whitmore blew open the front door of the farmhouse with a contained explosion. He entered with three agents and was killed by machine gun fire from the second floor.

Mullen raced around the side of the farm and encountered a group of *Kilij* agents with automatic rifles. They exchanged fire, and everyone fell dead.

Combat continued for another two hours.....

By sunrise, the hills of Tuscany were quiet. Silence permeated the ground and air. The early morning white fog mixed with the acrid black smoke of war. The gray smog blotted out the sun. No birds flew near the farmhouse.

A fire in the main building burned uncontrollably. US Army firefighters worked to put it out.

The bodies of many dead men were scattered across the hilltop. There had been only five American survivors. No Brits were alive.

By mid-morning, the misty rain had stopped. The first day in November would be warmer and sunnier than usual. There were no clouds in the sky, as the sun lit the valley below the killing grounds with natural light.

The nukes had been lost. Anwar and Claudia were gone - destination unknown. Like Mitrano had expected, the battle would go on..... But where?

A large transport helicopter approached the hill from the north. It landed in front of the burned out farmhouse. Five heavily armed men, dressed in black, rushed out of the copter. CIA Director Joseph Mitrano stepped onto the field of battle. Dark smoke, blown by the wind in all directions, still shrouded the field of the dead. Medical teams had already removed the few survivors.

The chief took his time, and stopped by the final resting place of each CIA and MI6 agent on the Tuscan hill by the Arno River. He prayed for all of them.

He finally came upon the body of Daivat Kakkar. The courageous Indian lay on his back in a grassy area near the farmhouse. His eyes were open to the sky, searching for heaven. He had fallen with a single gunshot to his heart. Mitrano had never met Kakkar personally, but he knew much of him and his exploits.

The director knelt by the Indian intelligence officer and kindly closed his eyes. He prayed over his body, paying final respects to another brave warrior of freedom.

The American noticed something in Daivat's clenched fist. He found the heart-shaped locket, and stared at the photograph of Daivat's wife and children. He gently returned the sacred piece, closing the freedom fighter's hand over his torn heart.

Joseph Mitrano looked up into the Tuscan sky and whispered more than once, "The people we fight and die for."

CHAPTER 26

Sarah and the Knight

Julius and Michael Stansfield reached the top of Monte Solaro in the late morning. It was a slow difficult climb up the steep 2000 foot high limestone peak. The highest point on the isle of Capri had a commanding view of the deep blue Tyrrhenian Sea to the west, the Gulf of Salerno to the southeast, and the Bay of Naples to the north. The Marina Grande on the north coast laid slightly northeast of Solaro's base. The entire island was visible from the peak. Topographical details of Capri, and the waters around it, were exposed to the naked eye. One could visually scan the island from the Punta Carena Lighthouse on the southwestern tip to the ruins of Villa Jovis, three miles away at the northeastern end. The remains of the Roman villa, built by

Emperor Tiberius in 27 AD, sat 1100 feet above the sea on Monte Tiberio. No ship could sail by Capri in any direction without being spotted from the top of Monte Solaro.

The Stansfields set up monitoring equipment in an old blockhouse fort, used by both the English and Napoleon's French troops in the wars of the early 19th century. Filled with dagger-scratched inscriptions by warriors of the past, the stone fortification provided shelter from the strong wind gusts swirling around the summit. A nest of Peregrine falcon hatchlings, protected by their mother, sat along the side of the blockhouse.

Computer connections to orbital satellites allowed the Stansfields to track position of the *Kilij* ship, Last *Sultan of Granada*. The 140 foot-long luxury yacht had left Malta, early the day before, and was expected at the marina on Capri by late afternoon.

Binocular telescopic photography from the top of Monte Solaro would identify some of the characters on the ship for the CIA. Their digital physical identifications would be traced back by analysts in Langley and London, permitting the CIA to make connections to other terrorist cells around the world. Information was critical to the CIA. More information saved more American lives in the never-ending Global War on Terrorism.

Julius looked out through the binocular telescope over the Tyrrhenian Sea to the southwest, waiting to capture the first glimpse of the terror ship. Michael sat next to him with the satellite equipment and monitored the ship's approach.

On the stone wall next to Michael, there were hundreds of doodles. Some were in English, others in French; but one caught his eye. A large spinning black tornado contained a message in bright red letters, *L'ODYSSEE DE SOLDAT.*

"A soldier's odyssey," whispered Michael.

Being a warrior himself, Michael understood the meaning of the sketch. He was familiar with the long wandering voyage of a soldier. The adventures and changes of fortune were filled with uncertainty and doubt; but also, the odyssey contained great wisdom and knowledge. For him, as for the French lieutenant of Napoleon's Grande Armee, it had been a quest for the truth in a whirlwind of black.....

"Mitrano hasn't given any orders for what happens after this ship docks," said Julius, peering intently through the scope. "We still haven't been informed of the operations in Florence. We don't know if Anwar and the nukes have already been taken down by Mullen.

"If so, Michael, do you think they'll still order us to strip this ship clean and take out the bastards on it?"

Michael laughed..... "With Mitrano, you never know..... The cat always has something up his sleeve. He's in charge, and his old brain is always working overtime. I'm sure he's cooking up something.

"Heaven knows what went down in Florence. If he'd been confident the bombs were easily seizable, he would have ordered us all to be there. He would have concentrated his forces in Florence, and not placed us here in Capri and Mark in Naples.

"We're in safety-valve positions because he expects twists and turns in this operation. He's still unsure of this freak, Anwar Nejem. He considers the *Kilij* to be an agile, intelligent opponent.

"I'm certain Mitrano has several contingency plans, and he likely has us both in the center of most of them. If we are on Capri, Mitrano expects the final action to occur here.

He has Mark and his team in Naples for eye identification of the SOBs as they arrive. Mark's squad will follow them in on the ferry. In the end, the show will come down to this island. He has over 40 agents sitting around at Marina Grande. The curtain will rise on the final act of the play in that little harbor to the north. You can count on it, Julius."

"You don't think Mitrano is saving our asses because of his friendship with Father?" asked Julius. "Perhaps, he's protecting us a bit? Wishing to keep us out at the end rather than throwing us into the action?"

"Give me a fucking break," laughed Michael. "He wasn't protecting me at Sevastopol a few months ago, or you at the Totenkopf Castle, or us both at Lorely Rock in Germany.

"What about Mark on the Red scum's boat in Como?

"Our brother's in a wheelchair, for God's sake..... The old man threw Mark into the fire because he believed in him. He was the right man, at the right time, at the right place.

"That's what the CIA is all about..... Choose and pick your fights with your best warriors.

"Old friendships aside, Mitrano would throw us into hell if he needed to rub off the devil himself. That's the only way he can have it.

"Dad functioned in the same manner, and so do we.

"He's put us on this rock because the *Kilij* and Anwar will successfully arrive on Capri In the next 24 hours. The dudes on the ship we see on the satellite image will soon be dead. You and I are the players he's chosen to lead the final action against this clan."

Julius caught the first sight of the *Last Sultan* at twenty miles out.

"There we go, baby..... Come to papa..... Let's see if we can identify any of these fuckers."

Captain Stansfield scanned over the deck slowly, from bow to stern. He counted twenty men, visually exposed, and began sending digital information of each by satellite to Langley. Data profiles quickly returned on Michael's computer.

"We've got three Libyans, two Yemeni, four Syrians, two Egyptians, three Iraqis, a Pakistani, two US nationals, and three rogue Russian military," said Michael, "a goddam United Nations team on a world cruise..... Little do they know what's coming their way..... We're going to put fire up their little asses, and sink their white ship into the Mediterranean..... These bastards are shark food."

Julius pressed his eyes tightly against the telescope..... "Wait a second here..... The ship's not turning towards Capri, Michael! It's going north into open ocean! What the fuck?

"Notify Mitrano and instruct we have a loose ship heading north along the coastline. Transmit coordinates, speed, and direction. Let them follow by satellite and estimate possible destinations.

"Maybe we got the bastards in Florence, and these fuckers are heading home.

"Communicate with the teams down in the harbor and have them prepare for rapid transfer..... Let's see if Mitrano has a contingency for this twist..... Let's get downhill and wait for orders."

Earlier the same day in Naples - I left the hotel, across from the Piazza del Plebiscito, and pushed my wheelchair two blocks to the promenade along the bay. The 3000 year-old city was full of historic sites. Hundreds of old churches dotted the ancient center of culture.

Reaching the bayfront, I found the beautiful "Church of the Seven Virtues". The late 15th century Renaissance architectural masterpiece was a feast for the eyes. A massive red-brick dome rose high above the street. The majestic facade - with cylindrical columns, Corinthian capitals, and Roman arches - was impressive from every angle. A large central triumphal archway, flanked by Corinthian pilasters, greeted all visitors to the sanctuary.

I sat in front of the church for a few minutes, alone in thought. I entered the place of worship as its three large bells tolled. At this time of the morning, the church was empty.

I rolled onto the golden yellow marble, under the coffered barrel vault of the interior nave. I slowly passed through the church, staring at all the art around me. Life-sized and idealized human bronze statues, depicting the seven virtues, were aligned along one side of the church's interior. Wisdom, Justice, Humility, Courage, Faith, Hope, and Love were captured in essence by the Renaissance sculptures.

I stopped in front of the glorious depictions, one by one, and studied them. I came to the statue of "Love" and stayed for a long while. I looked at the details, pondering their beauty and significance.

A mournful young female figure sat in a flower garden with her eyes closed. She held a baby in her arms, close to her bosom. On the ground next to the fair lady, a small dove looked up to her with its head tilted to one side. Opposite the mother, a male figure in powerful knight's armor knelt with his head bowed and eyes closed. The knight offered his right hand to the lady and child. A plea for forgiveness, it seemed.

The sculptures of the lady, child, and knight meant many things to me. Thoughts of life passed through my mind like flashes. Childhood and adulthood memories came to me in no particular order. Emotive apparitions of Mother, Father, Brother, Sister, Husband, Wife, and Child materialized in my sight, and then disappeared.

Most strongly, memories of Sarah and my sons filled me. All were wrapped in love and joy, peace and hope. The thoughts, rather than strengthening me, depleted energy. Exhaustion overtook me in the montage. I bowed my head, closed my eyes, and offered my open hand like the knight......

Much later, I exited the church and crossed the street to the promenade. I quietly looked out across the blue Gulf of Naples to the island of Capri. I thought of home, Sarah, and my sons.

I pulled a piece of paper from my coat pocket and scribbled a note to Sarah.......*Dear Baby... I desperately needed to speak to you... I'm sorry for everything. I'm sorry for getting hurt. I'm sorry for leaving you alone again... You deserve much more... I love you. I've always loved you, and will forever. Forever is a long time, but our love demands it... Take care of our boys, like you always have. Tell them, I love them... I hope to be home soon... There will be no more sep-arations. No more loss of words. No more regrets... My life is what it is. And I only wish to spend it with you... You are the only thing... Like the amaranth, I am yours eternally.....Mark.*

I received a scrambled emergency text-message from Director Mitrano. I quickly decoded the notation. It read, "Captain Mark Stansfield..... *Kilij* ship north of Capri, destina-tion unknown..... The Condor moving to coast with nukes, destination unknown..... Will inform with further planning..... Hold tight."

I erased the secret CIA transmission, and sat thinking. In a moment of serendipitous epiphany, I remembered three communications tapped from Anwar in St. Moritz in August. The calls had been placed to "Madre Sacre" in Piombino, Italy. Three of several thousands of messages transmitted by Anwar in August, they had not been fully deciphered or understood at the Pentagon.

The true meanings of the secret cables suddenly dawned on me. Anwar Nejem had sent messages to his mother, an Italian national whose whereabouts had been unknown to the CIA for the past year.

I could bet Anwar's mother was now living in Piombino. The ancient Italian city was situated on the north-central Tuscan mainland coast, on the border of the Ligurian and Tyrrhenian seas, across from the island of Elba. It was a short distance from Florence. Anwar wanted to see his mother a final time, before departing for the USA and martyrdom.

It became clear to me. Emotion and love could even pass through the veins of a killer terrorist. One man's strength could be another's weakness.

I encrypted a call to Jim Thomas..... "Jimmy, get me a transport heli from the NATO airbase in town. Tell them, it's CIA confidential... Tell Alvarez and Westcott that we're leaving immediately... I need everyone fully armed but in plainclothes... We're going north about three hundred miles, Jimmy. Can't tell you where exactly, right now... Don't communicate this with Mitrano, just yet. I'll know when to call and inform him... We're going to fix this thing. We'll all be home soon."

CHAPTER 27

Peace on Earth

"So that's how I met your father, my 'Noble Prince'," gently said my mother, with a weak and breaking voice.

She barely had energy to whisper the words, as she lay with her eyes closed in bed. I sat next to her, holding her hand in the dim light of early morning.

With every word expressed, a measure of physical life escaped from her. Her soul would soon escape also. I understood this. Years earlier, I had seen it with my brother and father. Like them, living had taken its final tolls.

My mother hung on only for me. Her surrender was an emotionally painful process for both of us. I'd help her release peacefully without a struggle. I wished no more struggle for her, only tranquility.

The story of my mother and father's early life had been kept secret from Bobby and me. I didn't quite understand why at the time. I was too young, I suppose, to understand the deep sanctity of such things. Romantic love was a complicated matter. Its emotions required secrecy. Like war, love could only be experienced by those in it. It was impossible to explain its essence to those not consumed by it. All the great poetry of the world had been born from the sacred secrets between lovers. The special bonds between two people in love could be truly understood only by them. They were rare gifts, reserved only for the lovers to share and cherish. The invariable nature of the very holy communion between two souls could only remain unspoken. I would understand this truth a short time later in my own life.

My mother took the deepest breath she could and continued to speak to me. She needed me to know what she knew. Like peeking through a slightly open secret door, she allowed me into her world.

"Time plays with one's mind, and memories can take on more vivid color. But meeting your father, in the way I did, was magnificently unique. It didn't require of me to infuse more color with time. My recollection is pristine, untouched by fantasy or passionate addition. It was what it was, a moment of divine intervention when I needed it most. In all the horror and despair of war in a faraway land, glory came to a lonely young girl from rural Minnesota in one fateful instant. In all the confusion, there was a moment of clarity and security. What I saw and experienced was not imaginary. It was real, and hopeful of mankind's greatness. Man could show unlimited compassion for his fellow man, even under the most dire circumstances. The actions I saw that day symbolized the very reasons for my toils. After all the pain I had seen, all the young lives I had taken from me, all the misery, all the disillusionment and disappointment, there was still hope that man could withdraw from the cruelty and do what was right and noble. Instead of taking lives, man could save lives and inject a little grace to his existence on this planet. It could not be all bad. There was also goodness in this world.

"Your father personified these truths to me. In one shining moment, he captured the glory and love in man. His strong force drew me closer to him. Through the black smoke and distant din of battle, I walked into the torn surgical tent and to his side, without hesitation or fear. I was invited into Heaven. His goodness allowed me in, and I loved him forevermore. He never left my side, since that day at Anzio. Except sadly, for that day at the end."

My mother stopped speaking. She closed her eyes as her lips trembled. Tears flowed lightly down her face.

"Open the window, Julian, and let me breathe the fresh morning air. I want to see the bright light of the sun one last time.

"Watching the sun rise is special. It doesn't bring regrets like a sunset. It's interesting how a sunrise seems so peaceful, and hopeful of things yet to come. It was the case even during the war. We would operate through the night and stop for a break at dawn. We smoked a cigarette while perched on an Italian mountainside, or stretched out on the grass in a valley. Soaked in our boys' blood, we would watch the sun rise over the eastern hills and think today would be a better day. Not even the roar of cannon in the distance could make us think otherwise. We sat in our own personal space and silence, like in a trance, secure in our hope for a better day. It seldom was, but we would think so. Early morning allowed us to survive and prepare emotionally for the day to come. It was our way of coping with things you couldn't change..... And there were so many things you couldn't change."

I opened the window for my mother. I stared at the sun as it broke over Lake Geneva in Wisconsin. My beaten eyes were strengthened by its energy. I could feel a warm hope in its light.

A cool summer breeze passed into the room, setting sound to the wind chimes in the corner. The soft tinkling of the metal tubes echoed gently off the walls. The music generated a surreal feeling for me. In the sorrow of our mutual dream, there was peaceful glory. The sounds of Bach or Beethoven could not have been more beautiful. Nature was supreme to my mother, and the chimes produced a special universal song.

Mother turned her head towards me and listened..... "Those were your father's..... He hung them outside his sleeping tent at Anzio on the first day he arrived with the 95th Evacuation Hospital. He loved their poetry. The songs brought peace with every blow of the wind..... It's funny how we get pleasure from the simplest things. Short interludes of beauty allowed him to endure..... He'd often say those chimes were the cause of our meeting....."

"What do you mean, Mother?"

I wanted to learn everything about my parents. It was inspiring to me.

"Your father arrived on the Anzio beachhead in late January 1944. He was injured in a bombing raid on February 7. The hospital was destroyed.

"His commanding officer gave him a day to rest and recover from a superficial leg wound. While lying on his cot, on the evening of February 8, he thought about the 95th's orders to retreat back to Naples. The 15th Evac Hospital would take their place in Anzio on February 10.

"He didn't want to leave Anzio. He sensed his services were more needed there, than in Naples. He had just arrived on the war's frontlines and wasn't comfortable with an early departure.

"While he lay in his tent, a long strong wind from the sea passed through his chimes outside. He listened to a beautiful symphony for several minutes. With the music came the decision to transfer to the 15th.

"As his crew shipped off from the beachhead, he stayed and operated. I appeared in his life soon afterward.

"He believed the chimes had brought us together..... Maybe so," said my mother in halting speech.

Her shortness of breath had worsened. Conversation was difficult. She realized the end was near. My mother was not afraid of death. She was serene in its anticipation.

"Solitude is difficult," said Mother. "Losing loved ones from your life leaves a deep black void. You miss their joy. You don't hear their laugh, or see their smile. Their closeness of being cannot be replaced. Their love cannot be replaced. Nothing can fill the absence. It is too complete..... I know you understand these things, Julian."

My mother paused to regain her breath, and mustered a last bit of strength and courage.

"Julian, how was your father that last day?" she asked in a gentle voice.

Her face expressed a profound love for him, and also many questions. She was anguished. I gathered much from her look. She wished to know if he had suffered. She needed to hear his final thoughts.

Mother had never asked these things of me. She'd been afraid to think her 'Prince' had passed from life with any unease. She couldn't accept the thought of his pain and discomfort. She only wished for his peace.

I came from the window and held her hand. I leaned over and whispered into her ear, "In love with you..... He was madly in love with you, Mother."

She closed her eyes and smiled..... Another tear ran from her left eye, and dropped innocently from her cheek to the pillow..... Bliss in heartbreak.....

"We woke early that morning and set sail north on Lake Michigan towards the Wisconsin coastline Father loved so much. He was more quiet than usual, as if concerned about something. Perhaps, he hadn't been feeling well.

"An hour into our trip, we sat together and talked of Bobby. He repeated many times how sorry he was, that he hadn't decided on Bobby's surgery sooner. His passing had been so sad for all of us; particularly you, Mother. That he had lost him; another young life had escaped his grasp..... He cried..... I embraced him, and assured him of our love..... I forced him to see he had done everything possible.

"Father said he loved you with all his soul, Mother; that we were the most important things in his life, and he had let us down. He repeated Bobby's name many times.....

"He looked into my soul and gasped, collapsing into my arms. His last words were of love for you and me. I saw his adoration for you, Mother, in his eyes..... He took a final breath and passed away from us.....

"I held Father for more than an hour, while our boat drifted in a calm breeze on Lake Michigan.....

"His last thoughts were of you, Mother....."

Ann Nelson Stansfield had no remaining energy to cry. Her breathing became more labored. I felt the pulse in her wrist become weaker beneath my fingertips. I sensed her life escaping.

I tenderly caressed her face and kissed her forehead. I whispered in her ear that it was alright to let go; that I would stay next to her until she crossed to the other side with Bobby and Father.

My mother opened her eyes for the last time. In her true essence, she looked at me and said, "Peace on earth." She whispered again slowly, "Peace on earth."

She took a deep breath and requested, "Please play for me, 'Amazing Grace'."

I kissed both her cheeks and walked to the old record player by the window. As I placed the music to play, the wind chimes softly sounded behind me. I knew her spirit had gone to my brother and father. I was alone now.....

I looked at the rising sun and hoped for a better tomorrow.....

Julius Stansfield closed Ann's diary. He tried to assimilate what he had just read. He now knew the deep spirits of his grandparents, Robert and Ann. He had seen their love form in the vortex of war. He could see the eternal nature of love in them.

Julius could also now better understand the character of his father. He had absorbed his father's early development as a human being. He appreciated the love his father had expressed for Olivia.

They had all been extraordinary people in unique times.

Julius thought of his brothers and sister. The essence of 'eternal love' was in all of them. They were also extraordinary people living in unique times. They were now responsible for living that love and passing it on.

Julius checked his gear, and looked across at Michael as he placed a magazine into his M4 rifle. He smiled at his brother, and the smile was returned. They, with twelve other heavily armed men aboard the transport helicopter, raced north across the Tyrrhenian Sea from Capri. They were only minutes away from their rendezvous with four more CIA helicopters south of Elba. Together, they would stop a ferry from Piombino to Elba, and help Mark Stansfield and his team confront the Condor.

The show would end here, near Elba, and all the Stansfield boys were ready.

CHAPTER 28

Take Me Home

I sat in my wheelchair at the docks of Piombino, receiving and transmitting encrypted text messages. It was dark, and a cold 43 degrees, an hour before dawn.

Jimmy sat a block away, at a bench by the ferry scheduled to leave for Portoferraio at 6:40 AM. The port on the island of Elba was only an hour trip by boat.

The early morning transport would be nearly empty on a Friday in November. Only a small group of day-laborers waited to board for the rocky island made famous by Napoleon's first exile.

I read the confirmation from Alvarez and Westcott, "Anwar and his men left his mother's apartment two minutes ago... Claudia is with them... They seem headed in your direction, just as you had hoped... Will follow them in... Any orders?"

I responded, "They're coming to the ferry for a short ride to Elba... I expect them to rendezvous with their ship on the island... We'll take them on the boat, before they reach Elba."

Another message from Mitrano read, "*Kilij* ship - *Last Sultan* - appears headed to Portoferraio, just as you deduced... Will arrive by 7 AM... We have a task force heading to Elba to intercept... Another task force headed your way, to assist on ferry takedown... Do not engage Anwar until help arrives... I repeat - do not engage enemy until help arrives... You were right, Mark... Great job... This is last communication until interception... Good luck and good hunting."

I turned the obsidian lucky charm in my hand. The inherited relic of fortune had been true to me once more. I felt its smooth polished surface, and thought back to my father, Annapolis, and the day of my graduation. I had gone early in the morning to the chapel......................

"I knew I'd find you here, Mark," said Father, sitting next to me in the silence. He wore a formal white uniform, and held his admiral's cap under his arm.

"You're early," I smiled. "Graduation and commissioning are still hours away."

"I know," he said. "I needed to see you in dark blue Marines. You look good as a second lieutenant," he beamed.

"How did you know where to find me, Pops?"

"It was a lucky guess, I suppose..... I came to the chapel also, on my graduation morning."

"Why?" I asked, almost afraid to learn.

"To pray, just like you, Mark..... To pray I'd have the balls to defend my country and honor..... To pray for the strength required of me in a critical situation..... To pray for courage to always do the right thing....."

"Were you afraid, Father?"

"Not any less than you," he smiled.....

"I wanted to pass on a small gift, Mark. It's a token of fortune, given to me many years ago by your mother's grandfather – Raul Sierra. I've carried it with me to the four corners of the earth, and the charm has always brought me back home. It's seen a lot of battle."

Father pulled a sharp and shiny black stone from his pocket. He gently placed it in my hand.

"It doesn't look like much, but it has great significance for me. It's an ancient obsidian spearhead, more than a quarter million years old. The black volcanic glass comes from central Ethiopia's Rift Valley. Once it sat at the end of a long wooden stick, the killer point of a javelin in the hands of primitive man. It's the oldest known projectile of war.

"I suspect Raul received it as a token of appreciation in one of his many wars against Communism. He hoped it would bring me more luck than it had for him..... It did, and I've saved it for you.

"Let it serve as the tip of your spear, Mark, in defense of honor, family, and country."

My father embraced me. He shook my hand and began walking away.

In his mid-stride, I shouted to him, "Father! Did you really know I'd be here?"

"It was the only place I looked!" he laughed. "You inherited my double helix!"

"That I did, Father," I smiled. "That I did."

"By the way, Son, let Mother catch your hat..... She deserves it as much as you," said my father softly.

"I'll do my best!" I shouted.

Father saluted, and I saluted..... He left me to pray in our chapel....................

I signaled Jimmy with my right hand to begin operations. He went to the group of construction laborers and quickly disbanded them. They departed their separate ways from the ship.

Jim boarded the small ferry and headed towards the pilothouse. The boat's captain and two crew soon stepped off into the dark. A small van dropped off three CIA auxiliary team members to help Jimmy man the boat. I waited.....

I pulled a photograph of Sarah and the boys from my coat pocket. Taken on Christmas Day two years ago, Robert and George seemed happy. They had grown up much in these two years, I thought. Sarah looked beautiful as always and full of joy, watching our boys open gifts.

I had not been there with them. My Marine raiders and I had been training at Pickel Meadows in the Sierra Nevada Mountains for our secret operation into the Hunza Valley of northern Pakistan.

Sarah had been brave, enjoying Christmas with her boys without me. She didn't know where I was, or where I was going. My Sarah was a woman in the extreme.

I had been gone from them much, I thought..... Too much.....

I hoped conditions would change for all of us. This Christmas, I'd be home to relive all that I had missed. There was great catching up to do.

I had no time to lose; no time to obsess over being crippled. My legs were weak, but not my heart. I could love, as

I had loved. I could enjoy, as I had enjoyed. This was my life to live, and there was no time to waste.

I slowly passed my finger over Sarah's face in the photograph. I closed my eyes, and sensed the soft contours of her nose, cheeks, and lips. She was with me now; allowing me to love her, as I had loved in the past. I opened my eyes, kissed her image, and returned the photograph to my coat pocket for safe keeping. I'd be home soon, where I belonged.

I closed my coat to keep out the chill. It had been a long day. I'd been awake for more than twenty-four hours. I leaned back and rested my mind awhile.

I stared at the dark sky. The stars seemed close and bright. They hypnotized me with their natural beauty.

I wondered if the twinkling suns had planets orbiting them with the social difficulties of ours..... How could Earth's mankind be so ugly in such an amazing universe? Could other planets harbor such creatures?

Yes, we are insignificant in the largeness of the cosmos..... Yet, our greed and pride could destroy our world for future generations. Our self-destructiveness was a crime against the laws of nature.

Could human beings learn to live together on this planet peacefully, and stop killing for conquest and control? Could a better world be possible in the future?

I dreamed and hoped for a future with justice. I prayed for the happiness of my children. I blessed them and Sarah in my mind.

Somehow I had drifted from Sarah to the cosmos. How appropriate, I thought.....

Sarah was my universe. I could see her face in the stars. She beamed more inside of me than all the suns in the sky.

But I couldn't touch her any easier than I could touch the cosmos. They were both outside my physical range.

In my mind, I kissed Sarah and my sons. I prayed for the safety of my men and brothers - Julius and Michael. I prayed for my country and mankind..... We could all use the Almighty's grace.....

I returned to the action at hand. I mentally prepared for battle. I hoped my body would follow.

The waterfront came alive.....

Anwar and his terrorist team arrived at the ferry. Yousef, Aqeel, and Ameer walked onto the ship. Minutes later, the Mole Rat waved for the Condor to board. Three more *Kilij* agents ran onto the ferry, carrying the steel nuke cases. Anwar followed with an apparently drugged and subdued Claudia.

Rafael Alvarez and Simon Westcott came along the docks and also boarded. The stage was set, I thought. The inevitable final act of *Project X* would begin.....

Julius and Michael Stansfield sat quietly in their transport helicopter to Elba. Julius received satellite confirmation of *Last Sultan of Granada's* arrival in Portoferraio. A CIA ground squad was already in position at the port to prevent any movement from the *Kilij* ship.

"What are you worried about, Brother?" asked Michael, in his own concerned apprehension. "I can see it in your face..... Don't screw with me..... What's in your head?"

"Mark's on the ferry with his team. They've been told to stand down until we arrive.....

"What are the odds of Mark standing down, Michael?

"There's not a chance in hell that's going to happen..... You know Mark has never stood down to anything..... I don't imagine he will today either..... He will take charge before we arrive..... He'll save his brothers the trouble if he can.....

That's one variable he'd like to control - save his big brothers from the danger of a combat interception at sea..... You know it, and I know it.

"That's what you see in my face, Little Brother.

"I don't know how much warrior there is still left in him.

"It's not his heart and mind I worry about. He has much of both..... It's his body and soul that concern me. He may not have the physical combat reflexes to confront a young enemy; and his soul won't allow the endangerment of his brothers, if he can prevent it altogether.....

"Do you understand me, Little Brother?

"We'll arrive on a finished battlefield..... Silence will greet us when we board the ferry..... That's what worries me..... A war will start in the next few minutes, and you and I won't be there for the finish....."

Sixty miles south of Elba, four additional helicopters joined the older Stansfield brothers. An orange glow filled the eastern horizon at dawn. Julius opened the transport's door to get some cold fresh air. Stars were still visible to the west. Sirius was bright as always.

Julius pointed at the family star and shouted above the noise, "Remember?"

Michael smiled and gave Julius a thumbs-up..... "Everything will be fine, Big Brother! Just wait and see..... The cavalry is on its way! Don't despair! Mark can still take care of himself..... He may be our little brother in a wheelchair, but he's one tough son of a bitch! If he moves before we arrive, God help those bastards!"

Michael tried to relieve his own tension and concern. So did Julius..... They lay by each other on the floor of the helicopter and looked out at the western horizon - counting stars.

316 | *American Requiem*

The ferry entered the channel between the mainland and Elba. The Condor and his men sat inside to avoid the cold wind. They kept Claudia in a corner, guarded by the Gremlin – Aqeel Sultan. Windows faced the deck outside, where Alvarez and Westcott smoked a cigarette.

The sedated Claudia played her role superbly. She knew by intuition that things were about to go down.

"I need the bathroom, now!" shouted Claudia, slurring her words. "I'm about to piss in my pants, you mother-fuckers!" she screamed.

Anwar yelled at Aqeel, "Take the dirty bitch out to piss, and take Ameer with you! Don't fuck her! She's only mine to fuck before I kill her!"

Claudia was escorted outside by the *Kilij* barbarians. They walked down the gangway to the bathrooms at the stern of the ship..... Rafael Alvarez followed them into the darkness of twilight's shadows.....

"I'm gogogogoing ouuuttt fofoforrr a smoke," stuttered Yousef in English, smelling trouble and looking anxious.

"Speak only Arabic, you fool!" said the Condor angrily. "Don't take long!"

Anwar Nejem remained in the parlor with the nukes. Three more *Kilij* agents sat across from him.

Yousef walked nervously past Westcott to the bow of the ship. The CIA agent, disguised as an old man, stood near the entrance of the ferry's parlor..... Suddenly, the American fell to the floor in a fit of convulsions.....

The Condor stared at one of his aides and pointed to the old man, "Go see what the hell is going on!"

Miles away, Julius stood by the open door of the transport and hand-signaled three of the helicopters to descend toward the *Kilij* ship in the harbor of Portoferraio. He saluted them, as they sped to the west for the combat assault on the *Last Sultan*. He ordered the fourth transport, flying next to him, to increase speed to target.

"Stand and make final preparations for combat!" Julius commanded the men inside his transport.

As the copter flew low over the rocky peaks of Elba, Captain Stansfield looked down at the pebbly beaches and secluded coves of the island. It was still twilight..... He looked at his watch for the last time and shouted above the noise, "Five minutes to target!"

Rafael Alvarez walked toward the bathrooms. Ameer Samara, hearing footsteps behind him in the hall, turned as Alvarez fired one round into his head. The click of the trigger was the last thing the Libyan heard before dying.

Claudia, sensing the situation, round-kicked Aqeel Sultan in the chest. Falling to the floor, the North African saw Alvarez pump silent 9mm rounds into his chest and head.

A *Kilij* agent walked over to Westcott and helped him up. The American drove a combat knife into the terrorist's left chest, pinning him to a wall.

The door to the parlor swung open; Jim Thomas entered and fired multiple rapid shots. The *Kilij* agents around Anwar dropped dead. Rising defiantly from his chair, the Condor was ordered to lift his hands in the air.

I pushed my wheelchair in front of Anwar Nejem.

"He's clean," said Thomas, after searching the Arab.

"Secure the nukes, Jimmy."

The Egyptian *Kilij* terrorist and I faced off. A great tension formed between us.

"Sit down here," I pointed, "where I can see you in full splendor, Anwar."

"You mean at your eye level, American."

"Yes..... At my eye level," I responded firmly.

Jim Thomas removed the cases from the room and prepared them for transport. Simon Westcott entered the parlor and stood close to Anwar with a pistol ready.

"My original orders were to confiscate the contraband and neutralize all of the *Kilij* agents on board this ferry," I said to Anwar. "Just recently, my orders were changed. I was to capture you alive, if possible, and bring you back for interrogation. My chief is interested in all you know about counter-American intelligence in Turkey, Egypt, and Europe. Perhaps, you are worth more alive than dead."

Anwar sat back in his chair, staring at me. His internal rage was palpable. The carotid arteries in his neck were visibly pounding.

"Shouldn't you be in Lourdes rather than here, dipping in holy water? What is a man in a wheelchair doing in an operation like this? They're sending cripples to chase me down? The CIA can't get better men than you?" asked Anwar with a sick grin. "America must be in sad shape if they can't get complete men to solve their problems..... This is sad..... It's pathetic to my eyes."

"Don't cry for me, Arab..... America is a land of equal opportunity, even for cripples in wheelchairs," I smiled. "Besides, In my country the worth of a man is not measured by the strength of his legs. It's based on his courage and honor. That's our standard, Egyptian. Like it or not, you are mine today. You have lost your struggle to destroy my country. You will never see the light of day again. You will be a prisoner of the United States of America until the day you die; and even then, we will not let you rest. There is no martyrdom for you, Arab, only hard life in prison."

Anwar snarled, "How did you find me here, American?..... I was the only man in the *Kilij* that knew of our final plan to leave Italy..... I didn't activate the order until after your attack in Florence..... Our secret transmissions indicated Capri was the exit point for us..... You didn't fall for that..... Why?"

"Your 'Madre' contact in Piombino," I answered.

Anwar looked perplexed..... "I used the 'Madre' pre-fix for all my secret contacts and communications..... There were thousands of them..... How did you conclude this location?"

I remained silent for a long moment. I then laughed and said, "Yes, you did use the pre-fix 'Madre' for all your contacts - Madre Rossa, Madre Gialla, Madre Viola, Madre Nera, Madre Rosa, Madre Inglese, Madre Russe, Madre Generosa, Madre Piccola, and many, many more. But you used 'Madre Sacre' for your contact in Piombino. I know as the world turns that there can only be one 'Sacred Mother'. It made sense to say goodbye to her before dying in martyrdom. I certainly would. So I deduced your mother, lost to the CIA for over a year, was hiding in Piombino. We tracked her down and waited for your arrival. You didn't disappoint me. You arrived as expected, and led us to the ferry for Elba. Our satellites tracked your ship, *Last Sultan of Granada*, on a course for Portoferraio. It all made sense. Even a terrorist, wanting to destroy my country, was entitled to love his mother. She was your 'Achilles' Heel', Anwar....."

The Condor, angered by American intelligence and intuitions, slammed his head against the wall. Bleeding from above his right eye, he screamed, "You pernicious vermin! You wicked American snake! You used my mother against me! I can't believe this..... How could that be my weakness?"

I calmly explained..... "It's a common weakness, Arab. It's a weakness for us all. It is not difficult to accept. It simply is. My job was to find debilities in your designs which America could use to destroy you. The little love in you provided all I needed. You are now legal property of the United States, and your evil scheme will not bear fruit. The *Kilij* plans are dead. This reality is all that matters."

"I will not talk!" shouted Anwar. "I will not speak against my movement. My people will not be enslaved by the 'Crusader'. We will continue the struggle until we are victorious. Soon America will die, and we shall live!"

I answered, "America's interest is that all people should live. Our intention is only to destroy those who want to destroy our way of life. We cannot allow radical movements to plan the destruction of our constitutional republic. If you leave us alone, we will return the favor. Freedom will not die, Egyptian - today, tomorrow, never..... It's the only form of government that works..... Your ideas of governing are not consistent with advanced societies. They do not allow for the personal freedoms necessary to live a full and productive life. If we are 'Crusaders' - it is only for freedom and justice, and the maintenance of our republic."

The support helicopters flew over the ferry. Jimmy Thomas and Rafael Alvarez signaled them to approach without concern of counter-fire.

Looking out through the windows at the approaching helicopters, Simon Westcott took his eyes off of Anwar for a split second. It was enough. The Condor jumped off his chair and grabbed Westcott's pistol, firing it into the American's belly. Westcott fell to the side unconscious, bleeding to death internally.

Anwar turned the pistol towards me. I pulled my weapon. We fired our guns simultaneously. The bullets found their marks. Anwar died with a head wound.

The bullet entered my left chest, shattering my lucky charm. It broke skin, muscle and bone. It punctured my left lung, and a major blood vessel near my heart. Hundreds of sharp fragments of ancient black volcanic glass cut through me like razors in a tornado. I bled from a thousand internal cuts. I was aware of all this.

Still conscious, I thought for a moment that I could survive. But as my warm blood puddled around me, I realized it could not be. I would die soon.

There was not much pain, while I sensed my blood leaving me. The rush of red next to my heart slowly drained my strength and consciousness. I weakened as my blood pressure dropped.

Still in my thoughts, I saw Sarah loving me forever - giving me the life I had hoped for - filling my dreams with hers - never leaving me..... I could feel my sons' breaths on my face. Their kisses and embraces, I had longed for, would never be again..... How could that be? I wondered..... I had worked so hard for my boys, to give them the life they deserved. I should be part of their future dreams as well..... The costs of freedom, I thought.....

I heard my brothers speak to me. I was in a haze, but both their voices were clear. "Stay with us, Mark," they said, over and over again..... "Stay alive!"

Julius and Michael worked on me..... "Breathe!" they yelled.....

Julius had placed me flat on the floor. He gave me air by mouth. Michael compressed my chest, not realizing I was bleeding to death inside from a thousand cuts. They had the fear of losing me in their eyes. They cried. Neither of them surrendered. Much effort for nothing, I thought. I was dying, and nothing could be done about it.

Jimmy Thomas hovered over my head, holding both my hands. His tears fell like raindrops on my face. He loved me, and realized my end before my brothers. I had loved him also.

I opened my eyes wide as a gush of blood came from my mouth - exudation from my lung. My heart was making a last valiant effort to keep me alive.

In my mind, I whispered to my brothers, "Take me to the sun." They could not hear my wish, while struggling for me to live.

The rising sun beamed through the window in front of me. Its warm rays landed on my face. The sky and sea were the bluest blue.

My soul wished to ask Julius, "Did you read Ann's journal?" I hoped he had, as I had..... "You must give it to Michael," I whispered. "He should read it also..... The Stansfields have always been sentient beings, but Robert and Ann were unique..... So too were Mother and Father..... Weren't they, Julius?"

I was ceasing to be..... Again in my mind, I asked Julius and Michael, "Have I been strong enough? Have I done for my family and country as I should have? Were they proud of me?"

My brothers stopped their efforts..... They knelt to each side of me and wept..... My soul smiled at both and said, "Take me home."

Sarah came to me with my sons. She bent down and kissed my lips. She whispered in my ear, "What do you see?"

The waters are a dark sapphire. The sky is azure and oyster shell white. A band of pumpkin orange beams between them..... A lonely star, here and there, can still be seen bright in the darker shades of blue..... A fading moon tries to hide away..... A melon of a sun rises to shine on a new day; its brilliance squints my eyes..... There is glory in what I see.....

"The power of words to love, and to be loved," softly said Sarah. "From my open heart to yours, I love you, Mark, and always will. You are my knight, and I forgive you. Please wait for me."

My sons kissed my face.

The images disappeared from my mind. I closed my eyes and went away.

Darkness greeted me. I fell into it..... Then there was light - peaceful light.

I walked into a colorful landscape of green meadows of grass, tall cypresses, and blue sky. Sun, stars, and moon, all mixed together above me. A deep cobalt blue ocean sparkled in the distance. Flowers were everywhere - massed fields of violets, white and orange lilies, pink and red roses, purple gladiolas, blue irises and lavender. Tall sunflowers curved toward the sun. The scent of lemon and tangerine was in the air. Figs and palms swayed in gentle breezes.

I climbed a sandy hill. I could see my father and mother calling me home. Like the young boy of my past, I ran and embraced them. They appeared as I had remembered - strong, warm, and loving. They both smiled and held my hand. I was in Elysium.....

CHAPTER 29

American Requiem

In the early afternoon, a long caravan of cars passed through the guard gates at Annapolis on their way to Bancroft Hall. Nasrin stared out her window, through the bright summer sunshine, at the tall branches of leafy oaks, maples, and poplars. A giant yellow buckeye stood apart, appearing alone but brave. She held her son's hand.

"Thank you, Mother," said Alex, "for explaining everything to me."

Alexander Stansfield closed the two journals. He softly placed them on his lap.

"John, when we arrive, please escort Alex to Memorial Hall. I'll wait outside."

"Certainly Mrs. Stansfield," said the security agent from the front seat.

The front cars drove up to Bancroft Hall. Security teams fanned out in all directions. A midshipman first class honor guard stood at attention, presenting swords, as the Stansfield car came to a stop.

"Go Alex," said Nasrin. "You need each other at this moment."

Alexander walked away, leaving his mother in quiet tears.

The young man walked up the steps to Bancroft's entrance, looking at the US Naval Academy crest above the doors. He passed with John up the marble stairway to the second deck and Memorial Hall.

"Here we are Alex," said the agent, stepping to the side and joining two more security personnel.

Young Stansfield slowly walked the length of the hall, past the captured enemy battle flags from America's prior wars. As he moved, the boy glanced at the "Honor Roll" with the names of Annapolis' war dead. He saw 'Mark Stansfield' inscribed on the bronze plaque, with the notation: *Captain-United States Marine Corps, United States Naval Intelligence, CIA; Killed in Action, Italy, Global War on Terrorism.*

Finally, Alex arrived at the only place in the world he wanted to be.....

"Hello Father," he whispered.

"Alex," said Michael gently, struggling to his feet with the aid of his cane. "You have a red amaranth on your jacket."

"As do you, Father."

They embraced warmly, and sat together by the portraits in silence.

Alexander had not known his grandfather and uncle, but he was in awe of them. He knew of their achievements, and also, of their character, integrity, and love.

The boy stared at Admiral Julian Stansfield's portrait. With his father, he bowed his head and prayed for several minutes.

He then faced the opposing wall, looking at Captain Mark Stansfield's life-sized oil painting. The Stars and Stripes of the American flag filled the picture's background. His uncle was depicted centrally in Marine combat camouflage uniform, holding an assault rifle with bayonet. Poised in action, with the point of the bayonet in front of him, Mark pushed forward over rocky terrain. The eyes were fixed straight ahead like a man possessed by duty to his country. There was no hesitation in the movement, no fear or regrets. Honor and courage were identified easily in the portrayal. The hero's uniqueness was captured.

Next to the portrait, a plaque commemorated awards and decorations – a Navy Cross, a Medal of Honor, and a Distinguished Intelligence Cross. He had been the only American in history to win both the military's and the CIA's highest decorations for bravery beyond the call of duty. He was truly a warrior in every sense of the word. Alex bowed his head again and prayed for several more minutes.

"Father, I read Mark's journal, and Ann Nelson's too..... Why hadn't you shown them to me?"

"It's a delicate matter," said Michael to his son. "I've tried to put the words out of my mind for many years."

"But those words, Father, are not lost to you..... You've spoken them to me as long as I remember..... They're in your speeches..... Mother calls them 'American Amaran-thisms'..... They are a part of us, Father....."

Michael Stansfield smiled at his son. For a young man, about to start his education at Annapolis, Alex was aware and intuitive. The boy understood his family's legacy.

Michael pulled a letter out of his coat pocket. "I'd like to read you something, Alex."

Both father and son firmed up. They wrestled with their emotions, like gladiators in combat.

"This is a letter sent to Director Mitrano of the CIA by your uncle, Mark. He had requested a transfer to dangerous duty in Europe. At the time - my brother was in a wheelchair, after injuries sustained in Medal of Honor actions in Pakistan the year before.

"*Dear Director Mitrano: Thank you for your expression of faith in my abilities to serve my beloved country. I understand your possible trepidation in receiving my request for transfer to hazardous duty in defense of the United States. I want to reassure you of my devotion to America. I may not be whole physically, but I am mentally and spiritually. My desire to help my country is deep in its origins. I hope it is suffice to say that I am completely committed to protecting and defending my country. There are no limits to where I will go to complete my mission successfully. My lack of mobility will be compensated for by my atypical presentation. I will not be looked upon by the enemy as a potential threat. They will not expect my coming. My tame, humble exterior will hide an eagle warrior heart. The best attack is the one the enemy doesn't expect. Stealth is our friend, and I can provide it. So again, my heartfelt thanks for receiving my request for the opportunity to get back into the fight. I hope you accept me into your mission plans. The 'field' is where I feel most comfortable, most alive. Among my comrades and brothers in arms, I am free."*

Michael carefully folded the letter and placed it back into his pocket. He turned and looked at his son.

"As you see, Alex, fighting men come in all packages. It's the spirit of the man that matters. His dedication to the mission is the critical factor. His mind is more important to me than his body. Even a man in a wheelchair can contribute immensely to the success of an operation. In this case, my brother upheld the greatest traditions of the Naval Academy, the United States Marine Corps, and the Central Intelligence Agency. He was the key factor in the favorable outcome of our mission. He is an American hero. The eternal flame over his gravesite at Arlington should stand as a beacon for all of us. Its fire will always remind us of the sacrifices required to keep our great republic free....."

"Why did you leave the CIA, Father?"

Michael closed his eyes for a moment. He gathered his mental energies.

"It was my leg, Alex..... My wounds from Iran eventually got the better of me. It became difficult to walk."

"How about the pictures of you and Mom, and me as a baby in a backpack, climbing the Rockies, the Alps, Himalayas, and the Andes? Your leg seemed well then..... Why did you go from the CIA to politics?"

"It was the last mission," said Michael, revealing the truth to his son. "I found it impossible to continue after losing Mark. I blamed myself for his death. I couldn't quite shake it off and maintain my duties as an agent.

"I went to Mitrano after returning from Europe. I resigned from the CIA in his office. The director accepted it without argument. He asked what I'd do next. I told him I didn't know. He suggested politics, and I laughed. He urged me to help change our country from the inside, that our government needed people like me. I smiled, and promised I'd consider his recommendation.

"In all honesty, I found politics unappealing. It was unfamiliar to me.

"I spent the next two years sailing the world with you and your mother. We climbed mountains on every continent. I grew a long beard.

"Mother tolerated all this from me, understanding the reasons. I needed to do these things to get into a special flow of mind. It took a while; but eventually, I accepted reality and moved on.

"One thing led to another..... I ran for Congress and won. I became governor of Florida; and like they say, the rest is history."

"You've been able to keep peace, Father, in yourself and the world," smiled Alex. "I'm proud of you."

"It's kind of you to say those words, Son. But, you couldn't be as proud as I am of you."

"I'm sorry, Sir," interrupted the Secret Service agent, "but we better get going to the chapel, or you'll miss the meeting at the White House this evening."

"Thank you, John," said the President of the United States.

Michael Stansfield got up from the bench slowly, using his cane for support. Alex tried to help him, but the president refused. The young man stood silently at attention behind his father.

"The world doesn't stop and wait for us to catch up with it. We must be prepared for the fight at all times and never fall behind. Always, we must continue to move forward.

America depends on us. Let honor and duty dictate. We must all be leaders of quality like your uncle," said Michael in a quiet voice.

The president stepped forward and stood alone in front of the admiral's painting. He got real close to it, away from his son's earshot, and gently whispered, "I'm sorry, Father..... Please forgive me for making your boy a 'Ghost of Annapolis'. I need you to know that America also loved him like a son. I am so very sorry."

Michael kissed his right hand and placed it over his father's heart. He lowered his head, closed his eyes, and wept. Alexander could hear his father's lament. He too bowed his head and wept.....

Together, side by side, father and son walked back to the courtyard in front of Bancroft Hall. The president and midshipman passed in front of the First Lady's car on their way to the chapel. Tears flowed down Nasrin's face.

"America needs her heroes, like we need air to breathe," she said softly to herself.

One of the president's aides by the car asked, "Would you like to drive, Sir?"

Michael turned and smiled at the assistant. He paused and lifted his cane, pointing it forward, "No, I don't believe I would. I need to exercise and numb my mind a little. Besides, I love to take walks with my son."

They walked into the chapel. The president's aides stayed outside. Father and son moved slowly down the dark central aisle to where the "Holy Stones of Annapolis" were displayed. A tender stillness permeated the sacred shrine.

A beam of subdued light came down over each of the statues, isolating each individually in a radiant cone. An area of shadow remained between the two statues, keeping each separate.

Michael and Alexander stood quietly in front of the massive stones. Holding the cane in his left hand, the president steadied himself upright. The place and moment demanded it of him. There was deafening silence – a peace that seemed eternal. It was a hush found only in the presence of greatness. They stared at the admiral's pale gray rock on a large pedestal of dark granite.

Admiral Julian Stansfield stood tall and erect. Four dark gray stars blazed prominently across his battle helmet. A patch covered his left eye. Binoculars hung down on his chest, as he pointed with his right index finger into the distant horizon. A horizon only he could see. His left hand laid to the side, slightly open in the dark shadow.

On the wall behind the statues was a bronze plaque, with the following inscription dedicated to the Brave WARRIORS OF FREEDOM – Descendants of Pericles, Washington, and Lincoln – A FUNERAL OATH FOR OUR TIMES:

Alexander Stansfield read aloud -

"So died these Americans in defense of their country..... Father and Son..... It is a tale of great hardship and sorrow, but one that must be repeated often and loudly for all to hear. Giants of their time, but still flesh and bone like you or I. We should have as unfaltering resolution in the field as they had on this earth. They were not content with ideals alone. They were men of action who put their ideals in motion. Filled with love of country in their hearts, they realized the power of true 'Freedom' and the true potential of America. We should all do the same. As displayed by these men, it is by courage, honor, and a keen sense of duty that patriots like these enable our great republic to survive

and prosper. They did not deprive America of their valor. Rather, they laid it at her feet as the most glorious contribution they could give, leaving her with the last full measure of their sacred devotion. For this offering of their lives, made in common by them both, they each individually receive that renown which never grows old and remains that noblest of shrine wherein their glory is laid up to be eternally remembered. For heroes like these, America will never forget."

President Stansfield wiped a tear from his face. He stared at his brother's marble. The echoes of "Semper Fidelis" played in his head. The music followed his eyes as he looked over the stone.

Mark's statue was slightly back of the left side of the admiral. He wore his Marine combat helmet with loose chinstrap. A field uniform covered his body; combat boots were on his feet. His left knee touched the ground; his right leg appeared to lift him from a stumble. His eyes were fixed forward in attack. Mark's left hand held an assault rifle with bayonet. His right arm outstretched in front of him, as if reaching. In the dark shadow between them, Mark's right hand clasped his father's left. The base of the statue was nearly covered in red amaranth; flowers dropped by respectful mourners and admirers of an American champion.

Michael could see enough of the granite pedestal to read its inscription, *"Never fade, never die, American Amaranth."*

Father and son removed the amaranth flowers from their jackets and tossed them beneath Mark's image into eternity. Together, they whispered, "For Peace on Earth."

Selected Sources

The novel, *American Requiem*, is a work of speculative historical fiction. Any resemblance of characters or situations in the novel to real persons, living or dead, is purely coincidental and not intentional. Set in the past, present, and future, it is the third book in the *American Amaranth Anthology*.

Along with numerous internet information sites, these selected sources were instrumental in creating the novel, *American Requiem*.

- The Day of Battle by Rick Atkinson

- Monte Cassino by Matthew Parker

- A Half Acre of Hell by Avis D. Schorer

- The 56th Evac Hospital by Lawrence D. Collins, M.D.

- A Surgeon In Combat by William V. McDermott

- Fighting For Life by Albert E. Cowdrey

- And If I Perish by Evelyn M. Monahan and Rosemary Neidel-Greenlee

- Hospital At War by Zachary B. Friedenberg

www.ingramcontent.com/pod-product-compliance
Lightning Source LLC
Chambersburg PA
CBHW030635260626
47157CB00007B/2335